MW00942370

Crash Shadow

A Tale of Two Addicts

Jeffrey

Vernon

Matucha

Many thanks to

Mary Kam Oi Lee

Sabrina De Mio

Holly Goodwin

Editor extraoridnaire
Cassandra Chaput

and

Supreme Scene Queen
Dani Dassler

Yes, I not only
let my mother
Virginia Langdon
read this book,
she helped me edit and
proofread it as well!

Copyright © 2015 Jeffrey Matucha
All rights reserved.

ISBN-13: 978-1516910014
ISBN-10: 151691001X

I

Looking For Jake

Skye

Staring at her fingertips, she was looking for any signs of blood.

She carefully picked up the razor blade and ran her eyes along the sharp edge.

Looking at the table and then back at her fingers, she took stock of the row of small plastic baggies, all of which had been split open and laid out like skinned carcasses.

Skye didn't know why she felt sharp twinges in her fingertips. She couldn't get over the feeling that she had accidentally cut herself as she had scraped out all of her old baggies. She was trying to consider the possibility that the pain was a result of her sleep-deprived imagination.

Fuck. I can't believe I slept with Deep.

Ever since late last week, her mind had been constantly bringing up the same torturous thought, the sincere wish that she had not slept with her speed dealer Deep. She wondered why her traitorous psyche insisted on continuously recycling that regret.

She leaned forward and put her face in her hands. A little more than a week ago her high spirits, as well as a good deal of Bacardi and a generous amount of speed, had gotten her into enough of a mood to consent to having sex with her tall and emaciated speed dealer.

If she thought about it long enough, he wasn't that bad looking. It was just that she would find him much more attractive if he only bothered to bathe more often. She also knew that Deep would probably be a lot more appealing if she didn't possess the foreknowledge that he would generally consent to sleeping with just about anything that moved, and he had the absolutely ugliest looking penis she had ever seen. It had probably looked fine at one point, but the raised, dark blue veins and rough, purplish skin indicated that he had put it through a lot of abuse before he had gotten around to using it on her. Her head spun as her mind forced her to imagine all of the orifices, inanimate objects, and marathon rounds of speed-induced masturbation had beaten his member into its presently sorry state before he had put it inside of her.

Wobbling to her feet, she looked at her clock and saw that it was close to six. She had to think for a moment to remember whether it was six in the morning or in the evening. The dull haze coming through her windows was not giving off a good enough clue.

Before she had fallen asleep, she had been awake for nearly two straight days.

Her clothes, which she had slept in, felt as if they had soaked up all of the oil from her skin. She quickly took them off. Standing still in the middle of her room, it felt as if there were a thick residue covering her body, though feeling even the still, cool air of her room felt good on her skin.

Then she caught a whiff.

"Yeeush!"

Her ripe odor helped snap her back into her senses.

She wrapped herself in her blanket. She wasn't about to put her oily clothes back on. It was only a short walk down the hallway to the bathroom.

In the shower, she lathered herself over three times, trying to get the ripe, oily feeling off of her body. Her hair felt like dry weeds as she wrangled shampoo into her twisted locks.

Wrapping her damp body back up in her blanket, she skittered out into the hallway and back into her room. She eyed the kitchen and hallway as she maneuvered back to her quarters. Her roommate Jane was hardly ever home, preferring to spend most of her time at her boyfriend's place. Her other roommate, the hyper-reclusive Arden, was usually shut inside her room, where she spent most of her time.

Her body felt hollow. Flopping down onto her futon and rolling onto her back, she looked down at her stomach. Her stomach was looking better as she lost weight, but her steadily deflating breasts were not holding up as well. She thought about trying to get in some sort of exercise, other than sex, once in a while.

She looked back at the ceiling. Her head was swimming. She thought about what she was going to do to get more speed. She didn't know if she wanted to get any more from Deep.

She thought about calling her former housemate Preston and finding a new dealer, or at least a new source, via a go-between. It had been some time since she had talked to Preston, but she was fairly confident that he was probably still getting wired. He had been pretty heavy into the speed scene the last time she had seen him, which was only a few months after she had left her former residence, the burnout crash pad known as the Hell Nose House. She had run into Preston at the club Shinra shortly after leaving Hell Nose House and he had given her his number at his new place.

His number had to be somewhere in her room.

After spacing out for a few more moments, she felt an unfamiliar pang of hunger. She forced herself off of her futon and staggered into the kitchen. Looking around the cupboard, she scanned her food supply.

Oh God, I can't believe I slept with Deep! Fuck!

She ended up searching the better part of her room. It had been a long time since she had called Preston, and the small, crumpled piece of notebook paper that had his number on it would no doubt be buried deep within the flotsam of her room. That is, if it was even still in her room.

She usually kept her phone numbers in the top left-hand drawer of her dresser. It wasn't there. It wasn't until she got to her bottom dresser drawer, where she crammed all of her miscellaneous papers and baubles, when she found it. She knew it was his number the moment she saw its thick blue and faded ink.

Her heart skipped a beat. A light feeling went through her chest. She picked up the phone and carefully dialed the number.

Her arm tightened up as several buzzes and clicks came over the receiver.

A pause.

A click.

Another click, a buzz, another click.

"The number you have dialed is no longer in service…"

Her shoulders became heavy.

She decided it was just another roadblock.

She knew enough tweaks. It should not take long to find someone who could go-between a deal for her.

Skye contemplated that she might have dialed his number incorrectly the first time. She picked up the phone and carefully dialed again.

"The number you have dialed is no longer in service…"

She was thinking of asking her friend Mercy, and if she needed to, she could always try her coworker Paige, though she was reluctant to go that route.

She called Mercy.

She answered on the second ring.

"Hello?"

"Hey Mers."

"Hey. Wassup?"

"Whatcha doin'?"

"Nuthin'. Just watchin' TV and doin' some redecoratin'."

"Yeah, I was callin' 'cause I was lookin' for Jake. Do you know where he is by any chance?"

"I might know where Jake is. He's probably at my friend's house. Why don'tcha stop by."

"A'right. I'm takin' off in about five. Is that cool?"

"Cool."

Jake was their code word for speed. They had gotten the idea from a gang of stoners they knew who always referred to marijuana as Bob. That way they could talk to each other in a room full of cops without letting on to what it was they were referring to. *"I'm looking for Bob." "No kiddin'? Bob's at my place. You want to talk to Bob?"*

She got out her jacket and sunglasses. It was a twenty minute walk to Mercy's new place.

Stopping short of the door and doubling back, she picked up the crumpled slip of paper.

"The number you have dialed is no longer in service..."

Yuri

It was one of those things that had really changed.

He couldn't get over how different it had become.

Lying on his bed, he would turn his head, looking up from his flat pillow and beaten mattress, and follow the grain of the wooden wall up to the ceiling.

He had woken up an hour ago, but still had not moved from his bed. He had found the perfect position.

Trying to focus his tired eyes on the fine lines was a convenient distraction. He would spend each night shifting his body around on his thin bedding, trying to find the best position for his slim body, trying to find those spots where his bones wouldn't press so much against the floor. He usually woke up several times during the night, trying to get comfortable, and it was always a chore to fall back asleep. He was most uncomfortable around his hips. His hip bones would always dig through his aching skin, as they pressed against the hard mattress.

Only in the morning could he go numb. Squinting at the wall, he always tried to gauge the weather. He felt as if he could see the temperature and wind outside. If the wind was strong enough, he could feel it through the sliver-wide gaps in the shack's boards.

Even after he got to the ceiling, he oftentimes still had a hard time believing he wasn't in the San Francisco anymore.

It had been a little more than two months since he moved out of San Francisco. It had been a very long two months for Yuri, especially since he wasn't using heroin to kill the plodding time anymore.

He had gotten a place in South Berkeley, down in the heart of the East Bay, where the rich folk looked down on the commoners from the long backdrop of hills that ran alongside the urban flatlands by the San Francisco Bay. If you were in just the right place, looking down a long westerly street, you could just make out the skyscraper tops across the bay in San Francisco. On really clear days you could make out the blinking light of Nob Hill, the girdered transmission tower atop Sutro Hill, and the Transamerica pyramid point.

His new home was a tall, thin, and plain wooden shack, located in the very back of the backyard of a much larger house. The main house was one of the dilapidated punk houses that dotted the East Bay flatlands.

The place in the back did manage to qualify as a living space, even though it did not have very much floor space. The bathroom was a closet, containing only a toilet and a sink. The kitchen, with its ancient stove and antique refrigerator, was only slightly larger than a walk-in closet. Yuri's room did not have a lot of space, but that wasn't really a problem. He had very few personal possessions. Aside from his clothes, he only had a clock and a small boombox, and one cardboard box of random items such as books, personal papers, and his small music collection. Technically the place had two rooms. A thin wooden ladder that had been nailed into the wall led to a small loft where his roommate lived. It was enclosed, secluded, and the preferred spot in the place.

Despite its small size and plain wooden surroundings, it was not altogether a bad place to live, especially when compared to Yuri's former abodes. The rent was very cheap. Yuri was embarrassed to tell people how little he paid for his place. It was also cleaner than his former places. It lacked the random bits of crud, trash, and grime that infested so many punk pads and wage-slave dives that Yuri had been forced to live in. The housekeeping was just a matter of dealing with minimal dust. The wood was dark, but not old. There was no peeling paint, frayed wires, or rotting wood, at least not yet. The fridge and stove, even though they were old, were still in good working condition. The best part for Yuri was that his friend and roommate Zatch was hardly ever there.

The most prominent aspect about his new place was its high ceiling.

It was at least fifteen feet in the air.

It was all a drastic reminder of how much his life had changed.

A tremor went through Yuri's shoulder. He quickly sat up.

Straightening out his back and looking at the far wall, a wave went through his head. He put a hand to his temple.

His head began to spin. The floor threatened to tilt on its edge. He carefully laid back down on his mattress.

What the fuck.

His flesh was wrapping around his heavy bones as the tapping of rain against the wood lulled him back to sleep.

Yuri decided to surrender to fatigue.

Even if it was reminding him of junk.

Pint Walk

It had been three weeks.

Once the novelty began wearing off, the sights and sounds of the low-rise East Bay city of Berkeley began seeping into the background.

"How d'ya like it?"

Yuri kept walking. He did not looking in his direction.

"Rare!" yowled the shaggy haired lunatic with a barbaric yawp.

Yuri was only slightly concerned about the loud and unkempt man who kept howling about the street to no one in particular. Just another crazy street person, decided Yuri, even though he looked a lot healthier and stronger than the average street person.

Yuri eyed one of the local pubs along the main drag. There were far more cafe's than bars around Telegraph Avenue, but Yuri had already tried all of the downtown bars. He was beginning to feel desperate. Ever since he had moved to Berkeley from San Francisco he had been trying to find a decent place to drink.

"Hot n' tight!" greeled the lunatic.

Yuri crossed the street as the shaggy hair man continued his rant. For a moment, he wondered if the lunatic had been yelling at him.

Yuri was surprised that there were no Casa Lomas, Zeitgeists, or other hip young bars in the East Bay. He had not been able to find even one black-walled bar full of punks and throckers and hip young adults with tattoos, body piercings, expensive shoes, and ridiculous attitudes. There were a few funky dives in South Berkeley that had appeared somewhat promising, but they were usually patronized only by old winos and run-of-the-mill dope fiends. It baffled him, since there were more than enough hipsters in the East Bay. Where did they hang out all of the time? How long could coffee sustain such people? In San Francisco those kinds of people needed to drink.

The frenetic pull of his old San Francisco haunts kept tugging at his back. Wallowing in young memories: a Sierra at the Zeitgeist with his friend Jenny tending the bar, being a dope fiend wraith in a corner of the Casa Loma, checking out all of the speed freaks, or squinting through the darkness of Noc Noc at the slick new wave hipsters sitting beside stacks of old television sets.

He needed a replacement for all of those old haunts. He needed an East Bay replacement. Yuri knew he could not go back to San Francisco, not even for a casual visit. It was only a short subway ride out to San Francisco, but he had managed to stay off of heroin for two entire months. The pull of the bars was nothing compared to the pull of the Tenderloin, the back alleys of the Mission district, or even the lower Haight.

Far too many junkies. Far too many dope fiends. He had been in the game way too long not to be able to recognize them.

It had not simply been the cheaper rents that had pulled him across the bay. Berkeley was not that far away from San Francisco, but it was far enough.

Yuri spied the front of a pub. It had dark green wood paneling on its exterior. It appeared as if it might be another rich college kid place, but Yuri also thought it might have some potential to end up being a decent watering hole.

Yuri wasn't encouraged when he first walked in. The wood was too polished, the place was too spartan, and the bar stools were brand new. There were the prerequisite pullover yuppies and rich-looking suburban college students hanging about, making dull conversation over beers and bar snacks.

He went up to the bar and eyed the taps. They had the standard Sam Adams and Guinness. His nerves were asking for a drink more than his skin.

"What's Orlando ale?" asked Yuri as he spied a foreign tap.

"It's from the Special Forces brew pub down in Santa Cruz," chirped the well-groomed bartender. "It's pretty good stuff. I can give you a sample glass if you like."

"I'll try a pint."

He didn't want to suffer the saccharine bartender any more than he had to. Yuri usually didn't try out new brews since pints were fairly expensive, but the monotony of the East Bay was starting to grate on him. He needed to throw in a little variety every now and then, even if it was just trying out a new beer.

He sat at the bar rail by the window. The window seats were just high enough so that Yuri could be inconspicuous to the passersbys below as he casually observed the street scene.

Telegraph was a crowded place, especially on the weekends. Scores of people were always passing by, to and fro, marching in a continuous urban parade. In every passing moment, all manner of people would be walking by at any time: college students, college punks, college preps, college suburbanites, old hippies, young hippies, middle aged hippies, street people, street lunatics, punks, fashion punks, gutter punks, young punks, old punks, pseudo punks, burnouts, winos, college bohemians, artiste' bohemians, second hand clothes store bohemians, cops on bikes, cops in cars, cops on foot, tourists, plain Janes and John Does, throckers, suburban throckers, burnout throckers, baby throckers, hipsters, posties, and a fair amount of people who could not be classified.

If you watched the street long enough, you would see most people who had walked by once before walking by again in the other direction. Yuri noticed one or two people who kept walking back and forth, going North and then South, and then North again and back South again and again, caught up in the beehive current of the main drag.

A warm rush went through Yuri as he sippedd his pint. A dull pain began snaking its way through his forearm and into his chest.

Yuri waited for a moment, holding himself still.

The ache was just a twinge, nothing a few hits from the pint could not quell.

The swirling throng underneath the barroom window was starting to blend into the background when a familiar fluff of dark burgundy hair came bouncing along the edge of the window.

He watched the bouncing fluff, trying to place it. It looked all too familiar.

Yuri jumped to his feet.

"Rebar!" shouted Yuri as he jumped out of the pub door.

Looking for Jake

Skye's legs felt light and quick in the afternoon wind. She was walking with a purpose. The streets didn't seem as crowded as usual.

Mercy was living in her own studio just off of Valencia. It was very rare for any of Skye's friends to have a place without any other roommates or significant others crowding the space. She remembered that it was a small studio and it had a lot of the typical inner city homestead problems such as peeling paint and suspect plumbing, but it was still a place Mercy could call her own.

Skye's latest ongoing speed binge was lasting a lot longer than usual. She would usually go on a weekend binge or an occasional three or four day tweak, but her current binge was verging on an entire week.

This time it was different. She was on a roll. She wanted to keep her high and silver speed streak going. She was enjoying the light and hollow feeling in her limbs, along with the clear and clean feeling in her head.

Perhaps it was just the times that had her going for the moment. Shortly after she lost her job at Sabrina's messenger service, she received a small inheritance from a recently deceased aunt. It wasn't a fortune, but it was enough money to keep her going for a good six months, give or take a month or two, without her having to work.

Nevertheless she did get a job, a part time job at a small video store only a few blocks from her flat. She was only working on call, working as many as twenty hours a week, and sometimes as few as eight. Once in a blue moon she would work over thirty hours in a week, but that was rare. She didn't feel the temptation to ride out her inheritance money. Large sums of cash like that were rare, at least for people such as herself. She had budgeted the money quite carefully, and still had a good deal of it left, especially due to her part time income.

The rays of the late afternoon sun were coming in sharply as Skye approached Mercy's apartment building.

"I haven't done any in about a month," explained Mercy.
"But you still gotta connec'?"
"Sure, but what about the other guy?"
"Other…?"
"Your regular guy. What's his name, Ditch or Dip or something like that?"
"I ain't buyin' from him anymore."
"Ah."

"Long story. Things are gettin' too tweaked at his place."

"Yeah."

Mercy picked up another trash bag. She was sitting on the edge of her futon, cutting black garbage bags into long thin strips with a pair of extra long scissors while her girlfriend slept behind her. Skye was sitting cross-legged on the floor, nursing a beer.

"I was actually gonna call you about that stuff," said Mercy. "Gish was asking me if I knew where to get any, an' I thought about askin' you for some of your dealer's stuff."

"Don't you have a dealer?"

"I know a couple of people I can call."

"Can they get the good stuff?"

"Yeah, sure," replied Mercy, sounding uncertain. "I don't do it often enough to have a really solid connection."

Mercy continued to slice long thin strips out of the black garbage bags. Skye craned her neck around to observe the dead sleep of the thin bleached blonde lying behind Mercy.

"What does she do again?" asked Skye, indicating Mercy's slumbering partner.

"She's an actor. At least that's what she wants to be. She's doin' some phone work on the weekends to pay the bills."

"Hm."

"She's in a play right now, but she doesn't want me to see it."

"Why the fuck not?"

"She says it really sucks, that it's really stupid and lame, and she hates her lines. She's got this one line where she has to say, 'Party city!'"

"What?"

"'Party city!' She says it after someone tells her about a party."

"What the fuck are you talking about?"

"She said it was a stupid play."

Standing up, Mercy went into her kitchenette. Skye was looking at the peeling paint on the ceiling. She was wondering how long Mercy would be living there. Skye's current place had originally been Mercy's room. Mercy had agreed to share the room with her several years ago when she had suddenly left her former residence, the infamous Hell Nose House.

Skye kept glancing at the sleeping girlfriend. She had not budged an inch since she had gotten there, at least so far as Skye could tell.

"So you know where we can score?" asked Skye as Mercy was setting up a stepladder in the middle of the room.

"Yeah. I'll call someone in a couple a' minutes."

Mercy grabbed a pile of garbage bag strips and climbed the stepladder. She started tacking the strips onto her ceiling.

"How much did you want to get?" asked Mercy.

Skye stood up. "At least a half. I'll score for you too if something goes through."

"Hell yeah!" exclaimed Mercy. Skye glanced at the bleached blonde again to see if she would stir.

"What's her name again?" asked Skye.

"Linette."

"A white girl named Linette?"

"Why not?"

"Hm."

Retrieving another beer from the kitchenette, Skye was still feeling the effects of her come down and burnout. Her skin began to harden up again, pressing Skye in on herself.

Mercy kept tacking black strips to the ceiling. They looked like black pieces of akimbo seaweed. Skye paced as she thought about other people she might be able to contact if Mercy could not get a connection.

Skye began looking through Mercy's stack of books and checked out her show flyers to keep herself distracted. Mercy's red Destroyer X guitar was sitting proudly on its stand. She wondered if Mercy had been keeping up with her music. It had been some time since Mercy had been on stage. Her last band had been really good, though they only lasted a few months before breaking up, and that had been more than a year ago.

As Skye continued pacing, she kept a corner of her eye on Linette. She was wondering when she would finally stir. Perhaps she would remain that way until they left.

She looking at the phone as Mercy kept pinning strips of shredded plastic bags to her ceiling with a sophomoric impishness.

Mercy got down off the stepladder and plugged in a large room fan.

"What are you doing?" asked Skye.

"Check this out."

Mercy turned on the fan. All of the strips started waving and undulating, whipping around like long grass in a strong wind. It made a soft rustling noise.

"Cool!" exclaimed Skye.

They stood still for a moment as they watched the sea of black garbage strip snakes coil around the ceiling.

"What the fuck are you doing?"

Linette was awake.

Underground

Rebar was driving to Carl's Place, a small dive situated on a side street in North Oakland. Rebar liked to gun his rusty old Chevette down the street as he weaved in between slower cars. Rebar's driving could occasionally be aggravating, but Yuri was enjoying his impatient driving style, at least for the moment.

Rebar's driving habits had not changed one bit, not since Yuri's earlier days in San Francisco when Rebar had been going out with Mercy. Yuri had only known Mercy through his then girlfriend and roommate, Skye. Even though Rebar had not been one of his closer companions, they had always gotten along.

"I've been off of it for four months at least," explained Yuri as he braced himself for another quick inter-lane weave.

"No shit?"

"Yeah."

"I thought you would never get off that stuff. Why'd you quit gettin' loaded?" asked Rebar.

Yuri had been asked that question once before since he had kicked his heroin habit. He was also wonderedwhy the answer shouldn't have been more obvious to him.

"Well, I just, didn't want to get wasted anymore," said Yuri. "I wasn't getting anything done. I was just layin' around, getting loaded. I just couldn't deal with it anymore."

"Uh huh."

Yuri tried to catch some of the names on the quickly moving street signs. "What about you? What you been up to?"

"I hadda move to the East Bay when I lost my chair at Chrissy's."

"That place over in the Castro?"

"Nu uh. That was Becky's place. The last place I worked for in the city was over on the Haight."

"I didn't even know you were in the East Bay until I saw you through that pub window."

"Yeah. What the hell were you doin' drinkin' in that place?" snapped Rebar.

Yuri scrunched himself down in his seat. "I don't know anythin' about the places around here. I was just tryin' to find a decent place to drink."

"Man, you were way off. Only stupid college peckerwoods ever go to that bar."

"At least the beer was good."

Suddenly turning down a deserted side street, Rebar quickly parked the car. Yuri followed Rebar as he walked impatiently up the street and around the corner. As they walked up to the bar, Rebar explained that Carl's Place had been well known as an old wino bar, but it had been slowly taken over by the local punks, skinheads, and neighborhood speed freaks over the past several years.

Carl's Place looked like a working class bar: a plain wooden exterior with high windows and a few neon beer signs. There were several faded paper shamrocks stapled above the entrance.

Walking into the bar, Yuri suddenly found himself off balance as he came out of the sharp sunlight and into the black cavern that was a poorly-lit bar. Once his eyes adjusted, he saw that the place was kitschy enough. There were many faded old black and white pictures of athletes hanging on every wall. A lot of the frames were cracked or on the verge of falling apart. There were old sports pennants and neon beer signs decorating every wall. There was also plenty of punk graffiti and band stickers stuck in various nooks and crannies around the place.

A couple of docile skinheads were playing pool at the bar's only pool table. Most of the crowd was made up of young working class punks, Ben Davis and Red Wing punks who didn't have enough money for Doc Martens or new flight jackets. A few old rummies were at the far end of the bar, defiantly hanging onto the last piece of wino territory.

In another corner, the corner which was the farthest away from the front door, a pair of punks hunched themselves over a table, as if they were trying to conceal themselves. They kept their eyes under their wilting black hair. Their edges were especially dark and sharp. Yuri could tell that they were the kind of screw-ups that had already gone well past the line that defined standard junkies and speed freaks.

Rebar and Yuri sat against the wall near the front door, right across from the long wooden bar, after getting pints of Sierra.

"You really got off th' stuff?" asked Rebar as he leaned back in his chair.

"Yeah."

"Not even a taste once in a while?"

"Hell no. I'm strictly off that junk."

"Shit. I don't know if I could do it."

"You don't use junk, do you?"

"Fuck no. I'm talkin' about gofast."

Yuri leaned on their small round table. "You're pretty much just a drinker though."

"Yeah, but I've been hittin' the crank a bit more, here and there."

"Okay."

"I was thinkin' about gettin' a half for this weekend. You could go in on it with me if you want to."

Yuri sat up straight and glanced over at the skinhead pool game. "That's okay. I never was big on speed." He looked around and then down into his drink. "I gotta stay off the hard stuff anyways."

"Fuck dude, I bet those two know where we could get some Jake." Rebar tossed his head in the direction of the burned out punks who were haunting the very back of the bar.

"No fuckin' way," replied Yuri quickly. "Even if I was looking to score I wouldn't wanna ask those guys."

"So how come you ain't livin' in the city anymore?" asked Rebar.

"I kind of had to leave my place."

"Kind of?"

"I was living in the back of this dive full of punks."

"Sounds familiar."

"Anyways, I got laid off from my part time job and, yeah, to be honest I was hitting the junk too much."

"Couldn't pay your rent?"

"Well, I was getting by, but then everything fell apart, just like, boom! Everything. All at once."

"How so? Gimme details."

"Lessee, first my sort-of girlfriend took off. I don't know what happened to her. Then my shooting partner really sunk. Last time I saw him he was rippin' people off and turning tricks for his junk."

"Fuckin' a!"

"Yeah. Even I never sunk that low. Then I lost my dealer. I don't know where he went. His place was empty and his phone number didn't work no more. Then in one day, my bicycle was ripped off and I lost my job. I don't know why, but I just kept tryin' to find my dealer all the time instead of looking for a new job."

"That's why you left your place?"

"Naw. My landlord went crazy."

"Crazy how?" Rebar leaned back in his chair, tilting his drink attentively.

"He showed up one night all drunk and blitzed on something. I wasn't there, my roommate was. But from what he told me it sounded like he was on something else besides alcohol."

"Yeah, okay. But so what if your landlord got wrecked?'

"He wasn't just wrecked. He was screaming that we weren't paying the rent, and he was waving a gun around."

Rebar leaned onto the table. "Fuck!"

"Yeah. We all got out of there before the next night."

"You weren't paying your rent?"

"I was. Maybe somebody else punked out. Who knows."

"Damn. So that's how you ended up over here?"

"Yep."

Rebar seemed a little more rough around the edges since Yuri had last seen him in San Francisco. He was trying to remember how long ago it had been. He knew it had to have been at least six months, maybe even more than a year. Perhaps Rebar had started a deeper descent into the tweaker lifestyle. Yuri wouldn't have been all that surprised if he had started going in that direction. He had the personality for it.

He could never imagine Rebar becoming a junky.

Yuri decided he liked Carl's Place well enough. Still, he never would have gone to a bar like Carl's Place if he was still in the City. Carl's was not a young person's place, it had only been taken over by young burnouts. He was still pining for the pseudo-dives that sported cattle skulls, glass Jesus candles, Johnny Cash and Johnny Thunders on old jukeboxes, stoic fruitbetties, mood swinging bartenders, and dorks in Danzig t-shirts who would brag about their previous roles in Richard Kern shorts, always in the scenes that Kern decided to cut out at the last minute.

Looking around once more, Yuri decided that places like Carl's Place would have to be his lot. If he had to endure kitschy wino dives for his pints in order to stay out of San Francisco, then that was what he was going to do.

Yuri's shoulders tightened when one of the Skinheads walked up to their table, gripping his pool cue. He was tall and wiry, wearing a long olive green overcoat.

"One a' you guys wanna play some pool?" asked the overcoated skinhead.

"Yeah, I'll play," drawled Rebar.

There was a buzz around the pool-playing skin, an aura around his eyes and stance that told Yuri that the tall and lanky baldy was drunk.

The skinhead set up the pool table as Rebar circled around, looking for a decent pool cue. The other skinhead, tall and lanky's former opponent, sat back at a table near the burned out tweaker punks.

The beer began to go to Yuri's head. He looked around the terminally scuffed floor and spaced out as he listened to clattering pool balls and Rebar's bantering.

Rebar sauntered by, Leaning on his pool cue in the midst of the game.

"Are y'winning?" asked Yuri as he lifted up his head.

"Fuck no," drawled Rebar. "I'm gettin' my ass kicked."

Yuri watched as the skinny skin sank a few more pool balls.

"Did ya run into Dex on the Ave?" asked Rebar from behind his pool cue.

"Nu uh. Should I have?"

"He's up there a lot."

"He's over on this side?"

"Yeah. He hadda move outta the city a few months ago. He's crashin' near my place."

Rebar took his turn at the table. He was soon back by Yuri's table.

"Dex's been hangin' out with Sweez a lot."

"Sweezy? She's out here too?"

"Yeah. Her an' Pel came out late last year."

"Fuckin' a', it's a goddamn epidemic."

"No shit. No one can afford to live in the city anymore."

Rebar got another turn at the table. Yuri had lost touch with most of his San Francisco friends when he started sinking deeper into his heroin habit. But there was also another reason why he didn't know about so many of his friends leaving the city: their method of moving out. Yuri did not go out of his way to tell anyone that he was pulling up his city stakes to live in the East Bay. No doubt they had gone the same route.

"So what ever happened to Mercy?" asked Yuri as Rebar sidled away from the pool table yet again. "She's not over here too, is she?"

"She's still in the city, as far as I know. I haven't called her in a while. I don't even know if the number I have for her works anymore or not."

"Damn dude, you went out with her for a long time."

"Yeah, I sorta did. She still went out with a lotta girls when I was with her. The last time I saw her she was still hangin' aroun' Skye."

"No shit?"

"Yup."

"They've been hangin' with each other for a while."

"I know. They're probably talkin' about us right now."

"Fuck. I wonder what she's doin' these days?"

"Mercy or Skye?"

Yuri shrugged. "Either one a' them, I guess."

The Skin sank the eight ball and put down his cue. "Y'wanna play 'nother game?" asked the skin.

"Fuck no. I suck at this game."

"C'mon, you ain't that bad."

"You're just saying that so I'll play again."

"Well you ain't gonna' get better unless you play."

The skin walked up to Yuri. He was practically standing right in front of him.

"Hey DT, you wanna play?"

A strike went through Yuri's head. He froze as he looked up at the skinhead.

"What?"

"Y'all wanna play some pool? C'mon. Nobody else wants ta play."

Yuri shook his head. He could feel his skin tightening around his skull.

"Nobody wants to play because you're too good at it," blurted Rebar from behind the skin.

"What the fuck?" barked the skin in a rather aggressive manner. "You pussies. I ain't that good."

"Well we're that bad."

"Buncha' pussies!" growled the skin. Yuri could tell the punks in the corner were watching the tall and lanky skinhead as he paced around the bar, even though they were not looking directly at him.

Rebar sat back down at their table. "We should go by McGee's sometime."

"Is that another bar?"

"Naw. My friend's place."

The skin was still stalking around the table. He flexed and twisted his crossed arms, glaring around the bar at no one in particular.

Yuri glanced over at Rebar. Rebar was slumped in his seat.

Yuri turned his head to look over towards the bar, where the bartender was busying himself with drinking glass arrangement. Yuri could not help but notice a bearded wino in an old leather jacket, who stared out over the bar, looking straight ahead.

Out to cop

Skye kept quiet, gripping her beer bottle as Mercy continued to make small talk with her contact.

"Yeah, Linette's still here. Hell no. Yeah. She's been here since Thursday morning. No, I don't think so. Why should I? Oh come on."

Mercy's feet hovered in the air as she lay on her stomach, cradling the phone against her ear as if she were a gossiping teenager. The skin wrapping itself around Skye's forearms grew tighter as she tried distracting herself by continuing to observe Linette, who had fallen back asleep.

The fan was still on and the gentle rustling of the ceiling-tacked plastic strips continued in the background.

Finally standing up, she walked right in front of Mercy. Crouching down, she slowly waved her hands at Mercy.

"Hey Wink, we should get goin'. Okay. Okay. Yeah? At Sylvie's. In an hour? Half an hour. Yeah, sure."

Skye sat down on the floor, gripping her beer bottle as if it were a club.

"In half an hour. Yeah. Sure. Okay. You too. Bye."

Skye's tension eased only slightly as Mercy put down the receiver.

"We're gonna meet Wink at Sylvie's," said Mercy.

'Sylvie's? What's that?"

"It's a little cafe offa' lower Haight. Let's go."

Skye pointed to the comatose Linette. "What about her?"

"She'll be alright. She'll probably be asleep for a couple more hours. We can give her a few lines when we get back."

Skye tried using the walk to Sylvie's to grind out some of her frustration. She kept thinking about how a quick call to Deep would most likely have gotten her a deal by now. Even when Deep was at his worst, he would still get her something after only a few hours. If nothing else, he would have treated her to a few free lines before making any deals.

Sylvie's was a long and thin corridor-like cafe, having two long and thin rooms separated by a narrow doorway. It was made out of plain, unpainted wood and had very high ceilings, almost two stories tall. Sylvie's was situated on a side street off of lower Haight. It was the kind of place located in one of the many big city nooks that was usually only well-known by local denizens who had a good lay of the land. The place was a bit too thin for Skye's tastes, at least on this occasion. She didn't relish the idea of making deals in such close quarters.

There were only a few people in the place. A couple of deadheads were behind the counter.

Walking into the next room, the tall and gangly Wink was already waiting for them, having crammed himself into a corner table near the back of the cafe.

"Hey Wink."

"Hey Mers."

"You remember this schluff here," said Mercy as she pointed to Skye.

"Hi Skye."

"Hey."

Skye had met Wink a few times before. He gave the impression of a second-hand clothes store Bohemian, except that he was not an artist or a musician, at least as far as Skye knew. He always wore the same dark gray tweed blazer.

"So, how's Linette doin' these days?" asked Wink.

"Come back to my place and ask her for yourself."

"What? She's awake?"

"Ha!"

"I thought so."

"About the stuff," gritted Skye between her teeth.

"So whatever happened to that Australian broad?" asked Mercy as she sat down next to Wink.

"What Aussie broad?"

"Y'know, Joan or Jen…"

"Jane."

"Mers."

"Yeah. Aussie Jane."

"She went back home."

"Oh."

"Yeah."

"I thought you two were going out."

"Oh no. Not really."

"What?"

"Hey Mers."

"We rolled in the hay a few times, but it wasn't serious."

"Aw, man, you shoulda' gone for her."

"Not really."

"Why not?"

"She was a really lousy lay."

"What? No way! Not her."

"Hey Mercy."

"It's the painful truth."

"She was? Damn. That sucks. She was totally fine!"

Skye looked down into her coffee.

They were walking to Wink's place. More walking and more time, as Skye wondered why they could have simply gone to his apartment in the first place.

Wink lived in a small apartment on the top floor of a tall and square apartment building. Skye did not mind the six-story broken elevator stairway climb. The physical exertion was helping cool her impatience.

His dark apartment, with its narrow corridors and cramped rooms, was fairly disorganized, but it was not a chaotic and compressed mess like so many of her friends places. Still, the close spaces kept pressing the heat back into Skye.

"Can I open your window?" asked Skye once Wink had finally gotten off the phone.

"Sure. I gotta go meet my connec' in a couple a' minutes."

"Where you meetin' him?" asked Mercy.

"Over at his place. It's only a few blocks away."

"Should we come with you?"

"Naw. Y'better wait here. There's some Mickey's in the fridge. Feel free to play some music or just watch the street."

"Watch the street?" asked Skye.

Walking over to his closet, Wink reached inside and started struggling something out of the crowded closet. He finally produced a small telescope on a metal stand, positioning it right by the window.

"Cool!" said Skye.

"We're so high up that people on the street never notice you lookin' at 'em."

Wink double checked himself in the mirror.

"How long will you be gone?" asked Skye, just as Wink started out the door.

"It shouldn't take too long."

Cruise

"It's the one thing I've always wanted," said Rebar as he was driving to hid place. "Joey's got one."

"What?"

"Huh?"

"What's the one thing you've always wanted?"

"A convertible. He's got an ol' '68 Cadillac."

"Who's Joey?"

"The drummer for my last band."

As long as Yuri had known him, Rebar had always talked about starting a band. He was constantly forming new bands. The reason he was always forming them was because his band projects would always fall apart before thcy cvcr got off of the ground. His musical projects would be lucky to get in three or four full practices before they split up. None of Rebar's bands had ever made it to any stage, or even a show at a party or warehouse, yet he would always talk about the killer band he would eventually put together.

"He was a pretty solid drummer. He let me crash at his place when I hadda leave my flat on lower Haight. Man, that car totally kicked ass."

"So is Carl's Place the only thing goin' on?"

"Fuck no. There's other stuff. The Square's all right, an' Gilman is okay if you really feel like bein' punk. The best thing is the warehouse parties. A lotta guys in West Oakland throw rent parties with bands an' kegs. Usually they're pretty cool."

"Any a' those warehouse deals coming up?" asked Yuri.

"What?"

"Those rent parties, anything like that coming up?"

"I could call aroun'. They happen all the time."

They stopped at a corner liquor store before going to Rebar's place. Yuri disregarded the Mickey's for a couple of tall bottles of Budweiser.

Rebar lived in a small one-bedroom apartment in an old three story building in West Berkeley. A disheveled sofa bed occupied the living room. Rebar quickened his pace through the somewhat unkempt living room. On their way through the apartment, Yuri noticed an unfurled sleeping bag on the white linoleum floor in the kitchen.

Rebar's room was small, occupied only by a bed, a small table, and an old office chair that looked as if it had been ground-scored from the street.

Rebar took a huge bottle of Jack Daniel's out of his closet. He took a swig and handed it to Yuri. Yuri took a quick swig to be polite.

Yuri sat down in the office chair as Rebar thumbed through his small black phone book. "Lemme' give ya Sweezy's number. You should give her a call and let her know you're over here now."

Yuri gripped the bottle of whiskey and took another swig. "I don't know if I jus' wanna call her up outta the blue."

"Why not?"

Yuri shrugged. "I dunno. It would just be weird. I haven't seen her in a long time."

"So what? Give her a call."

"I've never actually called her on the phone before."

"Whattaya mean? You used to hang with her all th' time, right?"

Yuri kept shrugging. "Well, I was always runnin' into her all the time. She was roommates with Mercy for a while."

"Tell me about it. She was livin' with Mercy when we went out."

"It'd just be weird to call her up all of a sudden, that's all."

"Okay, be a pussy."

"Fuck you."

Rebar put down his book and stood up. "I was gonna' have some people over soon anyways. I'll just invite her an' Dex over."

"Sure."

Yuri handed the bottle of Jack Daniels back to Rebar. He tried to recall if he had ever been around Sweezy or Dex when he had not been buzzed, drunk, or pinned.

"Should I call Sweezy right now?" brightened Rebar.

"Naw dude, don't call her right now. I can jus' see her later."

"Suit yourself."

Yuri took a long swig of whiskey.

Wait

She had read five comics, had thumbed through at least ten magazines, nosed through three books, looked through his music collection at least three times, and studied the flyers on his wall for a long time before succumbing to his telescope by the window, yet again.

Skye was finding the telescope to be fairly fascinating. With it she could get a very clear and close up view of people walking by, walking along the street, or simply standing in place. The people on the street usually were not doing anything out of the ordinary. Once in a while you would catch a couple of people meeting up and conversing.

It was addicting in any case, since she concentrated on people who did not know they were being so closely watched. It was addicting enough that it absorbed most of the waiting time.

Finally leaving the telescope for a moment, she picked up a few of Wink's cassette tapes.

"What should I play next?"

"I dunno. What's he got?" asked Mercy from behind one of Wink's comic books.

"Fuck, I've already played everything I can stand."

"Come on, he's gotta have something else."

Skye took a reluctant glance at the rest of Wink's diminutive music collection.

"Jesus, I didn't think I knew anyone who listened to this shit."

"What?"

"He's got the worst taste in music."

Mercy corrected her horizontal position on Wink's bed. "Lay off man. He's doin' us a favor."

Skye held up a tape. "Tell me you like Howard Jones."

"I like his musical equipment. I wish I had it."

"Uch."

She looked through the four tapes she had already played.

"So it's Mary Chain or Motorhead."

Mercy didn't say anything, slumping her head down as she turned the comic around at various angles.

Scanning the room yet again, Skye found herself contemplating his Bret Easton Ellis books.

"I'm gonna get another Mickey's," announced Skye.

"Ain't there only a few left?"

"There's one left."

"Damn, we shouldn't drink all his beer."

"Fuckit. If he don't want us drinkin' all his beer he shoulda' been back by now!"

"I know it's takin' a while," said Mercy as she struggled into a new position on Wink's bed.

"He's been gone for four hours! We shoulda' eaten all his fucked up girl scout cookies by now!"

"He has girl scout cookies?"

"Yeah. On top of his fridge."

"Hmm."

"I'm drinkin' the last beer."

"Damn Skye, at least leave him one beer."

"I'll buy him some more when he gets back."

Mercy followed Skye into the kitchen.

"Damn," said Mercy. "He really does have Girl Scout cookies."

"What the hell's he been doin' with Girl Scouts anyways?"

"I don't wanna know."

"You wanna split it?" asked Skye as she held up the last beer.

"Naw."

Sitting down at the kitchen table, she started drinking the Mickey's. Mercy took down the box of Girl Scout cookies and was cautiously looking inside.

"I should go out and get another six," said Skye.

"How would you get back in?"

"I could buzz the door."

"I don't know if the buzzer even works."

Wink's apartment and the apartment building itself had a typical rundown feel to it, meaning that much of the building's equipment may or may not work. Too often such places were plagued with defunct doorbells and dead door buzzers. Skye knew there was a decent chance that she could find herself standing outside of Wink's apartment building, hopelessly pounding on a broken apartment buzzer if she dared to leave the building.

"I could give you a call," said Skye. "I can call from a payphone and let you know I'm on the way up."

Mercy carefully extracted a Girl Scout cookie, as if her careful removal of the item would conceal its disappearance. "I don't know if I should be answering Wink's phone."

"Well shit, he went an' left us stranded here. Besides, I shouldn't be too long. There's a store just two blocks from here."

"Okay. Just try to be quick."

She downed the rest of the Mickey's and quickly dashed into Wink's room to grab her Derby jacket. She was starting for the front door.

"Don't you need Wink's number?" called out Mercy as Skye was grabbing the door.

"Right."

It was a quick walk to the corner liquor store. She grabbed a six of Budweiser talls and waited behind two people who were taking way too long to make their purchases. One fellow couldn't find his change, and a short, throcking woman couldn't figure out which brand of cloves to buy. Skye grabbed a three pack of Ho Ho's while she was waiting.

As she bought her beer and mass-produced pastries, she couldn't stop thinking that the cashier bore a striking resemblance to Michael Hutchence.

Walking back to Wink's apartment, her shoulders began to soften and her back unfurled as she ate a Ho Ho and felt the cold six pack through the paper bag cradled in her arm.

Skye remembered that she needed to find a payphone. She was half a block away from the apartment and there were no pay phones on his block.

Walking back to the liquor store, its payphone refused to accept her money. The coins just kept clinking through, coming back out into the change slot.

She maintained a slow simmer as she walked towards a nearby retail street. Finding a gas station with two payphones, she found one was missing its receiver, the stripped cord hanging down as if the phone had been ripped out. The other phone was not working either. It refused to give up a dial tone.

After a long search, she eventually found a working payphone, one that was a eight blocks away from Wink's place. By now she was out of Ho Ho's, and her shoulders were curling up with tension.

Quickly dialing the number…

Busy.

Wink's phone was busy.

Skye hung up and stood in front of the phone. She only waited a few moments.

Dialing again, it was still busy

Mercy could not have been making a call. She must have answered the phone. She was probably talking to Wink. Maybe he was giving her an update.

After another few moments Skye called again. Still busy.

Abandoning the phone, she decided she needed to keep walking to work out the tension. She searched for another working payphone. She was getting close to the Haight, and Golden Gate Park was just a few blocks away. She would pass by more than enough payphones.

Trying a few more phones on Haight Street, one phone didn't work and another one gave her the busy signal again.

"Fuck! What could she be doing?"

Skye didn't want to walk around upper Haight for too long while carrying a six pack. Too many punks and transients would be hitting on her for a beer.

Wandering back to the first working phone that she had found, she discovered that it was now occupied. She did not want to wait in case they were going to have a long conversation.

She decided she would go for a longer walk this time. She would walk over to one of the residential streets, pretending as if she were going back to an apartment, and do a good eight block wind back to her starting point. She did not want to wind up at the original working payphone and see that someone was still talking. She would probably brain the unsuspecting citizen with the six pack in that event.

She killed at least another fifteen minutes with her roundabout stroll. The beer was getting heavier, and its frosty chill was starting to fade.

Finding another working payphone...

Busy.

"Fuck!"

Skye slammed the phone down.

Her thoughts were spinning around and crashing into each other. She felt like screaming at Mercy. She felt like getting back into Wink's kitchen and eating all of his food. She felt like going back to the man on the payphone and punching him.

She cracked open one of the beers and started chugging it. It was still fairly cold.

The colliding thoughts in her head began slowing down. Making her way back to Wink's apartment building, she knew that Mercy had to be wondering where she was and possibly go downstairs to check for her.

Sitting down on the apartment building steps, she cracked open another beer. Her arms and shoulders became even more tight when she realized she had not bothered to remember Wink's apartment number so she could at least try the buzzer. There was no Wink to be found on the doorway directory, as she did not know his surname. Someone walked by and went in. She knew better than to try asking a passing tenant if he would let her in.

Quickly finishing her second beer, her neck and shoulders felt as if they were going to split apart from the tension.

A cool wave went over her as she saw Wink walking down the street.

"Hey Skye," said Wink.

"Lemme in. I really gotta take a leak."

"Yeah yeah."

"Where've you been?"

"My friend was hella late, and then we had to go an' meet his connection. I had to do a lot of shmoozing. What are you doing out here?"

"I went out to buy beer. I kept callin' your place so Mercy could let me in but she's been on the phone."

"She's using my phone?" he asked as he opened the front door.

"For more than half an hour already."

"What'?"

Quickly trotting up the stairs, Skye was sorely tempted to say something about his lack of punctuality, or perhaps hit him on the side of his head with the remaining Budweiser talls.

She dashed into the bathroom once they got inside. When she came out, Wink met her in his narrow apartment hall.

"The phone was off the hook," said Wink. "Mercy never noticed. Someone must've kicked it over"

They went into his room.

"Sorry Skye," said Mercy meekly.

"Whatever," groaned Skye.

"Did you get the stuff?"

Wink sat down on his bed. "Why don'tcha put on some music?"

Skye pursed her lips together.

Mercy put on the radio. Skye breathed a silent sigh of relief.

Wink took some money out of his pocket and handed it to Skye. "His dealer was almost out. I was only able to get a half for the three of us."

Skye's ribs felt as if they were curling into her lungs as her stomach sank.

Walk

Yuri turned down Rebar's offer of a ride so he could walk home. He felt the need for a walk to help clear his head and work out his tight limbs. He was concerned about his health since he had not gained very much weight after quitting his habit. He assumed he would start filling out once he began eating real food again, but as far as he could tell, he had not gained even a pound since he had left San Francisco.

He was beginning to wish he had accepted Rebar's offer. Too much exercise was not going to help his weight problem.

The sky was gray and cool. Dashing, darting, turning, the thoughts in his head were running around in a shallow storm. His eyes ran along the lines of the sidewalk, glancing at the gray concrete roads. He tried to let the row of houses form into a corridor, but the random plants and trash, the too-many cars and wandering people, and the tightly packed houses were all breaking up any symmetry that the streets could have offered his cluttered head.

He looked back down at the ground, tugged up his loose pants, and wondered if he would ever have anything resembling a stomach. If nothing else, he would have liked to have gained enough weight to have at least some of his clothes fit properly.

The thoughts began dying down. His legs felt hollow. A twinge was going through his knee. He tried to keep the churning of his legs to an absent rhythm, as his tired and thinning mind descended into a fog.

Suddenly a rush went through him, snapping his head around and trembling his hands. He saw something that shook his bones.

A subway station.

It was the station that was just down the street from his place. A momentary glimpse was all he needed to send his legs and arms to quivering.

The wallet in his left pocket suddenly felt like a stone. He knew enough to know that he had just enough. All he had to do was hop on a train and take a quick ride to the city.

A string in his forearm started to vibrate.

His head whirled. Urges and hunger and future regrets running into each other. His nerves snaked into his body with pure junky instinct.

Quickly walking into a corner liquor store, he bought two bottles of Coke and a couple of Snickers bars. Back at his place he felt his left arm go weak. He slowly ate the candy bars and nursed his soda. The running sugar quelled him, just enough. Resting back his heavy head, he concentrated on the high ceiling overhead.

Tease

"His name's not even Yuri."

That was the remark that finally got Mercy to look up from the guitar she had been incessantly plucking.

"What?"

"That's not his real name."

"It ain't?"

"Nah."

Skye was sitting cross legged on the floor, polishing off another Bud tall. Mercy and Wink sat on his bed as he chopped up lines of speed on a TV tray.

"I kinda wondered about that," said Mercy.

"What?"

"That whole Yuri thing. It sounded too Russian."

"Uh huh."

"So?"

"So what?"

"So what's his real name?"

"Hm?"

"What is it?"

"Not tellin'."

Mercy put down the guitar. "What?"

"I'll tell you after we score."

"Man, that's bullshit."

"What?"

"You're jus' fuckin' with me."

"Yeah, sure I am."

"I bet his name really is Yuri."

Skye struggled to sit up. She had been sitting on the floor for too long. "He's been goin' by Yuri as long as I've known him, but that can't be his real name. I just know it."

Standing up, she tried to cool herself down. Her tension began washing back, warming her skin.

She would have been a lot more worked up about the outcome of the deal, but Wink insisted on paying for the half himself since he had been unable to get them their requested supplies.

"So what ever happened to Rebar?" asked Skye.

"The last time I saw him he was living in a flat over on lower Haight, but I ain't seen him around in a while. I'm not sure where he went." Mercy carefully sat up and slowly set the guitar aside. "I should try to call Rebar," said Mercy. "I haven't talked to him in some time."

"You still got his number?"

"I have a number. I don't know if it's still good or not."

Skye eyed the television tray. It was an old tray with thin metal legs, the kind of furniture you would expect to find at a grandmother's house. Wink seemed to enjoy his line sculpting duties. He kept corralling bits and pieces of crank as they disobediently tried to scatter around the dull beige tray top.

"Okay then." Wink picked up a rolled up dollar bill. "Who wants to go first?"

Mercy looked at Skye. "You first."

"Okay."

Bending herself down towards the TV tray, Skye attained just the right altitude to snort her line. The tray didn't seem very sturdy.

Skye put bill to nose and touched it to the line. Quickly snorting up her portion of speed, she stood up and handed the bill to Mercy.

She did not get too much of a sting. It had the traditional battery acid taste, but it had not been very grainy or rocky.

Skye sat back down on the floor. Wink got up and put on the Howard Jones tape.

A light throb went through Skye's temples. She looked back down into her beer can and sniffed a couple of times. She was trying to taste the stuff in her throat, trying to figure out if it was any good. It had been quite some time since she had done anything that wasn't Deep's speed.

She finally felt a slight electric current going through her eyes.

Mercy did her line and handed the bill to Wink. "Thanks Wink."

"Sure."

"Whatever happened to Yuri anyways?" asked Wink. "That guy kinda just disappeared."

Skye looked out of the window.

Crawl

Yuri gathered up his clothes. He fished out enough change from his coat and pants pockets to do one load of laundry. He had at least three loads of laundry, probably more, but he could only afford to do one load. There was the temptation to simply recycle his less odiferous clothes for a few more days before he got his paycheck, but Yuri did not want to go through that routine anymore. He wanted to force himself to take care of his business when he could.

When he was using heroin, his clothes would go unwashed for weeks, at least during his later years of using junk. He would use up all of his clean clothes, and when they were all out, he would just sniff his way through his shirts and socks, seeing which ones were the best one to wear. He would do that until his clothes would get too unbearable, even for him, before he went to the trouble of washing them.

He simply did not want to live that way anymore. That was why he was forcing his tired body and his beaten monetary funds up for the five block walk to the nearest laundromat.

Walking down the street, slightly bent from the bag of clothes, he thought about Rebar's question. His thoughts faded in and out like an indecisive fog as he pondered the subject.

Trying to settle on some good reasons, he decided one of them was his recent desire to be in a band again. He had been in a few bands, years ago, but they were hardly anything more than disorganized jokes. He had never jammed with any serious musicians who were truly dedicated to getting a band going. His former bands would be lucky to get in a few practices, let alone an actual show, before they fell apart.

Yuri felt quite embarrassed when he recalled that he had only performed in two shows, and they were both punk house parties. He had never played on a stage in a club.

Thinking about it was making him angry.

Angry at his former bandmates who never tried to apply themselves, angry at his old girlfriends who taunted his efforts, but mostly he was angry with himself.

His shoulders and temple tightened at the thought.

He could only remember one person who had gone out of their way to encourage him to get going with his music. It was one of his exes, the one time he had lived in an actual house back in the city. He had not felt as if he had lived in a house, since he had only rented one small room there, but it still had a much different feel from all of the warehouses, apartments, and ghetto studios he had lived in before.

Then he remembered that it had really only been a flat. Yuri and his crowd of roommates had only occupied the first floor.

Back then she had asked him why he didn't practice more, and why he wasn't looking for people to play with, since he had always talked about being in a band. She had even offered to introduce him to other musicians she knew. She had been one of the few people who had not taken his expressed desire to be in a band as a joke, or just a passing fancy.

She had come to encourage him at the worst possible time, however. He had been getting deeper into junk. He was not the full blown junky he would become a year later, but he had more than enough bad habits besides his burgeoning heroin habit to keep him from getting anything done back then.

Yuri arrived at the large and spacious laundromat. The working class washery was not very full. The few patrons that were there had spaced themselves out at equal distances.

He ran into yet another old urge. In the old days, Yuri and his friends would wash their clothes in laundromats without adding any soap. They would look into the soap wells on top of the machines, and there was usually enough leftover laundry soap encrusting the edges of the well opening to create a decent amount of suds. They would scrape the edges to loosen the soap residue so they would be spared the additional financial burden of having to buy soap.

He bought a small box of detergent from the vending machine. He wanted to do his clothes right, even though it meant cutting into his Thursday money, the money he was sequestering for the day before his paycheck.

That was another thing Yuri pondered when he thought about why he was getting himself cleaned up. He was thinking about an apartment.

It could be a one bedroom or a studio. It didn't have to be large, just empty. It had to at least have hardwood floors, even if the floors were old and scruffy.

He wanted to have his own place. It was a dream of decency, of privacy, of finally getting to live like a decent human being. He had been poor all of his life, moving from one slum to the next, ever since he was a child as his mother dragged him and his brother and sister from one dump to the next. Each place only lasted a few months, and occasionally a year or two, but they always had to move.

He wanted a place he didn't have to share with anyone. A place where the plumbing worked, where the paint was less than fifty years old, where the wiring was not in danger of shorting out, where strange bits of crud and dust didn't just keep appearing out of nowhere, even after you cleaned up, and where you could not hear drunken domestic arguments every other night or semi-automatic gunfire in the distance.

He imagined having friends over, or just being alone. He imagined keeping things in their proper place, and cleaning up a little bit every day. He imagined being able to bring a woman back to his place, someone he chanced to meet at a club or a bar, and not worry about what the place looked like or what his unpredictable roommates might be doing.

But part-time wages and the bone breaking rents of the Bay Area made that goal a faraway dream. It would be hard enough for him to work up the wage ladder just to be able to comfortably rent a room in a decent flat, let alone a place all to himself.

His clothes were spinning. He wondered if he had added too much soap. The water was completely white.

He spaced out on the spinning, foamy waves.

He could not remember the name of the flat where he and Skye had lived. He only remembered that he had thought that it had been an incredibly stupid name.

Desperate

"You still want to cop?" asked Mercy.

"Yeah."

Skye was distressed at the surprise in Mercy's voice.

They walked along Market, coming down from the Castro district. They made a quick stop to see if some of Mercy's friends were home, which they weren't. Skye had hoped to get another possible connection to buy some more speed.

"I dunno," said Mercy, "It's pretty dry out there. I think we should just wait until next weekend."

"Fuck. Getting that bullshit line from Wink just made me want it more."

"Didn't that stuff get you wired?"

"A little. Not really."

"Well, I feel awake."

"Yeah, I'm awake, but that's it. That's all. I wanna get wired!"

"Well," paused Mercy as she looked down at the sidewalk. "If you find anything, I guess you can jus' go ahead. I'm not into it right now."

"Sure."

"Maybe next weekend."

"You want me to call if I find anything tonight?"

"Naw. Jus' go ahead. I'm gonna' get back to my place and kick it with Linette."

"A'right then. I'll call you in a couple a' days."

Mercy started down a perpendicular street, heading back to the Mission. Skye did her best to hide her disappointment as Mercy left. She momentarily considered the notion of skipping the whole venture altogether, but when she thought about all of the trouble she had already gone through that day, she would nearly tremble with indignation.

She had to score. She wasn't about to let a flaky Howard Jones fan get away with ruining her good time.

Skye decided it was time to bite the bullet, and face her mistakes.

She decided she was going to go see Deep.

Walking up to Deep's street-level apartment, she could see a thin frayed curtain fluttering in a half opened window. She would be able to look inside if she walked up to it.

She hesitated. The air around the curtains was too still.

Remembering that the doorbell didn't work, she gently rapped on the front door with carefully choreographed knuckles. The door started moving, gently swaying inward from the force of her light knocking. Clenching her right hand, she nudged the door open with her foot.

"Deep?" she breathed quietly.

Standing in the doorway, she could feel herself being pulled into the apartment as well as back out onto the street. She opened her ears and listened. The silence was overwhelming.

A slight rustle. The curtain had caught a gust of wind.

Stepping slowly into the apartment and carefully looking around, the coffee table was covered with beer cans, soda cans, fast food wrappers, magazines, newspapers, and two ashtrays overflowing with cigarette butts. Skye could not see any speed paraphernalia, but she reasoned that there had to be a few razor blades and patches of white dust buried underneath all of the coffee table clutter.

Walking up to the coffee table, treading lightly, she tried to get a better look at the overall apartment. She stood in the middle of the living room and craned her head around. Both the kitchen door and Deep's bedroom door were open.

She rolled her eyes around and searched the floors and the walls, peering into the corners, to see if she could spot any telltale clues of what was going on. Stepping around the coffee table and glancing into the small kitchen, she approached Deep's bedroom.

The light was out in his bedroom. It was pitch black.

The stillness became thicker as she slowly moved into the doorway, waiting for her eyes to adjust to the darkness.

And then she saw Deep.

Lying stiff as a board.

Passed out on his bed.

She could tell he was in a dead sleep. No doubt he was sleeping off a binge.

Skye's stomach sank as her heart lightened.

Cautiously stepping back, she paused and looked at the coffee table. Creeping up, she moved aside a few scraps.

Underneath a few junk food wrappers was a small and empty plastic baggie. Its insides were covered with a thin white residue. She could take it home and scrape out the remnants.

Pocketing the baggie and treading out of the apartment, she was careful not to make too much noise, even though she was certain that a freight train running through the living room would probably not wake up Deep.

Slowly walking out of the apartment, she made sure that his place was locked up as she quietly closed the door.

Back out on the street, her heavy steps were only lightened by the baggie in her jacket pocket.

Get Together

Rebar invited Yuri over for a get together at his place, and it was a quandary for Yuri. He knew he would enjoy the company of other San Franciscan expatriates, but the circumstances of the situation made him uncomfortable. He did not really know Sweezy and Dex that well, and the added embarrassment of having had to flee the city, for himself and them, would most likely make the initial encounter awkward.

Rebar called Yuri, only a few days after he had run into him, to inform him of a get together at his place. Dex and Sweezy were going to be there.

Pacing his steps to Rebar's place through the cold and dark air, he walked with a measure, letting the cold forty ouncer of Mickey's cool his hands through a brown paper bag.

Walking up the stairs to Rebar's place, he knew he would need the Mickey's before the evening was over. In the past few months, Yuri had been maintaining his ghetto nerves on regular beer, like Schaefers and Meister Brau, but he suspected for this evening he would need something stronger.

Rebar answered the door with a huge bottle of Jack Daniel's in his hand.

"Wassssssssssup!" squawked Rebar. Rebar's eyes were rough and wide with weekend energy. "Come on in. Everyone else is already here."

Walking into the apartment, Yuri tried following Rebar's festive vigor. They took the quick route through the roommate's living room, going straight into Rebar's room. He could hear Sacrilege blaring through the door.

Rebar's room was brightly lit. The first thing Yuri saw was Sweezy's bright, curly red hair, followed by Dex's weeds of spiked black hair. Sweezy and Dex were sitting on the far side of the room, away from the door. Sweezy was scrunched up into the easy chair, curling her thin yet sinewy legs up against herself. Yuri could see nearly every inch of her legs, as she was wearing one of her many trademark mini-skirts. Dex was sitting on the floor, his back against the wall.

"Hey Sweez. Long time no see."

"Hey Yuri."

"Wassup Dex."

"Nuthin' much," drawled Dex over his bottle of Newcastle.

Sweezy had not even glanced in his direction. She appeared to be hiding her eyes under her wild red curls.

Yuri thought back to one particular night, when he had washed himself out with a good deal of Bacardi and hash at a house party deep in the Mission. Back then he only rarely had gotten so wasted on alcohol and smokeables. The only part of the night he could remember was kissing Sweezy in the middle of a dark side room. He remembered waking up in Sweezy's studio the next day, back when she had been friends and roommates with Mercy.

He never found out just how far he had gone with her that night

Dex looked pretty much as he had back in the city, except that he appeared as if he had lost some weight. His hair was still black and spiked, though a bit longer than before.

Standing in the middle of Rebar's room, Yuri unwrapped his Mickey's. "So what's goin' on tonight?"

"Jus' gonna' have a few," said Rebar. "I heard somethin' was goin' on over at Genoa house."

"We don' know that for sure," said Dex from behind a cloud of cigarette smoke.

"I'm sure somethin's goin' on," replied Rebar with a hint of optimistic bravado. "I heard Generator was gonna play there tonight."

Yuri opened his Mickey's. He felt the lines in the room were too sharp. He needed to calm his nerves.

"I had no idea so many people are living out here now," remarked Yuri after hitting his Mickey's.

Sweezy and Dex did not say anything. They sat quietly and sipped their drinks.

"It sucks," replied Rebar. "I'd rather be in the city."

"Hey Rebar, you still got them extra strings?" blurted Dex quickly.

"Yeah, I gotta whole pack of 'em." Rebar went to his dresser and started rooting around. "I thought you didn't like these strings though."

Rebar kept looking for his strings as Dex picked up Rebar's guitar and started plucking it. Rebar eventually started talking to Dex about music, and the two got lost in their own conversation as Sweezy curled herself further into the easy chair, shrinking into an ever tightening ball.

"Hey Sweez," said Yuri. "Whatcha been up to?"

"Just workin'," she replied over her sinking shoulders. "I gotta job over at Gaylord's"

"Yeah? What's that?"

"A cafe' over on Piedmont."

Sweezy took another sip of her beer. He took a swig from his forty. Sweezy had fallen silent. Yuri searched his head for another subject to keep up the conversation.

"It's been a while since I last saw you," said Yuri, who immediately felt ridiculous for saying so.

"Mm hm."

"When was the last time I ran into you?"

She shrugged. "I dunno."

"I think it was like, a year ago, at the Casa Loma."

She didn't say anything. She took another sip of beer.

"When was the last time you was there?" he asked.

"What?" asked Sweezy, as if she had just realized he was talking to her.

"Have you been to Casa Loma lately?"

"No."

She started watching Dex jam on Rebar's guitar. He finished plunking through a few progressions and scratched out some power chords.

Taking a big swig off of his Mickey's, Yuri listened to Dex rake out a song.

Eventually Rebar retrieved the last of the Newcastles from the kitchen. "We need more beer," announced Rebar. "Come on Dex, let's get to th' store."

"Yeah."

"Practice your chops," said Rebar as he handed Yuri the guitar and walked out with Dex.

Taking another swig off of his forty, he was trying to shake off the air, but the air was still too thick. Sweezy was still curled into the easy chair. Yuri stood up and sat on Rebar's bed, cradling the guitar and trying out a few chords.

"I totally suck now," said Yuri as he strummed a few chords.

"What?"

"I've completely lost my guitar playing ability."

"You gotta have something left."

"You play?"

"Naw. Not really. Mercy showed me a few power chords a long time ago, but other than that I can't do anything." She started unfurling her legs.

"Was it this?"

Yuri mashed the pick against the strings as his hand strained against the power chord. He could feel how long it had been since he had played as the strings cut into his fingers.

Now she was grinning. "What was that?"

"Toxic dog. That was one of her songs, wasn't it?"

"One of whose songs?"

"Mercy's."

"Fuck no it wasn't. That Dave guy showed us that song, what's his name…"

"Oh yeah, the guy from Public Enema?"

"Yeah."

"Wait, did he write that song?"

Sweezy shrugged. "I dunno."

"I don't wanna piss anyone off."

"What? Copyright infringement?"

"Of course." He mashed the strings a few more times. Stealing a quick glance at Sweezy, Yuri could see her legs slowly beginning to stretch back out to the floor. She leaned her drinking arm on the armrest of the chair.

Sweezy finally let one leg loose, dangling it towards the floor. "I didn't want to talk about the Casa Loma. Sorry about that."

"Okay."

"I like the East Bay okay. Being in Berkeley is a lot better than Fremont, but it's just like, fuck."

"Yeah, I know."

"I stayed as long as I could," she finally confessed. "I finally got wrung out. I spent the last two months in the city just couchin' around at friends places, lookin' for a new place."

"Well, it's not that bad out here."

She stabbed out her cigarette. "Fuck. There's nothin' to do over here. There's some okay parties once in a while, but I always just end up doing boring shit I would never do out in the city, like hanging out in goddamn cafes all fucking day long."

"Yeah, I know what you mean."

"It's getting ridiculous. I can barely afford to live in the hole I got right now."

Yuri put the guitar down. "I dunno. I think it's not so bad to get away from that stuff."

"What? What stuff?"

"Y'know, the whole scene out in the city."

"Oh," she replied, sounding perplexed.

"I mean, sometimes there's too much stuff to do," he continued. "You get caught up in it too much."

"I guess." She lit another cigarette and watched it burn for a moment. "You were really getting caught up in it, huh?"

Yuri's skin bristled.

"Yeah," he replied meekly.

Sweezy watched the smoke rise from her cigarette. "I guess that's true. I've been getting' a lot more readin' an' writin' done ever since I got out."

"If that's what you like to do."

"I think it's a good thing. I may be bored, but I guess you are right about getting things done."

"Were you still livin' in that studio last summer?"

"What studio?"

"You know, the one you an' Mercy shared."

"Hell no. We lost that place a long time ago. I was couchin' around after crashin' at Hell Nose House before gettin' that last apartment.."

Yuri felt goose bumps going over his scalp. That had been the name of his old flat. "No fuckin' way! You were actually there?"

"Yeah."

He remembered that he had started going out with Skye shortly after moving into Hell Nose House. It had been a rather strange affair, going out with someone who had only lived a few rooms down from him.

"When were you there?" he asked as he put the guitar aside.

"Like, I was there for a little more than a month. I moved out of there last year."

"Were any of my old roommates still there?"

"Skye wasn't there."

"Yeah, she moved out before I did."

"I don't think any of your old housemates were still there. The place was really fucked up."

"More fucked up than when I was living there?"

"Hell yeah. There was way more graffiti on the walls, way more junk and garbage, an' they kicked a lot more holes in the wall. It was basically just a buncha gutter punks. They had punks sleepin' in the kitchen."

"How didja end up in that place?"

"My friend Jason was livin' there. I was all crashed out in his room for the last month I was there." Sweezy's feet finally reached the floor. "I forget who exactly was in that place when you were livin' there."

"Dan and Pel were sharin' a room, and Surly Sue was living in the small room in the back, just by the kitchen."

"Yeah, I remember Sue. She wasn't there no more. Dan and Pel were way gone. I think they moved out when they broke up."

"Holy shit!"

"Yeah. I never thought those two would ever call it quits."

Yuri leaned forward, "Hey, whatever happened to Preston?"

"Who?"

"Y'know, that guy who was always practicin' all th' time. We made him shut off his amp so he wouldn't drive us crazy?"

"Fuck, I have no idea. I haven't seen that guy in ages."

Gasp

Stopping by a drugstore, Skye bought a pack of razor blades on her way back to her flat. She didn't want to use her library card to scrap out the baggie she had lifted from Deep's place. Back in her room, she split the baggie along its seams so she could get to the dusty insides. She managed to scrape out at least three decent lines worth of second hand crank onto her mirror

The dull resonance of the lines she got from Wink still fluttered around her head like a teasing mist. She felt as if she were awake, but that was it. No charge, no high, no electric buzzing. She realized how poor Wink's speed was when she took a whiff of one of the freshly scraped lines. She got a charge, feeling a jolt go through her eyes and crackling towards the back of her skull as she snorted up a line. A white glow ran down her spine, through her gut and into her feet. A shallow electric buzzing set the bottom of her feet tingling, prompting her to stand and pace.

Feeling her dry throat, Skye wasn't feeling any guilt over snatching three lines worth of crank from Deep. She wondered if Deep had told anyone about their impromptu tryst. It was not news she was anxious to hear from third parties.

She found herself grinding over Wink and Mercy's efforts, but she could only blame them so much. Her own current contacts, outside of Deep, were not much better than theirs, and losing her one good source was only her own fault. She thought about how she should have kept another source on hand, how she should have kept in semi-regular contact with another dealer or go-between, someone she could buy off of every once in a while so she would have a backup source. She had been buying from Deep for so long that all of her other contacts had dried up.

She knew that eventually she would be able to make inroads to a new dealer. Most likely she would have to get to know a go-between first, and then get to the point where she could meet an actual dealer. After that, it would take time to get to know him well enough to the point where she could get the good stuff that wasn't full of B12 or baby laxative or whatever else they would use to cut their stuff.

But that always took time.

She did not feel like waiting. There was only one other person she could think of who was really down with the speed scene and who might still be around.

She did no really care for her chances of finding Preston. She had lost contact with all of their old roommates and mutual friends. On top of all of that was her ignorance of Preston's current status. For all she knew, getting in touch with him might not be any help at all. He might not be living in the city anymore, and there was also a chance that he didn't have any contacts himself. There was even the possibility that he might not be doing speed anymore. He may have graduated to heroin abuse, or perhaps he downgraded to simply drinking.

She wondered about getting a word on other dealers she had known a few years back, like the street dealer Vance, or the cafe dealer Phil, but those possibilities were even longer shots than finding Preston.

Going to the kitchen to quench her parched throat, she decided she would hang around a few select Haight street cafes and bars, just linger for a while to see who she might come across. She would always run into someone she knew if she hung out long enough at a few choice hangouts. Perhaps she could find someone who could get her a line on finding Preston or Vance or Phil. Perhaps she would run into Nuph the Priest, or Mittens, or Sex Dwarf, or one of the other facetiously named bohemian burnouts who occasionally wandered into Nishifu's or Beller's Cafe.

Skye startled. Someone opened the front door.

Jane's baby-fat face appeared in the kitchen doorway.

"Someone's here!" exalted Jane.

"Hey Jane."

Jane brought the rest of her exploding bleached blonde head into the kitchen.

"Wassup?" asked Jane as she walked into the kitchen.

"Nuthin'. How's Stash?"

"Okay. I left him crashed out back at his pad."

"You wore him out?"

"Me and his job wore him out. Mostly his job."

Jane was a hairdresser at a Castro street salon. She was the one who had introduced Skye to Rebar. Jane was one of her two seldom-seen roommates.

Jane was scarcely seen because she was almost always at her boyfriend's place. She would usually stop by the flat once every two or three days. One or two days out of the week she would actually spend the night in her own room.

In Jane's case, it was a love interest that made her appearance a rare occasion. There was quite a different reason why Skye would hardly ever see her other roommate Arden. Arden spent most of her time sequestered in her room, and Skye rarely ever saw the wraith-like Arden except for a daily sighting in the kitchen or the hallway. On those occasions when Skye would see her, she would always be wearing the same thing: her thick, white terry cloth bathrobe, topped by her head of flat, stringy black hair. Oftentimes Skye was not sure if Arden was there or not. On occasions she had suspected that she was absent, only to find out she was mistaken. Skye had never even seen Arden's room, a room far in the back of the flat, around the corner at the end of the hallway. Jane had warned her when she first moved in that Arden's section of the flat was very private, and she would get extremely touchy if she ever caught anyone so much as even looking into her room.

A few times Jane and Skye had wondered what it was that Arden did for money. Not that it really mattered to them very much. Arden was the leaseholder on the place and she always paid for the utilities, in addition to always paying her rent, so they rarely ever bothered with the idea of asking.

"You stayin' here tonight?" asked Skye.

"Yeah. I gotta give Stash a break. He's been gettin' ten hour days on his site this past week. I'm guessin' I'll just be wearin' him out even more."

Skye's dry throat was coming back. She downed the rest of her water.

"What you been up to?" asked Jane.

"Nuthin'. Jus' screwin around."

"Still workin' at Levigate Video?"

"Yeah. Just part time though. I'm doin' alright."

Jane started leaving the kitchen.

"You don't know where I can find any crank, do you?" blurted Skye suddenly.

Stopping in the doorway, Jane thought about it for a moment. "Stash might know somebody. We usually jus' grab some pot an' X, so I don't know if he knows anybody who deals crank."

"Yeah. I'm jus' kinda desperate, that's the only reason I'm askin', otherwise I wouldn't bug ya about it."

"Don't you have a regular dealer?"

"Not anymore," deadpanned Skye.

Jane paused and then brightened up. "I know guys that can get you all the heroin you want."

"Fuck no. I'd never touch that shit."

"Just kidding."

"I hope so."

"I know you tweakers are a minority around here."

"We're doin' okay." Skye started out of the kitchen.

"If you have any East Bay contacts you might try them."

"Yeah."

"I could ask Stash if y'like. I won't be able to ask him until tomorrow though."

"If ya think of it. It's no big deal."

Skye was making her way back down the hall as Jane went to her room. Skye did not know anyone in the East Bay. Supposedly there was a lot more speed out there, but all of her contacts were in the city.

Looking at the hallway floor, she wished she had not asked Jane about trying to find speed. Skye should have known that she would not know where to get any.

She was wondering just how desperate she wanted to get.

The bones in her forearms were getting heavy. They were trying to bring her arms back down to the table. She took a long drag off of her coffee.

Slowly tilting her head toward the table, she kept her eyes on the street as wisps of black hair fell in front of her eyes like attacking spider legs.

The weight of her skin was settling back down as the rays of the sun drew shadows on her table.

She reflected on her recent attempts to secure a source, and she could see Wink's face again as she ran the whole episode through her mind once more. What did Wink know about speed and speed dealing? Did he even have a clue? He might have been too dense to really know what was going on.

Skye mused on the idea that the whole experience might be trying to tell her something. Perhaps the whole scene was just over the top, that it was no longer worth the trouble it took to find her supplies. Perhaps she should stay off of the tweak altogether for a while. Her craving for the stuff was dying off, at least for the moment.

The sun's rays were coming in sharp, making the front half of the coffeehouse too bright and the back half too dark. In the few hours that she had been sitting there, she had not seen anyone she even recognized, much less someone she knew well enough to ask about drug contacts. Skye tried to console herself with the knowledge that having gone back to her place and sitting around would have driven her crazy.

Leaning back in her chair, she decided she would drink the rest of her half-finished luke warm pint of coffee and head back to her flat. She was finally starting to relax. She wanted to get home and cull the feeling and see if she could manage an early evening nap.

As she was beginning to settle into her wooden cafe chair, her eye caught a grungy punk sauntering past the window, bobbing her baseball cap about as she took a cool turn into the cafe, walking forward with dead eyes front.

A shot went through Skye.

"Gwen!"

Gwen had Preston's new number. Gwen was one of the old scenesters, someone who knew almost everyone because she spent virtually all of her time hanging out in cafes, bars, and clubs. She told Skye, who plied her with a latte, that she had been hanging out with Preston late last year, and she still had a phone number for his place.

Gwen said she had not called him in a few months, so she was not sure if it was still a good number for him or not.

She made some small talk with Gwen after getting Preston's number, just to be polite, but even that short amount of casual chatter had been excruciating.

Once Skye made it home she made a beeline for her room.

Taking in a deep breath, she picked up the phone and carefully dialed the number Gwen had written down on a napkin. The last number was a little smudged, since the ink bled into the soft paper, but she was almost certain it was the number five.

She finished dialing the last number.

A pause.

A click.

Another click.

Skye's skin stood on edge when she heard a ring.

Another ring.

Ring, ring…

A click.

A short scratchy pause. An answering machine had picked up. A thrash song started playing. That was a good sign. It was a scratchy, static thrash instrumental. It played for a few more moments.

The music stopped and the machine beeped.

"Hey Pres, this is Skye." She was stuttering. "I got your number from Gwen and I was wondering how you were doin'. It's been a while since we talked. Gimme a call, if y'like. We can catch up."

She left her number and hung up.

Now she really felt desperate. For all she knew it was not even Preston's number anymore. Someone would listen to some weird message from some spaced out tweak and wonder why she had been calling them. She had left her number, so now some stranger could start calling her place, bugging her about why she had called them.

The mirror next to her futon kept pulling at her. She was thinking about taking a blade and scraping together some of the mirror's faint speed residue to try and form a small line.

"Fuck, it's just tweak," she muttered to herself as she put her head down. She tried turning her thoughts to more practical matters. She had to go to work, for at least a few hours, in the next couple of days. She had not been getting as many hours at work as she usually did. The extra time was fueling her recreational cravings, she mused.

She knelt down on her futon and checked her water bottle. She was trying to remember when she had last eaten.

The phone rang. Lying down on her futon, she answered it.

"Hello?"

"Skye!"

It was Preston.

Home

Yuri stumbled into his place with his duffle bag full of clean clothes. It had started to lightly rain as he was walking back from the laundromat.

"Yo!"

Yuri started. His roommate was home.

"What th' fuck?" greeted Yuri.

"Whatcha doin'?" bellowed Zatch as he looked down from the rafters.

"Did mah laundry."

Yuri put down his duffle bag, just as the patter of rain could be heard hitting their shack.

If there was ever a time when he really enjoyed his place, it was when it was raining. He was only sorry that it wasn't raining harder so that it would be more satisfying to be inside. It was one of the few places he had ever lived in that managed to stay warm during cold and wet weather. Zatch had turned up the small yet powerful old gas heater in the kitchen.

"Come on up," invited Zatch.

"Jus' a sec." Yuri took out his bath towel which was still damp. He draped it over the single chair in his place, an old wooden kitchen chair that he had borrowed from the main house.

Yuri climbed the sturdy wooden wall ladder up to Zatch's loft. Zatch was still wearing his studded leather jacket. A woman was curled up in the corner of Zatch's loft, her eyes peeking out from her impossibly straight and long dark red hair.

"Wassup Yuri," said Zatch.

"Hey. Long time no see."

As Yuri clambered into Zatch's very low-ceilinged section of the place, Zatch held forth a can of Mesiterbrau. Yuri did not really feel like drinking, but he wanted to be polite, so he took the Meisterbrau.

"You remember Carrie," said Zatch.

"No I don't."

"What?"

"He hasn't met me yet," said Carrie.

"Oh, right."

"Hey. I'm Yuri."

"Hey."

"Whatcha guys doin' here?" asked Yuri as he cracked open his beer.

"I live here, remember?"

"No."

"Huh?"

"I hardly ever see you in here."

"Yeah, that's right."

"Carrie's place gettin' too boring?" asked Yuri.

"There's this big fucked up party goin' on there right now," replied Zatch. "We're too burnt to put up with it."

"I need to get some sleep tonight," said Carrie darkly from behind her straight red shield of hair.

"Don't worry about me," said Yuri. "I'm crashin' out tonight."

"Sure thing," said Zatch. "We'll try not to make too much noise."

Carrie shifted around in her corner. "What noise?"

"Aren't we gonna make noise tonight?" pleaded Zatch.

"Fuck no. I'm way too tired."

"Aaaaaw," moaned Zatch.

"Go ahead," said Yuri. "You won't be able to wake me up."

"I dunno dude," said Zatch. "She's a real screamer."

"No way," said Carrie. "You're the one who does all the screaming."

"Oh yeah, right." Zatch nodded towards Yuri. "I'll try and keep it down."

"S'cool," said Yuir. "I might check out the Stab party if it turns out I can't sleep."

"Why do they call it the Stab House?" asked Carrie. "Does it have to do with that singer?"

"The one from the Misinformed?" remarked Zatch.

"I only knew him from when he was in S.F, when he was in that band Toxic Intercourse," said Yuri.

"How come they don't call it the Toxic House anymore?" asked Carrie as she leaned forward.

"They used to," said Zatch. "They just said Toxic. Like in, 'Let's go to Toxic.' Not even 'Toxic House'."

"That was only one of his bands," said Yuri. "He was in so many bands that they finally just called it the Stab House."

Yuri tilted back his beer. He chugged it down. He wanted to get back down and tidy up his space.

"Thanks for the beer," said Yuri.

"Hey, four for a twelve you can't go wrong."

"Nice meetin' ya," said Yuri to Carrie.

"Yeah," groaned Carrie as she slumped down in her corner.

"I'll see ya in th' mornin'," said Yuri as he started climbing back down the ladder.

Yuri was only halfway down when Zatch stuck his head out again. "Hey, some guy called for you earlier."

Yuri stopped on the ladder. "Yeah?"

"Somebody name garbage or litter or somethin'."

"Trash?"

"Yeah."

"Johnny Trash?"

"That's it! He wants you to call him back."

A shudder almost knocked Yuri off the ladder.

Quickly skittering down to the floor, he wondered why he had shuddered when he had heard the name Johnny Trash.

He went to the fridge and grabbed another beer.

Reminisce

"I hardly seen you since you took off," said Preston.

Leaning down, carefully holding onto the straw, Skye snorted up her line. An electric charge throbbed through her face.

"Fuck yeah," drawled Skye as she leaned back.

"I remember comin' home an' you just wasn't there."

"I just got tired of the place," said Skye before Preston could ask. The rush had vastly improved her mood.

"Yeah? So?" he chided as he cradled his blue Fender Guitar.

"Shit, this is some good stuff!"

"Hell yeah it is. I got a good source."

"I just got way tired of Hell Nose House," said Skye. "It was always a fuckin' mess, there was never any quiet, an everythin' was broken all the time. I just couldn't take it anymore."

"But that's what alla' our places have been like."

She shrugged. "I know. I pretty much figured at the time that I'd probably end up in the same kinda place."

"Didja?"

She tilted back her beer. "Not even. My new place is cleaner and quieter, an' most of the stuff works pretty well."

"Actually, this is the quietest place I've ever lived in."

"No shit?"

"I got this place all to myself, and the neighbors usually aren't too noisy."

She had scrunched herself into an old easy chair that sat in the middle of Preston's room while Preston sat on his bed. He had put the mirror on the edge of his bed, as his cramped room didn't leave much space for other kinds of furniture.

Preston was living in a small and dark apartment in the top corner of an old and sequestered apartment building. He lived fairly close to the industrial section of town, a somewhat modest walk from Skye's flat. The building was sandwiched between a large warehouse and a machine shop.

The room was crammed and cramped with a wide variety of objects. The major pieces were his bed, the chair in which Skye was sitting, an old wooden desk that took up way too much of his bedroom, and a bookcase next to the door that was filled to capacity with all manner of objects, few of which were books. There was a row of shelves behind Preston that contained even more items, including a very impressive stereo system.

She was quite surprised by his room since his place back at their former residence had been quite spartan. The only object Preston really cared for back then was a small music collection and his guitar. He now had three guitars.

"So when did you leave the house?" asked Skye.

"What house?"

"Our old place with the stupid name."

He looked at the ceiling as if he had to remember what had happened. "I just remember leavin' after Pel and Dan had left. Once Dan was gone the whole place became way too chaotic."

"I'll bet."

"I moved to this weird little house near the waterfront. It was a trip. It was this little house with about three bedrooms and it was hella' old. It was all fucked up and it was sittin' next to this big ass warehouse in the middle of nowhere. Half my friends could never find it when they tried to visit me. Couldja' open that window?"

"Huh?"

"That little window. I need some air."

"Where?"

"Back there," said Preston as he pointed.

One of the windows had been blocked off by a shelf. The window next to the bed had been taped up with a flat black material. The only source to the outside world was a small window next to the large wooden desk, which Skye spotted only after squinting around the poorly lit room. Her head tilted as she stood up.

"Fuck," groaned Skye.

"What?"

"I am really fuckin' wired!" she said as she danced around to keep her light feet steady.

"Yeah. Sorry to make you get up and deal with the window. My head's out there too."

She struggled with the small window. The wood was rough, splintering along the faded white paint. Wrenching the window halfway up, a cool blast of noisy air wafted into the room. She had no idea just how stuffy it had been inside of the dark room until she felt the rushing city air.

Maneuvering carefully back to her chair, Skye moved her beer aside. She wondered how she was going to handle the next line, which Preston was already forming. The first line had been quite large, and the next line he was making for her was even larger.

"So can you get me a half?" she asked in a casual voice.

"Hell yeah I can."

Stretching himself out and over the edge and reaching under his bed, he brought out a wooden box that was about the size of a large shoebox.

"Just a half?" asked Preston.

"Yeah."

He took a small scale out of the wooden box, along with a very large plastic bag full of white powder.

Skye's eyes went numb.

She could not believe her luck.

The size of his supply told her everything that she needed to know.

Preston was a dealer.

II

Clean and Mean

Another Score

Skye was sorting through her change jar, looking for quarters. It was time to do the laundry, which she would tend to after a quick stop by the large corner drug store to buy some more cheap underwear. After sorting through her clothes, she found she was forced to part with two more pairs of panties that had been worn and frayed to the point where they had become unwearable.

Skye was riding a maintenance line, a line she had just snorted, not to get high, but simply to stay awake and alert after having worn herself out with another speed binge.

She kept thinking about her list of chores as she counted quarters: laundry, underwear, eat. She had to remind herself to eat, just a little something to thicken her blood and get her going again.

The door buzzer went off. She ducked into the hallway and got on the intercom.

"Hello?"

"Hey gorgeous, where you been all my life?"

"Hey Mers. Come on up."

Skye buzzed Mercy in. Quickly grabbing a couple of beers from the fridge, she led Mercy into her room.

"So whatcha been up to?" asked Skye as she sorted through her widely dispersed laundry.

"Nuthin' much. Jus' hangin' out with Linette."

Skye leaned down on her futon. "Okay, what's her real name?"

"Linette."

"Naw, I mean her real name."

"That is her real name."

"Bullshit," smiled Skye. "It's something else."

"Why th' fuck would anyone want to change their name to Linette?"

"I dunno. Maybe she's got somethin' to hide."

"Pshh."

Skye pushed her laundry into a corner and sat down on the futon.

"Did you find a new dealer yet?" asked Mercy.

"Oh yeah!"

"So how is he? Do I know him?"

"He's got some pretty good stuff," she said as her bones started sinking into the futon.

"Cool. 'Cause I was lookin' to score. Linette wanted to try some."

"I could work that out."

"She's never tried it before."

Skye sat up. "No shit?"

"Nope."

"That's a surprise."

"Whattaya mean?"

"I thought she would've tried everything by now."

"Yeah. I guess that's a reasonable assumption."

Mercy sat down on the floor, crossing her legs and leaning over the edge of the futon.

"We jus' wanna get a half."

"Sure, no prob. Just lemme make sure my guy is up."

Skye went into the kitchen to make the call, leaving Mercy in her room. If Preston was just dealing nickel and dime bags, or even if he had simply been selling quarters grams and half grams, she probably would have told Mercy about Preston.

But Preston was a serious dealer. He was selling significant supplies. His minimum weight for sale was a teenager, a gram and a half of speed. Usually he sold eight balls, and eighth of an ounce, which was the kind of supply nickel and dime dealers would buy to sell. Considering the level of dealing he was engaged in, it was better to keep his current activities on the under, rather than spread it around.

When Skye thought about it, Mercy was more than just another friend. She had admitted to herself that she had always looked up to her, as if she were her older sister. Mercy was about a year younger than Skye, but she always seemed so much more calm and collected, as if she had a few more points of life figured out than the average person.

Skye though about it as she started dialing Preston's number.

Underwear, underwear, remember to buy underwear.

Phone calls

Yuri was going through his fridge.

His bread was going stale. He had forgotten to eat all of it before it had become uneatable.

Carefully inspecting the bread, perhaps some of the slices in the back of the bag were still edible. There was almost half a loaf left. He was thinking about groceries. He had tried to budget himself, but he had indulged in one too many cups of coffee on the Avenue, and one too many pints at Carl's Place. He kept running into Dex up on Telegraph Avenue, and they would invariably end up hanging out at the Bottega or the Med. They would have two or three cups of coffee and then score a slice of pizza at one of the local pizza stands. It was not much, but he would usually end up spending four or five more dollars than he had expected to whenever he ran into Dex, which was becoming a more frequent occurrence.

He was halfway through his bread inspection when his phone rang.

Lying down on his mattress, he answered his phone.

"Yello?" sang Yuri into the phone.

"Hey Yore-ee," pronounced Sweezy deliberately.

"Wassup?"

"Just wondered if you wanted to go see Special Forces tomorrow night."

"Hmmm," he moaned noncommittally. "I dunno. That last show…"

"It won't be like that show, honest! The Calm's singer was just really drunk."

"So? So was Cleave at the Bartap show, and he was still entertaining."

"Hey, it's Special Forces. Have they ever let you down?"

"Yeah. Orlando owes me a dollar."

"He does not!"

"Does too."

"Come on. Come to the show."

"Make me."

"I will. I'll come over there and beat you."

"Ooh ooh! Yes do."

"How about it?" asked Sweezy seriously.

"Yeah, sure, what the hell," confessed Yuri.

"Cool."

"If I get Rebar to go he can drive us."

"I thought Rebar wasn't into Gilman."

"He goes there sometime. Besides, He's got his drummer's van for a few weeks. We could toss a buncha people into the back."

"Sweet."

"Should we come over there?" asked Yuri as he casually eyed his ceiling.

"If you want. You could also just meet us at the Med."

"Rebar would probably want to meet up at Carl's Place."

"Carl's Place? That dive with all the fucked up skinheads in it?"

He sat up. "Yeah."

"Why would he want to meet there?"

"They're not all skinheads."

"I know, but some serious fuck ups hang out there," she worried aloud.

"He still likes to go there. The screw ups never get on his nerves."

"No shit? Is he copping?"

"Hell no. He just drinks."

"Weird."

"Why don't we just go by your place," suggested Yuri finally.

"Do that."

"What time?"

"Mmmm, about seven?"

"Okay. I'll give him a call."

"Sweet. See you later."

"Not if I see you first."

Yuri put down the phone.

Suddenly he remembered his bread inspection. Hopping to his feet he dashed back into the kitchen.

Inspecting a few more pieces of bread, he determined that the entire half loaf was inedible.

His hand unconsciously moved to his stomach.

He was still very thin.

Another deal

"A half this time?"

"Yep."

Skye was sitting, yet again, in the easy chair. This time she straightened her legs out. Her skin was warming in the cramped atmosphere.

"Can I open the window?" asked Skye.

"Let's snort a few lines first. I don't want the wind blowin' th' stuff around."

Preston dumped a pile of crank out onto his mirror. Skye was buying a half, but she would eventually do at least that much in free lines, and most likely more than that by virtue of Preston's casual generosity.

Skye looked at her legs as they stretched out from the old easy chair. She had on her faded black jeans which were beginning to turn gray. She recalled that the last time she was hanging out with Preston, back in their Hell Nose House days, she would wear all kinds of colors: shocking blues, bright greens and red plaid skirts. She would wear just about anything, as long as it was painful to look at. Now there was barely anything in her wardrobe that wasn't black, or at least dark gray.

She was quite grateful that he had turned out to be such a good direct source for good crank. A lot of small time crank dealers would buy grams and teens from dealers like Preston for their supplies. Those kinds of dealers usually cut their stuff, mixing in an inert substance to make their supplies artificially larger, just to get another couple of quarter grams or dime bags out of their stock. They had to be cautious, however. Some dealers would get carried away with cutting their supply and end up diluting it to the point where it wasn't very powerful at all, leading to too many disgruntled customers.

Those kinds of dealers usually did their small time dealing around cafes or bars on the main drags. Other dealers, the ones who usually dealt with trusted contacts, would buy eight balls for their supplies, selling quarter and half grams to people from their homes and their friends homes.

Then there were dealers like Preston. Preston would sell teens and eight balls, one and a half grams and three gram portions. He was a dealer who would sell to major tweaks who bought large personal supplies and to small time dealers. Skye knew from her knowledge of the speed scene that Preston's dealer was even more hardcore. He sold speed by the ounce. That was the man who knew the true source of the drugs they were consuming: the manufacturer. Somewhere, deep in the

East Bay suburbs, there were several speed labs continuously churning out the popular white powder.

Skye did not know exactly how speed was made. She knew a few details, such as some of the preliminary products that were needed, and she also knew that it created a lot of chemical waste, but she did not know anything specific about the manufacturing of the drug. She was reassured by a friend that she didn't want to know.

"I know you don't usually sell portions this small," apologized Skye.

"I know." He leaned back and grabbed one of the guitars next to his bed. "I'm only doin' it because you're a friend."

"I appreciate it."

Preston strummed out a quick ska rhythm.

Skye leaned down and snorted up her line. This time it did not hurt so much. She sat up, feeling light from the crank filling up her head.

"I don't mind doling out halves for you, but do you think you might ever want to buy up a teen?"

She tilted her head back to catch the drain. "Maybe. If I get some people to go in with me. It'll happen eventually I'm sure."

"You still know a lot a' tweaks?"

Skye shrugged. "A few. Not really, I guess. The only ones I really knew were the ones who hung around my last dealer."

Yuri's work

The echoes eventually faded into background noise as Yuri's lone footsteps reverberated throughout the warehouse.

Yuri's workplace was a block long and a block wide cavernous concrete structure with a low ceiling. The entire place was basically a concrete basement under an old five story office building near downtown Oakland. It was his job to record and catalog books, magazines, and records, which comprised the back stock for a small chain of independent book and music stores. Yuri only remembered that Moisette had a store in Berkeley. He could not recall where her other two stores were located. He had never even been to any one of her shops, despite being one of her employees.

The place was full of ceiling-high metal and wooden shelves of various designs and styles. Some of the shelves looked brand new while others looked old and worn, and some appeared as if they had been found on street corners or junkyards. The aisles were inefficiently lit, some having just barely enough light to make things out, which only made his job more difficult. Most of the inventory were books and magazines, requiring him to squint through the darkness at various titles and print. Yuri thought it looked more like a bomb shelter or a gangster's hideaway than a warehouse.

He had been working at the warehouse for several months. The first few weeks had been a trial. Aside from his first two days on the job, when the owner Miss Moisette had incessantly chattered during his training, he spent virtually every work day completely alone.

Technically, Yuri was the warehouse manager. That's what Moisette was always calling him. Despite his grandiose title, he had no underlings to command. He would have appreciated the title a lot more if he was not the only employee. Once in a while he would run into Garrick, the delivery man who usually came by in the mornings to drop off inventory.

He wasn't used to being alone without something coursing through his veins. Isolation would oftentimes bring back all too recent memories. Occasionally, when he was far back in the dark warehouse, he would get a few shakes, a shiver or two, up his back or down his arm.

The farther back one got into the place, the darker it would get. Once, about a week into his job, he got the shakes so fiercely he wondered if he would be able to keep working. Fortunately he was able to snap out of it after a few moments. He once considered bringing a small bottle of something, such as rum or vodka to work, to calm his nerves down during such events, but he decided it was too risky.

Most of the stock was brought in during the week, usually during his many days off. Yuri was continuously organizing and cataloging all kinds of books, magazines, records, and cassette tapes.

They also managed to always bring in an odd assortment of items, presumably on the whim of the owner Moisette, and he would have to decide how to organize them. The delivered items included such things as old toys, kitchen appliances, boxes of clothes, boxes of office or carpentry supplies, old buttons and paper binders, along with all manner of other random items. Once they delivered a stuffed boar's head, and another time he had to sort through random mannequin parts: arms and legs and random torsos, all without a mannequin head in sight. He wondered if they sent him the seemingly random items as a joke, or as some kind of bizarre employee aptitude test. He also wondered if perhaps they had a benign intention, that they brought such random items as a way to make his job more interesting.

At the moment he was carrying an armload of records, taking them to the back of the warehouse where he kept the discontinued LP overstock.

His footsteps echoed louder as he got deeper into the warehouse. The shadows were getting darker.

He organized the records by genre, only he wasn't sure how to categorize recordings of Hungarian flute concerts and Scottish skiffle music.

As he carefully indexed the records into wooden milk crates, he was startled by a loud noise at the other end of the warehouse. Light was pouring in from the front of the warehouse.

Quickly walking down the aisle, Yuri recognized the trademark stomping of Garrick. He had backed up the van to the warehouse doors.

"Hey Gar," greeted Yuri as he walked up to the warehouse entrance.

"Moisette really don't like it when you leave the doors open."

"I need the extra light and the air to work."

"She doesn't like it. Help me unload this stuff."

They unloaded several crates of records, a few cardboard boxes full of cassette tapes, and a small bundle of books. Garrick also brought out a shoe box full of old super 8 film reels, a cardboard carton full of old clothes and plastic hand puppets, and a metal crate full of old fashioned doll clothes.

"She says this stuff might be worth somethin'," said Garrick. "You should store it in the back somewheres so it'll be safe."

"Is it?"

"Huh?"

"Is it valuable?"

"Is what valuable?"

"This stuff." Yuri wagged his finger in the direction of the various items they had just unloaded.

"Fuck if I know. Just make sure it don't get messed up."

Garrick turned, slamming van doors shut as he started walking back to the driver's seat.

Yuri decided to handle the potentially valuable random objects before getting back to the usual filing of books and records. The new arrivals did not appear to be worth very much, even though he knew his pedestrian opinion was not very helpful in determining the value of old hand puppets and antiquated super 8 film.

Walking towards the back of the warehouse, he decided the alleged collectibles would be best kept on one of the high metal shelves in the back. He echoed down the dark corridors as the ceiling lights filtered their way through books and records and random shelving. The air got thicker and the darkness got darker. As he walked, he wondered what he would have thought about the warehouse if he was still using, if such a place would make it harder to get high, or perhaps if it would be the perfect heroin hideaway.

At first it was just a slight tinge in his right forearm. After a few moments it quickly shrunk into a knot, a tight point right on one of the strings in his arm. For a moment, it felt as if it would just be another momentary spasm, but the knot kept getting tighter. A few more breaths and it started to ache. He kept moving, quickly trying to get himself to the back of the warehouse.

Suddenly he started losing his grip on the crate. Shooting pains shot up and down the bones in his arm, scurrying into his palms and his fingertips. He stopped and put down the crate as his arm started convulsing. Stopping in his tracks, he looked at the crate which kicked up some dust that was now settling onto the doll clothes. Leaning over to pick up the crate, the spasms got worse. His hand shook.

He grasped his forearm with his left hand. The spasms were not going away. The fierce and concentrated vibrations caused his hand to go numb as the spasms moved into his fingers.

He clenched his teeth and knotted his temples. He saw the wire metal crate filled with dusty miniature dresses and frocks, and could not shake the demeaning thought that he was incapable of carrying a box full of toy clothes.

Turning around, the daylight from the faraway warehouse doors seared right through his tightly shut eyes.

Forcing himself to stand up, he held onto his arm as he walked out of the warehouse. Out on the street, he squinted his way to the nearest liquor store.

Getting into the liquor store, he tried to straighten himself up as he hoped the quick walk would calm down the spasms, but they were still plucking at the muscles in his forearm, as if a frantic violinist were trying to rip a tune out of the inside of his arm. Yuri bought a small bottle of Stoli's and dashed out. He noticed a few winos out front who made it a point not to look directly at him.

Getting back to the warehouse, there was still a wriggling in his forearm as he pushed the doors open. The spasms were subsiding, but he also began to realize that the strain had snaked itself through his other arm and was moving into other parts of his body. His right knee ached, his temples were tight, a drop of sweat ran into his eye.

"Hey DT."

Right after locking the doors, he went over to the brightly lit shipping desk. He placed the vodka on the desk and watched it for a moment.

He kept the bottle in the bag as he took off the cap and took a quick swig. He barely registered the sting of the vodka. He could feel its warmth move through his throat and his chest, but the kick never washed back on him.

He turned his head and squeezed his eyes shut. Keeping his eyes closed for a few more moments, he opened them again and took another swig on the vodka. The light was not so bright this time.

But the darkness was still there.

Work Plane

Her head felt hollow. Her feet were light and heavy at the same time. She would not have felt her arms, if it had not occurred to her to try to do so.

She was still wide awake.

Two days and she was still awake. She was not just awake, but very wide awake, as if she had just awoken from a long and restful sleep.

Which was fortuitous for the circumstances. Skye was at her part time job. She was only supposed to work a four-hour shift, but the manager had asked if she could stay on for another two hours.

Skye leaned on the counter next to the cash register as a few customers wandered the aisles. The place was quite a popular video store, even though it was in a very small and cramped storefront. More often than not, Skye could not see most of the customers from the counter through the tightly packed maze of shelves.

Skye could feel the weight of her maintenance line, which was inside a small baggie in her right inner coat pocket. It was cold enough inside the store for her to keep wearing her Derby jacket.

Usually she would take the empty free time on her job to busy herself with the shelves, rearranging videos or checking customer records, but she did not feel like moving in her current state. The manager had already gone home for the day, so she did not have to force herself to look busy.

"How's it goin'?"

Turning around, it was her short and short-haired coworker Chasey.

"How's it goin' today?" asked Chasey again.

"Okay."

"Cool."

Skye wondered if Chasey could tell she was strung out.

"How was your weekend?" asked Chasey with widening turquoise eyes.

"Pretty good."

Chasey straightened up. "I was wonderin' if you could help me in the back with somethin'."

"Yeah sure," said Skye, taking a quick glance around the store before following Chasey into the back.

They walked into the small back room of the store. It was a long and narrow room with black walls and poor lighting. Chasey went over to the long plywood shipping desk.

"I gotta put labels on these new vids," explained Chasey as she indicated two boxes of videos.

"Okay."

Chasey started opening one of the boxes. She leaned towards Skye and spoke quietly. "I was just wondering, you wouldn't happen to know where I can score any crank?"

Skye though it through. She usually did not worry about people asking her about drugs. She either agreed to help them out because she knew them well enough, or she just shrugged them off, telling them she didn't know where to get any.

With this particular coworker she had to think about the risks. She was definitely a borderline case.

"I might be able to find some," said Skye meekly.

"I was just looking for some for me an' a friend, for next weekend."

"Well," Skye cast the corner of her eye towards the door to make sure the other coworker was not close enough to hear them. "How much were you lookin' to buy?"

"Just a half. That'd be enough for us."

"Okay."

"I can turn you on to some really good pot if y'like."

"That's okay. I think I know where I can get some."

"It's pretty killer bud. I even got some back at my place if y'wanna try it."

"That's cool. I'm not really into bud. Just gimme your number," said Skye, "an' I'll give you a call in the next day or two."

"Sure thing."

Underground

Skye had made the call. Preston told her to come over.

It was starting to become routine. All Preston had to do was hear Skye's voice on the phone and he knew she wanted to come over.

Skye was starting to feel a guilty about their new ritual. Preston wasn't just another dealer, he was also an old friend. She decided she needed to go over to his place for a social visit, at least once in a while, just drop by without asking for any supply. Skye believed she owed him that much.

Skye even had her eventual social visit planned out. She intended to drop by his place in the next few days with a six pack of Red Hooks or Newcastles and talk about the old days and music.

Walking up to the dark and old apartment building, Preston buzzed her in and she made the four-story trudge past the perpetually broken elevator.

Preston opened the door. Preston had left his hall light on. He almost never had it on.

"Hi Skye."

"Yar' Pres."

"Get on in here," smiled Preston as he stepped aside.

Turning the corner of the short hallway, There were two leather jacketed long hairs in Preston's kitchen. One was seated next to the small round kitchen table while the other was standing next to the fridge, sipping a tall can of Olde English 800. The standing one had a thin mustache and full, long wavy dark hair. The sitting long hair had a cracked and worn black leather jacket, a thicker mustache, and longer flat hair.

"Jus' hang loose," said Preston. "I gotta complete some biz in the next room."

"Sure."

Preston disappeared into his room.

The apartment did not have a large kitchen. The younger had to stand in front of the fridge in order to give the elder enough room to sit at the table. Skye backed herself up against the edge of the sink.

"Y'wanna a eight ball?" asked the younger rivethead.

Skye was tempted to make a joke. She knew they were offering her a beer. "Sure thing, if ya can spare one."

"Show 'er th' fridge," rasped the elder.

The younger opened the fridge door. There were four six packs of beer crowding Preston's fridge.

"Okay, I suppose you can spare one," said Skye.

"That's just for starters," said the elder.

Accepting the Malt liquor, she quickly opened it and took a long drag.

The younger rivethead seemed to be fairly mellow, but Skye wasn't completely comfortable with the way the elder was looking at her.

"So how long you known Pres?" asked the younger.

"Long time."

"You ever jam with Preston?"

"Eh. Kind of."

"You play?"

"Yeah. I play guitar, and bass sometimes. But I suck."

The elder laughed.

"I was just thinkin' of those bands Pres' had been in, like Free Chuck," said the younger.

"I never played with any a' those guys."

"Who did ya play with?"

Skye shuffled her feet. The younger's question sounded a little pointed. She took another drag of her beer, trying to keep her cool.

"You ever heard of the Dynamite Chicks?" asked Skye.

"Nuh uh."

"Well, asides from the Dynamite Chicks I jammed with the Ex-Girlfriends, and I also filled in for my friend Spider in Triple-T."

The younger straightened up. "You played with Triple-T?"

"Only for three shows."

"Fuckin a', that band fuckin' kicked ass!"

"People only say that because the singer was always takin' her clothes off."

"Hell yeah!" volunteered the elder.

"Even so, they were a good band, asides from the nudity," said the younger.

"Yeah, it's the closest I've ever been to bein' a rockstar," said Skye.

The Younger straightened his gait. "So how you know Pres?"

"From the scene. We used to be roommates."

"Yeah? Back in the Lower Haight days?"

"Naw, not that far back. After that, at Hell Nose House."

"No shit? I think I remember you now."

"From Hell Nose?"

"Did you ever see the band Hammer Party?"

Skye rolled her eyes towards the ceiling as she thought about it. It suddenly struck her.

"Was it a show at Ruthie's?" she asked.

"Yeah."

"And some industrial band was playing?"

"Yup."

Skye stood up straighter. "I forgot the industrial band's name."

"Greenway's band. I forgot their name though. Something about a hamster."

"I can't remember either."

"We were pretty good that night, huh?" asked the younger with brightening eyes.

"Beats me. I was too damn drunk to remember anything."

The younger shook his head. "That's what everyone says."

"That's because it's true," snarked the elder. "Th' only people who'd listen to you were drunks."

"No way. They just don't want to tell us what they really thought."

"I heard you guys were pretty good," said Skye.

"Who told you that?" smiled the elder.

"Some guy who stayed sober long enough to remember the show."

"Fuck, that was the best band I was ever in," lamented the younger as his posture relaxed.

"When'd you guys break up?" asked Skye.

The younger turned around and grabbed another beer out of the fridge. "Somethin' like, six months after we got started. Nobody could take it anymore."

"What? Musical differences?"

"Naw, nothin' like that. Like, almost every fuckin' show, somethin' fucked up would happen."

"Isn't that par for the course?"

"I mean like something really fucked up, somethin' really out there. It was usually somethin' that would keep us from playin'."

"Like what?"

"We had one show at Carny's where we was playin' right before the headliner. Right as we were settin' up, a buncha Nazi skins showed up, and this full blown riot started up right outside the club."

"It stopped the show?"

"Naw. Everyone was out fightin' in the lot when we were playin'."

"At least it was for a good cause."

"Then there was the Case Street House. Some asshole dropped a toilet on our bass players head."

"What?"

"We're bringin' our stuff into the Base Street House when this toilet drops out of the second story window, an entire fuckin' toilet! An' comes down right on our bass player."

"No fuckin' way!"

"The guys upstairs were replacing a toilet, and they just chucked the old one out the window."

"Without even lookin' first?"

"That's what I said. Those assholes even tried to talk us into still doin' the show with one a' their roommates on bass."

"That's too much."

Preston's head popped into the kitchen. "Hey Skye."

"Thanks for th' beer," said Skye as she made her way to Preston's room.

Preston closed the door behind her. There was another long hair in the room. He was sitting in the old beat up easy chair that Skye usually occupied.

She stood uneasily against the wall next to the television and the stereos. The long hair in the chair was wearing an old blue denim jacket. His long hanging hair was shrouding his face as he was fiddling with something in his lap.

"Whad'ja want to get again?" asked Preston as he sat cross-legged on his bed.

"A teen," said Skye.

"Right."

Preston started weighing out her stash. With a great shnuffing of air, the denim rivethead raised his head suddenly, sending his hair flying back. He was holding onto a long and thin glass pipe full of white smoke. The rising wisps of curling smoke gave the air a metallic smell.

Skye knew who he was. His name was Ratchet. He was the singer for Landshark, a thrash band made up of seasoned burnouts that were making it big in the metal and punk scene.

Carefully maneuvering herself around the small and crowded room, she sat down on the corner of Preston's bed.

Leaving his scale for a moment, Preston picked up his mirror and started making some lines. "Lemme do us up and then I'll weigh out your teen," said Preston.

Ratchet took another long hit off of the pipe. It was a long and thin pipe made out of clear glass. There was an upturned bowl on the end of it where he melted the speed. He breathed in a long white line of snaking smoke and then holding held it in, slumped into the chair with his lips pressed together so that the speed would congeal in his lungs.

Skye could smell the steel exhale as Ratchet blew out the smoke.

"Those dumbfucks out there didn't talk too much shit, did they?" asked Ratchet.

"Huh?"

"Those guys in the kitchen," said Preston.

"I woulda come here by myself, but they were my ride," remarked Ratchet with a dry raspy voice.

"They were okay. They weren't obnoxious at all."

Preston handed Skye his metal snorting straw. She leaned over and did her line quickly. Had she been alone with Preston, she would have snorted it much more slowly, but she did not want to look like a wimp in front of Ratchet.

Skye brought her swimming head back. She downed the rest of her Olde English 800 to try and get the tightening throb in her face to calm down.

Ratchet held the pipe out to Skye.

"I've never smoked it before," said Skye.

"You ever smoke crack?"

"A couple a' times."

"Well smokin' this makes crack feel like a jerk off."

She accepted the pipe. He handed her the lighter.

"Jus' heat the bowl until it starts to melt."

She remembered the glass pipe smoking routine from her very early days, when she was living in South Berkeley across the bay. She had hung around a few crack houses back then.

She moved the lighter underneath the bowl, trying to remember the old crack rush. A quick stream of smoke shot up the stem and she breathed it in too quickly. Taking the pipe from her mouth, she tightened her lips to hold in a cough as well as the hot smoke. Her lungs felt as if they were filling with steel wool. A silver coat came up through her lungs, into her throat, and then danced on the back of her teeth, making them tingle and sting.

She let out the smoke, releasing a large plume. She was surprised at how much she had breathed in.

A wave lifted her head and her eyes started floating

Skye tried to keep her neck stiff. Her head felt as if it were going to fall over backward. Tilting her head around, she saw Ratchet snorting up his line.

Concentrating on keeping her head straight, she handed the pipe to Ratchet.

"Didja get a hit yet?" asked Ratchet as he reached out for the pipe.

"Oh yeah."

Ratchet pocketed his pipe and stood up. "Thanks man." He walked out of the room, making sure to close the door behind him.

"Fuuuuck," moaned Skye.

"Got a good hit offa' that pipe?" asked Preston.

"Fuck yeah. My head feels like it's about to float away."

"I like smoking it once in a while, but I wouldn't do it all th' time. It makes people psycho."

"Yeah?"

"Shit yeah. People who only smoke it tend to get too crazy. It's almost worse than shooting it."

Leaning over the side of the bed, Preston picked up his speed kit. "Can you see if those guys left yet?"

"Yah sure," she replied, as she wobbled to her feet.

"Make sure the front door is locked."

Skye actually had to prop herself up as she was stood up. Staggering into the hallway and peering into the kitchen, she saw the trio was gone. Looking down the hall, the front door was closed. Into the kitchen and opening the fridge, they had left a six pack behind. She grabbed one more Olde English 800 and went back into Preston's room.

Sitting down in her usual spot, she saw that Preston had resumed weighing out her teen.

"You getta lotta rockstars in here?" asked Skye through her gossamer eyes.

"Who's a rock star?"

"That Ratchet dude. A couple a' his shows were almost riots."

"He ain't nuthin'. I've met musicians way bigger than him."

"Yeah? Like who?"

"Like none a' your business," smiled Preston.

"Name me somebody. Just one guy."

"Okay, like someone from Neunzig."

She sat up. "No shit?"

"Yeah."

"Where'd you meet them?"

"I run into people like that when I go out to my supplier."

Leaning back into the chair, Skye opened her tall of Olde English 800. She was trying to will the light out of her head.

Brew

Yuri had run into Dex on the drag. Pel, Yuri's old roommate from the Hell Nose House days, was with him. Yuri accepted Dex's spontaneous invitation to have a pint in the basement bar of a local restaurant.

Yuri was sorry he had not found out about the basement bar sooner. The place was literally a basement with a very low ceiling that had criss-crossing wires and pipes. The lighting was dead poor, making for a very shadowy existence. A professional looking wood polished bar looked out of place at one end of the dark cavern. The place was sparsely populated with small wooden tables and chairs, all painted black. A couple of glowing pinball games haunted one corner, and there was also a low wooden stage, which only rose about six inches off of the floor.

Yuri liked the place, even if it was reminding him of his place of work.

Pel had not changed much. Her bleached blonde hair was still exploding from her head, her owl eyes and bird nose were still the same, and she was still criminally thin. He was surprised to see her. The last time he saw Pel was when she had left Hell Nose House.

"You really broke up with Dan?" asked Yuri.

"Eh. It was kinda mutual. I haven't seen her in months."

"Man, you two used to be inseparable."

"Who's Dan?" interjected Dex.

"She was my girlfriend back at Hell Nose House."

"She was a cop," added Yuri.

"Fuck!" blurted Dex. "How the fuck could you live with a cop?"

"It was easy," said Yuri.

"Easy for you, maybe," commented Pel.

"Weren't you always gettin' pinned back then?" asked Dex.

"Where'd you think we got our drugs from?" said Yuri.

"She only brought home stuff a couple of times," corrected Pel.

"Yeah, but it was damn good stuff."

"She didn't bring home any H though."

Dex looked at the table. "Man, you people used to live some kinda crazy." He stood up with his empty pint glass. "Anyone want another one?"

"Yeah."

"Sure thing."

"Okay. Next round."

Dex grabbed their pint glasses and went to the bar. Pel leaned back in her seat.

"I was surprised to hear you came across the bay," said Yuri as he leaned on the table.

"Same as everyone else. Got forced out by the rents."

"You seem a lot more mellow now."

"Shit, you almost have to become more mellow when you move out here."

"Yeah, I know what you mean There's hardly anything to do out here."

"I guess that's kinda good," she remarked as she brought out her cigarettes. "It's cool to just kinda calm down an' get away from that scene."

"I know that one too. It is nice to get away from all those bad influences."

"If you think about it, all those places an' everything that goes with 'em, it just starts to rot your brain after a while."

"Among other things."

"Sometimes the whole city thing is just too busy. Y'know, too many bars an' clubs an' stuff," puffed Pel from her now-smoking cigarette.

"Sure. Like the UFO Landing."

"Oh God, I spent way too much time in that place."

"That place was kinda' popular."

"No shit. That's 'cause Jeek let people do small deals in the back."

"As long as it wasn't the hard stuff."

"The only thing he considered hard stuff was heroin."

"Then you went to the Del Ray," emphasized Yuri.

"Where was that?"

"You know, that little dive that got took over by a buncha Danzig boys on upper Haight."

"Hell yeah. Dan loved that place. We used to go there on the weekends to check out all the cycle girlies."

"Shit. We went to the Collander for that."

"That place was cool, but it was no Muttertag."

"Remember when we went there an' you played pool with those skin chicks in the Scottish kilts?'

"Yech. I thought she was gonna brain me with that pool cue."

"That was the night after we saw the Meatbangers play the I-Beam."

"The night Dan went off on the Jagermeister."

"Oh God, don't remind me."

Dex came back carrying a pair of pints. "I gotta go back for the third one."

"You wanna come to Gilman with us?" asked Yuri. "We got Rebar comin' with us. He's got his drummer's van."

"I dunno," said Pel. "I gotta watch my money."

Dex came back carrying the last pint.

"Sorry I took so long. There were a couple of sore whores in front of me who couldn't decide what they wanted."

"S'aright," said Pel.

Dex looked at Pel. "You comin' to Gilman with us?"

"I dunno," shrugged Pel. "I'm thinkin' I might just stay home."

Gilman

"So I had these Snickers bars an' a bag a' Dorts, right?" explained Rebar.

"Uh huh," acknowledged Yuri.

"And it's really fuckin' hot, so all the chocolate's melted. You eat the candy bar with your fingers, and then, y'know how you lick the cheese dust offa your fingers after you eat Dorts?"

"Ew!" groaned Sweezy.

"I do that," commented Dex.

"Anyways," continued Rebar, "You leave the chocolate on your fingers and all the cheese stuff sticks to the chocolate."

"YUCK!" howled Sweezy.

"Gross dude," moaned Yuri.

"I gotta try that sometime," said Dex.

Rebar leaned forward. "You know how you get the string caught in your teeth?"

Everyone fell silent for a moment.

"What?" asked Sweezy.

"That string. It gets caught in your teeth when your girlfriend forgets to take out her tampon."

A howl arose from Rebar's small audience. Dex was laughing. Yuri was wincing. Sweezy had gotten to her feet.

"That's too fuckin' gross!" threatened Sweezy.

"You know it's true," smarmed Rebar.

"You wouldn't make jokes like that if you knew what happened to those things," laughed Sweezy as she jumped out of the van.

Everyone tilted back their beers. Rebar had brought along a twelve pack of Mooseheads along with his gratuitous bottle of Jack Daniels.

They had been passing around the Jack, gulping down quick boilermaker shots.

The Van shook as Sweezy bounded back in. "There's a big crowd outside the club," she said as she grabbed another beer. "They're still between bands."

They had parked a few blocks away from the Gilman club so they could consume their weed and liquor before going over to the clean and sober punk club.

Dex turned to Yuri. "I heard you was talkin' to Johnny Trash."

"Who told you that?"

"Zatch did."

"Oh."

"So didja?

Yuri looked around the van. "He left me a message. I ain't called him back yet."

"Is he still in the city?" asked Sweezy.

"Yep."

Rebar whirled his head around. "You were talkin' to Trash?"

"Not yet. I'm going to though."

"You wanna talk to that fuckin' burnout?" blurted Rebar.

"Fuck dude," said Dex. "You guy's are practically twins."

"Fuck no we ain't! How am I anything like Trash?"

"You got the same accent," suggested Sweezy.

"So fuckin' what? We're both from L.A. Big deal. That don' mean we're the same."

"You're both drunks."

"And who do you know who isn't?"

"Lessee," said Dex, "You're both drunks, you're both from L.A., you both have long hair, you both listen to Guns and Roses…"

"Hey man," interjected Rebar, "Trash would never come to a Gilman show!"

"You only came because we dragged you," sneered Sweezy.

"It's true though," said Dex. "Trash would never come to a Gilman show."

"Hell yeah!" exalted Rebar.

Sweezy examined the dwindling number of beers. "Should we get more booze after Crimpshrine?"

"I'm gonna take this in," replied Rebar, as he waved around a small bottle of Jack Daniels.

"Fuck no dude," blurted Dex.

"Don't take that in," said Yuri.

"Fuck that pussy clean an' sober shit," spat Rebar. "Half the punks in there are so fucked up they don't even know what's goin' on."

"So what?" replied Dex. "You just do your stuff before goin' in, y'don't bring it in there."

"Fuck it." Rebar put the bottle in his pocket.

"Jus' leave it here," protested Dex.

"Fuck no."

"Rebar," groaned Yuri.

"Awright." Rebar took out the bottle and put it in the glove compartment. "Are you fuckin' pussies happy now?"

"Yes," said Dex. "We fuckin' pussies are very happy now."

"Fuckin' a'."

The group clambered out of the van and sauntered down to the club, walking slowly down the street as they carefully observed the scene. Rebar occasionally stopped a few times to say a quick hello to a few people he ran into as they made their way towards the club.

Yuri and Dex decided to hang around outside of the club as Rebar and Sweezy went inside.

Gilman was a small box of a club on the corner of an industrial street in West Berkeley. The place did not even have a sign, except for a hanging wooden sign that read "The Caning Shop", indicating a small shop that was directly behind the Gilman club in the same building.

Despite its obscure location and nondescript appearance, it was not a hard place to find. All one had to do was drive around until one spotted a large group of punks hanging around on the corner. The crowds sometimes got so large that the crowds of denim, leather, and Doc Marten boots would start to spill out onto the street.

Yuri was sticking close to Dex. He didn't recognize a lot of the faces swirling around the street.

Most of the crowd were done up very punk, at least on the surface. Virtually everyone had dyed hair, frayed cloth jackets, denim jackets, or black leather jackets. Almost everyone was wearing boots, except for a few who were wearing plain cloth soles or sneakers. Most everyone was wearing a band t-shirt, a t-shirt with a band name or logo on it. Most of the shirts were advertising very obscure bands that were not so well known to people outside of the hardcore underground.

To Yuri's puzzlement, he could not spot any Danzig t-shirts.

The general youth of the crowd began to make Yuri uncomfortably aware of his age.

His thoughts drifted back to hazy memories of the I-Beam, of the Crucifixion, of the Crab Louse Club, and of all of the other clubs he had habitually haunted back in San Francisco. Whenever he had been in those places, he remembered that he felt as if he recognized everyone he saw, whether he knew them or not. Gilman was strictly a punk club. One look would tell you that, but you could not look at a Nightbreak crowd or a Zeitgeist crowd and say it was punk, or Heavy Metal, or just a Rude Boys hangout. Those select San Franciscan places were always filled with people who touched on all of those subcultures, but none of them were completely awash in one or the other. They were the kind of people who had gotten past the idea of submerging themselves into a specific genre. They had either already gone through the turnstiles of countercultures, having already made their way through heavy metal and punk phases, or they had never bothered to sink into one specific subculture in the first place.

Dex strolled through the crowd, looking relaxed and confident.

Yuri was still following Dex's lead.

"Hey Chute!" bellowed Dex suddenly.

"Dex! What th' fuck?"

Dex approached a short button-nosed woman drenched in long and frayed black clothing and white face makeup. She had a plume of hair-sprayed black hair frothing from her head.

Dex and Chute embraced.

"What you doin' with all these silly punks?" asked Dex.

"What? Aren't I a punk?"

"Fuck no. You know how to read."

Chute tossed a quick glance at Yuri, quickly turning her eyes back to Dex. "Hey, I saw Alicia's pubic hair."

"What? You saw her naked?"

"Nu uh. I just saw one of her pubic hairs."

"What the fuck are you talking about?"

"Dolan has it."

"Dolan?"

"Yeah. In his wallet."

"What, does he have it framed or something?"

"Naw. He has it in one a' those clear plastic credit card holders in his wallet.

"No shit?"

"He was showin' it around to everyone earlier."

"How'd he get it?"

"He got together with her last night."

"Well, okay, but, I mean, did he ask her for it?"

"What?"

"Did he just pluck it out or what?"

"He told us he got it caught in his teeth."

"Is he here?" yawped Dex.

"Yeah."

"I wanna see it!

"Fuck dude, it's just a pubic hair. It looks like an eyelash or something."

"I wanna see, I wanna see!"

"C'mon."

Dex and Chute quickly disappeared into the crowd. Yuri began wandering in their general direction for a moment before he stopped himself.

Heading towards the club, he decided he might as well get inside and check out the scene while trying to hunt down Rebar and Sweezy.

There was a small line to get into the club. More people seemed to be pushing their way out of than into the club. At the entrance, Yuri could hear the raspy resonance of a semi-competent thrash band.

The first few rooms only had a few milling people. There was a small crowd in the dark main room where the bands played. The main room at Gilman was the size of a small club, with a high ceiling full of wooden rafters. The air was thick with smoke and body heat. Every square inch of the place was covered with graffiti. There was even graffiti on the floor. Along one wall a few people had set up some tables where they were selling band patches, t-shirts, and records.

Walking slowly around and squinting through the darkness, he half-heartedly listened to the band as his eyes wandered at the dark faces.

He finally saw Sweezy. She was huddled with a couple of war-painted punks, short and chubby teenage women wearing thick makeup. They were standing in a semi-circle, leaning into each other while talking and laughing. Yuri wandered off in a new direction.

He went into one of the back rooms, a small graffiti-covered place where they sold sodas and snacks and earplugs. He sat down on an old couch across from the drink and snack counter.

With his wandering and bored gaze, he eyed the rack full of photocopy punk zines when something hit his shoulder.

"What th' fuck dude?"

Rebar had flopped down on the couch next to him.

"You wanna see someone's pubic hair?" asked Yuri.

"What? You're gonna show me your pubic hair?"

"No."

"Fuckin' a, this band really sucks!" yarked Rebar.

"They're okay."

"No they're not. They totally suck. They reek, they bite, they blow! I could sound better if I spit on a Gibson."

"They're just another dumb ass thrash band. They ain't that bad and they ain't that good."

Rebar's kept turning his head around as if he were a club radar. "I knew I shouldn't a' let you queers talk me into coming to this fucked up club."

"Hey, it's just one a' the first bands. The other bands'll be a lot better."

"Yeah, right. Alla' these fuckin' punks are the same."

A passing Mohican let out a razz at Rebar. Rebar razzed back.

"Still, it's better than hangin' out at Carl's Place," said Yuri.

"Fuck, we should just take the van out to the city. We'd have a lot more fun out there."

Yuri held in a shudder.

Yet Another deal

"You playin' for anybody?" asked Skye as she cautiously approached Preston's Stratocaster.

"Naw," drawled Preston.

"May I?" she asked as she started reaching for the pristine guitar.

"Sure."

Skye picked up the guitar and brought it back to the easy chair.

"What about you?" he asked, looking up from the mirror. "You been in any bands lately?"

"Naw. Not since Gutter Folklore."

"Wasn't that Johnny Trash's band?"

"Yeah."

"How did that work out?"

"We kinda got off to a bad start. Johnny went and invited all these transients to our first show, and the club owner got hella mad at us."

Skye lightly plucked the strings as she tried to keep the chords right. She felt self conscious playing in front of Preston. She felt it was an understatement to say she was a bit rusty, and she had more than enough respect for his playing ability.

"Whatever happened to that band you were in," she asked, looking up from the Stratocaster.

"Which one?"

"The one you were playing for when I left Hell Nose House."

"Oh yeah. Shit."

"What?"

"I can't remember what we were called."

Preston looked at his hands.

"I don't remember either," said Skye.

"Fuck. I should remember, but I'm totally blanking."

He was still looking down at his hands.

She stood up and gently put the guitar back on its stand. "So I was hopin' to get a gram."

"I fuckin' hate it when I forget stuff like that. It's just really fuckin' lame."

The buzzer in the corner of the room went off.

"I'll be back." He carefully moved off of his bed.

"That line is yours," said Preston as he walked out the door. He had pointed to one of the large dealer lines on the snorting mirror.

She leaned down and quickly did her line. Preston had rigged it so that the door buzzer, which was located by his front door, would set off another buzzer in his room. There was a long and twisted red wire that ran through his hallway apartment and into his room.

Throwing her head back into the easy chair, she realized she had done her line too fast. A wave of dizziness bent the sides of her skull and set her spine to tingling. She could feel the amp dancing in her feet.

Picking the guitar back up and holding it close to her chest, she braced herself for an entrance by a new stranger. Perhaps one of the longhairs had returned, or some other customer, or perhaps even his supplier.

Her eyes buzzed as she stopped strumming so she could hear what Preston was doing. A click, a door opening. "How are you." Someone else's voice. After some shuffling sounds she could only hear hushed voices.

Preston came back in with an impossibly tall and thin woman. She was dressed head to toe in form fitting black clothes, which was surprising given how slim she was. Her skin was dead white pale, and her short bleached blonde hair was sticking straight up towards the ceiling.

Preston matter-of-factly went back to sitting on his bed, being careful not to jostle his speed kit and mirror too much.

"Sorry there isn't much room," commented Preston.

Skye pressed the backs of her leg against the chair, hoping she would not have to give up her spot.

"I still gotta weigh out your supply," said Preston.

"Sure," replied the tall and slim woman in a deep voice.

Skye was not sure what to do. The woman was standing before the door as Preston fiddled with his speed kit. She was standing perfectly still. Skye's head was still swimming.

She was looking at the fretboard, thinking about what to play next. She was deliberately not looking in the tall woman's direction. Pressing her fingers against the fretboard, she could feel how long it had been since she had practiced, considering how the strings were cutting into her fingers.

"Katla, this is my ol' friend Skye," said Preston as he suddenly looked up from his speed kit.

"How do you do," smoothed the deep voiced Katla, as she bent her upper torso down to extend her hand.

"Hey, how's it goin'," she replied, shaking her hand.

Katla righted herself again and resumed her tall and quiet stature.

After quickly weighing some of his stash out, he held out a baggie full of speed. It appeared to contain at least a teen of speed. "Here y'go."

"Thanks," deeped Katla, who then turned towards Skye. "It was nice to meet you."

"Likewise."

Katla left the room.

"That was quick," said Skye.

"Yeah it was. Some people never stick around to kick it, and other people I can't get rid of."

"Which one am I?"

"You're neither, really. I guess that's 'cause I don' mind you hangin' out."

Skye felt the skin on her arms warming. She assumed it was the speed washing back on her.

"If you check the front door I'll give you another line," said Preston.

"You were gonna give me another line anyways."

"True, but it would be nice if you could make sure Katla locked the door."

Gently placing the guitar back on its stand and wobbling to her feet, she wondered how many more people she would meet at Preston's place.

Rapport

Skye was eating a microwave burrito at the shipping counter when Chasey casually wandered into the room.

"Hey Skye."

"Hey."

"Thanks for th' gofast last weekend," said Chasey as she sat down at the other end of the shipping desk.

"No prob. Anytime."

"It was pretty killer. It tasted like it was pure."

"It's the good stuff. I know the dealer pretty well so he don't give me none a' that cut stuff."

Chasey looked down at the table. "Do you think you could get a bigger score?"

"Whatcha mean?" asked Skye as she eyed the doorway for eavesdropping employees.

Chasey tossed a glance over her shoulder. "I was thinkin' of getting a teen."

"Really?"

"Yeah. I'm havin' a little shindig at my place, and I wanted to get a buncha stuff for my guests."

"Okay. When's the gig?"

"This Saturday. You can join us, if y'like."

"You sure this ain't all for yourself?" joked Skye.

"Okay, you caught me," smiled Chasey.

Skye's head was clicking. She was riding maintenance lines after having finished a binge on Tuesday and it was already Thursday. She would have Friday to rest up at home, as long as she could make Chasey's buy on Saturday.

As she downed the last of her burrito, she wondered what Preston's disposition would be and how well his supplies would be holding out so close to the weekend. She was pretty sure it was a safe buy, that he shouldn't be too burned out or lost when Saturday rolled around. He always did his best business on the weekend.

"Where's your place at?" asked Skye.

"I live in an apartment on Nali street, just off of Valencia."

"Holy shit! You live like, three blocks away from me."

"No way."

"Well fuckin' a', I can just bring the stuff by your place."

"Okay."

"I need to get the money first."

"How much will it run me?"

"I can get you a teen for eighty."

"Cool. Can I give you the money tomorrow?"

"Hell no. Give it to me on Saturday. I'm gonna be burned out tomorrow."

Social score

Waking up...

Squinting at the clock, it was close to noon. She lifted her head for a moment and then put it back down.

Drifting….

Her eyes popped open.

She quickly lifted her head.

It was close to four o'clock.

Shooting a quick glance at her curtained windows, Skye breathed a sigh of relief as she realized it was not four in the morning.

Sitting up, she was surprised at how spry she felt.

Her clothes were warm. She had piled herself under a generous amount of blankets as well as a cloth sleeping bag. It had been getting colder, and she found herself having to encase herself in more covers in order to get warm enough to sleep.

Shuffling the covers off and standing up, Skye estimated she had just enough time for a quick shower before running over to Preston's and getting Chasey's teen.

She stripped off her clothes and picked up the phone.

"Hello?"

"Pres, it's Skye."

"Hey."

"I was gonna stop by in about an hour, is that cool?"

"Yeah."

"Okay, see you then."

Hanging up, she darted for the shower.

Skye paced herself along Mission while eating one of Arden's homemade bran muffins. Realizing that the small organic muffin would not be enough to sustain her, Skye stopped at a McDonald's for a few cheap cheeseburgers.

After quickly wolfing down a few fast food burgers, her pancake stomach felt as if it had a blob of clay in it as she finished up the last few blocks of her walk to Preston's place. Even though her body was trying to manage the rough digestion of sticky organic bran muffins and fast food starch, she refused to slow down. She had to be at Chasey's by eight, and she was trying to make sure she would have enough extra time to hang around Preston's place for some decent conversation and a few free dealer lines.

Stopping just long enough to look into a used bookstore window to find a clock, she saw it was slightly past five, enough time to get in a good two hours at Preston's if she hurried. Continuing her quick walk, she could feel her tightening thighs pushing against her tight black jeans as cool air creeped into her leather jacket. The cold and aches were prodding her giddy energy.

After a few more blocks she was practically skipping up to Preston's apartment building. She buzzed Preston's apartment.

After a few moments, a barely audible buzz and few static clicks emanated from the door speaker.

"Preston?" puzzled Skye into the speaker. The door buzzed open.

She tried to remember not to be too enthusiastic as she darted up the stairs.

Arriving at his door, she straightened her posture and cautiously rapped on the door.

There was a loud thump, somewhere in the back of the apartment, followed by a moment of dead silence.

Another moment. Skye thought she heard someone shuffling around behind the door.

The door opened.

"Hey," groaned Preston.

His gait was bent. His eyes were dark and shrinking

He turned down his hallway as Skye walked in. She was careful to make sure that the door was closed and locked behind her.

"What's up Pres?" asked Skye in a pronounced voice.

"Fuckin' burnt," he murmured as he ghosted quickly back to his room.

Preston's room was heavy. The light and the air were pressing in on Skye, more so than usual. Sitting on his bed, his body threatened to curl in on itself. Skye stood in the small clearing by the door of his room.

On the bed were his scale and two large baggies of crank.

"I already weighed out your stuff," he rasped. "It's a teen plus a gram an' some change."

"You alright?"

"Yeah, I jus' burnt myself out too much durin' the week. I got on a binge with Riff an' we jus' kept goin'."

"Riff?"

"Yeah. My guy."

Skye's skin snapped to attention as she straightened herself out. Either he was too burnt to know what he was doing, or he had decided that he could trust her enough to let her know the name of his supplier.

"I need to crash," moaned Preston.

She dug the money out of her leather jacket. "Dude, do you need a maintenance?"

"Naw. Jus' put the money on th' table n' make sure the door's locked when you leave."

He did not even bother to count the money. He simply lied down on his side and started curling up.

She put down the money and picked up the baggies. Taking off her leather jacket, she carefully placed the baggies into her inside pocket and slung her jacket over her shoulder.

Slowly and quietly stepping out of the room, Skye could have sworn that he was already asleep.

Outside of his room, she cautiously shut his door. She tip-toed down the hallway and into the kitchen. She extracted the baggies and inspected them. She had Chasey's teen and her own gram. It was a heavy gram. Skye thought it looked more like a teen than a gram.

Scanning the kitchen, his place was a little more chaotic than usual. There were a few more newspapers, beer cans, and ballpoint pen tops than usual. Looking it over once again, she decided there was nothing too amiss about it.

She made a quick line on the kitchen table. She made a decently sized user line from her baggie.

Snorting up her line, she snapped her head back. She felt a wicked spin as the rush pressed against her skull.

"Fuuuuuck."

Skye plopped herself onto one of the kitchen chairs. Sitting for a moment, the high wire came on quickly.

Finally standing up, her head was still swimming as she felt her eyes throb. She re-examined her baggie. The flakes were crystal clear.

Carefully looking at Chasey's baggie, she could not tell if it was the same stuff that Preston had given her.

If it was just as good, she might never get Chasey off of her case.

Skye decided she would ride the spins during her walk back to Valencia and find another place to do some more lines. She carefully re-stashed the baggies back into her coat and did a quick inspection of the kitchen and the hallway before she left. When she shut his door, she tested it a couple of times, turning the knob and pushing on the door to make sure it was shut and locked.

Back out on the street she felt a cold sting. It had gotten even colder in the short moments that she had been at Preston's.

Glancing inside a corner liquor store, she saw that it was only half an hour before six.

Her heart sank even further when she thought about going back to her place to kill a few hours. She knew she would not be able to relax if she was alone.

She stopped at a payphone.

"Hello?"

"Chasey?"

"Yeah."

"This is Skye."

"Hey Skye. Is everythin' cool?"

"Oh yeah, more than cool."

"Okay."

"Actually, I was wonderin' if I could make an early delivery."

"Sure thing. I'm just sittin' aroun'. Come on over!"

"Okay."

"You got the address?"

"Yeah.

"Cool. When will I see you?"

"In like, twenty minutes?"

"Okay!"

Skye hung up the phone and started down the street.

She tried not to walk too quickly.

Chasey's Place

Walking up and down Nali street a few times, the building numbers were either missing or obscured in dark doorways. She knew she was on the right block, she just could not find the right apartment building.

Skye started walking up to one of the apartment buildings.

"Hey Skye!"

She wheeled around.

"Skye!" repeated the disembodied voice.

She finally spotted Chasey leaning out of a second story window. She was one building over.

"Hey!" yelled Skye.

"Come on over. I'll buzz you in."

She walked over to Chasey's building. The door buzzed as she approached.

"I didn't expect you til' eight," called Chasey from her apartment doorway as Skye walked down the hall.

"I managed to get th' stuff earlier than I thought I would."

Walking into the living room, she saw that Chasey's place was fairly well kept. There was a large television with a few old vinyl chairs and what appeared to be a brand new couch. One wall was covered with a bookshelf full of videos.

"Fuckin' a'," exclaimed Skye. "Where'd you get all these videos?"

"Where d'ya think?" smiled Chasey as she went into the kitchen..

The kitchen was very narrow and very long, appearing to run the length of the apartment. There was an old wooden diner booth built into the far end. The large refrigerator was covered with flat magnets depicting old movie and book posters. Glass Jesus candles and old liquor bottles lined the tops of the long row of cupboards.

Chasey opened the fridge. "Red Hook?"

"Fuck yeah."

They sat down at the wooden booth with their beers.

"I've been workin' there for some time," said Chasey. "I usually nab a video or two every week."

"Cool." Skye took a drag off of her Red Hook. She didn't realize how parched she was until she tasted the cool brew. "I'm gonna need a glass of water," gasped Skye as the beer stung her dry throat.

"Sure."

As Chasey got out a large red plastic cup and filled it with water, Skye eyed the doorways to the living room and hallway. "Should I bring it out now?"

"Go for it. My roommates won't be here until late tonight. They're still out workin'."

She took Chasey's stash out of her jacket and carefully laid it down on the table.

"Damn," exhaled Chasey.

"Hm?"

"This is the first time I've bought this much speed all at once."

Get Together

They had moved from the kitchen into the living room Skye sank into the couch as Chasey made more lines on the coffee table.

"You don't have to," commented Skye politely.

"Sure I do. I can't do all of this myself."

Chasey made fairly large user lines. As Skye bent down to snort her line, she felt the weight of her own supply which was still in her jacket.

Skye's head took a swim after doing her line. She was already high from the lines she had done in the kitchen, which was still riding the back of her preliminary line back at Preston's. Leaning back on the couch, she let her head slowly fall backwards.

"Fuuuuuck," moaned Skye.

"This is really good stuff."

"I'm gonna need another beer."

"No prob."

Skye tilted her ballooning head forward. "I can score another six pack."

"No way. I've got plenty of beer."

"Beer an' tweak."

"Fuck yeah. I wanna get wired an' drunk and have a fuckin' good time!"

"How many people are comin' over?"

"Just about four or five close friends, give er take. Who knows."

Sky leaned forward, resting her elbows on her knees. "Is all that tweak for them?"

"Not all of it. Some people are bringing their own stuff. I coulda got some through one a' them, but the stuff you got for me is so good I wanted to try you before going through them again."

Chasey sat in her chair and melted into her seat, collapsing her folded arms on her legs as she sat forward in a half slump.

"You should stick aroun'," slurred Chasey.

"Yeah?"

"Kick it with me an' my buds."

Leaning her head back again, Skye's spins were calming down. She let her body go limp, swimming in the electric buzz that kept slithering and wrapping around her body.

A loud metal buzzing noise startled Skye into sitting up straight.

"Somebody's here," said Chasey as she struggled to her feet to answer the door.

Skye leaned back, trying to get her arms to go limp and let her chest unfurl.

Several footsteps came into the room.

"Hey Skye!"

Linette walked in, followed by a tall and lanky Throcker. Skye recognized the tall Throcker. His name was Hatch.

"What's up Lin?" greeted Skye as she lifted her head.

"Linette."

"Yeah."

"Nothin'. What are you doing here?"

"I'm one of Chasey's coworkers."

"Hey Hatch," greeted Skye as Hatch sat down next to her on the couch.

Hatch squinted at Skye, looking blank for a moment. Suddenly he pointed a finger at her.

"Oh yeah, you're, Ski or something?"

"That's Skye you fuckin' doofus," laughed Chasey.

"Whatever."

Skye had run into Hatch a few times at local Throcker parties and a couple of shows on the upper Haight. He used to be a friend of Yuri's, and she also remembered one particular night when she ran into Hatch at a warehouse party. They had done a few lines together and had gotten fairly buzzed off some Stoli. At least she had gotten buzzed. She did not realize just how drunk Hatch had gotten until she brought him home with the intention of sleeping with him. Her attempted one night stand with Hatch never got off the ground, as he passed out only a few minutes after she had gotten him through the door.

She had not seen him since that night of failed casual sex.

Hatch fixed his eyes on Skye. "Didn't you used to start fights alla' time?"

"Mm, I got into a few punch outs when I was younger."

"Yeah. You still scrape?"

"Naw. I don't get into fights anymore. I'm always the one who breaks them up now."

Chasey took out her bag of crank. "Who wants a line?"

"Me!"

"I do."

"Skye?"

"What?"

"You want a line?"

Skye shrugged. "Sure, why not?"

Swirl

After another hour, six more people had shown up at Chasey's. Once a decent crowd had congealed in the living room, the speed had moved into Chasey's bedroom.

Everyone in the place took turns disappearing and then reappearing to and from Chasey's small yet cozy bedroom. The central coffee table in the living room had become the base for milling beer cans and smoldering cigarettes.

At one point Skye found herself haunting the bedroom for quite some time. She had formed a few lines on a large bedroom mirror which had been placed in the center of Chasey's bed. People kept coming in and dumping out portions of speed from their own stashes. Skye had become the official line-former, chopping and shaping all of the speed on the mirror into lines.

By virtue of lording over the party's snorting surface, she met the get-together's guests one by one as they came in for hits of speed. There were a few Danzig boys, as well as a feathery Throck gal named Ninotchka, who had arrived in a white floor length antique pattern dress. Also attending were a plain Jane and Joe couple who seemed out of place, at least as far as their appearance. They were wearing light colored jeans and had on light blue and yellow shirts. They not only appeared to be fairly square, but were also acting quite square, their conversation remaining fairly proper and cuss-word free, very different from the other guests.

Even though she did not know any of the guests, other than Linette and Hatch, the members of Chasey's entourage treated Skye to lines from their own supplies.

From all of the complimentary lines she had been getting, Skye was beginning to realize just how good Preston's supply really was. She had sampled quite a wide variety of speed from many different sources. She was able to get a good feeling of the amperage from the complimentary lines, but too many of them had the chalky residue of too much cut.

Chasey came in and sat down on the bed, followed by Ninotchka. Chasey was pouring out some of her supply.

"Here," said Skye, handing Chasey the blade. "I'm getting tired of lining up."

"Sure thing."

Skye made her way into the living room which was filled with the gray air of cigarettes and speed smoke. The Danzig boys had broken out a long piece of foil and were smoking speed.

Retrieving a Red Hook from the kitchen, she was trying to figure out what band was playing on the stereo.

Walking up to the couch, Skye approached one of the Danzig boys.

"Can I get a hit offa' that?" asked Skye.

"Yep."

Taking another quick hit, he carefully handed over the foil, the lighter, and a short plastic straw he had been using to suck in the smoke. "There's still some left in there," he gasped.

She ran the lighter closely along the underside of the long and thin piece of foil, sucking up the smoke through the straw.

"Damn," exclaimed Danzig boy number two. "That's what I call a dope fiend."

Skye held in her hit. The metallic smoke wavered in her mouth and sent her head spinning. The high went down and back up into her throat. It swirled around in her head. She was getting lighter.

She was still trying to figure out what band was playing on the stereo. It was a loud, harsh, and rhythmic industrial song.

"Acid Bath," she suddenly blurted as she released a cloud of speed smoke.

"What?" stoned one of the Danzig boys.

"Acid Bath. Alien Sex Fiend. That's who's playin' on the stereo."

"Oh. I was wonderin' who th' fuck that was."

Skye took a few more hits off of the foil before going into the kitchen. Linette was sitting in the wooden booth, making up a line on the kitchen table.

"How's it goin'?" asked Skye.

"Eh," moaned Linette as she corralled a few rocky grains of her crank on the cover of an old photography book. "I'm jus' snortin' the last of my stash. I didn't feel like doin' it in front of everybody else."

Skye opened her Red Hook. "Ya shoulda gone into Chasey's room."

"Yeah, but that's too obvious." She put down her library card and started rolling up a dollar bill. "I was kinda bummed by this stash. It's not very good."

"You didn't get it from one a' them street dealers, did ya?"

"No way. I got it from someone I know over on Haight. His stuff's usually okay, but once in a while he gives me a bunk batch. I'm just sorry he gave me this shit for Casey's bash."

Quickly snorting up her line, Linette leaned back in the booth and sniffed a few times.

"I thought you never tried this stuff before," said Skye.

"That's just what I told Mercy."

She could feel herself shake, ever so slightly, just under her skin.

Skye sat down in the booth, opposite from Linette.

"Keep this between you an' me," said Skye. "I got another stash with me."

Linette's eyes brightened up. "Y'mean like the stuff Chasey's got?"

"Yeah. I can do you a line."

"Cool!"

"Is that stuff you got from Haight having any effect on ya?"

"Kind of. I mean, it gets you wired, sort of, but it's got no kick at all."

"I hate shit like that."

"Yeah."

Skye palmed her baggie as she brought it out. She put some out the on the book that Linette had been using as a surface. Squinting at the faded cover, Skye saw that it was some antiquated picture book of old racing cars.

Making up two large user lines, Skye gave Linette a bit more than she gave herself. Her head was still buzzing.

Linette leaned back and let out a heavy breath after snorting her line. "Do you know where we could score some more of this? I mean, like maybe for next weekend," emphasized the wide-eyed Linette.

Looking down into her baggie. "Yeah, sure."

"I mean, like this stuff," emphasized Linette as she pointed to the faint dusty remnants of her line.

"Oh yeah, I can get the same stuff. Sometimes it varies a little in quality."

"Y'mean like it ain't as powerful?"

"Sometimes it's a little less powerful, but it's still good. Sometimes it's more powerful."

"Okay!"

"Y'gettin' into this stuff?"

Linette was breathing heavily. "Fuck yeah. I could seriously get used to this shit."

"Y'got my number?"

"Hell no. Why would I have your number?"

"Because a' Mercy."

"Nah. She didn't give me your number. I suppose I could get it from her, but then she'd get all suspicious."

Skye tipped a little more crank out onto the book. "You really don't want her to know you're doin' this stuff?"

"She's been giving me a hard time about alla' my partying. I don't know what she's bitchin' about. She knew what the fuck she was gettin' into when I let her seduce me at Langer's house. We've known each other long enough."

Skye was thinking about Rebar as she worked out a few more lines. Back when she first started hanging out with Mercy, Mercy had been seeing a Los Angeles rocker named Rebar. Skye had always gotten along with Rebar, even when other people were not so crazy about him.

She was thinking about Rebar because of Linette. Something about her prompted Skye to remember him. The way she was talked, the way she leaned on the table, the slope of her pronounced Californian drawl, and the fact that she was sitting at the kitchen table all by herself.

Taking her baggie out of her coat, Skye tipped some more speed out onto the book. Linette tipped her head so she could see how much she was putting out.

"Fuck dude," replied Linette in quiet awe.

"How's your play comin' along?"

"How'd you know I was in a play?"

"Mercy told me."

"Goddamit, I told her not to tell anyone."

"Why not?"

"Did she tell you it was a stupid play?"

Skye leaned over the book, making up lines with her library card. She kept one eye on the door in case anyone came in.

"Did Mercy ever tell you about Rebar?" asked Skye.

"No. Who the fuck is Rebar?"

Skye had contemplated the idea that Linette and Rebar might have been related.

Dopes and Blokes

"Skiiiiinheeeeads smoke DOPE! Thaaaaat ain't no fuckin JOKE! Yooooooooou are a stupid BLOKE! Skiiiiinheeeeads smoke DOPE!"

Almost everyone in the room was bellowing out the chorus amid the fog of cigarette smoke and floating speed resin. Only the straight couple sat out of the sing-along.

"Best punk song ever!" declared the first Danzig boy. Skye had discovered that his name was Paul.

"Are you fuckin' crazy?" spouted the straightlaced man.

"Fuck yeah."

"That song sucks."

"What the fuck are you talking about?" flexed Paul.

"'You are a stupid bloke?'"

"That's what the man told you."

"Why the fuck am I a stupid bloke?"

"You're the stupid bloke?" yarked the other Danzig boy. Skye had not learned his name yet.

"No, I didn't mean me," groused the straightlace as he started to become irritated. "Why is the person listening to the song a 'stupid bloke'?"

"What the fuck are you talking about?" asked Chasey.

"The singer calls the guy listening to the song a stupid bloke. Why?"

"Because it rhymes with joke," volunteered Skye.

"What's the point of having a line in a song if it doesn't mean anything?"

"You are a stupid bloke," declared Paul.

"Why?" scraped straightlace.

"Because skinheads smoke dope."

"What?"

"You are a stupid bloke because skinheads smoke dope."

Skye eyed the rest of the room. People were holding their heads down, holding back their laughter.

"So anyone listening to the song is a stupid bloke because skinheads smoke dope?" pronounced the straightlace.

"No, just you," announced Paul with a demonstrative finger.

"What?"

"He was talking about you when he wrote that line."

Straightlace stood up. "What are you talking about?"

"You are a stupid bloke because skinheads smoke dope. So there."

"That's ridiculous! It makes no sense at all. Why would anyone be at all entertained by something that doesn't make any sense?"

Skye and several others broke out laughing.

"What is your problem?" snapped straightlace as he took a step forward.

"Hey," cautioned Paul as he held up his hands. "Don't get so excited." Paul was holding his hands out flat as if to indicate he was backing down, but Skye knew differently. Her instincts told her that Paul ready to counter the straightlace, should he lash out or become too aggressive.

Skye's shoulders squeezed together. She braced herself to jump in between the two of them if anything actually started.

"This is the dumbest fucking argument I've ever heard," said Skye.

"Hey!" snarked Paul. "You sayin' I'm dumb?"

"Yeah. You're dumb and he's stupid," replied Skye as she pointed at Paul.

"Them's fightin' words!" grinned Paul as he twisted his face around.

"Back off man!"

"She means it," said Chasey.

"You ever beat up guys before?" asked Hatch of Skye.

"Sure."

"Uh huh," grinned Paul.

"I'm talkin' about the ones that didn't ask me."

"Oh," replied Paul, pretending to be humbled.

"You actually fight with guys?" asked the white-faced Throcker.

"I used to fight all kindsa' people."

"What's it like to fight a guy?" asked the plain Jane.

"It's easy," scoffed Skye. "One kick in the happy sacks and they're down for the count!"

"Hey!" exclaimed Paul. "No fair!"

Straightlace had retreated to the kitchen. Everyone else was tittering and giggling as the music kept playing in the background.

The cigarettes and heated tinfoil started up again. Skye leaned forward to grab another beer off of the coffee table

As she opened her beer, Paul leaned towards her.

"That was some good stuff you brought."

"What?'

"Chasey gave me a line of th' stuff you got her."

"Yeah."

"You know where I can hook up with some more a' that stuff?"

Skye took a sip of her beer. She put the beer can on the table.

"Sure."

Scavenger Hunt

Yuri was putting away his laundry.

He had obtained several milk crates for his room. This time he had gotten some from a friend, rather than snatching them from behind a store.

One milk crate for his pants, two crates for his shirts, and a large metal crate for his socks, underwear, and other miscellaneous clothing items.

Outside it was gray and calm with a slowly moving wind.

He was contemplating the bizarre new practice of separating out his socks when his door suddenly shuddered and thundered with a boisterous round of hyperactive knocking.

"What the fuck?"

A round of facetious animal noises came from the other side. He thought one of them sounded familiar.

Opening the door, it was Rebar and Sweezy.

"Come on!" beckoned Rebar.

"What?"

"You gotta come with us," said Sweezy.

"Do you know where Hack is?" asked Rebar.

"Who?"

"You know," said Sweezy, "the guy who used to hang out with Johnny Puke and Asshole, the guy who used to play for Stinkhammer."

"Oh, that guy. Fuck if I know where he is."

"We gotta find him," snapped Rebar.

"Why? You really need a greasy rivethead that bad?"

"He's on the list!" bounced Sweezy as she waved a piece of paper at Yuri.

"What?"

"Scavenger hunt," said Rebar.

"Come on!" barked Sweezy.

"Scavenger hunt?"

"Yeah!"

"So what do you need Hack for?"

"He's one of the items on the list!" said Sweezy.

Yuri soon found himself in the back of the off-white van that Rebar was still driving.

"I thought you were supposed to give this van back," asked Yuri loudly over the vans grumbling motor.

"He's still out of town!" shouted Rebar.

"How come?"

"He hasn't come back yet, so I'm still driving it."

"Won't he get mad?"

"Fuck it! If the fucker wants his van back he should come and get it."

Sweezy handed the list to Yuri so she could dig a few beers out of her backpack. Hacker Salem, better known as Hack, a well known East Bay heavy metal drummer, was indeed an item on the scavenger hunt list. Apparently, from what Yuri had gathered over Rebar's quick and animated explanation, they were competing against three or four other teams of punks, metalheads, and local throckers who were familiar with the Berkeley and Oakland scene.

Sweezy handed Yuri a beer as he looked over the rest of the list: a twelve pack of Pabst Blue Ribbon, a video copy of a film called The Incredible Kung Fu Guy, a magazine other than Maximum Rock and Roll that mentions the local new wave band Hat Confusion, a used baggie that had formerly contained coke or speed, a vibrator that costs less than five dollars, a copy of Cometbus that was at least a year old, a button that contained the word 'bitch', a band patch of a punk or thrash band that wasn't black…

Several of the items had various conditions set to them. During the hunt, you were required to obtain one ground-scored piece of furniture, an abandoned piece of furniture that was good enough to take home and use. You were also required to obtain one bottle of Robitussin cough syrup that had to be obtained through the act of shoplifting. There was also a bottle of hard liquor that had to be obtained from a liquor collection of one of the team member's parents or grandparents, and which had to contain at least twelve ounces of liquor. Yuri thought that one to be a long shot. No one in the van was still in regular contact with their parents, or their parents did not live in the Bay Area.

Rebar had taken the van up to Telegraph Avenue where Sweezy quickly jumped out of the van to search the local cafes for Hack. After a few quick and fruitless searches, Rebar quickly took the van South, away from the main drag.

The van started slowing down.

"Fuckin' a'!" exclaimed Rebar.

"What?" asked Yuri.

. "Gust!" shouted Sweezy.

"What?"

"Look out the window."

Yuri climbed up next to Sweezy and looked out of the window. He saw a short red haired woman and a young shaggy-haired man pushing a passed out green-haired Mohican in a clattering shopping cart.

"What the fuck?" yelled Sweezy to the bright red head.

"Hey!" yelled Gust. The young woman walked up to the van.

"What the fuck are you doing?" yelled Sweezy.

Gust stuck her face into the window. She was short and young and had a lumpy pile of painfully bright red hair coming out of her head. Her thick black eyeliner was starting to flake and crack around her eyes.

"Shim passed out in the park."

"What?"

"Shim passed out in the park. He killed a whole bottle a' Cuervo."

"Bullshit," snorted Rebar. "That wimp would be dead by now if he did that."

"Why are you pushing him around in a shopping cart?" asked Yuri.

"We gotta get him home."

"Why?" asked Rebar loudly.

"Well we jus' can't fuckin' leave him in the park!"

"Dump him in the van!"

"Shouldn't you find out where he lives first?" asked Yuri.

"What for?" dismissed Rebar. "We got all day."

Yuri struggled to open the side door. Gust and her companion were pushing the cart over the curb and towards the van. They almost tipped over the cart as they wrenched it off of the curb.

"Careful!" cautioned Yuri. "You'll break his head open."

"Fuck," groaned the shaggy-haired young man, whose hair covered his eyes.

"We're pretty fuckin' plowed dude," spitted Gust.

Yuri and Sweezy carefully lifted the dead weight Mohican out of the cart and brought him into the van. They laid down the unconscious young drunk on a pile of old tarps that were in the back of the van. Yuri thought the tarps were rather filthy, but considering the condition of the young man, he didn't think he would mind, at least for the moment.

Gust sat in the back of the van near her passed-out friend. Sweezy shut the door and the van lurched back down the street..

"Where the fuck were we goin' again?" harkened Rebar.

"We need to get some of this stuff," shouted Sweezy as she pointed to the list.

"What?"

"Stop at a liquor store."

Gust shot a look at Yuri. "What the fuck are you looking at?" asked Gust as she tried to hide her grin.

"You."

"Why? You wanna fuck me?"

"I dunno. I'd have to fuck you first to give you an answer."

Yuri glanced at the stoner who was staring to nod off in the corner right behind the driver's seat.

"What's up with your other friend?" asked Sweezy pointing at the now sleeping shaggy hair in the corner.

"I don't know. He had like, two beers, but then he took alla' these little white pills we found in the park."

Suddenly Rebar wrenched the van to the left, swerving off of the road and stopping abruptly in a parking spot.

"What the fuck?" yelled Gust.

Sweezy jumped out of the van and ran into a liquor store. Rebar turned around in his seat. "Scavenger hunt," said Rebar loudly.

"What?" asked Gust.

"We're on a scavenger hunt." said Yuri. "Here's the list."

Gust snatched the list and carefully looked it over.

"Hey! I know where he is!" jumped Gust.

"What?"

"I know where Hack is!"

"No shit?" said Rebar.

"We should go get him before someone else finds him," said Yuri.

"Where is he?" asked Rebar.

Lunging forward, Gust pressed herself up against Yuri as she leaned onto Rebar's seat. "He told me he was crashing at Karina's."

"Fuckin' a'!" exalted Rebar.

Sweezy came darting out of the store and jumped back into the van. "They don't have Pabst Blue Ribbon."

Rebar began driving up the street again. "There's plenty a' liquor stores on the 'ave."

"Go two blocks and stop up at the corner!" shouted Gust who was still pressing herself against Yuri, so much so that he could feel her body warmth.

"Do they have Blue Ribbon up there?" asked Yuri.

"There's a porno shop up there!"

"What?"

Gust pointed to the list. "We need a cheap vibrator."

"Let's go!" jumped Sweezy.

Rebar gunned the van. He jammed it up the street a few blocks and stopped at the corner as Gust directed. In the middle of the block was a plastic sign announcing the presence of an adult bookstore.

Sweezy hopped out of the van.

"What the fuck are we doin' here?" yelled Rebar.

"Vibrator!" yelled Sweezy.

"Whattaya need a vibrator for? You got me!"

"She needs something that lasts longer than two minutes," said Gust as she climbed out of the van.

"I'll put twenty minutes up your ass!"

"We need a cheap vibrator," reminded Yuri. "It's on the list."

"Come on!" commanded Sweezy.

Yuri sided up to Gust as they were walking towards the shop. "Shouldn't someone watch your friends?"

Gust shrugged. "They ain't goin' nowhere."

Looking overhead as they were walking down the street, Yuri saw that the sky was still gray. The air was still keeping its cool edge. Looking back up the street, Gust ran up to Sweezy while Rebar walked alongside Yuri.

"Just pretend you're my boyfriend," said Rebar.

"Right. We're looking for some strap ons."

Sweezy and Gust had already disappeared into the shop as they walked up to the entrance.

Carefully stepping into the shop, Rebar remained just behind him.

Right by the doorway to the shop were a few clear plastic stands stocked with small plastic bottles and feathers. To the right was a wall covered with brightly colored magazines. Behind the plastic stands, dominating the center of the store, were rows of shelves filled to capacity with pornographic videos. The wall on the right side of the shop were covered with a myriad of sex toys, hanging from hooks and placed on shelves.

Glancing over the video displays, Yuri took note of the scores of video covers sporting collages of various sex acts as he was trying to spot Sweezy and Gust.

There were a few men in the store, squeezed up against the magazine shelves, looking straight ahead in silent contemplation.

"Hey Yuri!"

He tried to hide his embarrassment as he quickly skittered between the racks of porno flicks, moving quickly towards the wall of sex toys.

Looking around, he could still not spot Sweezy or Gust.

"Down here!"

Theys were kneeling on the floor, looking through a box of vibrators and rubber phallic moldings.

"What are you doing?" asked Yuri quietly.

"The ones on the wall are too expensive."

"What?"

"We have to find one that's under five dollars," said Gust.

"Under…?"

"The list says the vibrator we get has to be under five dollars. You gotta bring the receipt as proof."

"Help us look through these," said Sweezy sharply.

Gust stood up as Yuri kneeled down. Gust wandered off as he started looking through the box of shrink-wrapped plastic vibrators.

"What are we looking for again?"

"We need a vibrator that costs less than five dollars."

"Do they make stuff that cheap?"

"Hell yeah they do."

He cautiously picked up a small white plastic vibrator. Its shrink wrap was fairly loose. He turned it over, trying to find a price.

"That's not a Johnson," said Sweezy.

Sweezy leaned up against Yuri. "Look at this one!" Sweezy was holding up a huge rubber vibrator, decorated with small plastic animals that were strategically placed around the base.

"Fuckin' a'."

"Isn't that crazy?"

Now Sweezy was pressing up against him. He could feel her voice vibrating through her frame as she talked.

"Are you going to buy it?" asked Yuri, as he was leaning back into Sweezy. He could feel his cheeks getting warm.

"Why? Do you want me to use it on you?"

Suddenly a magazine flew into his face.

"Look at this!" squealed Gust.

"What the fuck."

"Look at this!" said Gust as she held up an open magazine. There was a photo series of two very pregnant women fondling each other.

"You don't like it?" asked Gust.

"Hell no. It's gross."

"I think it's sexy."

"She's just saying that," said Sweezy as she put the animal vibrator back in the bin.

"Am not. Ooh! Preggo lesbians!"

"Let's get out of here," commanded Sweezy as she stood up. "This place is too high class for cheap vibrators. "

"Wait a minute, can it be a vibrating bullet?" asked Gust.

"What the fuck are you talking about?" asked Yuri.

"A vibrating bullet."

Gust held up a plastic package with two small plastic oval objects attached to a plastic control box.

"I dunno," replied Yuri. "Ask Sweezy."

"I think it has to be the traditional phallic vibrator," said Sweezy.

"Come on, these things vibrate!" said Gust.

"You'd have to ask Rizz."

"Who's Rizz?' asked Yuri.

"He's the guy who's running this thing."

"What thing?"

"The scavenger hunt."

"Let's call him!" squealed Gust.

"Forget it," dismissed Sweezy. "Come on."

"Are they under five dollars?" asked Yuri.

Gust looked at the package. "Oh. Never mind."

Standing up, Yuri could see Rebar being uncharacteristically nonchalant, as he carefully looked over a copy of Playboy.

As they were walking back to the van, Yuri turned to Gust.

"I thought you weren't old enough to go into those kinds of places."

"I'm not."

"Oh."

"So when ya fuck me you'll have to keep it quiet."

"They'll throw you in jail!" said Sweezy to Gust.

"Why?" asked Gust with newly thrusted hands on hips.

"Corrupting a major."

"Ha!"

"No judge would ever convict him."

"Ha!" sharped Gust again. She grabbed Yuri by the collar and put her nose right up to his. He could smell her rum breath. "He looks pretty corrupt to me."

"He is," said Rebar.

"I would have been offended if you said I wasn't," said Yuri.

Everyone climbed back into the van. A dashing Sweezy made sure she got to the front passenger seat before anyone else could take it. Gust flopped back down to the floor of the van. "We need to find that damn Pabst."

"What about Hack?" asked Yuri.

"Fuck! Get to Karina's!"

"Where is it?"

Gust jumped to the front, wedging herself between Rebar and Sweezy, and gave Rebar directions. It took about twenty minutes of maneuvering the coiling Oakland streets to get to Karina's place, a run down two story punk house not too far from the edge of the East Oakland warehouse district. Gust and Sweezy ran into the house, only to emerge a few minutes later.

"He left this morning," said Sweezy.

"Hack actually got up in the morning?" asked Yuri.

"They said he's wired off his ass."

A shiver went through Yuri. He hunched his shoulders together.

Sweezy and Gust clambered back in and the van started up again.

Rebar drove the van in seemingly random directions for quite some time as Gust and Sweezy discussed scavenger hunt strategy.

Yuri looked at Gust's friends. Gust's shaggy-haired friend was now completely out cold as well as the Mohican who was still crumpled up on the tarps.

Yuri distracted himself by watching the van's windows. There was a gray sheen to the side windows of the van, as small droplets of mist gathered on the panes. A slight drizzle was coming down.

"I told you they'd have it," chided Gust.

"Yeah, yeah," dismissed Rebar.

"Nyah! I was right, you were wrong!"

"Shut up ya little beeyoitch."

All the members of the van that were still conscious were standing in the liquor aisle of a local Safeway, looking over a row of Pabst Blue Ribbon twelve packs.

Sweezy lifted out a twelve pack.

"Let's get two," said Rebar.

"Fuck dude, haven't we had enough already?"

"It's on sale."

Gust grabbed another twelve. Yuri picked one up as well.

Back in the van, Gust and Sweezy sat in the back, sipping on Pabst. Yuri took advantage of the opportunity to sit in the passenger seat.

"I can't believe we wasted all that time just for this stupid beer," sneered Yuri.

"Fuckin' a'," agreed Rebar as he drove the van out of the parking lot.

"Where are you goin'?"

"To Mira's place."

"Why you goin' there?"

"That's where Hack is."

"How do you know Hack's there?"

"Karina said he was getting wired, so if he wants more wire he'd go there."

Craning his neck around, Yuri saw that Sweezy and Gust were huddled in the very back of the van. He couldn't hear what they were saying to each other. The van's engines were too loud. Both of Gust's friends were still unconscious.

Seeing the two young men so dead to the world made his skin heavy. He found himself eyeing them a little closer to make sure they were still breathing.

Suddenly Sweezy started bellowing from the back of the van. "Hey! Where the fuck are we going?"

"Mira's place," answered Yuri, shouting so he could be heard over the van's engines.

"What for?"

"Rebar says Hack's there."

"Whatever."

Turning around in his seat, Yuri looked to the back of the van. "You still got the list?"

"Yeah." Sweezy took the list out of her coat and stood up long enough to hand it to Yuri.

Yuri looked over the list. There were about twenty five items on it, and they had only managed to collect a few of them.

Rebar hit a few quick turns, snapping the van around quickly enough to make the unconscious punks slide back and forth across the van floor.

Yuri noticed the shaggy-haired young man waking up as Rebar parked the van. They were in front of Mira's house, an old run down Oakland house situated on a small slope of a hill in between two plain stucco apartment buildings.

Everyone piled out of the van. Sweezy and Gust carried in the twelves of Pabst. They left the Mohican behind, still passed out on the floor of the van as if he were just another one of the tarps.

Yuri climbed out of the van just as everyone ascended the creaking wooden steps to the faded red shingled house.

"Fuck yeah!" exclaimed a short woman with long dark dreadlocks at the top of the steps. "People with beer!"

"Is Hack here?" asked Rebar.

"Yeah. He's passed out in Cory's room. Come on in."

Walking into the house, the place was dark and musty. Going from the bright gray light into the dark domicile, Yuri carefully followed Rebar, as it was dark enough to prompt him to be cautious.

They walked into a large and sparsely furnished living room. The ceiling was nearly two stories high. The room was furnished with old wooden chairs, a few faded easy chairs, and a beat up dark red couch. A very old and large television set was in front of the fireplace. A coffee table was buried beneath a collection of beer cans, cigarette butts, and assorted magazines.

There was a lone short and slender skater in the room, sitting in the far corner of the room, leaning on his skateboard and smoking a cigarette. He looked as if he was trying to blend into the background so he would not be noticed.

Everyone quickly made themselves at home, finding places to sit. Yuri commandeered an old easy chair at the far end of the room. Sweezy and Gust put the twelve packs upright at the end of the coffee table. They filled in Mira on the details of the scavenger hunt.

"Don't let Hack get away," emphasized Rebar.

"I don't think he's goin' anywhere," said Mira. "He's too burnt."

Mira looked small enough when she was standing up, but when she sat down on the couch she almost seemed to disappear into it.

Before long, everyone was chatting away. Somehow Yuri managed to get lost in the crossfire conversations. Rebar chatted with Mira, Sweezy talked to Gust, and the now conscious shaggy haired youngster had managed to strike up a covert conversation with the reclusive skater, even though the skater was still sticking to his corner and talking under his baseball cap.

Yuri sipped on his Pabst, following the wall up to the ceiling. He admired the height of the ceiling. The space was so large you could watch the air swirling around. The floor was scuffed and the walls were old, the paint was faded and the windows were gray with age. It had all the looks of a place that had been quite nice and regal at one time. He wondered what kind of history the house had suffered to bring it to its current status as a burnout crash pad.

Up to the ceiling, he was finally managed to let his mind go blank, just for a few moments.

After a short while, he turned to Sweezy.

"What about the scavenger hunt?" asked Yuri.

"What?"

"The scavenger hunt. Are we still gonna finish it?"

Sweezy looked around and shrugged.

She went back to her conversation with Gust. He went back to concentrating on his Pabst.

The warmth of the cheap lager went through his arms and started softening his hard skin. The fading light in the windows let him know that it was creeping from late afternoon to early evening.

Supply

"You've been getting' a lot of stuff lately."

"Yeah."

Preston strummed his white Stratocaster. Skye always thought the instrument looked quite delicate since it was in such good condition. The white color was completely unfaded and unmarred, and the neck was so straight it looked as if you could play pool with it. She had learned that Preston had received the guitar as partial payment from a dealer who had owed him quite a bit of money.

She thought about picking up one of Preston's older, less pristine guitars and grinding out a few slow chords, but she wanted to get a line in herself first. A tight spot in the middle of her torso kept squeezing itself up, curling her chest inward.

"Why don'tcha line us up," said Preston as he concentrated his Stratocaster.

"Huh?"

"Grab th' bag an' make some lines."

"Okay."

Leaning forward, she picked up the wooden supply box and carefully opened it. Picking up one of the large bags of speed, a quiet, feathering quiver went through the strings in her forearms. She had never had that much speed in her hands at one time.

"You've been scorin' a lot of stuff for your friends lately," interrupted Preston.

"Yeah." She gingerly shook out some powder onto Preston's mirror. "Don't worry, I haven't' told anyone I've been getting' it from you."

"Fuck, I'm not worried about that. I know you're careful enough."

"I haven't even told Mercy."

Preston thrusted his pointing finger towards the mirror. "Hey, put out more than that! Jeez, whattaya think's goin' on here?"

Skye shook out some more.

"Is Mercy buyin' a lot?" asked Preston as he concentrated on a new power chord.

"She only scored the one time. I've been gettin' a lot of stuff for my friends at work."

Pushing the crank around on the mirror, her fingers started to ache as she pushed the congealing grains back and forth with her library card.

Preston leaned back against the wall. "How is Mers doin' these days?"

"Pretty good. She's got her own place now."

"No shit?"

"Yeah, a fucked up little studio over near Mission and 16th. It's kind of a mess, like our usual places, only she has the place all to herself."

"She still got that girlfriend?"

"Linette?"

"Who's Linette?"

"Some art junky she's been seein'."

"Oh. I was thinkin' of Leslie."

"Leslie is ancient history. She scored for Linette too, that one time."

"Why don't you just start buying regular supplies from now on?"

Skye stopped herself for a moment, putting down her library card and picking up the straw.

"You mean do my own dealing?"

"Sure. Why not?"

She quickly snorted her line out of impatience.

"Different stuff?" gasped Skye as she pointed to the lines.

"Naw. Same stuff. But if you buy in bulk you get a better price and make some money"

Skye held in her breath, watching the far wall, as her head started swimming.

A Visit

It was the third time in the last twenty minutes that she had wandered from her room to the kitchen. She could sense Jane's presence somewhere in the flat. The door to Jane's room was shut. Skye was reluctant to knock. It was Sunday, and for all she knew Jane was sleeping off a long weekend.

She got another glass of water as she was getting ready for another binge. The reclusive Jane was still unaware of Skye's new and steady speed supply, and Skye was starting to feel guilty about not letting her in on some of the action. Jane was not really into speed, but she did enjoy an occasional foray into other substances besides her preferred liquor and pot.

Walking slowly back to her room, she thought about Chasey's new supply. She had her own teen, and she had an eight ball all ready for Chasey, as Chasey had gone in on a larger supply with several friends of hers.

Skye got out her own supply and lied down on her futon, hanging over her snorting mirror. She made herself a fairly large line. She wanted a good jolt to start off her new binge. She would make an even bigger line later.

She was just about to snort her line when the door buzzer went off in the hallway.

Carefully laying down the straw, she got to her feet and went into the hallway.

A high pitched and scratchy voice came over the intercom. "Is Skye there?"

"What?"

"Skye."

"Who's this?" she sharped as she leaned into the intercom.

"Linn."

"Who?"

"Linn. I just thought I'd stop by."

"What?"

They said something again, but Skye could not make out what they had said.

"Hang on," said Skye into the intercom.

Going back to her room and grabbing her keys, she made her way down to the front door. She was being very cautious as she approached the strange voice that knew her name and her place of residence.

Slowly walking down the steps, there was someone in light colored clothing, with her back half turned to the door, wearing a thin white skirt that came down to her pale knees.

Slowly creeping down another few steps, she squinted for a few more moments. Her eyebrows climbed her forehead in surprise.

It was Linette.

Skye opened the door. "Hey Linn, wassup?"

"Hi. I hope you don't mind me stopping by," said Linette in a light and pleasant voice.

"Come on up."

Skye led Linette up to her flat. "Mercy musta told you where I lived."

"We stopped by once before, when we had been cruisin' Valencia. She wanted to see if you were here."

She brought Linette into the kitchen. "You want some water or a beer or somethin'?"

"I wouldn't mind a beer."

"We only got Lucky Lager."

"The bottles?"

"Naw. Cans."

"I like those puzzles under the cap."

Skye led Linette into her room. "I was jus' about to do a line. You want one?"

"I wouldn't say no."

She quickly doubled back to the kitchen to grab a chair for Linette. Linette sat down as Skye moved the mirror to the center of her futon.

"Damn," exclaimed Linette as she looked down at the mirror. "That's a fuckin' big line!"

"Yep. That's kinda standard for me these days."

Linette limply nodded her head. "I can give it a try if you don't mind being generous, but don't tell Mercy. I'm already getting enough shit from her as it is."

"Fuck, I'll tell you some stories if you want to get back at her."

Linette slouched further into her chair. "I dunno why she gets so unwound about it."

"Mercy always did have a habit of going out with people who were more intense than her."

"You mean more fucked up than her."

"Hey, it's not exactly difficult to be more out there than Mercy."

"I knew what you meant," smiled Linette.

Corralling a few free range grains of speed, Skye mused over Linette's rather abrupt appearance. The impromptu visit from someone who was technically still an acquaintance should have been more disconcerting, but Skye found herself pleasantly surprised by her visit.

"So what brings you by?" asked Skye with her nose still pointed to the snorting mirror.

"I was in the neighborhood. I'm jus' spinnin' an' spacin', an' I thought I'd just drop by, see if maybe you wanted to hang out an do a deal."

"You lookin' to score?' she asked as she rolled her eyes upward from the mirror.

"Yeah, maybe."

Looking back down at the mirror, she took the bag and poured some more out. "You shoulda come by earlier. I just went to see my dealer."

"Your supplier?"

Skye kept her eyes on the lines as she pushed them back and forth on the mirror.

"You want me to make your line smaller?" asked Skye.

"Um, naw, you don't have to do that. I just might not be able to snort it all up at once though."

"So how much were you lookin' to get?"

"What?"

"How much crank did you want to buy?"

Linette straightened up in her chair, squeezing her knees together. "Well, I wasn't thinkin' about just myself. I was thinkin' a half for me an' another half for a couple a' friends of mine."

"Okay, I'll give my guy a call."

"Cool."

Skye put down her blade and picked up her straw.

Pull

"Dude, it's been way too fuckin' long."

"Yeah."

There was a pause at the end of the line.

"Hey man, you sound kind of down."

Yuri didn't know what to say. The only times Johnny Trash had ever called him was when he wanted to go clubbing and drinking in San Francisco.

"I ain't talked to you in a long time."

"Yeah."

"Yeah yeah yeah!" hawked Johnny. "That's all you can fuckin' say!"

Johnny Trash's Southern California drawl had an infectious quality. It was relaxing and stimulating at the same time. Johnny was always energetic, yet he also managed to keep a persistent kicked-back air about him.

Trash was still living in San Francisco.

"Fuckin' a', y'oughta come out here," drawled Johnny enthusiastically.

"Hm."

"Me n' D was gonna hit up Remington's and then go by th' Crucifixion."

Yuri knew the place well. The Crucifixion Club was a large converted warehouse where all kinds of scenes taking place, with all of its various floors and rooms. He remembered the place as being ideal if the band that was playing was not to your liking, since one could wander away from the main room and find a myriad of other distractions in one of the numerous side rooms.

It was just the kind of place Yuri was missing during his East Bay exile.

"Charge n' Harlot Blade are gonna be playin'," said Trash.

"I don't know if I can make it."

"Why not? You don't gotta work, d'ya?"

"I might. The boss was gonna be taking inventory."

"No way. Not on a Saturday night."

"Yeah, well, I might be kinda' tired afterwards. You know, 'cause a work."

"Shit. Get out of it."

"What?"

"Call in sick or somethin'."

He shuffled his feet. "Dude, I can't do that."

"Aw man."

"It's a lotta work."

"Just come out!"

"I also gotta lotta stuff to do asides from work."

"Do it some other day."

"It's a lot of things I have to do at home."

"Just come out," exasperated Trash.

"Well, lemme' think about it."

"I'll see you tomorrow."

"Okay, maybe."

"Come by my place at eight."

"Lemme call you tomorrow."

"Just come over."

"I'll talk to you tomorrow."

"Ya mon."

He felt a wave of relief when Trash finally hung up. He went into the kitchen and retrieved a forty ouncer of Budweiser that was still in the fridge.

Sitting on his mattress and swigging his beer, he wondered if he could go by Trash's place and say hello without proceeding to the club. Perhaps he could just get off at the 16th street subway station and go over to his place for a little while, just for a couple of drinks and some conversation. He could admit to himself that it would be refreshing to see Trash and Domina again.

But there was no way he was going to the Crucifixion Club.

Too many tweaks, too many junkies. There was simply no way he could handle it.

Underground

His head felt numb as he sat down on the San Francisco bound subway train. He had finally decided accept Trash's request that he come out for a visit. When Yuri had called Johnny Trash back, he had reiterated, several times, and with various levels of forcefulness, that he would not be attending the Crucifixion Club. Trash had promised not to cajole him further, but Yuri knew it was an empty promise.

He clutched a forty ouncer of Budweiser which he had bought before he got on the train. He had been tempted to get a Mickey's or King Cobra, but he erred on the side of lighter fare.

Watching the details of West Oakland zoom by kept him distracted until the Train went underground, into the transbay tunnel that ran underneath the San Francisco Bay where all there was to see outside of were intermittent blue and white tunnel lights.

He resisted the urge to tap the forty and take a few sips.

The train operator announced the first San Francisco stop over the loudspeakers. The train passengers were displaying the San Francisco bustle that was just a little more quick, a little more intense, and a lot more serious than the walking gaits of East Bay citizens.

Yuri's eyes ran along the metal window frame, slowly tracing out the line surrounding the dark windows, killing time as the train quickly shuffled from stop to stop.

They arrived at the Civic Center station, the last stop before the 16th street station.

The train moved slowly.

Looking around, he saw that the subway car had become a lot more crowded. No one had bothered to sit next to him despite the diminishing seat space. He opened the forty and took a quick swig, keeping the bottle firmly wrapped in its bag.

The train stopped at 16th street, right in the middle of his old South of Market stomping grounds. Yuri was still dealing with the head rush from his quick liquor hit as he left the train in the midst of the quietly shuffling crowd. The warmth of the alcohol still reverberated inside his mouth, making its way to the top of his head as he stood on the escalator.

Stepping out onto the street and stopping, he saw a gutter punk hanging out near the entrance. He was sitting against a wall, with his thin plaid legs curled up against himself. He looked as if he hadn't had a change of clothes in weeks. All of his punk gear was gray and dingy. His arms were folded together and resting on the top of his knees. He was trying to keep his head up. The tip of his nose and the tips of his flayed hair kept bumping into his arms.

A quick quiver scattered through every part of Yuri's body.

Yuri started down the street. He needed to get over to Valencia. He slowed his pace when a sharp twinge went through his arm. It was a long and stabbing string, going right through his left forearm.

Shutting his eyes and stopping, he clasped his hands together.

Opening his eyes and shaking his head, his arm became warm and numb. He resumed his pace.

He uncapped the bottle and took another rush of the lukewarm lager.

His mind wandered around his limbs, trying to make sure he could still feel all of his bones. The alcohol rush kept waning in and out, waxing his head with a dull, stinging throb.

The sun was going down. The hills and buildings shrouded the streets with a premature dusk. Yuri turned down Valencia, away from the main part of the Mission. Both sides of the main drag of Valencia were walled off by apartment buildings that had small stores and restaurants on the first floors. Some of the small restaurants, used book stores, and machine repair shops had brightly lit windows. Other places were dimly lit or completely dark.

Most of the apartment windows gave off soft and eerie glows. It was rare to see an apartment window that was unabashedly open. Curtains were almost always drawn, sometimes completely blotting out the light or giving off only the dimmest glow.

His head took a swim. Capping the bottle, Yuri realized he had been walking too fast and swigging his beer too quickly. The orange and blue glow of the popular Beller's cafe indicated that he was only a few blocks away from Trash's place.

The closer he got, the more the memories and pseudo-memories would swim around his head. Some of the nights he had spent with Trash had left only faint blurs in his memory.

He remembered the night they went backstage at the Cult show, where Trash had managed to con themselves backstage. There was the night they tried ecstasy, and the night he mixed speed and acid. There was also the night that Trash promised him they would be getting laid. They went to a club and Trash talked several women into going back to Trash's place with them, and sure enough he had followed through on his promise. On another night, high on speed and booze, they broke into Trash's ex-girlfriend's house so that Trash could retrieve some nude photos of himself. Trash ended up taking more than just the photos.

He also remembered that Trash had talked him into every single one of those adventures. Looking back on it, he doubted he ever would have tried the drug combinations, one-night stand adventures, or breaking and entering without the encouragement of his bacchanalian friend.

Stopping in the street and looking up at the familiar apartment, he wondered how it was that Trash managed to hang onto that one apartment for so long.

A dull yellow glow came out from behind the windows. The curtains were always drawn at his place. Yuri could feel his energy through the brick building walls.

Standing firm, his feet felt as if they were bolted to the ground. A pull on his back made his shoulders heavy.

He opened his bottle and took another swig.

Closing the bottle, he turned on his heel and started walking back toward Mission. He would keep walking, get back on the subway, and go to Telegraph Avenue. He didn't want to go home. He didn't want to hear the phone ring. He didn't want Trash talking him into a night out.

Sidling up towards the buildings, he wondered if Trash might have already spotted him through his window.

Just before the subway entrance, Yuri tossed his bottle of beer into a trash can, even though it was still half full.

Detour

She loaded up her backpack: a flannel shirt, a copy of Animal Farm, just in case she needed to kill some time, and a couple of cassettes that she would offer to play at Preston's place. She wanted to play her old demos from her Dynamite Chicks days.

The cassette cases were also a good place to hide her speed.

She was supposed to call Preston at three o'clock, but she knew she would not be able to stand the press of her four walls until then. Skye had been burning out for the past few days, and even the amphetamine residue in her mind couldn't keep the walls from closing in on her.

She had called Preston the night before about making another buy. He told her to call him back at the aforementioned time. She wasn't sure why he had picked that specific time. She knew he had to get a new stash from his supplier, and she was assuming he had done so the night before.

It was those few details that were burning the back of her head, along with Chasey and the Danzig boys, as she could hear their faraway foot taps as they waited for word of their supplies. Zipping up her backpack, she grabbed her Derby jacket and headed for the door.

Stepping outside, the cold wind brushed back her hair and stretched her t-shirt out against her chest. A refreshing chill went through her. She resisted the urge to put on her Derby so that the rushing winter wind could wake up her skin.

Stirring her legs, she briskly walked towards Mission and Valencia. She decided she could always set herself up at Beller's cafe or Zeitgeist to kill some time, but for the moment all she wanted to do was walk.

Skye let her mind fog up with the wind and the stretching of her limbs. The streets were sparse enough. Coming up on 16th street, her legs were no longer rigid. She was slowing down.

She ducked into the Captain Chlorine video store. Finding a clock, she saw that she still had half an hour to kill. Knowing that she would need more than half an hour to kill off a cup of coffee, she casually browsed the magazines. Captain Chlorine was a lot like Levigate, only they had a lot more videos, and they also carried magazines and a few books, unlike Levigate, which had only videos.

Keeping one eye on the clock as she was thumbing through a movie magazine, the press of her intended business was returning.

The idea of getting back to her place started to become appealing. Skye was growing frustrated with her ever-changing desires. Her moods simply gave her no fair warning of where they were going to go next.

Putting down the magazine, Skye decided she would call Preston early. She was now thinking about playing Preston her Dynamite Chicks tapes. Walking briskly up the street to the nearest pay phone, she thought about getting back into playing music.

Calling Preston, she got his answering machine. She hung up without leaving a message. A nearby McDonald's made her wonder if she should eat something. Feeling a slight pang of hunger, she went in and quickly lost her appetite when she smelled the frying hamburgers. Walking out, she saw that it was just past three o'clock. She called again. His answering machine. Once again, she did not leave a message.

After killing a few more minutes in Captain Chlorine, she tried calling again. Once more the answering machine.

She was not going to duck into the video store again. She decided to walk back down Valencia, at least a good five blocks. She wanted to kill a decent amount of time before trying to call again, but she couldn't resist the urge to try calling again after the first few blocks. Answering machine.

She walked very briskly now. Looking inside of a used furniture store for a clock, she saw it was quarter past three.

She measured herself, keeping a steady pace going back towards 16th street. Her eye caught the Sinclair cafe. She quickly made a decision. She would call Preston and leave a message this time, letting him know that she was at the cafe.

Grabbing a corner pay phone, she called Preston's again.

A busy signal.

Hanging up, at least she knew he was there, Hopefully he would not be on the phone too long.

Walking down 16th this time, she grabbed another pay phone after a few blocks. Still busy.

The muscles in her forearms were getting tight. Her feet started burning from all of the walking.

Starting back to Valencia and 16th, Skye held herself back as she passed by a few more pay phones. Finally grabbing a corner phone at 16th and Valencia, she hunched herself as she put the phone up to her ear.

 A bristling of relief went through her shoulders as the phone rang.

It kept ringing.

His answering machine again.

"Preston, Preston, are you there? Pick up. Preston!"

Holding the welling expletives behind her tongue, she made it quick and to the point. "I'm in the Sinclair cafe. It's already three thirty. Find me there."

Hanging up the receiver with a bang, she started crossing the street towards the Sinclair cafe.

There were only a few people in the Sinclair cafe. Skye noticed someone watching her as she made a beeline for the coffee counter.

She ordered a bianco. Looking for a table near the window, she could see that the someone sitting at one of the wall tables was still looking in her direction, some dark woman sitting near the front corner. Skye tried pushing the burning sensation out of her back. She was not interested in being stared at.

She was about to give the still staring woman the business, one of her rare outbursts of "*What the fuck are you looking at*?". She didn't say it that often. Usually she didn't need to.

Turning around, Skye found herself shrinking.

It was Mercy.

"Hey."

"Hello Skye," said Mercy.

"What th' fuck Mercy. How's it goin'?"

Mercy was sitting with her arms folded and her legs crossed. She had the back of her chair up against the wall.

"What's up Mers?"

"Nuthin'." Mercy's eyes were looking back at her with a dull sleepiness. "What are you doing?"

"Jus' killin' some time."

"Walking over to the industrial section?" deadpanned Mercy.

"Yeah, I was hopin' too," said Skye as she sat down at Mercy's table.

Putting down her coffee and leaning on the table, Mercy looke around the cafe.

"Mers," intoned Skye, "Were you lookin' to talk to Jake?"

Skye realized someone was standing right next to her. They pulled up a chair and sat down.

It was Linette.

"Oh. Hey Linette."

Mercy was about to say something when Linette held up her hand.

"Don't," groaned Linette.

"What took you so long?" asked Mercy, looking at Linette.

"Fuck."

Linette lowered her head onto the table. Mercy kept her eyes on her.

"Hey Mers."

Mercy snapped her eyes up at Skye, enough to make Skye stop herself.

"What I was askin'…"

Mercy shook her head.

Linette lifted her head . "How's it been goin' Skye?"

"It's goin' all right," replied Skye.

Skye kept still in her seat. She picked up her coffee and took a long sip.

Linette looked down at the floor. Mercy was still staring straight out.

Skye leaned on the table. "Mers."

Mercy turned, softening her eyes a bit.

"I gotta go catch up," said Skye.

Linette looked up again. "Where ya goin' Skye?"

"Just to see a friend," she replied as she stood up.

Skye started walking out.

"See ya Skye," said Mercy in a softer voice.

"See ya."

"Bye," chirped Linette.

Out on the street, Skye felt cold. She saw a pay phone, but was in no mood to call him again. She still had a small maintenance stash of speed in her backpack. She thought about wandering over to the Edit or the

Momento to grab a drink and do a line in the bathroom.

She spotted the neon sign for the NunStuck lounge.

She felt nauseous.

Skye kept walking to Preston's.

Another pint

The week had driven his funds bare, and he was trying to stretch out the last of his cash for the next four days. Yuri was taking the long walk home from work. It was several miles from his house to work, but the bus fare he saved over the next few days would allow him to buy one or two extra small meals right before payday.

The excursions to the Med and to Gilman were draining too much of his money. He would have been in a much worse bind if Zatch had not unexpectedly shown up at his place with an extra large pizza the other night.

Sweezy, Dex, and Rebar had been a bad influence on him. They had cajoled him into going out several times, even though he wanted to rein in his spending. He wondered how much money he had saved by skipping out on Trash and the Crucifixion Club.

He felt the damp insides of his shirt and pants getting thick from sweat. His left hand unconsciously touched his shirt where his diminutive stomach was. His fingers kept lighting on the hanging shirt that seemed to never touch his slim midsection.

His thoughts floated to Sweezy. Even though she was just as slim as he was, it did not seem to bother her.

Sweezy and Yuri had known each other for years, but it was not until they had become East Bay exiles that they really started to click. He could not help but wonder why it was that they had not gotten closer before.

His eye caught a familiar faded sign with the dull neon green glow. It was Carl's Place.

He squinted in the wind as the sun was slowly blotted out by the clouds. A sharp wave went up his back. His skin was cold from the damp insides of his clothes.

He found himself detouring into the bar.

It took a minute for his eyes to adjust. The dungeon dive dark wrapped around Yuri as the front door slowly eased shut. Yuri could see that there were only a few patrons in the place. The bearded wino was sitting in his usual spot. A couple of young and scruffy bikers were the only ones sitting near the front, bent over cocktail glasses at a small round table across from the bar. There were the requisite shadows haunting the back of the bar.

"What'll it be?"

"A pint of Sierra."

As the bartender was drawing Yuri's pint, he realized that he was in Carl's Place for the first time by himself.

Taking his pint, he observed a small round table near the door. It was near the only window that gave off any kind of real light. There were several stacks of free newspapers and a large Carlsberg neon sign in the window that provided enough cover so that he could watch people wandering back and forth on the street and still remain relatively unnoticed.

Yuri squinted through the dingy window. The Sierra tasted somewhat bitter, more bitter than Sierra usually did. Looking through the diffused light, he could barely see the street outside. His eyes and his tongue began stinging and his temples started to throb.

He cautiously cast a glance to the back of the bar.

Another hit of the amber brew, which tasted even more bitter. His temples became tight.

He thought about getting home. There was a good chance that the eye on his answering machine would be blinking with a message from Dex, or Rebar, or Sweezy, or maybe even Pel, who had also started calling him on occasion. Most likely it would be Rebar on his machine. Rebar still had his drummer's van and he had been talking about taking everyone out to San Francisco, a hip field trip with Dex and Sweezy. Rebar had suggested the idea, without even considering that Dex and Sweezy would probably not want to go.

Sweezy would probably try to throw off Rebar by asking Yuri to go to another show at Gilman, or possibly the Berkeley Square. Sweezy had been making the rounds of the East Bay music scene, going to at least two or three shows a week. She had been around the scene so much she had been catching many of the house party and warehouse shows as well.

Then there were the coffee outings with Dex. For some reason, Dex had been steering away from the bars and shows. He always wanted to haunt the cafe scene. He knew Dex well enough to know that he wouldn't be going anywhere near a coffee house if they were still in San Francisco.

There was a slight amount of movement in the very back of the bar, in the deep dark pitch where the tweakers were lurking. Taking a very light sip, the sickly taste curled behind his lips.

Quickly putting the pint glass down and holding in a wince, he kept his place. He looked away from the window. The light was too bright.

Suddenly Yuri felt his throat coming up. He had to stand up. He kept his head away, trying not to look at the bartender or patrons, moving around the table so they could not see his half empty glass. His twisting throat forced him out of the door and onto the street.

He went down a side street, the small alley-like street that was right next to the bar. His mouth was still bitter and stinging. He wondered if he would have to throw up. Siding up to a large rusty dumpster, he stood still for a moment, trying to feel his insides. His gut was numb. The bitter sting was making its way up and down his throat.

He turned the corner of the dumpster, getting behind it in case he had to throw up.

He wasn't sure why he wasn't more startled. His bitter throat and numb insides kept their place and he took a few steps back from the body lying on the ground.

He knew who it was.

It was the skinhead, the one who had challenged him and Rebar to a game of pool, the first time Rebar had brought him to Carl's Place.

He was wearing the same trench coat. He was lying next to the dumpster, stomach down, with his face turned sideways against the pavement.

Yuri stood in place, looking down at the unconscious skin. Leaning on the dumpster, Yuri winced. The skin had thrown up, and he was lying next to his floating pile of clear viscous insides. He was, most likely, simply drunk. The bitter sting came back up to Yuri's throat.

Folding his arms on the edge of the dumpster, he put his head down. A dull pain went through the underside of his skull. He listened to the urban background noise, the sounds of the traffic, the sounds of the swirling air, and the random voices stirring in the distance.

He banged his elbow against the dumpster when he flinched. Something had grabbed his leg.

"What th' FUCK?" slurred the skin.

Yuri tried stepping away, but the skin had a firm grip on his pants leg. He was dragging the skin part way out of his spot as he kept trying to pull himself away. The skin kept yammering at him incoherently. Yuri's stomach curled up on itself as he felt the skin's fingernails digging into his pants leg.

"MOtherFUCKER!" slurred the skin, who was trying to pull himself up by Yuri's leg.

Looking down at the skin, the right side of his face was covered with specks of dull yellow vomit and dried blood.

"Leggo!" yelled Yuri, as he put a hand to his stomach. The skin now had both of his hands on Yuri's leg, tugging at him as Yuri tried to pry himself loose.

"Cockshucker! I'll FUCKIN' Kill YOU!!!" screeched the skin.

As the skin heaved on Yuri's leg, Yuri's stomach turned around and twisted his throat. He could feel his stomach starting to rise up.

Yuri startled. Someone had come up behind him.

"Let go of him!!" yelled a new and gravel voice in Yuri's ear.

Craning his head around as he kept balancing himself on the edge of the dumpster, a shorter skinhead was grabbing the drunk skinhead's hands, trying to pull him off of Yuri.

The second skinhead was shorter and wearing a dark green flight jacket. The shorter skin pried the taller skin's fingers off of Yuri's leg.

Yuri's leg was finally free. He stumbled along the edge of the dumpster. Bending over, he felt as if he was going to throw up.

Nothing came up.

Looking back behind the dumpster, the short skinhead was trying to lift up the tall and skinny skinhead, but tall and skinny was lapsing back into dead weight.

"Fuck!" snapped the short skinhead as he finally let the tall skinhead fall back to the ground.

Yuri righted himself, standing up on his legs.

The short skinhead looked at him. "What the fuck was goin' on back here?"

Yuri put a hand onto the dumpster to steady himself. "I thought I was gonna hurl, so I came out here to toss behind the dumpster. That's when I found him, an' when I tried to leave he grabbed me."

Kneeling down, the short skin checked over his friend. "Fuckin' a'. I don't suppose you wanna help me carry him?"

"Dude, I feel like I'm gonna hurl any minute."

The shorter stood up and turned to Yuri. "I'm sorry about all that. He just got all fucked up when he couldn't score any H."

Yuri stood still. The jelly went out of his legs. His stomach untwisted, letting go of his throat.

"Fuck," gasped Yuri.

"It's pretty fucked up," said the short skin. "I'm the only one who still deals with him. None of our friends can stand his shit anymore."

Yuri remembered where he had seen the short skinhead before. He was the other skinhead who had been playing pool with the tall skin.

"Sorry about that," said the short skin.

Yuri waved a hand. "Don't worry about it. I've been there myself."

The short skinhead started walking out of the alley.

"You just gonna leave him there?" asked Yuri.

"Don't get near him. He'll attack anyone that wakes him up. He's always gettin' fucked up like this these days."

The short skinhead walked out of the alley. Yuri took his hand off of the dumpster, standing himself straight.

The street was bright with the low reflecting sun. Looking straight ahead, Yuri walked out onto the main street.

Yuri started walking and kept walking, straight ahead, always walking, until he got home.

III

Jake's Place and the Cult

Twelve Step

He kept clasping and unclasping his hands as he tried to listen to the current speaker. He was finding it hard to concentrate. He was trying to keep up with what the man was saying. Looking down at his feet, which were pushed up against the back of the folding metal chair in front of him, he kept trying to focus, to really pay attention. The scrunge sitting next to him was shifting in his chair, yet again.

I wish he would fuckin' sit still.

Lifting his head, Yuri tried to see over the crowd. He had shown up late and had to settle for a seat towards the back of the long and crowded hall. There was not much to see through all of the baseball caps, bald heads, and the occasional fields of exploding spiked hair.

Why the fuck are there so many bald guys here? What's up with that?

There were too many people in the low-ceilinged room. His neck and shoulders were knotting up. His hands were aching from all of the clasping and unclasping they had been doing for the entire meeting.

The speaker sat down. Stretching out his stiff fingers, he reluctantly held up his arm. The chair for the meeting pointed in his direction. He had to shift his chair around in order to sit up.

He felt ridiculous, he felt ludicrous, he felt like punching himself in the face, but he had convinced himself that he needed to do this.

"Hello, my name is Yuri, and I'm an addict."

He winced as the unison response of saccharine voices filled the room. "Hi Yuri."

"I've been clean for 30 days now."

He was cut off by applause. He self-consciously nodded his head in response, trying to bend his mouth into a grin.

He started up again as the applause quickly died down.

"I'm really glad that today is my last day as a newcomer."

More applause.

God dammit.

At least he could admit to himself that he was glad he did not have to announce himself as a newcomer anymore, one of the traditions of the meetings. Anyone with less than thirty days of clean time was compelled to announce to the crowd that they were a "newcomer", as the label went.

That part was getting old for him, even if it only had been a month.

"It's been pretty weird," he continued in the midst of the staring crowd. "I mean, not doing any junk isn't that weird, I really wanted to get away from that stuff, but quitting everything, that's been tough. I mean, no drinking, no pot."

Someone coughed in the back. A few people shifted in their chairs.

"I'm glad I'm here though. I mean, just being around clean people, it's made all the difference."

I can't fuckin' believe I just said that!

"I mean, a lot of my friends ditched me when I got clean. I never suspected they would. My friend Sweezy stopped talking to me altogether once she found out I quit drinking."

That much was true. He never suspected that all of his friends would suddenly cut him off so abruptly once he had decided to stop indulging in any kind of excess whatsoever. It had been a pretty surprising turn of events for him, and quite demoralizing.

"But, I mean, I don't know what else to say. It's been weird, but I'm just glad I'm off the stuff."

Crossing his arms and lowering his head, the room watched him for a moment longer, and then people started clapping.

People always clapped whenever anyone said anything.

He quickly reviewed what he had just said.

He shuffled his feet as the room turned to a new speaker. Looking around the room, he saw people looking down into their coffee, others were staring out into space, and others whose eyes were wandering disinterestedly. A few people seemed to be paying attention, but many others acted as if they were hanging out in their living rooms, rather than attending a clean and sober meeting.

Most of the people in Narcotics Anonymous appeared to be fairly healthy, even if a few of them were a bit scruffy and worn. He could tell that most of them had been through the substance abuse wringer. There were a few people who looked as if they were still getting wasted, even though many of those people, so he had been told, had been clean for years.

And then there were a select, scant few, those people who looked as if they had been wrung between the hands of death itself, the ones who looked as if they had been trampled by a pack of wild horses and had just barely escaped with their lives.

They were in the program, but he could never tell how long they had been there. Blotchy skin, pale and thin, some of them appearing as if they were suffering from some sort of degenerative disease.

Those were the people that really goaded him on. Sometimes he would only see one or two of the walking dead at those meetings, and most often not at all. But the few pale corpses that occasionally made it to the twelve step gathering were what really inspired him to try and stay off of heroin. He did not want to end up being another pale, scabby skeleton, living or dead.

Even so, the entire twelve step business was all still rather odd.

He assumed he would get used to it all, eventually.

The meeting was breaking up. People were milling about. Yuri was standing next to his metal chair, waiting for the crowd to thin out before he tried making his way out of the hall.

Oftentimes meetings would empty out rather quickly, many people taking off right as the meeting concluded. Some people would hang around, socializing and talking. That's what was happening at this meeting. Most of the people were still there, even though the meeting had ended.

"Hi there. I'm Holt," bellowed a voice behind Yuri.

Turning around, he saw a large and tall man, wearing a blue army jacket and a wool cap. He had a wide smile on his face.

"Hey," replied Yuri.

"Thanks for your share," said the large and friendly fellow as he moved his arms around him. Yuri accepted the gratuitous embrace, as such greetings were the custom. Hugging was the twelve step handshake, as he had come to realize.

"So you're a newcomer?" asked Holt.

"Not anymore."

"Yeah, congratulations!" he smiled as he shook his hand.

"Thanks."

"Are you new to NA?"

"Yeah. I've only been in it these thirty days."

"The reason I ask is because not all newcomers are new to NA."

Someone had already told Yuri about the newcomer phenomena. Even if you had many years of clean time, and you went out and drank liquor or used drugs again and then went back to a Narcotics Anonymous meeting, you had to declare yourself as a newcomer, regardless of how much clean time you had before.

"Hey, lemme give you my number. You should give me a call

sometime."

"Sure."

He took out a card and handed it to Yuri.

"Hey Holt!" shouted a disembodied voice from the back of the crowd.

"Take it easy Yuri." Holt reached out to embrace him again. Yuri gave up a gratuitous hug. "Give me a call soon," beckoned Holt as he dashed off into the milling crowd.

He looked at the card. *"Call me before you use"* it said on the top. The name was simply Holt, no surname.

He put the card in his wallet. Perhaps he would call the tall and friendly fellow. He had only talked to people at meetings. He had not gotten around to calling anyone in the program just yet, and calling other members was a recommended practice.

The room was still quite crowded. He sat back down. He scanned the room for someone he might recognize. He had seen enough people over and over again in the past month that he was beginning to feel he might be able to go and talk to some of them at the spur of the moment.

The crowd was made up of small clusters of people, groups of two or more, standing in semi-circles and tight little huddles. A few people were milling in between the aisles, or in the back, standing or walking, appearing to be a bit lost as they wedged and pardoned their way through the conversing crowds.

Yuri noticed one man in particular who was trying to make his way through the crowd. At first glance, he appeared to be older. Looking through the deep lines and dark circles on his face, he realized he was actually a lot younger than he first appeared. He was short and thin, with gangly strands of black wisping hair. His eyes were large and constantly looking around the room.

Yuri looked the other way.

He was still trying to find a familiar face, or at least achieve eye contact with someone. Feeling his shoulders turning in, he started shrinking into his seat. Even though the room was still crowded, he felt a sudden urge to leave.

Picking himself up, he hunched his shoulders and pardoned his way through the packed throngs of chatting twelve steppers. There was another milling crowd on the church stairs.

Finally emerging, he made his way down onto the dark sidewalk. A few NA members were wandering away from the meeting hall, but most of them were still clumped together in groups, with a few strays straggling along the sidelines.

Contact

The clouds remained overhead, with the drizzle coming and going. Those were the days that were either slow or busy.

She did not mind that it was slow. Chasey was apparently feeling the same way. They were both smoking at the shipping counter in the back.

"Whatcha gonna do this weekend?" asked Chasey from behind her newly created nimbus.

"Seek an' tweak, as usual. What about you?"

Chasey leaned onto the counter. "I dunno. Might go see my friend Grace's band."

"Who's that?"

"The Scuzzy Kilts."

"That's a really stupid name."

"So what? Like the Fuck Ups is a better name."

"Hey, that's a decent name. It's a good name for that band, anyways."

Chasey took her arms off of the counter and leaned back. "Yeah, well I wouldn't go unless..." She made a subtle yet pointed sniffing noise.

"Of course."

"Can ya get me some before Saturday?"

"Mmm, It would be easier for me if I could get it to you on Friday night. That's when things pick up."

"Sure."

"I was wonderin' if my friend Trafe could give you a call."

"Trafe?"

"Yeah. He was askin' me if I could go-between for him, and I was wonderin' if I could just have him call you instead."

"Do I know him?" she asked through her cigarette smoke.

"He was at my party."

"Which one? One a' those Danzig dweebs?"

"No, the guy with the button up shirt and blue jeans."

Skye stamped out her cigarette. "Oh man, you mean that complete fucking geek who got into that stupid argument with one a' those Danzig boys about skinheads smoking dope?"

"Oh come on, he's not that bad."

Skye picked up her pack of cigarettes and then put them back down on the table. "I dunno. I don't think I want that guy calling me."

"Why not?"

"He looks pretty damn straight."

"Trust me. He's a total tweak."

"Yeah?"

"He wouldna been at my party if he wasn't."

Leaning back, Skye took a quick look at the front of the store. The new cashier was leaning on the counter, reading a magazine. Skye could not see any customers.

Chasey sat up. "Jus' because he actually bathes at least once a week don't mean he don't do no speed."

"Well, fuck it. I guess if you say he's cool you can give him my number."

"Cool."

Late afternoon, Skye knew who it was when the phone rang.

"Hey Chasey."

"Hey. Are you all ready?"

"Yep. I can be there in half an hour."

Skye had already made the walk back and forth to Preston's place. She had a new supply for Chasey. She also had some extra for Linette. Linette had not asked her to get her anything, but she had already anticipated that she would be calling on her. She also had her own gram, just for herself.

"Cool. I'll be here," said Chasey.

"You still goin' to see that band?"

A pause. "What band?"

"You know, that band you told me about." There was a long pause on the other end of the line. "You know, that stupid kilt band."

"Oh! Right. Yeah, I'm still goin' to that."

"See ya in a few."

Lying back down on her futon, she leaned over the edge of her futon and made up a line for herself. She would do the line and lie in amphetamine bliss for about five to ten minutes and then start towards Chasey's.

She carefully pushed the grains back and forth, crafting a large tweaker line.

She was putting the finishing touches on it, trying to make the long and thick line as straight as possible.

The phone rang.

" It's only been a couple a' minutes Chasey."

"I'm not Chasey," said a stern male voice.

"Sorry. I thought you were someone else."

"Obviously," irritated the voice.

"Who is this?"

"Is this Skye?"

"Who's this?"

"Am I talking to Skye?" repeated the voice impatiently.

"Who is this?" she asked as she carefully put down her cutting blade and sat up.

"Is this Skye?"

She hung up the phone, putting it down with a bit of a slam.

The phone rang again. "Hello?"

"Is this Skye?" growled the same voice.

"Who, is, this?" she enunciated deliberately.

"Are you Skye or not?"

She slammed down the phone. It started ringing again almost immediately. This time she ignored it.

Lying back down on the futon, she picked up the blade and started corralling a few disturbed grains that had been dislodged when she sat up. Her answering machine clicked on and her short thrash message played out.

The same voice came crackling through her answering machine's beaten speaker. "This is Chasey's friend Trafe. She told me I could give you a call."

She grabbed the phone. "Dude, you have to tell me who you are when you call."

"It's Trafe. Remember me?"

"Yeah. Chasey's pal, from the party. Skinheads smoke dope."

"What?"

"Nothin'. What's up?

"I was lookin' to score."

"You mean you're looking for Jake?" she emphasized sharply over the phone. She had instructed Chasey to tell him about the code word.

"What was that?"

"Jake. You're looking for Jake."

"What?"

"Jake. That's why you're calling me."

"Who... Oh yeah. Chasey said something about that."

She gripped the phone. She was getting ready to hang up again, after snapping out a quick, "*I don't know what you're talking about*".

"Riiiight," he drawled. "I'm looking for Jake."

She was sorely tempted to hang up.

"Okay, so you thinkin', what, a half?"

"More like a whole," he replied with a suddenly chirpy voice.

"Okay." Skye thought about how much she could get if she scored another teen from Preston. She could charge Trafe eighty bucks and keep the extra for herself. "I can do that, no problem."

"Awesome."

"I'm goin' over to Chasey's now. I'd need to meet up with you."

"Fine. I'm over in the Sunset."

"Sunset? Like where?"

"Close to 19th street. Can you come by our house?"

"Mmm, can I meet you halfway? Say lower Haight? Like at Casa Loma or something?"

"Casa Loma? Never heard of it."

"Well..."

"I could meet you at Rockin' Robins on upper Haight."

Her eyes rolled to the corner of the ceiling. "I guess I could do that."

"Cool! That'd be awesome."

"Lemme go to Chasey's and then I'll make my way up to Haight."

"Great! Also, I need to get this stuff in an hour."

She propped herself up on her elbows. "What?"

"I need to have this stuff within the hour or I can't do the deal."

She lowered herself back down onto the futon. "Dude, there is no way I can get you that in an hour."

"No?"

"No way."

A pause. "There's really no way you could get the stuff in an hour?"

"Do you mean an hour from now or an hour from when I get your dough?"

"Dough?"

"Money."

"Oh."

"Are you talkin' about an hour from now?" asked Skye.

"Yeah. I need it within the hour or I can't do the deal."

"There is no way I can score that for you in an hour," she announced.

"You mean there's no possible way you can do this deal in an hour?"

"Well, there's a possibility that it could take an hour, or a little less."

"Okay then."

"But most likely it's going to take more than an hour."

"Why do you say that?" He was beginning to sound exasperated.

She sat up. "What are you talking about?"

"Don't you know how long it's going to take?"

"I couldn't tell ya."

"Why not?"

"What?"

"Don't you know what you're doing?" he snided.

"Are you for real?"

"What? Why are you asking me that?"

She stood up, gripping the phone. "I don't believe this."

"Just tell me why you can't have it done in an hour."

"I can't guarantee that I can get it to you in an hour. It's most likely going to take more than an hour for me to get you that stuff."

"Well then I can't buy it," he replied flatly.

"Okay."

"So can you get it for me within an hour?"

"No, I can't."

"Well, you'll lose a customer."

"Okay then."

"Well, I don't see how you can keep your customers if you can't accommodate them."

"Fuck you Trafe."

She slammed down the phone. An aggravated jolt went through her.

A grimace shook through her chest. Her temples became tight. She had forgotten what she was supposed to do next.

She saw her line on the baking sheet. She remembered that she was in a good mood before Trafe called, that she was looking forward to a nice and silver high from her line. The thought of doing her line just to improve her mood was only making her more aggravated.

The phone rang.

"Hello?"

"Skye." It was Chasey. "I was jus' wonderin' when you were gonna come over."

"Yeah. I had a slight delay."

"Delay?"

"Yup."

"Oh. Um..."

"I'm going to be a little late."

"Oh. Like, how..."

"About twenty minutes from now at least."

"Okay."

"Then we talk when I get over there. Okay?"

"We do?"

"Yeah."

"Okay," replied Chasey uncertainly.

"See you soon."

She put down the phone.

She would do her line and relax for a few minutes, and then deliver the goods as well as a stern lecture to Chasey.

She would deliver the lecture first, before handing over her supply.

Surly Sue

The meeting was over.

Standing in the midst of the milling throng, he waited for the slowly moving crowd to thin out so he could maneuver out of the room. He had spotted Jes and Dorman, two tall and gangly clean and sober punks who were also friends of Holt, the ones he had managed to talk to the night before.

Shuffling around, Yuri was trying to make his way over to them. He had been tempted to share again at the meeting, but the chair for the meeting had never picked him to speak, even though he had repeatedly raised his hand.

He had probably not spent more than ten total minutes talking to Jes and Dorman combined, but at least he had been introduced to them and he had managed to remember their names. Yuri decided that was enough license to go up and talk to them.

Two guys had stopped in his aisle to chat. They were standing, hands in pockets, blocking his way.

"Excuse me," he said gently as he edged his way closer to the two.

"Excuse me."

They didn't budge.

Pushing aside a folding chair, he tapped one of them on the shoulder. "Excuse me!"

"Yes?" said the tapped man in an irritated voice.

"You're in my way."

The man looked at the floor and gingerly stepped aside, looking around as if he was annoyed that he had been interrupted. He left Yuri a small corridor with which to leave. Yuri made sure he bumped into him as he went past.

Just as he was getting through into the makeshift corridor of metal chairs, a hand fell on his shoulder.

"Hey Yuri!"

It was Holt.

"I'm glad to see you at another meeting," emphasized Holt.

"Thanks."

Holt's arms went around Yuri. As Holt let go of him, he self-consciously glanced down at his shirt which was fluttering over his still sunken stomach.

"How's it goin' man?" asked Holt with a big smile.

"S'aright," he replied as he cast a quick glance over his shoulder to see if Jes and Dorman were still there.

"You workin' your steps?"

"Yeah."

"You have a sponsor yet?"

"Huh?"

"You got a sponsor yet? Are you looking for somebody?"

"Kind of."

"Hey, don't let me keep you up."

Holt departed after giving him another pat on the shoulder. Turning around, Yuri could not see any sign of Jes or Dorman.

He went towards the church room door. He walked slowly, not wanting to barge his way through the crowd.

He was about to go out the door when he suddenly turned on his heel and doubled back. Perhaps Jes or Dorman had come back inside. Perhaps they had made a stop by the coffee table. Holt and his friends always seemed to move around quickly, especially after meetings. If Jes and Dorman had gotten outside, no doubt they were long gone or talking in an impenetrable huddle.

"Yuri!"

He had only barely heard his name. He wondered if it was Jes.

"Yuri!"

His ears perked up. It wasn't Jes.

It was a woman's voice.

Turning and looking through the crowd, his head weaved left and right as the voice kept repeating his name.

Suddenly, a short bobbing bald head came bouncing through the crowd.

"Hey Yur!"

A short, skinny, and steely-eyed woman popped out of the crowd.

He had to stare at her for a moment before he realized who it was.

He could not believe it.

"Damn Yuri, it's been a long time."

"Yeah. At least a year."

"More than two years," corrected Sue.

"No shit?"

"Yup," she confirmed as she picked up her coffee cup.

"You still go by..."

She cut him off. "No, I don't have <u>that</u> adjective in front of my name anymore."

She had been known as Surly Sue back at Hell Nose House. She had been one of his numerous roommates at the large and long flat back in his early San Francisco days.

"So what do you think of the program?" asked Sue over her raised cup of coffee.

"Hm?"

"NA."

"Yeah, I'm not sure. I just got here."

"Congratulations!" she smiled.

"Thanks."

"I'm really glad to see you've cleaned up."

"Yeah, thanks."

Back in the Hell Nose House days, Sue had always kept a large explosion of sharp dyed black hair emanating from her head. She had always endeavored to keep it as black as possible, repeatedly dying it, even though her hair was naturally black. She had been such a small and sharp person, and her ever present blast of knoxed black hair had been her trademark.

Surly Sue had not been one of the more obvious fixtures around Hell Nose House. Sue usually kept to her room, and was oftentimes not even home. She had rarely ever joined the front room television watching sessions or the forty ounce kitchen get-togethers. When he did see her there was always something about her gait, her steely eyes, and even her hair that told him she was a tightly wound person. She had the air of a person who was always ready to spring, or snap, or simply explode. It had made her quite intimidating, despite her diminutive size.

Now Sue was looking right at him. Her dark eyes were too bright.

"So who do you know in the program?" she asked as she cradled her coffee cup in her hands.

"Just you."

"Hm?"

"You're the only person I know in the program, really."

"Well, you must have met a few people."

"Yeah, well, I met this one guy named Holt."

"Oh yeah! He's really cool, isn't he?"

"Yeah."

"He's always hanging out at Trevor House."

"Trevor House?"

"That's the really cool Saturday night meeting. Haven't you been there yet?"

"Nu uh."

"Well Hell's bells, we gotta go. Are you busy next Saturday?"

"Not that I know of."

"Then we have to go."

Leaning back in his seat, he felt a warm wave of satisfaction. He had finally met someone he knew in the meetings.

Sue was acting as if they were old friends, with her high-toned voice and her bright smile.

"So, what have you been up to?" asked Yuri.

"Oh, you know, the usual stuff. Paying the bills, working my program, going to school."

"School?"

"Yeah. I'm working on my associate's at Vista."

Looking down into his coffee cup, he kept turning it around on the table. "Hey, do you remember why we gave our place that stupid name?"

"What place?" she perked.

"Hell Nose House."

"Yeah, that place." She grinned through a wince.

"I forgot why it was called that."

"That's what it was called before we moved in there. That stupid punk band, what were they called..."

"Yeah. I remember now."

"You remember that band's name?"

"No, just those guys that gave it its name. Didn't we used to know the reason?"

Sue leaned on the table. "There was a house full of Christian evangelists living across the street at the time. Remember those guys?"

"Those preppy idiots in the white sweatshirts?"

"Yeah, those people."

"Uh huh."

"They called their place the 'God Knows' house. Know as in k-n-o-w."

"Right."

"So that band called our old place Hell Nose House in response. Nose as in n-o-s-e, kind of like a protest."

"Heck yeah."

"They used to moon the Christians across the street and offer them beers and sex."

"Didn't one a' those Christian dorks try to sleep with one a' the punks?"

"That's what I heard. He came over one night and hit on the bald chick, because she kept telling him she'd give him a blow job and he was beginning to believe it."

"She was just kidding, right?"

"Hell if I know. Maybe she wasn't."

"Weren't you living there when that band was there?"

"No, Skye got me in there when I needed a place, remember?"

"Not really. There's a lot of things I don't remember about that place."

"No kidding."

His eyes wandered past Sue and towards the cafe scene in the background.

"So how long you been in the program?" asked Sue.

"Not long. Just about five weeks."

"Congratulations!"

She lifted her coffee cup as a toast.

"I'm still trying to get used to everything," he confessed meekly.

"Just stick with it. You'll do well. I know you will."

They both sat in silence for a moment, picking at their coffee.

"Hey, you wanna get something to eat?" she chirped. "You said you were in South Berkeley, right?"

"Yeah."

"I live just off of Ashby near Telegraph. We could get something and go back to my place."

It was not just Sue's smile and the friendliness. It was something else, something very different.

He was trying to figure out what it was.

Eliot's

"You wanna come with us?" asked Holt.

"Where to?"

"Eliot's."

"What's that?"

"It's a cafe on Durant."

"Okay."

He did not know what else to say.

Holt brought Yuri and a few chattering young women from the meeting over to Telegraph in his old station wagon. Yuri sat in the front seat as the two women talked between themselves in the back seat.

"A lot of us cruise by the Eliot's after meetings, especially on the weekends," explained Holt.

Holt had spent a lot of times at meetings, as Yuri had come to learn. He had also learned quite quickly that Holt was one of the social busy bodies in the East Bay clean and sober scene.

"So how long have you been in the program?" asked Yuri.

"I've got more than seven years clean now."

Yuri felt a bit flush when Holt mentioned his clean time. He was already feeling the weight of the six weeks he had been in the program.

"I had my seventh birthday a few months ago," continued Holt.

"Birthday?"

"My clean and sober birthday, not my belly button birthday."

"Oh. I asked 'cause…"

"Hey Holt!" bellowed one of the women who thrust her head between them from the back seat. "Did Eddie tell you if he was gonna be there?"

"I didn't have a chance to talk to Eddie after the meeting."

"Did you see who he was with?" bellowed the woman loudly again.

"I think he was with Stretch and Lidia."

Holt and the woman continued discussing the possibility of Eddie being at Eliot's. The other woman joined in on the conversation as well. Yuri resigned himself to admiring the urban scenery for the rest of their short trip.

Getting out of the car and walking down the street to the cafe, Holt and the two women continued talking between themselves.

Eliot's was a dark wood cafe located up against the side of a building on Durant street, just a half a block from the main drag of Telegraph. Outside, the few small sidewalk tables were crowded with teenage throckers and punks, some of whom were obviously homeless kids. The inside was much more sparsely populated, with a few bohemian college students studying in the back as a few scene burnouts lingered in the front.

Yuri trailed behind Holt and the two still nameless women. He wasn't too sure what he should do when Holt stopped to talk to someone at one of the outside tables. The two short and energetic women had disappeared into the cafe. Yuri was left standing next to the short stairs that led up to the entrance.

He stood for a moment, leaning back and forth in indecision. After shuffling his feet for a few more moments, he decided to go in.

Standing in line, there was a short, backpacked college student in between him and the two nameless women.

The nameless women got their coffees and went off to find a table. He grabbed a small coffee and started looking around the cafe. The Holt women sat in a wooden booth, having joined a tall man in black. The tall man deftly held up a cigarette while tilting his head in order to keep his well groomed hair to one side. Looking through the window, Holt was still in the same spot, talking to a few more people.

Taking his coffee to a small round table by the long cafe window, he discreetly watched some of the patrons outside of the cafe.

Turning in his seat, he let himself be distracted by the flyers on a nearby wall. Most of them were band and club flyers. There were a few extra flyers for an anarchist collective and a few holistic health seminars.

He also saw a few Gilman show posters. He was considering going to a show, but he was not sure who would go with him. He was not sure if he should try to ask one of his fellow twelve steppers. For all he knew, it might have been improper to ask someone in the program to go to a place like Gilman. He was still trying to get down all of the Narcotics Anonymous rules and rituals.

Someone tapped him on the shoulder.

"Whatcha doin' over here?" asked Holt.

Yuri shrugged in reply.

"Come on over," said Holt as he led him to the two nameless women and the tall well-groomed hair.

Holt took a seat at a small table next to the chattering Trio. Yuri sat across from him.

"Hey Rod, this is Yuri," said Holt to the tall and well groomed hair man.

"Hello Yuri," replied Rod in a quick and sedated tone. He had not even looked in Yuri's direction when he said it. Rod quickly resumed conversing with the taller of the two no-name women.

The shorter no-name started talking to Holt. Yuri nursed his coffee, trying to listen in on the conversation between Holt and the shorter no-name.

He quickly gave up on eavesdropping. They kept talking about people he did not yet know.

Drinking down the last of his coffee, Yuri leaned onto the table. "Holt."

He kept talking.

"Hey Holt."

He still kept talking to the shorter. Yuri stood up.

"Holt."

Holt finally glanced in his direction. Rod turned towards Yuri.

"How much clean time do you have?" asked Rod definitively to Yuri.

"What?"

Rod repeated his question, speaking slowly and deliberately this time. "How, much, clean, time, do, you, have?"

"A little more than six weeks."

"A little more than six little weeks?" said Rod.

Holt and the two no-names had stopped talking, looking to Rod.

Rod was holding still, his cigarette smoldering at an angle in the air. Yuri stood his ground.

"A gutter punk came in here today," intoned Rod. "I asked him if he liked speed."

"Okay," said Yuri.

"I told him that if I had any speed I would flush it down a toilet in front of him and all of his friends and go 'Ha ha ha'."

Yuri was not sure what to say. Something came to mind, but he held his tongue.

"Okay."

A shrill voice came from the back. "Hey Rod, don't give other people shit just 'cause you can't handle your drugs!"

A tall woman with long dark burgundy hair and a black leather jacket was standing across the cafe.

"Fuck you, scumbag," muttered Rod.

"Chad never did nuthin' to you," bellowed the woman with a sharp, jabbing finger. "Why you gotta act like a stupid asshole all the time?"

Rod turned around in his chair to face her. "If he was a real man he wouldn't need to do drugs!"

The tall woman stood her ground. Yuri felt there was something familiar about her by the way she was standing and the way she had her hands on her hips.

Rod turned back towards the table to stub out his cigarette. "This is bullshit."

Holt and the no-name women were sitting straight and still. A few of the grunged-out gutter punks were looking through the window from the outside tables.

Rod stood up. "I don't know why I even come here anymore."

"Yeah, take your clean an' sober ass on outta here!" emphasized the long haired woman with a toss of her hand.

Rod started out of the cafe. The tall leather jacketed woman deliberately bumped into Rod with her shoulder as he went by her.

"Scumbag," muttered Rod.

"Get your ass on outta here! Talk shit about people somewheres else!"

Rod kept coolly walked towards the door. He stopped and turned just before leaving.

"Give me a call tomorrow, Holt," he announced, emphasizing the word Holt.

"Will do."

The leather woman started walking towards Rod. Rod turned and left with a straight back and a steady gait.

The leather woman turned toward them.

"Why the fuck do you hang out with that loser?" asked the tall leather jacket woman.

"Lay off, Jen," dismissed Holt.

Jen turned towards Holt with a jut of her hip and a wave of her hand. "You were a lot nicer when you were gettin' loaded, you fuckin' wimp."

"Whatever," he replied, as he kept looking forward with folded hands on the table.

"I liked it better when you weren't walkin' around like you had a flagpole shoved up your ass. What the fuck did you have to do to get like that? Is it really necessary to become a prick to get clean?"

Holet did not say anything. He only gave her a quick upwards glance.

Jen confidently walked out of the cafe.

The taller no-name turned to Holt. "Damn, why the fuck did you let her talk to you like that?"

"Let her talk. Who cares?"

"She's lucky Rod didn't kick her ass," said the shorter no-name.

"Jeez, yeah," replied the Taller. "Rod was tellin' us about how he almost kicked this guy's ass over at the DNA Lounge the other night."

Yuri turned towards Holt. "Did you know that woman?"

"I used too, some time ago," he replied quietly.

"Rod shoulda fucked her up," interrupted the shorter.

"He should've. I could tell he wanted to, but he held back."

"Rod's not the kind of guy to do that kind of thing," said Holt. "I know that he wouldn't hit a woman, at least."

Yuri listened to the bluster of the two no-names, as they kept replicating more and more details about how and why Rod should have beaten the threatening Jen up. Yuri was especially interested in their fisticuff theories because of what he had just seen.

Yuri saw that Jen had not simply been posturing. He could not explain to anyone how he knew it was so. He had felt the way her arms and legs had been tensing up for a fight. All she had been waiting for was a decent excuse to hit Rod. Everything he had seen told him that Jen was someone who knew how to fight.

She reminded him of someone he used to know, an ex-girlfriend from his San Francisco days.

Looking at the wall.

She wasn't fond of the idea of repeating history.

Quite some time ago, when she was first living in the Bay Area, she had punched a hole in one of the walls of her room. She had done so because another woman had just confessed to her that she had slept with her then boyfriend, Zirk. In retrospect, she was embarrassed to think that she had made such a scene over someone who had never been much of a boyfriend.

The entire ordeal would not have struck Skye so much if the woman had not revealed Zirk's infidelity at a crowded Saturday night party.

This time, standing still in the middle of her room, she was only angry at herself.

She had planned on doing a few maintenance lines last night in order to do her laundry. Some random idea in her head had told her that she could get away with lying down on her futon for a few minutes.

She had fallen asleep.

The laundromat had closed and now she was left with a large pile of unwashed clothes. She had planned on getting her wash done so she could spend the day resting and crashing out after a long binge. She had plans to go out that evening, but she certainly wasn't in the mood to walk around in any of her currently grungy clothes.

Now she felt like punching the wall, though she was not sure if she could punch through this particular wall. The construct of the flat appeared to be quite a bit sturdier than the flimsy walls of her former abode, Hell Nose House.

Looking around her room, she tried to gauge herself, to see how far she could take her mind and her body on a round of errands and whether or not it would burn her out too much. It felt as if there were a large hollow spot between her lungs. Her head was tilting under the weight of her unwashed and matted hair. Her limbs were heavy enough, but her joints were stiff as well from having suddenly fallen asleep on the futon.

The thought of laundry brought other concerns to mind. She scanned her pile of shirts, trying to decide which one was the least offensive, as she thought about her food situation. She had already raided her cupboard of the last box of pasta a few nights ago. If she had anything left in the fridge, it was probably not edible anymore.

Her thoughts drifted to the bathroom as she got on her knees and started sorting through her laundry for a decent shirt. She wondered if she still had enough shampoo and soap. Arden never left any bathing articles in the bathroom. She knew her well enough to know that Arden was very particular about what she used in the shower, so she always kept all of her toiletries in her room.

Sitting up on her knees, she was startled by a round of sudden shuffling noises. A few sharp clicks got her to jump to her feet.

There was something in her laundry that was making that noise

She took a few steps back as the noises continued. Her heart jumped in her throat and her skin froze in fright. She heard another shuffle and a click.

And then a long and high pitched beep.

She felt flush when she realized the noises were being made by her answering machine. She dug through her shirts, searching for the machine. She managed to find the phone as the quietly whirring machine was recording the latest message.

Picking up the phone and carefully putting it down far from her laundry, she followed the cord, picking up shirts and laundry as she went, and found the still recording answering machine.

The caller finally finished leaving a message, as the machine clicked a few more times, rewound the tape, and beeped out another long beep.

Her heart sank when she saw there were eighteen messages.

Hitting the play button…

"Skye, this is Chasey. Could you give me a call when you get a chance? Thanks."

Click click…

"Hey Skye. This is Chasey again. I was wondering if you could…"

She hit the skip button.

"Hi Skye…"

Click click.

"Skye…"

Click click.

"Skye, hi. It's…"

Click click…

A new voice.

"Hey Skye. It's jus' scrungy ol' Linette callin' ya. Sorry the ol' lady's been such a bitch lately, but she's been gettin' on my case about you–know-what. Anyways, since she's not here I thought maybe we could hook up n' go like, y'know, check out the scene. Maybe do an act above the Zeitgeist or somethin' stupid like that. Y'know, get all fucked up an scrungy lookin' and impress all the stupid Danzig boys on lower Haight."

She enjoyed Linette's message, even though she knew that she was looking for the same thing as Chasey.

"Gimme a call when you're alive again."

Click click.

"Hi Skye, it's Chase..."

Click click.

"Hi Skye…"

"Damn!" she exclaimed as she pounded the skip button.

"Skye, this is Trafe. I need you to give me a call…"

She hit the skip button harder this time.

"I called you over an hour ago, and I don't see how you can keep up your business if you don't return phone calls."

With tightening shoulders and bristling skin, she carefully listened to the rest of Trafe's next message. "I need you to call me back because I need to score some gofast within an hour, so call me back immediately."

The machine started clicking to the next message as her skin grew hot. She reminded herself not to hit the machine.

She skipped over the next three messages which were all from Chasey. There was another message from her part time job at Levigate, someone asking her to fill in for an absent employee. She listened to the next set of messages.

Someone belching into the phone and hanging up. She assumed it was Linette.

"Skye, Pres here. Call me when you can."

She quickly hit the stop button and dialed Preston.

"Yo."

"Pres, it's Skye."

"Hey."

"How long ago did you call?"

"Just like an hour ago."

She eyed the machine. There were still a few more messages left.

"What's up?" asked Skye.

"Jake came over with a twelve of UFO Lager. I'm pretty stoked right now. Y'wanna come over?"

"Yeah. I'll be right over."

She gathered up her backpack and did a quick maintenance line. She would buy a supply from Preston and get back to Chasey and Linette and the inevitable friends of theirs that they were go-betweening for.

Thinking about what she needed to do, she would have to stop by the local head shop for a new collection of baggies. She had to remember to ask Preston if she could borrow his small scale. She needed to cash her paycheck so she could have enough for an eight ball.

And she needed to find Trafe.

She had to do something she had not done in quite some time.

Trevor House

The meeting took place in a very large and well hidden Victorian House, just a few blocks up the street from the North Berkeley urban sprawl.

Yuri and Sue had gotten off the bus at the main street and were walking up the hill towards the house. Yuri could see it from several blocks away. Its windows were glowing brightly between the tall pine trees that surrounded it.

Yuri felt a twinge of excitement as he saw all of the people milling outside. He would only admit to himself that he often felt out of place at NA meetings. Before him, milling about on the sidewalk, was a wavering field of black clothes, dyed hair, facial piercings, band t-shirts, Doc Martens and tattoos. It was an impressive gang of punks, throckers, rude girls, rude boys, and postie burnouts.

They had arrived early, a good fifteen minutes before the meeting was about to start. Yuri walked slightly behind Sue, carefully following her lead.

"Pretty cool, huh?" asked Sue as she glanced back at Yuri.

"Yeah."

Nearing the large and impressive house, Sue started wavering to the left side of the mini-mansion. She approached a group of tall, bald men. One tall baldy was turning towards Sue and Yuri.

"Hey! How's it goin'?" said one of the baldies.

It was Holt. He let out a bright smile and held a hand out to Yuri.

"Hey Yuri, you made it!"

"Hey."

Yuri was about to shake his hand when Holt embraced him.

Holt released Yuri and turned to Sue.

"How ya doin'?"

"Pretty good," smiled Sue.

Holt turned back to Yuri. "So, you made it to Trevor House."

"Yep."

Holt had his arm around Yuri. He was turning him around to the rest of his gang.

"That's Cory, Semi, Darren, and Tilden."

Each one of the tall bald men and the one short fellow with the green mohawk named Tilden first shook Yuri's hand and then gave him a quick embrace.

The baldies retreated to their former semi-circle as the Mohican stood his ground to speak to Yuri.

"How's it goin' Yuri?"

"A'right. Can't complain."

"Have you been in th' program long?"

"Just a few months actually."

"Well, congratulations! You doin' your ninety in ninety?"

"Yeah, well, I'm tryin', but I can't find a meetin' I can get to on Thursdays."

"It's really important to get that in."

"Yeah, it's just I gotta work that day, and there's no place nearby."

"I did my ninety an' ninety when I got in. You really should keep that up."

Yuri noticed the baldies drifting to the side, huddled in a quiet, almost whispering conversation. Holt and Sue had stepped off to the side to talk to each other.

Yuri talked some more with the Mohican, who abruptly pardoned himself after a few minutes to avail himself to a couple of overdressed punks who had just arrived. Yuri drifed towards Sue, but he stopped himself when he saw how she was talking to Holt.

Holt suddenly turned to Yuri. "Hey, you done your ninety in ninety yet?"

" I'm workin' on it right now."

"I think it's good to get that in. How many days do you have?"

Sue chimed in before Yuri could answer. "He's doin' good. He'll get there."

"All right, but you should really keep up that ninety in ninety."

"Of course," said Yuri with as confident a voice as he could muster.

Holt tossed his head towards the house. "I'm goin' up. Anyone comin' with?"

"Yeah," commanded Sue. Yuri walked alongside Sue as she followed Holt up the crowded wooden stairs.

The large Victorian appeared to simply be a house. The only thing that gave it away as a community center were the long fluorescent lights in the hallway and the bulletin boards riddled with Narcotics Anonymous and Alcoholic Anonymous flyers. The hallway was so crowded that Yuri could only shuffle his feet as he kept close to Sue. They kept shuffling along, moving slowly to the back of the house.

The meeting was being held in a wide and very long meeting room in the basement. The ceiling was low, and the room was interspersed with a few square pillars. The whole place was brightly lit by embedded fluorescent lights in the ceiling.

The walls were lined by couches and easy chairs, while the center of the room was dominated by a field of metal and plastic folding chairs.

Yuri was trying to keep up with Sue as they moved through the crowd. He was being pulled back by the smell of strong coffee. He spotted the coffee table, complete with three coffee brewers that were still steaming.

He snaked his way through the thick and milling crowd. Yuri grabbed a cup of coffee and turned to make his way back. Almost everyone had already seated themselves. Yuri could see Sue sitting towards the front of the meeting hall. She was waving to him. Walking over, Sue had saved him a seat.

"I hope you don't mind sitting in the smoking section," said Sue.

"Not at all. I could use a cigarette actually."

Yuri felt the weight of his presence as he sat down next to Sue. He was trying to imagine what the crowded meeting would be like if he had been there alone.

Yuri quietly sipped his coffee as the meeting started with the traditional reading of the fellowship credos. Even though the secretary had started speaking, there were still plenty of murmuring and shuffling people, creating a background of chatter and distractions throughout the hall.

Yuri was at the point where he was getting used to the traditional readings. He was not paying nearly as much attention to them as he had only a few weeks ago. He was looked around the crowd, trying to recognize faces.

After a few moments of preamble droning, his wandering eyes slowed down. He cast his glances around the long meeting hall, trying to focus on interesting scenes. There was a trio of punk chicks, all clad in leather and Derby jackets, sitting on a small two-seat couch, crowding up against each other. Closer to the front was Holt and another baldy, sitting with a pair of very skinny young women.

Towards the front there were a few biker looking types, and a couple of cowboy hats topping long grainy hair. The people sitting up front appeared to be older and more solemn than the rest of the crowd.

Sue had chosen a seat near a few baldies and young punks who were tittering and talking and fidgeting. They acted as if they were at a party or a club, taking very few pains to keep their voices down or their bodies still. Yuri casted side glances at them, hoping they would notice his glare and try to keep it down.

Yuri's also noted more than a few loners who dotted the room. People sitting alone, looking forward or askance, looking as if they were searching for something. Sometimes they were older people, sometimes they were younger. Yuri saw them all the time at meetings, the dour and searching singles.

The speaker started up. Yuri only knew that someone was starting to speak because of the sudden applause. He kept his covertly roving eyes going. He cast a few nervous glances at Sue, who alternated between watching the speaker and looking at her feet.

His searching eyes suddenly stopped, as if they had been snagged by a hook.

A tall woman stood in a far and dark corner. Yuri almost missed her, which would have been quite a feat, since she appeared to be at least six feet tall. She was wearing an old black leather jacket, looking steadily towards the speaker with dark and immobile eyes. She had short, neatly trimmed spiked black hair and a porcelain face of pale skin, save for a dull red scar that ran down her cheek and towards her neck. Her slightly plunging neckline revealed a chest covered with elaborate tattoos. Yuri could spy the curling tail of a writhing dragon tattoo, just above her collar.

She leaned back into the corner with her hands behind her back, standing straight. She was looking at the speaker, standing still and silent, paying cool attention to what was going on.

He darted his eyes away. He returned to his roving mode, looking down at his coffee and back up again to the crowd. He tried to listen to the speaker and quickly gave up. There were too many distractions to hear what he was saying.

Resuming his scan of the crowd, he hoped he would spot someone else that he knew.

Yuri lost Sue in the swirling crowd as the meeting was breaking up. Edging his way towards the outside of the house, he roamed through the milling twelve steppers until he found Sue again. He spotted her across the street, standing in one of the semi-circles with a few other women. Crossing the street, Yuri headed in Sue's general direction, but he also kept his distance. Her huddle of women appeared to be too exclusive for one of his intrusions. Slowing his pace, he kept an eye out for Holt or Tilden. He hoped he would be able to spot Tilden. He needed to make more new contacts.

He began drifting towards Sue.

That's when he saw her again.

The tall leather dragon woman stood within one of the huddles, a group of well groomed punk women, all of whom had neatly trimmed green, red, or bleached blonde hair. The dragon woman was standing at ease, but not talking, hanging out more on the edge of her semi-circle rather than standing within it.

Turning on his heel, Yuri stopped right next to Sue.

"Hey Sue."

"Oh, hey!" replied Sue. "What's up?" asked Sue as she turned around to face Yuri. The trio of women who were talking to Sue all moved a short step away.

"What's goin' on?" asked Yuri as casually as possible.

"Not much. You wanna go to a party?"

Yuri straightened up. "What kinda party?"

"Daphne's having a party. You should come with us."

"Sure."

"Cool," replied Sue. "We're about to take off."

Yuri put a hand on Sue's shoulder and leaned towards her.

"Do you know who that woman is, standing over by the Trevor house entrance?" asked Yuri quietly.

"Who?"

"That tall woman in the black leather," replied Yuri, casually pointing with his eyes.

"That's Zata. Pretty impressive, huh?"

"You know her?"

"Not really. I've seen her around at meetings, but I haven't talked to her that much."

"I see."

"Come on," said Sue as she took Yuri by the arm.

"Where we goin'?"

"Lindsey's gonna give us a ride to the party."

Party

Sue had introduced Yuri to everyone in Lindsey's car. He was warmly greeted with smiles and handshakes as he nestled next to the window, pressed up against Sue. There were three other women and another man in the car, not including Sue, all crammed into a long green station wagon..

Yuri tried to listen in on the conversations as he tried to remember everyone's hastily called out names. The only name he could readily remember was Lindsey since it was her car and she was driving.

One of the women in the front seat turned around, looking into the backseat.

"Hey, you into KMFDM?" asked the woman as her large nose poked through her bright green braids.

It took Yuri a moment for him to realize that she was talking to him.

"Hell yeah," replied Yuri after Sue nudged him.

"You should check out Shill. They're playing the Square on Saturday."

"That's Turner's band," remarked Sue.

"Is Jess still playing bass for them?" asked a disembodied voice from the other side of the car.

"No way," answered the other male. "He relapsed last week."

The group got back into a discussion. Yuri again tried listening in on the conversation as he gave up trying to remember the names of the non-Lindsey people.

After a few minutes of driving, Yuri did not recognize the neighborhood they were in, but he estimated that they were somewhere near Piedmont, one of the nicer neighborhoods in Oakland.

They parked in a residential neighborhood made up of well kept single story houses. Yuri followed the small crowd for a few blocks until they came upon other wandering people who were all headed for a large house on a corner.

A lot of people from the Trevor House meeting were already there, walking up to the bright doorway.

Yuri had to wait to get in the doorway. The members of Lindsey's group were being hugged and greeted by various people just outside of the front door. Finally getting inside, Yuri tried to keep himself in the general vicinity of Sue. Sue introduced Yuri to the hostess. The hostess gave him a quick welcoming hug.

The inside of the house was clean and orderly and spartan. It was furnished with expensive looking new furniture. The walls were so white and the carpet was so clean that it appeared to be more of a museum than a home. Yuri was hesitant to touch anything.

There were small squads of recovering addicts huddled in strategic positions throughout the house. A few lone wanderers stood in corners or against a wall here and there. All of it was reminding Yuri of the aftermath of a typical meeting.

Yuri kept his eyes sharp, looking for a diversion. Yuri suddenly saw Holt near the kitchen door, talking to a new batch of baldies and punks.

Yuri detached himself from Sue to watch a couple of fashion punks play a video game. As he spaced out on the flashing video game, Yuri thought back to his earlier San Francisco days, specifically the only other time he had been to a completely drug and alcohol free party. It was several years ago when some of the Hell Nosers decided to go across the Golden gate bridge to Marin to see if they could find a party or a club. They had all been interested in finding something that was not part of the typical San Francisco scene. The whole trip had been a real novelty, because many Marin County scenesters jumped out to San Francisco to go to clubs and parties.

They had gone out to San Rafael, himself and his roommates Pel, Dangerous Dan, and Preston, as well as his then girlfriend Skye, to dig up whatever throckers and punks they could find to try and scare up some kind of a scene. They got a line on a big house party in Larkspur from a Marin County throcker. Gunning out to Larkspur in Dan's beat up station wagon, the party turned out to be an alternative clean and sober party. Thinking back about it now, Yuri suspected it had probably been a twelve step get together.

They had wandered around the Larkspur party for only a few moments before they started to thirst for liquor. "This is fucking lame. Let's get the fuck out of here," someone had blurted out, quite loudly. Yuri couldn't remember who had said it. He only remembered that a lot of people turned around to stare at him and his motley crew.

Yuri was snapped out of his thoughts by a hand touching his shoulder.

"There's more food in the kitchen if you're hungry," chirped the passing hostess.

"Thanks," replied Yuri quietly, as he remembered that the hostess' name was Daphne.

Walking towards the kitchen, he found several people hovering around a snack table, grabbing food and drinks and chatting away. Yuri spied the bottles of soda and bowls of chips, ruminating on how strange it was to see a party table that did not have crowds of beer cans and liquor bottles.

His thoughts drifted back to the long ago Marin search for a party. He could recall that Preston, his former musician roommate who was constantly practicing, had been the driver. He also remembered Preston's friend Wink and his roommate Pel had gone along, and that Pel and Dangerous Dan had been the most social ones, the ones who had quizzed the local throckers about potential parties.

Then he remembered.

It had been his girlfriend Skye who had yelled out, "This party is fucking lame."

He recalled that he had responded "Hell yeah", quite loudly.

He found himself embarrassed by his own memories.

Reaching for a bowl of chips, Yuri wondered how he could have missed her when he had come into the kitchen. Zata was standing in a corner of the kitchen, a few feet from the edge of the snack table. She had her hands in the pockets of her leather jacket, squeezing her jacket shut with her arms as she stood tall and straight.

Rounding the table, he made his way to the drinks. He also searched the crowded kitchen for any sign of Holt, or Sue, or even Daphne.

Grabbing a can of soda, Yuri found himself pivoting on his foot. Turning around, he was looking at the tall Zata, standing still in her corner.

"Hi."

"Hello," deadpanned Zata.

Yuri felt flush. "How's it goin?" volunteered Yuri.

Zata did not say anything. Her dark eyes seemed to be watching something across the kitchen.

"You're tall," said Yuri suddenly.

"Yes," confirmed Zata.

"Are you a friend of Daphne's?" asked Yuri as he cradled a handful of chips.

Zata looked right at Yuri. "Who?"

"Daphne. She's the one throwing this party."

"No, I don't know Daphne," replied Zata, who returned to looking into the kitchen distance.

"I'm Yuri," he finally said. "I'm kind of new to the program." Yuri held out a hand.

"Susan dragged me here," blurted Zata.

"What?"

"Susan dragged me to this party."

"Dragged?"

"Yes."

"Okay."

"I don't really like parties," deadpanned Zata. "There's not much point to them if you don't get loaded anymore."

"You don't like this one?"

"What?"

"You don't like this kind of party?"

"What kind of party?"

"A clean and sober party."

"Hell no." Zata looked around and then leaned down towards Yuri. "Don't tell anyone I said that."

"Hmm?"

"Just keep that to yourself."

"Sure."

Zata stared down at Yuri.

"Would you get in trouble?" asked Yuri

"What?" asked Zata as she leaned in closer to Yuri.

"Would you get in trouble if anyone found out you said that?"

Zata leaned back, looking at the ceiling as if she were thinking about it.

She shrugged. "It just wouldn't be cool."

"Okay," said Yuri.

Zata settled back into her corner. Yuri took a step back as he looked down to the other end of the table.

He looked back to Zata. "Maybe I'll talk to you later?"

"If you really want to."

Yuri nodded and turned away.

He drifted towards the end of the table, considered the pastries, and then wandered out of the kitchen.

Yuri passed by several huddles of talking twelve steppers and went back to watching the video game.

Linette

"Can I come over?"

Linette's voice told Skye she was looking for a score.

"Sure thing."

"'Kay. I'll just come over?"

"Yeah, yeah. No prob."

Skye put down the phone.

Skye made herself a short line to get herself up for Linette's visit. Taking a quick snort, she picked up a few dirty dishes and headed for the kitchen.

Walking into the kitchen, she was caught off guard by an exploding bush of bright blue hair that was hovering by the fridge.

"Skye."

"Fuckin' a' Jane, you almost scared the hell out of me."

"I know, I'm quite scary lookin'."

"I haven't seen you in weeks."

Skye had been so surprised by the sight of Jane that she did not notice her boyfriend for a moment, who slouched his gaunt frame over the kitchen table, smoking a cigarette.

"Hey Stash."

Stash only nodded his head slightly.

"How's the paintin' goin'?"

Stash shrugged one shoulder. Skye put her dishes in the sink.

"What you two up to?"

"Stash had to sell his VCR, so we came over here to dig out mine."

"More midget porn?"

"I wish!"

"You gonna watch it here?"

"Sure. Why go all the way back to his place? Besides, I should probably spend some time here since I'm still payin' rent."

Stash got up and walked out of the room. He had not even glanced at Skye.

Skye leaned towards Jane. "What's up with Stash?"

"Some asshole fucked up all of his paintings."

"What?"

"Someone broke into his apartment and slashed up alla' his paintings. That's why he had to sell his VCR. He's spent alla' his money on new art supplies, an' he kinda forgot that he had to pay rent and buy food."

"Fuck."

"Jane," echoed a sullen voice from the hallway.

"I'll talk to ya in a bit," said Jane as she carted off two tall bottles of Sheaf Stout into the hallway.

Skye went back to the sink, listening to Jane's heavy boots clomping down the hall.

It suddenly hit Skye. She was not sure if she had left her door open or not. If so, they might be able to see the mirror, and possibly more than that. Skye's brain snapped to, coming out of its post-amphetamine fog just enough to race with itself, wondering if she had left out any bags of crank, or scales, or big plastic baggies full of smaller plastic baggies.

She cautiously listened to Jane's clomping footsteps. She wondered if they had quickened, out of surprise, or slowed down, out of curiosity.

Jane's clomping stopped. Skye heard Jane's door shut.

Cautiously walking into the hall, looked around her door frame.

Her door was slightly open. She stopped for a moment to study the slight opening to her room to see if they could have spotted anything.

Into her room, she saw that she had left the mirror by her futon. She had also left out a blade and a straw. There was a faint residue of speed on the mirror.

Kicking herself, Skye inspected the rest of her room. She had left the baggie for her main stash on the floor, on the other side of her futon. It was doubtful that it could have been seen through the door.

The door buzzer went off.

Skye let out a breath. Quickly but steadily walking into the hallway, she wanted to make sure she buzzed in Linette before she hit the buzzer again,

Skye quickly led Linette to her room. Linette carried out her newfound habit of retrieving a kitchen chair and sitting herself right by Skye's dresser. Skye had retired to her futon, lying stomach down and hanging just off of the edge of the futon so she could make lines for herself and Linette.

"Wassup Skye. What's goin' on?" Strands of ratted hair were drooping in front of Linette's face, threatening to ignite on her cigarette.

"Not much. Same ol' shit," replied Skye as she examined her personal stash.

"Fuckin' a'," moaned Linette.

"Watch where you step when you walk around in here," cautioned Skye. "I lost a blade in here somewheres."

"I ain't movin'. You heard from Mercy lately?"

"Nope. Ain't you seen enough of her?"

Linette dangled her head. "Fuck it. I dunno. Can I tell you somethin'?"

"Like what?" asked Skye as she was shaking out more speed onto the mirror.

"Well, don't tell Mercy I said any a' this, but hanging out with her is gettin' really fuckin' boring."

"Really? I never thought of Mercy as boring myself."

"I dunno. It's not really that boring. I mean, the sex is pretty good, an' once in a while she'll go with me to a club or a show, but usually all she wants to do is hang out at her place, or see some foreign film at the Roxie, or listen to some stupid ass dyke poetry at the bookstore."

"You're a dyke."

"Who wants to listen to that 'flowering essence of womanhood' bullshit? I mean, fuck, that an' fifty bucks will get me eaten out on Polk Street."

"I dunno. The only lesbian poetry I know is Tribe 8."

Linette's head weaved back and forth. "Shit, I don't really want to rag on Mercy, it's jus', she was givin' me a lotta crap about hitting the stuff too hard."

"Which stuff?"

"All of it. The horse, the Jake. She didn't want me hangin' around you too much."

Skye's face went flush. Looking at the lines, she tried to concentrate on what she was doing.

"Were you lookin' to score?" asked Skye as she kept her eyes down on the mirror.

"I wouldn't mind," moaned Linette as she leaned back in her chair. "As long as it ain't too much trouble."

"Naw. I gotta score anyways."

"I'm tryin' not to do so much horse," remarked Linette as she tried leaning further back into the chair. "I think I should stick to other stuff. I dunno. I gotta few rocks from my friend Shill the other day. I was thinking I could hook a few lines, maybe get me goin' up instead of down alla' time."

Skye got a few lines ready. "Just kick it an' we'll take down a few before I get goin'."

"You goin' out?"

"Yeah."

"'Cause I need to do somethin'," trembled Linette as she was picking her nails. "I'm gonna go stir if I just sit aroun'."

"Hang on a sec'," said Skye as she stood up and handed Linette the straw.

Skye went into the kitchen to make a quick phone call.

"Hey Pres."

"Hey. You comin' over?"

"Yeah, but I was wonderin' if I could bring someone with me."

"Like who?"

"My friend Linette."

"Sure. If she's cool, bring her on over."

Going back to her room, Linette leaned over the mirror and brushed the strands of her hair out of her face. Her eyes were a little more lively and she was sitting up straight.

Linette at Preston's

Linette was quiet during the Mission street walk to Preston's place. She kept her arms crossed tightly against her body for the entire walk.

She only brightened up when they were finally approaching Preston's building. She unraveled her arms and looked around.

Knocking on Preston's door, Linette bit her lip as Preston took his customary time wandering from his room to answer the door.

"Hey Skye," greeted Preston. Skye wandered in, quickly eyeing the kitchen to see if anyone else was there. Linette was right behind her.

As they walked into Preston's room, Linette plopped herself down in the easy chair.

"This is my buddy Lin," said Skye.

"Wassup," said Preston.

"Hi."

Skye sat down on the floor next to the entertainment center. "You been hittin' them chops?" asked Skye as she nodded towards his guitar.

"Fuck no. I've just been burnin' out." Preston took out his speed kit. "You keep asking me if I'm jammin'. What about you? You gonna play again?"

"Fuck, I'm so fuckin' rusty. An' I wasn't even that good to begin with."

Skye and Preston chatted about music as Preston made up some lines. Linette sat quietly in the easy chair, nursing a cigarette. She curled her arms and her legs against herself, her head getting lower and lower against her tightening limbs.

Preston turned to Linette. "Hey Lin, you play anythin'?"

"What?" snapped Linette, suddenly lifting her head.

"You play anythin'?"

"You mean music-wise?"

"Yeah. You hangin' out with a couple a' musicians you know."

Linette shook her head. "Naw. I don't have to. Alla' my girlfriends have been musicians. They play for me."

"Ah man, y'don't want someone else makin' your music."

"Fuck it. I'm too lazy."

Preston leaned forward and handed Linette the straw. Linette took the straw and stood up.

Linette looked down at the snorting mirror. "Holy shit!" gasped Linette. "Is all of that for me?"

Linette was pointing to one of the lines on the surface.

"Actually," replied Preston, "if you don't snort that whole line, you owe me money for the unsnorted portion."

"What?" shook Linette.

"Well, I figure there's gotta be at least ten bucks worth a' crank there. So if you only snort half a' that line on the first snort, you'll owe me five bucks."

Linette looked around as if she were following the flight of some invisible insect. "Are you serious?"

"Fuck yeah I'm serious!" snapped Preston as he held the straw closer to Linette.

Skye shook her head. Linette cautiously leaned down to do her line. "Hurry up," said Preston, "We ain't got all day." Preston couldn't keep himself from smiling this time.

"We do so have all day," said Skye.

"Right. Take your time then."

"I'll have to," cautioned Linette as she carefully leaned down to do her line.

Starting out slowly and then picking up her pace, Linette strained to do the entire line. Skye knew Linette was driving the rush.

Finally bringing her head back, Linette collapsed into the easy chair, letting out a groan. Skye took the straw, noting Linette's tearing eyes and red face.

Skye didn't know how tight her skin had been until she did her line. A warm wave passed over her, loosening the flesh around her bones.

"Hey Skye," harkened Preston.

"What?"

"What did you wanna get?"

"I need two teens."

"Okay. Hey!"

"What?"

"Linette didn't do her entire line!"

"What?" groaned Linette as she raised her swimming head.

Preston pointed to the remainder of her line. "Look at that! That's at least three bucks worth a' crank!"

"Dude," groaned Linette, "you can't be serious."

"Well, I'll have to think about this."

"I'll do the rest in a minute."

"Oh no you don't!" Preston leaned forward with his baggie and started sprinkling out some more speed. "I'm gonna reload this line and you'll do the whole thing next time."

"Oooooh God," scrawled Linette as she sank back in the easy chair.

Preston kept ribbing Linette as he made a few more dealer lines for them and weighed out Skye's supply.

"He's just kidding about the line," cautioned Skye as Linette leaned over to do another rail.

"The hell I was!" harked Preston, much to Skye's irritation.

Skye and Preston started talking about music again as Linette collapsed into the easy chair.

"Fuck," groaned Linette.

"Hey Skye, I think your friend ain't feelin' too good."

Linette crossed her trembling hands.

Skye kneeled down by the arm of the chair. "Lin, what's up."

"I'll be alright," trembled Linette. "It'll pass in a minute."

"You gettin' the horse shakes?"

"I can't fuckin' believe it," quivered Linette. "I gotta get this when I'm wired offa' my ass."

"Would a beer or two..."

Skye was cut short when Linette sprang to her feet. "Where's the bathroom?" she groaned.

"First door on the left," said Preston. Linette dashed out of the room, dashing through the hall and crashing the bathroom door shut.

"You didn't tell me you was bringin' a junky," said Preston.

"Sorry."

"That's all right. Don't worry about it."

"She's trying to convert."

"Well, she makes up for it by being a total babe."

"Yeah, Mercy always hooks up with total babes."

Preston looked up from the mirror. "What about Mercy's boyfriends?"

"Studs, of course."

"Of course."

Skye tried to keep up the conversation, trying to lighten the mood. Linette came back in after a few minutes.

"I think I did too much speed," Linette lifted her head, throwing out wide eyes of pure glass.

"Maybe we should go back to my place," said Skye cautiously.

"Mmmhh."

"I need to get my stuff."

"Yeah, sure."

Preston quickly bagged her first order and quickly started to weigh out her second teen. Linette collapsed into the easy chair.

After Preston was done weighing Skye's supplies, Skye carefully secured her substances in her backpack.

Skye slowly approached Lincttc.

"I'll be a'right," shivered Linette as she quickly looked up at Skye.

"Thanks Pres," offered Skye.

"Make sure you lock the door on your way out," said Preston as he looked back down at his mirror.

Linette walked ahead of Skye as they left Preston's place. Skye took a quick look into Preston's bathroom. There was no residual mess, but it smelled foul enough.

On the way home, Linette kept walking ahead of Skye, stopping quickly at a corner liquor store for a moment to grab a six pack of beer.

"Gotta calm my nerves," explained Linette.

Back at Skye's place, Skye prepared herself a line to calm her nerves. She would do another line and then nurse a few of the Meisterbraus that were left in her fridge.

Linette quickly downed a few beers. She sat back in her kitchen chair, looking at Skye's speed mirror.

"Can I buy some offa' ya?" asked Linette.

"Are you sure you want anymore?"

"Oh hell yeah. It was just a short DT. The beer helped a lot."

Skye shrugged. "It's cool. I can sport you a few lines if you like."

Home

The wind impatiently pushed Yuri towards his place as he sprinted through the backyard of the main house. The wind tried to follow him inside of his house. Shutting the door, slices of the wind kept whistling through the razor-thin cracks in the wooden wall. The floor was cold enough to make it feel damp.

The front of his face felt tight, as he tried sniffing away his running nose.

Putting down his small bag of groceries, he put away a few potatoes and apples he had bought from the corber market. He had been eating a lot of pasta and cheap McDonald's cheeseburgers, and he felt he should try eating more fruits and vegetables. Zatch had a few Budweiser talls left in the fridge, one of which was open.

Keeping his coat on, Yuri sat down on his bed. The tiny red light on his answering machine was staring back at him, still and unblinking.

Slowly lowering himself down onto his bed, he had only taken his shoes off. His chilled bones were cooling his flesh. Walking around had been easy, but bending his arms and legs to get down on his bed kept stinging his joints with pin cushion aches.

Looking back at the unblinking red light, his answering machine had returned to its old habit, its initial behavior when he first moved into his Berkeley home. When he had first moved across the bay, he may as well have moved across the country. He had lost touch with so many people. But after running into Rebar and reconnecting with some of his friends, he would rarely ever walk into his house without seeing his answering machine furiously blinking at him, indicating calls from Rebar, Sweezy, Dex or Pel.

The small and still red light kept looking at him as if it was asking him an accusing question.

A quick but sharp quiver went through his upper left arm. It quickly left, but the quiver had sharpened the sting in his joints. He went numb, and now Yuri could feel his aching bones. Yuri squirmed and turned, trying to find a comfortable spot on his bed.

Lifting his head, Yuri suddenly realized he had forgotten to buy milk for his coffee.

"God dammit."

Tired and cold and aching, Yuri did not want to struggle to his feet and make the three block walk back to the corner liquor store for a half quart of milk, but he had to go to work in the morning, and he could not stand the thought of trying to choke down black coffee or of going to work without any coffee at all.

Turning on his side, he decided he would try to rest for a few more minutes and then go out again. Perhaps the wind would die down in the meantime. A wicked whistling went through the wooden walls.

He quickly jumped through the door and slammed it shut, hitting back at the wind and the rain.

"Fuck!"

Just as he was getting to the store, a sudden downpour broke out. He dashed into and then out of the store and walked as quickly as his legs could carry him, trying to run ahead of the rain. By the time he got home he was soaked to his skin.

Getting out of his dripping wct coat, he resisted the urge to throw the milk across the room as an angry shudder went through his body. One thought after another kept crashing into other streaming thoughts as they flashed through his roiling mind. If only he hadn't forgotten the milk. If only he didn't need to dilute his rancid coffee in order to drink it. If only he didn't have to drink coffee in the morning to be halfway awake, if only he wasn't so burned out half the time that he needed to drink coffee to wake up, if only he didn't have to go to work so early in the morning, if only he didn't live in such a dump, if only he could get a decent night's sleep once in a while, if only he had a decent mattress, if only it was not always too cold or too hot, or too damp or too dry, if only he didn't have such a terrible job, if only if only if only…

He quickly put away the milk. Yuri was concerned that the urge to hurl it against the wall would become too great.

He stripped out of his soaking wet clothes and quickly dried himself off. The combination of his damp naked skin and biting cold air made him tremble fiercely as he struggled into a new set of dry clothes.

Still shivering, he thought about borrowing some of Zatch's bedding so he would not be so cold.

Picking up his blankets and spreading them out, he stopped.

The red light on his answering machine was giving off a slow, steady blink, indicating that he had at least one new message.

Yuri cautiously hit the play button. The last time he had gotten a message on his machine it had been a wrong number.

The scratchy tape started to play.

"Hey motherfucker, drop your cock and pick up the phone!"

It was Johnny Trash.

"What the fuck? Where've you been? I haven't heard from you in a while. Gimme' a call an' come on out. You know the number, motherfucker!"

Johnny ended his message with a high pitched barbaric yawp. It sounded like static on the machine's small and beaten speaker.

He had almost forgotten about Johnny Trash. He had not talked to Johnny since he had taken the plunge into full on sobriety.

Yuri wondered how Trash would react when he found out about his new lifestyle. Perhaps Trash would not have bothered to call if he had known beforehand.

Scrambling up the ladder, he grabbed a few of Zatch's blankets.

Wrapping his violently shivering body into a cocoon of blankets, he decided he would call Johnny Trash after work tomorrow. He did not feel like breaking the news of his newfound sobriety to Trash just yet.

Phone call

She found it while she was putting away her stash. Linette had left her wallet behind.

They had been around each other for more than twenty four hours, drinking and snorting until they had finally both crashed out on Skye's futon.

Linette had been coming by Skye's place more often. Skye enjoyed her company and Linette, apparently, felt Skye's company was a welcome relief from Mercy's atmosphere.

Looking around her bottom dresser drawer, she found the scrap of notebook paper with Linette's number on it.

Lying down on her futon and dialing Linette's number, Skye was not feeling too bad for having just finished off another speed binge. She had been up for two straight days before she had passed out.

After listening to Linette's phone ring for about the tenth time she put down the phone.

Looking inside Linette's wallet, she saw there was about a hundred dollars in it.

She picked up the phone.

Skye didn't even have to look up the number.

"Hello?"

"Hey Mers, what th' fuck?"

"Hey Skye."

"So what's up Mercy?"

"Nothing."

"Mm hm."

Skye paused for a moment.

"I thought I'd give you a call 'cause I hadn't heard from you in a while."

"I've been pretty busy," stated Mercy flatly.

"Oh yeah? With what?"

"With work and Jenelle."

"Jenelle? Who's that?"

"My girlfriend."

"Oh." Skye paused again as she was caught off guard. "I was kinda hopin' you knew where Linette was."

"I don't know where she is. I haven't seen her in almost a week."

"Hm."

"Is something wrong? Is there a reason you need to find her?"

"Naw. Not really too important," intoned Skye apologetically. "Jus', if you see her, let her know I'm trying to reach her."

"Okay."

"So what else you been up to?"

"I gotta go. Jenelle is waiting for me."

"Gotcha."

"Bye."

Mercy hung up before Skye could say anything else.

Skye lifted herself off of the futon and put Linette's wallet on top of her dresser. The weight of her bones pulled her quickly back onto her futon.

Staring at the ceiling and spacing out, she wondered if she should make the walk to Preston's. She wondered what kind of chores she needed to get out of the way in the next day or two. She wondered where her energy had suddenly gone.

Turning over on her side, she decided she needed to try and get some more sleep. Her increasingly heavy body was dragging her flesh into the floor.

Closing her eyes, she knew she wouldn't be able to sleep.

Proxy

"I have to go on a run."

"You mean out to your supplier?"

"Yup. Out to the East Bay. Jer's gonna be here pretty soon to drive me out."

Skye already knew that Preston's speed supplier was somewhere in the East Bay. She had previously gathered that he was in Oakland, since Preston had mentioned once before that his supplier was "just off of the other side of the bridge."

"I was wonderin' if you could hang out here while I'm gone," asked Preston. "Jus' while I'm out getting some more stuff."

"Why would ya want me to stay here?"

"I need someone to answer the phone while I'm gone. I gotta few calls comin' that I don't wanna miss."

"Yeah, I guess I could do that."

"You can hack on my axe an' hoach on my beer. There's also the TV."

"How long you think you gonna be?" asked Skye.

"An hour or so. Not more than two hours, tops. "

"A couple of hours?"

"I'll give you a half if you do this for me."

"Okay!" brightened Skye.

"When I get back, that is."

"Sure thing."

Preston gathered up his speed kit and his backpack.

"What should I tell people when they call?" asked Skye.

"Just take a message. Don't tell 'em where I am."

"A' course not."

"Tell 'em I'll call back as soon as I can, an' that's about it."

Just as Preston was strapping on his backpack the door buzzer went off.

"That's Jer."

"You trust me?" smiled Skye.

"Hell no! I've got the exact amount in my change jar written down, dammit!"

"Sucker."

"Just don't snort alla' all the dust offa' my floor."

"Why not? There's probably a lotta crank down there."

Skye followed the quickly skittering Preston down his short hall, locking the door behind him. She found a six pack of Mooseheads in the fridge. Taking two bottles, she went back into Preston's room and grabbed the black Gibson.

Sitting in Preston's traditional spot on his bed, she clicked on the television with the remote and opened a Moosehead while cradling the guitar in her lap. She made sure the phone was right next to her so she wouldn't have to eject any guitars from her lap or abandon any beers if it rang.

Sipping the beer slowly, she was still riding a clean sheen of a crystal meth high. She was just wired enough for the beer to take the edge off of her amp and give her a calm, floating feeling.

After a few moments of channel surfing, she found a daytime talk show. Putting the Gibson in her lap, she strummed it a few times. It was slightly out of tune.

Absentmindedly plucking out a progression, she began eyeing the window next to Preston's bed and wondered if it was possible to open it. Preston had covered the window by his bed with some sort of thick black cloth. She would probably have to wreck the covering and the window in order to open it. She decided to douse her desire for fresh air with Moosehead and the soft glow of the television screen.

She lingered on the talk show while her fingers continued to wander the strings. She kept plunking out tunes and dashing off quick three-chord progressions.

She muted the television so she could play out a melody she had absentmindedly discovered.

Suddenly it hit her, out of the corner of her mind. She was playing the opening from an old song without even having realized it. It was the opening of an old Annie Rage song, the one Annie had written for the Dynamite Chicks.

The harsh and shrill electronic pitches of Preston's phone rudely interrupted her musical meditation. Leaning over the guitar, she picked up the phone.

"Hello?"

"Who's this?" snapped a voice on the other end after a surprised pause.

"Ibskibit," answered Skye.

"What?"

"Ibskibit."

"What the fuck are you saying?"

"This is Ibskibit."

"Is Preston there?"

"Nope."

"What?"

"He's not here."

"What the fuck do you mean he's not there? What the hell are you doing there if he's not there?"

"This is Mister P's personal assistant."

"What?"

"He's not in at the moment. Can I take a message?"

"Really, who the fuck is this? How do you know Preston?"

"I'm his pal Lucy."

"Lucy?"

"Yeah."

"Lucy who?"

"Lucy Van Pelt."

There was a long, uncertain pause at the other end of the phone.

"Would you like to leave a message?" asked Skye finally.

"Um, naw. I'll call back."

He quickly hung up.

Getting back to her previous routine, she found a new song. It was a bare-boned thrash song, a three chord grinder from her earlier days of her musical pursuits. She was trying to find the tune she had lost when the phone rang.

The phone rang again, but this time Skye was ready for it.

"Hello?"

"Oh. Wrong number."

"Wait…"

They hung up before Skye could finish her sentence. She put the phone back down and it rang again a few moments later.

"Hello?"

Her answer was followed by a dead pause.

"Hello?"

Skye listened for a few more moments and then started putting the receiver down. Just before she was about to hang it up she heard someone say something through the receiver. She quickly put the phone back up to her ear. "Hello?"

Another pause, then a gruff voice. "Who the fuck is this?"

"I dunno. Who the fuck is this?"

"Where's Preston?"

"I dunno."

There was another impatient pause.

"Where the fuck is Preston?"

Skye leaned back into Preston's spot. "Well, I guess I can tell you.

Him and his friends had some ideas about primate cross breeding."

"What?"

"Him and his friends went to the zoo to fuck apes."

"What?"

"Don't tell Preston I told you."

"Who the fuck is this?" growled the voice on the end of the phone.

"Lucy."

"Lucy who?"

"Lucy Van Pelt."

"What? Who the fuck is this?"

"I told you."

"Lucy?"

Leaning back against the wall, she sank further into Preston's bed. "Yeah."

"Lucy from Freak Magnet?"

Skye had heard of Freak Magnet. They were an all-girl lush band that had haunted some of the local punk dives a few years ago. "Sure."

"What?"

"Yeah."

Skye remembered what they had looked like, the four skinny and sketched out punks, but she wasn't sure which one had been Lucy.

"Do you remember me?" groused the voice.

"No. I was too drunk," replied Skye confidently.

"What?"

"I was drunk. I don't remember nobody."

"What the fuck?" shouted the voice. "Where the fuck is Preston? Who the fuck is this? What the fuck are you doing on his phone?"

"They wouldn't let me go to the zoo with them."

The angry voice hung up the phone.

A few talk shows later, Skye let the channel wander to the evening news. The dead drag and drone of plucking guitars and hazy cable television was broken by the phone again.

"Yello?"

"Is Lucy there?"

Skye paused for a moment. She had momentarily forgotten her previous phone alias.

"Yes. Lucy Van Pelt speaking."

"Is Preston back yet?"

"Nope. He's still not here."

"Oh. Well couldja tell him to call Reese?"

"Yeah sure."

"Cool. Thanks Lucy."

"No prob Mister Reese."

"I'm not Reese."

"Oh."

"Thanks. Bye."

Putting down the phone, Skye looked at the clock. Preston had been gone for at least two hours.

Tipping her head to the side, she watched the television at a new angle. She wasn't playing anymore, simply cradling the guitar in her lap as she sank deeper into Preston's spot.

Leaning forward, she finally put down the guitar. Her fingers were sore and cramped from playing.

She went to the fridge for the last bottle of Moosehead. Earlier she had considered giving Linette a call, but she didn't know if Preston had call waiting.

But then again, Preston had been gone for an awfully long time. She wondered if that shouldn't allow her a few liberties with his place.

Skye turned off the television and picked up the phone.

"Hullooo?" graveled Linette.

"Linette! What's up?"

A pause. "Nuuuthin'."

Even her short pauses sounded dead.

"I'll call later. It sounds like I woke you up."

Linette hung up without saying anything.

Looking back at the television, she turned the sound back up and wondered if there was anyone else she could call. She considered calling Chasey, but she usually only wanted to talk about drugs.

Skye's shoulders suddenly shook. "Fuck!"

She realized she had been digging her fingernails into the palms of her hands. She unclenched her hands and considered leaving Preston's place altogether. Downing the last Moosehead, she looked at her backpack.

Getting off the bed, Skye paced around the small room, looking at all of Preston's various belongings.

She began to wonder if she could simply leave his place temporarily. Perhaps go to the corner liquor store for some snacks or more beer, if for no other reason than just to break the monotony. It was probably safe enough to leave Preston's apartment door unlocked for ten or fifteen minutes. She wondered if there was a way for her to get in and out of the building. That would be more problematic. There was also the possibility that Preston could show up in the short amount of time she was gone.

She heard the front door click.

Quickly skittering out into the short hall, she listened as someone was fiddling with the front door knob.

The door gently clacked open after some generous knob rattling. It was Preston.

"Dude," drawled Skye with more than a hint of aggravation in her voice.

"What?" replied a puzzled Preston as he took a quick detour to the fridge.

"Where've you been? You said it wasn't going to take more than two hours."

Preston brought his head out of the refrigerator. "You drank all of the beer."

"Fuck dude, you were gone for more than six hours!"

"Oh. Fuckin' a."

Preston wandered into his room with Skye trailing behind.

"Call Reese," said Skye.

"What?"

"Reese wants you to call him, apparently."

"Who the fuck is Reese?"

"I dunno. Some guy called and said to call Reese."

"Somebody named Reese called?"

"No, he said he wasn't Reese."

Preston started unpacking his backpack. "What the fuck are you talking about? Who the fuck called?"

Skye aimlessly waved a hand in the air. "You want me to try and explain it again?"

"No. I don't know who the fuck Reese is anyways. Did anyone else call?"

"Yeah, a couple of other people, but they just said they would call back".

Skye flopped down into the easy chair. Preston dug through his backpack, pulling out plastic baggies of powder.

"Do you want me to score you another six?" asked Skye.

"Don't worry about it."

Mirror

He could not help it. He kept glancing at the mirror, looking up and then and turning his head back and forth as he held his eyes steady.

He was in the main house. He had just taken a shower. It was midday and there weren't too many people inside the main house. It was a good time to use the bath and shower since he was less likely to be disturbed.

He was looking at his cheeks. They were too shallow, he thought. Looking at his nose, he decided it was too pointy. It was thin, just like his body and his face. There was no fat in his face. Looking straight into the mirror, he puffed up his cheeks, trying to imagine himself with a fuller face.

Yuri glanced at the top of the mirror. Usually Yuri spiked his short hair. It was wet and flat. He put his hand on the top of his head and wondered if he should just shave his hair off. Perhaps he would fit in better in the clean and sober scene if he did. There were so many bald guys at the meetings he attended. He wondered if it was an unwritten ritual or protocol, that there was some sort of implied clean and sober virtue to having your head shaved.

There were a few things he was finding out about the clean and sober scene that was not written on the cards they passed out at the beginning of each meeting. Various kinds of people in the program ritually asked him about his program habits, such as which step he was on, whether or not he had a sponsor, and whether or not he had done his ninety in ninety. Holt and Sue and Tilden would always ask him. People he merely recognized would always ask him, and then people whom he barely knew and even people he had just met would start asking him about sponsors and steps and ninety days.

Many of the speakers, the speakers at meetings, or simply people who shared, almost always talked confidently, with an overview of what you had to do in order to stay off of drugs. One subject that Yuri had heard about quite a few times was letting go of unrealistic expectations. One man divulged how he had a dream of getting rich and comfortable, about how he wouldn't have to work anymore, and how he came down to Earth to realize that his dreams were folly. Another speaker talked about how she gave up her dreams of becoming an example of feminist ideals, how she had been trying to model herself as an example of a strong and independent woman, until she realized that such endeavors were foolish.

It made him wonder how his desire to improve his lifestyle and his life, with new clothes and new furniture, and a decent place to live, were unrealistic.

He also found out that you were never supposed to admit, at least openly in meetings, that you ever had a good time taking drugs. He could not talk openly about how good he felt the first time he had shot up heroin, or how much fun he had having sex with his speed freak girlfriend Skye when they were both wired on speed. It was fine to talk about those kinds of things with people one on one, at least certain people, in any case. There were more than a few NA people who would get upset about someone saying such things, even in private.

He remembered why he had put his shirt back on before looking in the mirror. He did not want to see his gaunt body in the mirror.

Collecting his soap and towel, he thought about what other unwritten Narcotics Anonymous rituals and protocols he had not yet stumbled upon.

Thinking about shaving his head reminded him of Holt. He felt like calling him again. Yuri had already left a message on his answering machine. Yuri had called him a few times before, and several times Holt would call back fairly quickly, but on other occasions Holt would not return his calls at all.

Walking out of the house, the cool wind refreshed his damp skin as the sun warmed him.

Gathering up his money, he would go to McDonald's. He was going to get a full meal, and possibly a dessert, rather than just a few cheap cheeseburgers. He needed to gain some weight.

Thinking back to the bathroom mirror, he decided against the idea of shaving his head. It would only make him look thinner than he already was.

Sponsor

Holt told him he had to do it.

It was at the large Tuesday night meeting, the one in the church basement on University Avenue. For some reason it was always packed. It was just a few blocks away from a warehouse pool hall, the one that Yuri was always tempted to try out after meetings.

Holt had encouraged Yuri to get more phone numbers. Holt advised Yuri that he needed to branch out and start calling people. Yuri suspected it was good advice.

"You really should get yourself a sponsor," Holt had repeated to him at the meeting. Many members had been telling Yuri to get a sponsor.

Coming from Holt, it sounded more like good advice. Even so, the peer pressure was beginning to get to Yuri. He suspected he was losing favor with some of the regulars at several of the meetings because he had not yet gotten a sponsor.

For the moment, Yuri concentrated on just getting phone numbers. He tried an easy one first, asking Tilden for his number, which he readily gave. He had asked an old hippy for his number, a fellow whom he had met a few times before. He was an understated and calm man, a large barrel-chested bearded fellow whom Yuri thought looked like Santa Claus, if Santa had been a pothead.

Yuri had not asked anyone else. He barely knew anyone else. He strolled through the aftermath of the meeting, eyeing the various huddles and groups for people he knew.

The crowd was slowly making its way outside. Yuri drifted towards the door when he saw Holt walking up to him.

"Did you get any numbers?"

"Yeah, a couple."

"Good, that's good," replied Holt with an approving nod. "So now what are you gonna do?"

"Hm?"

"What are you gonna do now?"

"I dunno. Get more numbers?"

"You got some numbers, now you should call 'em."

Yuri was surprised by Holt's comment.

"Give these guys a call within the next few days."

"Are you my sponsor?" blurted Yuri.

Holt stood for a second, as if the question had surprised him. "I can be your temporary spons. But you'll still have to find a regular sponsor."

"Okay."

"If you want to do that, have me be your temporary sponsor, then you need to call me tomorrow, right after you call a couple a' other people."

"Sure."

"Okay? Then we'll get started tomorrow."

Holt gave Yuri a pat on the shoulder and made his way towards the entrance.

Yuri found himself floating near the door. He decided to wait for the crowd to thin out. Loitering near the coffee table, he half-heartedly scanned the crowd.

He knew that Holt was serious when he insisted he could only be his temporary sponsor. Holt did a lot of circulating, so it was only reasonable that a lot of people were asking him to be their sponsor.

A wave of uneasiness came over him. He lowered his head and leaned against the coffee table. Looking back up, someone was standing close by, looking at him.

It was Zata.

She was practically standing right next to him, standing in a relaxed stance, though she was completely still. Her dark eyes were looking straight at him.

"Hi," said Yuri.

"Are you feeling alright?" asked Zata.

"Sure. I'm all right. Just a little tired."

Zata stood for another moment. "I saw you talking to Holt."

"Yeah. He agreed to be my temporary sponsor."

"Just temporary?"

"Yeah."

"My, how generous of him," said Zata flatly.

Yuri felt a warm sting go through his arms. He straightened his back and brought his arms to his side.

"He says I need to get a regular sponsor," said Yuri.

"Of course," said Zata in the same tone as her last comment.

Yuri swayed on his feet. The hall was almost empty.

"Would you be my sponsor?" asked Yuri with a grin.

"If you want," replied Zata flatly.

"I was just kidding."

"You were? Why?"

Yuri took a moment to look at the corners of the ceiling. "Well, I was jus', y'know, tryin' to lighten the mood. I know guys are supposed to ask other guys to be their sponsors."

"Naturally."

"Yeah."

Zata put her hand out, flat against Yuri's shoulder. "Give me a call this weekend."

"What?"

"Sue has my number," said Zata, keeping her hand on his shoulder.

"Sure."

Zata turned and left. Yuri waited for a few moments before starting out of the hall. He found Sue talking in one of her traditional huddles.

"Hey Sue."

"What's up Yuri?"

"You goin' back home?"

"Yeah."

"I got me a temporary spons."

"Really? That's great!"

"Yeah. Holt said he would be my temporary sponsor."

"Cool. He's a good guy."

"Zata also told me to give her a call."

Sue looked up at Yuri. "She asked you to call her?"

"She said I could get her number from you."

"Did she really say that?"

"Yeah."

Sue watched him for another moment. "Okay. I can give you her number this weekend."

Sue offered to commute home with Yuri. It seemed that his revelation about Zata had renewed Sue's interest in Yuri, even though she did not talk about Zata again for the rest of the evening.

He was lying on his mattress. His hip bones felt as if they were stabbing right through his mattress and into the floor.

Picking up his phone, he felt somewhat stunned at the thought of calling someone he hardly knew. He had the number for the random Mohican whom he had only spoken to a few times. He had only met him because he knew Holt, and now he was going to call him up out of the blue.

Trying to make his mind go blank, he dialed Tilden's number.

Forcing down the uneasiness, he listened to the phone ring.

It rang several times, and then a loud click. A blare of thrash music came through the phone. It was an answering machine. The music played for a few moments and then the machine beeped.

Yuri hung up without leaving a message. He would wait until he actually got him on the phone.

Rolling onto his back, he wondered how long he should wait before calling Tilden again.

His mind wandered. Rolling onto his stomach, Yuri decided he would call Holt.

The phone only rang twice before Holt picked it up.

"Hello, this is Holt."

"Hey Holt."

"Yes?"

"It's Yuri."

"Oh, hey Yuri!" brightened Holt.

"How's it goin'?"

"It's all good. What are you up to?"

"Callin' ya like I said I would."

"Did you give anyone else a call?"

"Yeah, sorta."

"Sort of? What do you mean by that?" asked Holt as his tone became more serious.

"I just tried calling Tilden, but he wasn't home."

There was a pause on Holt's end of the phone.

"You know Yuri," said Holt very seriously, "you shouldn't try to hustle a hustler."

"What d'ya mean?"

"Well, Yuri, I talked to Tilden on the phone a few minutes ago, and I know he's home right now."

"Okay."

"I know you are probably uncomfortable with the idea of calling people up, and it may take you some time to get the nerve up to call, but this won't work out if you're not honest with me."

"Okay."

"So, are you going to call Tilden?"

"I told you, I just tried to call him."

"Yuri."

Yuri sat up on his mattress. "What do you want me to tell you? I just tried calling him. I got his answering machine."

"I know for a fact that Tilden always answers his phone. He doesn't screen his calls."

"Well, you can say whatever you want."

"You're going to have to get a lot more serious about this program if you want this to work," interrupted Holt.

"Holt, I'm not lying. I really did just try to call him."

Yuri could hear Holt give up a sigh. "So you say you got his answering machine?"

"Yeah."

"Did you leave a message?"

"No. I haven't called him before, so I thought I would wait until I got him on the phone."

There was another pause at the end of Holt's line.

"Have you thought about your higher power?" asked Holt.

"Yeah, I have."

"That's good."

Yuri took the phone away and then brought it back to his ear again.

"I haven't really told anyone about it yet."

"You haven't?"

"No. I thought about it for a while, what it could be, and I finally settled on what I believe it is."

"Okay."

"It's like, I think, it's the reason I got clean in the first place. I keep thinking about the life I want to have."

"How's that?"

"Well, the way I figure it, my real higher power is the life that I don't have. Right now I can't afford a lot of things, and the power is those things which are out of my reach, like a nice place to live, and decent clothes on my back, and not having to worry so much. I mean, I don't expect to be really rich or successful or anything like that. I just want to be comfortable."

"No, that's not your higher power," announced Holt confidently. "The program is your higher power. Concentrate on your program and your steps and worry about getting a more comfortable life later."

A numb feeling went through Yuri's face. There was a short pause on the phone.

"I want you to call me again tomorrow," said Holt.

Another pause.

"All right? Can you do that?" asked Holt impatiently.

"Sure," answered Yuri flatly.

"Okay, see you later."

"Yeah."

Yuri hung up the phone.

Standing up, Yuri decided he was going to the corner store.

He wasn't going to call Tilden again, at least not that evening.

Cut

"I can tell that stuff you sell is pretty pure."

Skye concentrated on the lines she was making as Chasey hovered around her living room. Linette was laid out in the easy chair, sinking into the cushions and nursing a bottle of Red Hook.

"You thinkin' of spreading it out?" asked Chasey as she started towards the kitchen.

Skye lifted her head. "What?"

"I mean, dealing halves and quarters and dimes."

"What are you talking about?"

"You could make a lot more money if you sold some smaller bags of cut stuff on the side."

"Just keep sellin' us the pure shtuff," slurred Linette with a smile.

"I'm just fuckin' around, I'm not trying to make a business out of it," replied Skye flatly.

Chasey grabbed a few beer bottles on her way back to the kitchen. "You want another beer?" asked Chasey as she looked back at Linette.

"Naw. I'm still workin' on this one."

Chasey disappeared into the kitchen. A combo tape of The Selecter and The Damned was playing at a decent volume, not too loud or too soft. The windows were shut and a few second-hand lamps were making the room glow with a dull yellow and orange light. Chasey didn't bother turning on the overhead room light. It was too bright and harsh for their tweaker eyes.

It was the early evening. Skye had brought Chasey and Linette decently sized supplies to distribute among their friends. They had also bought their own personal supplies for a weekend binge. Skye made sure she had gotten to Preston early in the week before all of his weekend orders started piling in.

Linette wobbled her head towards Skye. "I still gotta wicked buzz offa' that last line."

Skye put the finishing touches on a new set of lines, making sure they were good and straight.

"Did you hear what Chasey said about Mercy?" asked Linette.

"Chasey knows Mercy?"

"Yeah. They used to hang out at th' Penny Pasta all th' time, back when Mercy was livin' with some chick named Sweezy."

"That must've been a while ago."

"Chasey told me that Mercy has a magic cunt."

Skye lifted her head up from the mirror. "What the fuck are you talking about?"

"Chasey said that Mercy has a magic vagina, that if a guy was havin' problems with his equipment, all he'd have to do is fuck her an' they'd go away."

"Chasey said that?"

"Yeah. If a guy had th' clap, or a penis infection, or if he had broken his dick, Mercy' vagina would fix it."

"A broken dick?"

"Yeah, like ripped it on somethin' or bent it too far."

"Jesus, what the fuck are you talking about?"

"Haven't you ever known a guy who broke his penis?"

"No."

Linette waved her beer bottle for emphasis as she talked. "I knew one guy who tore his foreskin on some gal with this really small and sharp cunt, and another guy who bent his too far and hadda have it operated on. He like, busted up a buncha vessels in it when he bent his erect penis too far."

"Bullshit. You're making that up."

"No I'm not. Anyways, if any guy had something wrong with his pecker, all he'd have to do is fuck her and his peter would be all cured."

"Just like that?"

"Yeah, like magic! No infections or tears or breaks."

"Right."

"But there's a drawback!" said Linette as she sat up.

"Like what?"

"Guys can't see her cootch."

"Why not?"

"Because if they see it, they'll turn to stone!"

"Excuse me?"

"It's a Medusan cunt. Like, if a guy tried to eat her out, an' the lights were on, he would turn into stone. Chasey said she had to leave one of her places because of all the weird statues she had collected in the basement. Like, all these naked stone guys leaning over with their tongues sticking out."

"But I've seen her naked, and I ain't made a' stone."

"That's 'cause you're a woman, and because you really have to lean over an' really look at it, like see her clit an' her inner labeeeyahz."

"You can talk about a magic vagina but you can't pronounce labia."

"Chasey's right though," said Linette as she pointed at the mirror, "You could make a lotta money if you sold some cut quarters an' dimes."

"I make okay money as it is," replied Skye as she looked down at the mirror. "I don't need to be hangin' around fucked up cafes an' dealin' with those idiots on the drag."

"Fuck, I betcha you could get a couple a' geeks to go-between for ya."

"That's what I have you an' Chasey for."

"No way. I don' wanna deal with no death puppies on the upper Haight either. I'm only go-betweenin' for my friends."

The back of Skye's neck became tight. Jumping to her feet, she started towards the kitchen.

"There's another rail for you," said Skye to Linette as she pointed at the mirror.

"Thanks. I'll do mine after you guys do yours."

Skye went into the kitchen. Chasey was putting away some dishes.

"Your rail is on the table," said Skye.

"Thanks."

"Is it okay if I have another beer?"

"Oh gee, I dunno Skye. I mean, how can you drink two whole bottles of my beer when you've giving me giant lines of free crank?"

"Ya."

Chasey handed another beer to Skye and they went into the living room. Skye sat back down at her spot as Chasey leaned over to do her line.

Skye sat back against the couch, letting herself settle into the beaten springs. Her eyes wandered around the dark room. Chasey had cleared off one end of the coffee table for the snorting mirror. The rest of the table was covered by half empty beer bottles, cigarettes, and rolling papers. There was a baggie of pot at the end of the table.

Chasey leaned back after a mighty snort, tossing her head back to catch the drain and drive the rush.

"Hey Chase," asked Linette, "Y'know where I can get any hash?"

"Huh?"

"That weed was pretty good. I was wonderin' if you knew where I could score some hash."

"I might. I'd have to ask around."

Skye sat up and looked at Linette. "You gonna do your line?"

"Yeeeah," slurred Linette.

Skye sat back, drinking her beer. She could tell that it would take Linette a good snort or two before she could get down her line. Leaning down, Linette managed to get down a little more than half of her line before stopping.

"I know what you mean about askin' aroun'," said Linette through her sniffing red face. "My horse dealer was busted last week. Alla' his buyers were hittin' me up for stuff."

Leaning her head back, Skye wondered if Linette was still dipping into junk. She was puzzled by Linette. Skye had not recalled any junkies who went on to speed. At least some of them did.

Perhaps Mercy had exaggerated Linette's heroin habit. She considered that a real possibility, since Mercy had never really gotten very deep into any of the drug scenes.

"Hurry up Lin. I wanna do my line," said Skye.

"Just do it now," gasped Linette through her red face as she held out the straw.

"I'll wait until you finish yours."

"Fuck, more pressure."

Chasey wobbled to her feet. She picked up a joint she had rolled earlier. "I know what would go good with this." Chasey quickly disappeared into the next room.

Leaning over, Linette finished up her line with a loud and forced snort. Falling back with a gasp, Skye saw that there was a smidgen of her line left. Leaning over, trying to keep her head up, Linette handed the straw to Skye.

"You finish it off. I can't do no more."

Turning the mirror slightly so her line was facing her, Skye took up her blade and corralled the remnants of Linette's line into her own. Chasey came back in carrying a small leather bag with a zipper on it.

"When you're done with that," said Chasey pointing to Skye's line, "I got somethin' else for us."

"What is it?" asked Linette as she climbed back into her easy chair.

Unzipping the bag, Chasey brought out a small plastic baggie with some white powder in it.

"More speed?" asked Skye.

"Nu uh. The other stuff."

"Not H?" sneered Linette.

"Coke?" asked Skye. Chasey nodded.

"Oh, fuck," gasped Linette. "That's all I need now."

"You don't have to try it," remarked Chasey.

"Yes I do. I can't just sit back and not join in if you're gonna toss coke at us!"

Skye leaned down and quickly did her line. She barely felt any stings of the grainy crystals going through her nose, but she could feel the high crashing through her face, lighting her head and warming her face and chest.

"Fuck Skye, I don't know how you do it," said Linette.

"It's just practice," said Chasey as she leaned down to pour out some cocaine.

Skye watched Chasey make some modestly-sized lines on the mirror as she recalledthe few times she had done coke. She liked the way it made her feel when she had gotten high off of coke, but the high only lasted about half an hour with a decent line. She was not impressed with its longevity, and only ever bothered with cocaine when it was offered to her.

Leaning her head on the back of the couch, Skye watched Chasey lean over the mirror. She was looking at Chasey's thin cheeks and the arcs under her eyes. She was cutting her hair short lately, almost as short as a buzz cut. She had bleached her hair blonde, and there were still a few faded colors from her former dye jobs.

Skye kept playing with a random strand of her hair. She had been letting it clump up into dreadlocks. She wondered if she would have a better time with a lot less hair.

Skye's trance was broken by Linette's bellowing.

"You really should think about cuttin' some a' your stuff," suggested Linette.

"Maybe I should cut your supply," said Skye sharply as she lifted up her head.

"Hey, I'm jus' sayin'."

"Just drop the cuttin' bullshit. I don' wanna hear it anymore."

"A'right, a'right."

Putting her head down, Chasey quickly snorted up a line of coke. Chasey tossed her head back and let out a gasp.

Skye took the straw and leaned down to take in a line of coke.

"Fuckin' a'," groaned Linette.

Johnny Trash

Yuri had agreed to meet Johnny at the Beller cafe on Haight street. Johnny had originally suggested they meet at Zeitgeist near the Mission, but that particular bar was too close to his old junky stomping grounds.

As he was riding the subway into San Francisco, he kept turning over the memory of his East Bay friends, the ones that he had lost touch with after he had gone completely clean and sober. He kept thinking about Dex and Sweezy and Rebar.

He had been clean for nearly three months. He had talked to Sweezy only once in all that time, and that was shortly after he had decided to go full on clean and sober. Sweezy had offered him a few mild salutations, saying, "That's good. That's great," in a tone that made her sound as if she were talking to a potentially dangerous person.

The train reached a downtown stop. Yuri got off in the financial district. He could have gotten off two stops further, but he did not want to exit at a station closer to Mission street. He could still catch a bus to the upper Haight from downtown.

During the bus trip, the pull of his old haunts was not as strong as he had anticipated. He was able to space out on the changing street scenes as the bus rolled through the crowded Market street, through the upper mission shops, and then through the semi-dilapidated Lower Haight. He did feel a twinge, a sharp feeling in the pit of his stomach, when the bus went past Haight and Fillmore.

He got off of the bus while it was still a few blocks away from the cafe. He wanted to survey at least one familiar section of the city on foot. There were enough things for someone like himself to appreciate on the Upper Haight: The Nightbreak, the I-Beam, Reckless Records, and a few other small shops and interests. For the most part, the upper Haight was the tourist section of hip San Francisco. It was the one former haunt of his that had tacky souvenir shops and roaming tour buses.

Rounding a corner, he went into the Beller cafe.

"The coffee's better in Berkeley," explained Yuri.

"The drugs are better over here."

Yuri looked down at his half finished latte. "I wouldn't know about that. Not anymore, anyways."

Yuri bent over his drink as he leaned on the table. Johnny sat in the window, leaning against part of the window frame with his legs up on another chair. He was still wearing his sunglasses, even though his dyed black bangs were covering the top half of his face. He was still tall and slim, and his skin was still pale.

"The booze is better over here," Yuri added quickly.

"Fuck dude, we went out to Berkeley a couple a' months ago, an' there ain't no fuckin place to drink over there. Just a couple a' fucked up yuppie bars and a few skanky dives."

"No shit."

Johnny leaned back in his chair. "So what the fuck are ya doin' over there?"

"What?"

"Whattaya doin' out there in Berkeley anyways?"

Yuri turned his glass around a few times. "Workin' in a warehouse, an' livin' in this cool little place in South Berkeley."

"Fuck, my drummer said if his rent goes up one more time he's gonna end up out there."

"Out in Berkeley?"

"In the East Bay somewheres."

"Yeah."

Johnny suddenly leaned forward. "What about the dope out there? Is it any good? Or do you have to come out here for the good stuff?"

"Dope?"

"You try out any a' the crank connections? I hear there's some good crank in the East Bay. Here it's almost all H."

Yuri shifted in his seat and leaned farther onto the table.

"That's the thing," said Yuri. "I've decided to clean up."

"What? No more horse?"

"No more anything."

"Whatcha mean?" asked Johnny as he brightened up in sudden interest.

"I mean I'm full on. No horse, no crank, no booze."

"No booze?"

"Yeah."

"Fuckin' a'!" exclaimed Johnny. "I thought you would never get offa' that stuff. I mean, I can see ya quittin the H, but booze?"

"Yeah."

"What about ganj? Can you still smoke weed?"

"Nope. No weed."

"Fuckin' a' man, that's a trip. Hell, sometimes you used to get so wasted over at Hell Nose. I'd come over and you wouldna even known I was there."

A jolt went through Yuri's shoulders as he tried to hold himself still.

"You never told me anythin' like that before," said Yuri.

"Tell you what?"

"That I used to get that wasted.'

"Fuck it. What for? You was gonna do junk anyways."

"What?"

"I mean, if I had told you that you shoulda quit doin' junk back then, would it had made any difference?"

Yuri looked deeper into his coffee cup.

"Fuck this shit," blurted Johnny as he returned to his casual position. "We should go to the Nightbreak. Maybe there's a couple of throckin' skanks we can hit on."

Johnny stood up, picking up his black leather jacket and started out of the cafe. Yuri had an idea to protest, insisting that he be allowed to finish the remnants of his latte, but he decided to reluctantly follow.

It was a short walk to the Nightbreak. Johnny kept chattering as they walked. The upper Haight was unusually bare of pedestrians.

Johnny walked into the Nightbreak, went right up to the bar and leaning casually across the counter. The Nightbreak was a small and dark club. They had shows on the weekends and operated as a bar during the weekdays. It was thin and long, with a few patrons haunting various corners of the club.

Johnny ordered a Sake Bomb. Yuri ordered a soda. He was rather annoyed that his pint glass of cola came with a straw.

"You shoulda come to that club that night," drawled Johnny as he dropped his shot of sake into his beer.

"What club?"

"The Crucifixion."

"Right." Yuri had nearly forgotten why he had journeyed out to San Francisco before.

"It was pretty wild. It was even more crowded than before. I was walkin' around the upstairs room and there was this one place that had all these couples wrapped aroun' each other."

"What? You mean they were doin' it?"

Johnny shrugged. "I couldn't tell. It was too dark."

"A lot of people must've been pretty fucked up then."

"Most of 'em were on X. I think that stuff is bullshit myself. It's like bunk acid without the bad side effects."

"Mm hm."

Yuri looked down into his soda. He had barely touched it.

Johnny kept talking, going on about the old days. Trash could talk for hours. He always seemed to have an endless supply of experiences to talk about.

Johnny's hand came down on Yuri's shoulder. "Remember when Preston and Wink got that stash?" blurted Johnny.

"What stash? They had all kinds a' junk going on."

"Back at Hell Nose, when Twurk flipped out."

Yuri had to think for a moment. "Oh, oh yeah! That's right. Preston's dealer flipped out."

"He thought he was about to get busted."

"Right."

"But he was just too tweaked out to think straight."

"Yeah."

"And he ditched his whole stash onto those guys, for nothing!"

"I remember."

Johnny continued to talk, but Yuri was thinking about Skye since Johnny brought up Hell Nose House. He wondered what became of her. He remembered that she had been getting into the speed scene when they parted. All he could remember was that one day she had left Hell Nose House, simply moved all of her things out of her room when everyone was away. He later learned that she had gone to live with her friend Mercy.

He had not seen her since. Concentrating, he was trying to remember how long it had been.

Then he remembered. It was only a few years ago, shortly after the last time he had done speed.

The speed memories started coming back. Another quiver went down his left arm. He remembered the clean sheen high that went through his body whenever he had done speed with Skye.

Looking back down into his drink, Yuri tried to concentrate on what Johnny was saying. Johnny had gone off on another tangent, relating yet another drug story.

Chance

Preston almost ran into him as he rounded the corner.

"Fuckin' a' bitch, watch where you're goin'!"

Stopping in his tracks, it took Preston a moment to recognize him.

"Holy shit, Johnny Trash!"

Johnny playfully punched Preston in the shoulder. "Where th' fuck you been man?"

"Hey, y'know, same ol' shit, different day."

"Yeah, I'll bet."

"I ain't seen you in at least a couple a' years," gawked Preston. "Whatcha doin' now?"

"Goin' back to my place. What about you?"

"Goin' to practice," answered Johnny as he casually leaned against a telephone pole.

"Still tryin' to get a band together?"

"Fuck yeah. You still hangin' out with Jake?"

"Yup. I see him all the time."

"I'd like to meet him again sometime."

"Well give me a call. I'll hook you up."

"Sure. Gotta pen?"

Preston fudged around his pockets.

"Waitasec'." Johnny pulled a pen out of his leather jacket. Preston wrote down his number on one of Johnny's business cards.

"Hey, I was hangin' out with Yuri th' other day," said Johnny.

"Yuri? You mean Skye's Yuri from Hell Nose House?"

"Yup, the one and only."

"No shit? What's he up to? I haven't seen that guy in a long time."

"He's tryin' to clean up his act. He lives in the East Bay now."

"Clean up his act? Did he get off the horse?"

"That's what he told me. He's living in some dive in Berkeley or Oakland, one a' those places. I can't remember exactly. I have his number at home."

"Man, I'll have to tell Skye."

"Yeah. I think he was asking about her the other night. "

"Cool." Preston handed Johnny his number.

"I gotta run. I'll call you soon!"

"I know you will," said Preston with confidence.

Johnny dashed off as Preston continued lumbering down the street.

First

He kept trying to see the far wall

Wisps of smoke got in his way. Every time he started to focus on the wall and its details, a random curl of dead white smoke would slither in front of his eyes.

The woman was shoving something into his hands.

It was made out of glass. It was hot.

He grasped it between his fingers, even though it was almost warm enough to burn him.

Holding it up to his lips, he was still trying to see the far wall through the smoke.

The woman stared off into the corner, looking away through her thick rimmed glasses.

His chest was stinging as he drew in the hot smoke.

His limbs became empty.

He kept trying to see the far wall.

It wasn't a wall.

Through the smoke, it was another woman.

Quickly sitting up, his head was spinning.

He could not see the wall. It was too dark.

He could not see the ceiling. It was too far away.

Puffing out, his chest was heavy.

Shaking his head, he was in his room.

The wind was battering itself against the walls. It was dark because it was the middle of the night.

He had wrapped himself up in his blankets and sleeping bags to keep warm. His body was damp from perspiration.

Feeling the cold air slicing against his face, he did not want to get out from under the covers.

Looking at the glowing red numbers of his clock, it was just past four in the morning.

He wrapped himself tighter in his cocoon, curling his body against the damp insides of the sleeping bag. He kept shivering as he tried to get back to sleep.

"It was really fuckin' weird."

"What happened?"

Yuri tried sitting back on Sue's couch. He took a sip of his soda. Sue sat on the floor near her television. She was organizing her videotapes.

"I was smoking crack with these two women."

"Crack?"

"Yeah."

"I didn't know you used to be into crack."

"I didn't. I mean, I've tried it a couple of times, but I never got into it."

"Did you know who the women were?"

"No. They were like these two latin gals. They looked like businesswomen. One of them did, anyways. She was wearing a business suit and had these big glasses."

"Drug dreams can be pretty tweaked."

"It was really fucked up." Yuri leaned forward. "I felt like I had used when I woke up. I felt like I was high."

"I've had dreams like those."

"But a crack dream? What the fuck is that?"

"Whattaya mean?"

"I'm a junky. I should've had a dream about dope, or liquor at least. Even a speed dream would have made more sense."

"Hey, drugs are drugs."

"I'm still trying to figure out why I had that dream."

"It never makes any sense."

"Fuck."

"D'you still want to watch a movie?"

"Yeah."

"I've got The Loved One and Harold and Maude."

"Mmm, you pick."

"Have you ever seen Harold and Maude."

"Nuh uh."

"Then that's the one were gonna watch." Sue jumped to her feet with the tape.

"Doesn't it have a lotta hippy music in it?"

Sue sat down on the couch. "Now you're starting to sound like the old Hell Nose Yuri again."

A shiver went through Yuri's chest.

The Med

He had taken Sue to the Med a few times, now he was meeting her there again for the second time in a week. Haunting the Mediterranean Cafe was a new habit that he wanted to keep.

He had arrived early so he could grab the prized window table once it had been vacated. Looking out onto the Telegraph scene, his eye was always on the lookout for familiar faces whenever he went to the Med.

Watching the street scenes, a few older Berkeley denizens were sitting just outside the window. Just past the old denizens, down by the other window was a gang of throckers and punks. A trio were standing in the middle of the sidewalk, talking and posturing. They were quite young, and some of them had the criss-crossed eyes of the fast life.

The farther away Yuri got from substance abuse, the uglier the dark eyes of the burnouts were becoming. There was something too deep, too sharp, and too dark about the lines in the faces of the few who were obviously riding the edge of an excess cycle.

Even so, Yuri wanted to try and get back into some kind of scene other than the meetings. The meetings had been taking up a lot of his time. He needed to get his head out of the traditions and steps.

He glanced up at the clock. He still had half an hour before Sue was supposed to show up. Yuri noted that Sue was quite a punctual person, which was a facet of her current personality that was at odds with her old personae. Back in their Hell Nose House days she would oftentimes disappear for days at a time without informing anyone of where she was going. She was, by far, the most unsociable person who had lived there.

Yuri found himself looking down into his half full latte glass.

He suddenly lifted his head. It was as if he had just missed something.

Looking around the cafe, there were several people standing in line. Someone was paying for his coffee. He was tall and slender, dressed all in black with shaggy dyed black hair. He was looking towards the counter, standing at a somewhat odd angle.

The tall and slender man turned away from the counter. Yuri sat up in his seat.

"Dex!"

Dex kept walking as if he hadn't heard Yuri, even though Yuri was only a few feet away from him.

"Hey Dex!" emphasized Yuri as he started to stand. "Dex!"

Dex abruptly stopped and turned, standing still after turning to face Yuri.

"Oh. Hey Yuri," pronounced Dex.

"Whatcha doin'?"

"Just gettin' coffee," answered Dex as he stood his ground, standing right in front of the cafe door.

"Yeah, I see. How you doin'?"

"Okay," answered Dex quickly.

"So, how come I never hear from you guys anymore?" blurted Yuri.

"Us guys?"

"You and Sweezy."

"Well, it's jus' that we know you're trying to stay clean."

Yuri crossed his arms and looked back at Dex.

"Well, I gotta get goin'," said Dex. "I gotta meet this guy about a job I might be able to get."

"Yeah, sure."

"See ya. Take care."

"Yeah."

Dex quickly left the cafe.

Yuri sat down again and continued looking out onto the street.

Lost

As soon as he finished tuning his snare drum, he peered over his cymbals, trying to find his singer.

"Johnny! Where the fuck are you?" shouted the frustrated drummer.

"Over here," muffled the singer from a corner of the practice room. "I lost somethin'."

The drummer stood on his toes, trying to locate Johnny Trash. He finally saw him rooting through a pile of magazines and beer cans that had accumulated next to the bass amp.

"What the fuck are you doing?" asked the drummer.

"I fuckin' lost this card with Preston's number on it. Y'know, the one who can get us some tweak."

"Ain't it in your jacket?"

"Naw. I fuckin' took it out an' put it on the amp. It musta fell off."

"Dude, you're always losin' shit like that. You'll never find it in this mess."

Supplier

Snapping awake, something had caused her to stir.

A sharp ringing.

Jumping off of her futon, it took her a moment. She had to remember where she was. Another blast of the ringing sound.

She quickly realized she was in her room. Her phone was ringing.

She grabbed it quickly, to quiet its wretched jangling.

"Hello?" slurred Skye. Her mouth was dry.

"Hi Skye," chirped Preston.

"Wassup?"

"Did I wake you up?"

Skye blanked for a moment. "Don' worry about it."

"I'm in your neighborhood. I was wondering if I could stop by."

"Sure."

"Where are you?"

"What?" Skye was still trying to blink the fog out of her eyes.

"I don't know exactly where you live. I'm over on Valencia right now."

It suddenly dawned on Skye that Preston had never been to her place. Skye gave Preston the directions.

She shambled her traumatized body and mind into the kitchen to start up the coffee machine.

The door buzzer went off right as the coffee machine started percolating. Skye was a bit surprised. She thought it would take Preston longer to make it over to her street and find her house. Buzzing him in, Preston trotted up the stairs and they went into the kitchen.

"So what you doin' in my neighborhood?" asked Skye.

"Gettin' new guitar strings from Kirsch's."

"You want some coffee?" asked Skye as she poured herself a cup.

"Naw, I'm cool. Can we go talk in your room?"

"Sure."

Going into her room, Skye sat cross legged on her futon as Preston sat down in the kitchen chair that Skye had permanently commandeered for her room.

"You still got your license?" asked Preston.

"What?"

"A driver's license? Don'tcha have a license to drive?"

"Yeah, I still have a license, but I think it's about to expire."

"It's still good right now, right?"

Skye's eyes searched the floor. "I'm pretty sure it's still good. I'll have to check."

"Because I was wondering if you could drive me over to my supplier's place."

Skye straightened out her back and looked at Preston. "Yeah, I can do that," replied a wide-eyed Skye.

"Can you take a look?"

"What?"

"Can you check your license?"

"Sure."

Skye retrieved a bottle of Moosehead for Preston and set about digging through her bottom dresser drawer. It took a few minutes to sift her license out of her collection of papers.

"Yup," confirmed Skye. "It's still good. I got another three months left."

"Cool. I was wonderin' if you could drive my car out to my supplier's place."

"I guess. Where would we be going?"

"West Oakland."

"Mm, I haven't driven a car in some time."

"Like how long?"

Skye thought about it for a moment. "I think it's been like, almost a year now."

"Well, it's not like you really ever forget."

"When did you want to go out there?"

"Sometime tonight, maybe after seven when the traffic starts dying down, if you've got the time."

"Okay. Sure."

"I need someone I can trust to take me out there since my license is still suspended," continued Preston. "Riff doesn't like it when people are waiting outside his house, so I need my driver to be someone that I can bring inside."

"Didn't you always have Jer drive you out there?"

"Yeah, I used to, but he's gotten too flaky. He's showin' up way too late. He's just getting too burned out. It's not just his bein' late all of the time. The last time we drove out, he was fuckin' swerving and driftin' in the lane all the time. It was two in the morning and I was still worried he was gonna hit something."

"Can y'spare a line right now?" asked Skye.

Skye shifted the car around, inching it back and then forth. Preston's small compact had been boxed in by a couple of other cars.

Preston sat calmly in the passenger seat. He did not seem to be at all affected by the vehicular situation nor Skye's terse and nervous mood.

"I already told him I was bringin' someone new out there," said Preston. "By the way, don't let him know I told you his name. Wait until he introduces himself."

"Sure," answered Skye as she concentrated on the car's controls. "What's with this transmission?"

"The gear shift kinda sticks when it's in park."

Carefully looking over her shoulder, she pulled the car out of its place and drove it out onto the street.

Preston's car was a beat up old compact. There were a few dents and some small rust spots on the roof. The dented trunk was held down by a bungee cord, and the interior was covered with band stickers.

"Are you cool?" asked Preston after Skye had cautiously driven a few blocks.

"Yeah."

Suddenly her foot hit the brake, jarring the car to a sudden halt.

"Fucking jerk!" yelled Skye. A large luxury car had run a stop sign.

Skye gunned Preston's car.

"I'm cool," reassured Skye.

Skye was feeling quite confident by the time she pulled onto the freeway on ramp. She had a few driving flashbacks, remembering some of her driving adventures from a couple of years ago. There were the few times that she ended up dragging Dangerous Dan's old clunker to Gilman shows, or the time she went on midnight rides in a roommate's dilapidated old compact.

Preston was filling in Skye on Riff Raff's place as she drove. "He used to have people wait outside, like people who drove out his contacts. He wanted to limit his exposure to people because of his biz. He started to realize that it would look too suspicious to have people hanging around outside, especially sittin' around in cars looking anxious an' nervous, since these deals can take a bit of time."

Preston continued to explain the protocol. He asked her not to mention any aspects of the deal or anything about buying or selling.

That was always done in the back, away from the living room.

As Preston continued, she was getting the idea that Preston was a little nervous about bringing her over for the first time. That was no surprise. Suppliers were even deeper into the drug scene than people such as herself and Preston. No doubt Riff Raff knew plenty of rough and knee deep characters, people who were a lot more intense than herself or Preston.

"He can be a pretty funny guy. He also lines everyone up whenever you come over. But if you wanna have a few beers while were over there we should stop somewhere first. He don't have no liquor there, at least not usually. I don't think he even drinks."

"Sure. Let's grab a six on the way."

Preston kept chatting about various details of Riff Raff's place as she wound the car through the light bridge traffic.

"This is it!" snapped Preston.

"What?"

"The exit!"

Skye had to quickly veer the car to make it to the exit ramp. They were getting off at the very edge of West Oakland, right out into a field of truck yards and factories. It was one of the industrial sections of Oakland, just a few blocks away from the residential section of West Oakland. It had a few high streets populated by liquor stores, bars, and community organizations that were rarely open or operating.

Preston was now carefully directing her around West Oakland, telling her which lane to be in, when she would have to turn, and how far she had to go along on each street. They stopped at a gas station mini-mart for a six of Colt 45 talls and then proceeded to delve deeper into the residential sections of West Oakland.

After only a few minutes of driving, Preston directed her to the middle of a deserted street. It was a wide street sparsely populated by parked cars. Some of the stationary vehicles appearing as if they hadn't been moved in years. Most of the houses in West Oakland were packed closely together, but for some reason the houses on this street had quite a bit of distance between them. The rays of the far away factory lights gave the cars, houses, and yellowing patches of grass a deadly still look.

"You better take this," said Preston as he handed Skye the six pack.

Skye could smell dust and fuel in the air, as she watched out of the corners of her eyes for any signs of other people. A few of the cars parked on the street were missing their wheels.

Preston led Skye to a house in the middle of the street. It was the most run down looking house on the block. The faded white paint was peeling. The creaking wooden steps had already been laid bare and thin from wear and decay. The wood around the windows and door frame was starting to warp. .

The front door was a large black metal door, guarding a fragile looking wooden one behind it. A makeshift door buzzer had been wired onto the side of the doorframe. Preston pressed the buzzer, which activated a loud metal ringing inside the house. Preston stood still as they waited for a few long moments.

A shrill buzzing noise Preston opened the black metal door and they walked into a dark, steep, and narrow stairwell that led to the second story. The boards of the stairs were creaking loudly, echoing in the dark stairwell as they slowly trudged up the stairs.

They reached a closed door at the top of the stairs. Preston knocked.

"Who is it?" muffled a voice from behind the door.

"Preston."

A pause. A careful ruffling. The door opened slowly.

Skye saw a baseball cap and a mustache appear briefly in the doorway before the mustache suddenly stepped aside and disappeared into the room.

Skye was careful to follow Preston, but she also made sure she did not stand directly behind him. Preston himself followed the lead of the man who had let them in. He wore a black baseball cap and had a bushy beard. He was dressed more or less like a suburban working class type, with light blue jeans and a white t-shirt.

Walking into a long and wide room, Skye couldn't help but observe how high the ceiling was. The room was a long lane, the right wall covered with shelves containing televisions, stereos, and musical equipment. At the far end of the room was a huge mixing board sitting next to a drum set and a row of sleek guitars.

A tall and skinny black-leather-jacketed Mohican sat on one couch, while a balding and bearded biker sat in an easy chair towards the end of the room.

The Mohican concentrated on a joint he was rolling. The biker nodded to Preston. The baseball hat disappeared briefly into a door at the very back of the room and then quickly came back out. He looked right at Skye.

"Who's the DEA agent?" he barked.

"That's Skye," said Preston. "And she's trying not to blow her cover!"

Riff-Raff's comment threw Skye off for a moment.

"Fuckin' a', that means I have to make another line," groaned Riff

Raff.

Walking further into the room, Skye saw a small round table across from the drum set. It was next to two bookshelves filled with old paperback books and magazines. Riff-Raff sat down at the table. Preston took a seat as well.

Skye cradled the six pack, she wondered if she should offer any beer to anyone. Skye sat down next to Preston in an old but sturdy wooden chair, putting the bag of beer down on the floor.

The Mohican was still concentrating on his joint, staring intently at it as he tightened it up.

"Is that a six pack ya got there?" asked the biker amiably.

"Or are you just happy to see me?" barked out Riff Raff.

"What the hell was that?" groused the biker. "Was that supposed to be a joke?"

Riff Raff shook his shaggy head. "He's got no sense of humor."

"Fuck you bitch, I do too gotta sense of humor," smiled the biker.

Skye looked at the biker and held up a beer. "Y'want one?"

"Wouldn't say no," he replied.

Skye leaned over and handed the biker a beer. She took out a few more, holding one out to Preston and Riff Raff.

"No thanks," said Preston.

"Ain't drinking right now," answered Riff Raff. "You shouldn't drink and snort at the same time."

"Why not?" asked the biker.

"Because you might spill your drink," answered Skye.

"Fuckin' a'," muttered the biker.

Opening her beer and taking a sip, Skye tried sitting back in her seat. Preston was sitting straight up, his arms at his side. Riff Raff got up and disappeared into a back room once again. He came out with a plastic bag filled with a huge amount of white powder. Skye had to contain herself. Despite all of her experiences in the scene, Skye had never seen so much speed in one place at one time in her entire life.

She was trying not to stare as Riff Raff poured a large amount of crank onto the dusty mirror on the table. He was using a large box cutter blade to organize the congealing grains of speed.

"So Skye," started Riff Raff, "How d'ya' know Preston? Or did he jus' grab you outta some bar so you could drive him out here?"

"You drove him out here?" asked the Biker, looking at Skye.

"Yeah. Me an' Preston go way back."

"Don't you drive, Preston?" asked the Biker.

"He don't drive!" said Riff Raff.

"I do so."

"Then why'd they take away your license?"

"Aw man, that whole thing."

Riff Raff looked at Skye. "I started climbing the telephone poles when I heard he was drivin', an' I was still over here."

They kept going back and forth, mostly the biker and Riff Raff. Skye casually sipped her beer as Preston finally leaned onto the table, still keeping his back stiff.

Skye stood up, taking another beer out of the bag. She was not sure, but she thought she saw Preston flash her a look as she stood up. She walked over to the Mohican on the couch.

"Would ya like a beer?"

"Thanks," replied the Mohican who took the beer and then continued to obsess over his joint construction.

Turning around, Skye strolled back to the table, casually looking over the musical equipment and the large mixing board. The guitars were so pristine they appeared as if they had never been played before.

Looking back towards the table, Riff Raff was leaning over the large mirror. He gave a mighty sniff and lifted his head, handing the straw to Preston.

"I wanna get some a' that roach first," said Preston, handing the straw to the biker.

Preston gave a slight nod in Skye's direction. Skye stood up and walked back towards the table.

Just as she approached the edge of the table, Skye stopped in her tracks.

There were four lines, each literally a foot long, and at least half an inch wide.

She had never seen anyone put out a line of speed that was that big. She bumped Preston as he walked by.

"One a' those is for me?" asked Skye under her teeth.

"Yup."

Skye estimated there must have been more than a quarter gram in each line.

The biker leaned down. He snorted up his line all at once. Casually turning around, he handed the metal snorting straw to Skye.

"Thanks."

The biker nodded and sat back down. Looking down at the tray, The biker had snorted up his entire foot long line all at once as if it were nothing. The speed making up the lines was a fine, shining powder, heavy with crystals. Even a short line of pure crystal was enough to cause quite a bit of nasal pain and discomfort.

Skye could see from the corner of her eye that Preston was talking to the Mohican as they shared a newly lit joint.

Skye carefully placed the end of the straw at the start of her line.

She started slowly and carefully. She did not want to go too fast. The first grains were fairly painful, even with slow snorting. It was the good stuff, pure and crystal and sharp. She was not even halfway done when her nose started stinging and throbbing. Halfway through the line, her eyes were beginning to tear up. She held her tears in through sheer willpower.

She had another three or four inches of her line left when the bones in her face started squeezing together. Her eyes were stinging as the skin on her face stretched thin. It felt as if there were a tightening vise wrapping around her head as the wicked high started crashing and throbbing through her head, into her throat, and down into her heart.

It took all of her willpower to finish up the last bit of her line. Her face and chest felt as if they were going to burst as she quickly stood up.

Skye walked away from the table, tilting back her beer, trying to hide her red face as she staggered towards Preston and the Mohican. She squeezed her eyes shut, trying to push out the pain and pressure. She had to cross her feet as the room kept waning from side to side. Opening her mouth and trying to breathe, her chest and face went numb and became warm. The warmth was washing back up in her throat as her eyes expanded in their sockets and all of the fine lines of the room stood out, cutting into her eyes.

"Fuckin' a'."

Nostalgia

Yuri had gone to the Wall of Berlin with Sue, Holt, and one of Holt's sponsees, a rather short, thin, and nervous looking fellow named Reed.

Yuri could not help but notice how agitated Reed's eyes and expressions were. Even Reed's short, spiky hair looked nervous.

"When did you say you were going to school?" asked Holt.

"In the third week of January," answered Reed, as his short cropped hair vibrated to his bird-eyed words.

"Where are you going?" asked Sue.

"I'm taking three classes at Laney."

"You sure that's not too much?" asked Yuri.

"What d'ya mean?"

"Well, a friend a' mine said if you're jus' gettin' into school you should only take one or two classes, just to get the feel for it, before goin' full time."

Reed brightened up. "Hey man, I know that whatever I do, my higher power will be looking out for me."

Yuri knew Reed was a newcomer, and that he had been going to meetings for less than two weeks.

"What are you taking?" asked Sue.

"Oh, some algebra, a history class, and a video production class, just to see what I think of it."

"Oh man, I can't take those math classes," said Yuri.

"Well, I used ta' have a problem with math, like algebra an' stuff, but I know my higher power is lookin' out for me. I jus' stick with my program, jus' keep working my program and doin' the steps and' I'll be all right."

Yuri glanced around the table. Holt was leaning back in his chair. Sue was watching the smoke swirl out of her cigarette.

Reed turned to Yuri. "Have you done your ninety in ninety?"

"Well, there's this one day where I can't get to a meetin'," explained Yuri.

"You really gotta do you ninety in ninety," explained Reed.

"Well…"

"You really need it to get in with the program. It's really important for you to establish yourself in order to stay clean."

Yuri did not say anything. He sat back, looking more or less in Reed's general direction.

"You really should do your ninety in ninety," emphasized Holt.

Yuri decided not to go into his explanation again. There was one particular night, Thursday nights, when he could not get to any NA meetings without taking an extended bus trip. He was always working on Thursday, so he couldn't make any daytime meetings, and the night time meetings were too far away for him to get to in time.

He had tried explaining this to various members who inquired about his ninety in ninety. He had been tempted to just tell people he had been going to an unbroken string of meetings, but he did not want to start stretching the truth and lying to his fellow members.

Eventually Holt and Reed left the cafe. Reed seemed to have gotten himself in a state where he simply had to move, as he had become more tremorous as the night wore on.

Sue was still watching the swirling smoke come out of her cigarette.

"Hey Sue." Yuri stopped himself.

"Yeah?"

Sue turned and looked at Yuri.

"Do you ever miss it?"

"Hm?"

"Do you ever miss getting loaded?"

Sue's eyes moved around the cafe as she tilted her head to one side.

"Well," muttered Sue. "I kinda miss goin' out on the weekend. Why do you ask?"

"I was just thinking about some of those days in San Francisco."

"You aren't thinking about using again?"

"Oh, hell no. It's just all everybody talks about all the time in the meetin's is fuckin' drugs. It makes me think about the times when I was usin'."

"War stories."

"Like, you remember when Skye filled in for that bass player, that one time. What the hell was that band's name?"

"Triple-T."

"Yeah, fuck yeah. Remember that night?"

"Amazingly enough I do. And I got really plowed at that show."

"Remember all those rails we had done?"

"Hell yeah. I remember how we got that stuff."

"That's when Wink and Preston went to see Wink's dealer, and his dealer was flippin' out."

Sue sat back and studied her cigarette as she recalled the event. "Wink's dealer was hella tweaked out. He had been up for somethin' like, four or five days."

"He was way paranoid, right?"

"He was convinced he was going to get busted, that someone must have ratted him out and the cops were going to storm his place any minute."

"How did it go?"

Sue leaned closer to Yuri. "Since he was convinced the cops were gonna be crashing down his door any minute, he asked Wink if he could help him out by getting rid of his stash."

"Yeah."

"He practically shrieked at them to take his stuff. Those guys walked out of there with something like, a quarter ounce of crank, or something ridiculous."

"That's why all that fucked up speed was around the house for so long."

"Yup."

"It was pretty good stuff, wasn't it?"

"Fuck yeah it was. I got hooked on that shit later, but that was some good stuff."

"I never did so much speed in a week."

Sue leaned closer to Yuri. "Why are you asking me about this now?"

"I dunno. I mean, everyone talks about the old days, but no one's got anything nice to say."

Sue looked at Yuri with serious eyes. "There's nothing nice about what we were doing."

"No, there isn't. But sometimes it was fun."

Sue looked off to the side.

Riff Raff's

Preston had gone into a back room with Riff Raff, disappearing through a dark doorway. They had been gone for at least twenty minutes.

"Hey, I'll trade you a spliff for another beer," volunteered the biker. "What?"

"That's my stuff over there," said the biker, pointing over towards the Mohican who was still fiddling with a bag of marijuana and a pile of rolling papers.

"Eh. You can jus' have another one."

"Let's go bother the silly punk," said the Biker as he accepted another beer.

Skye chose a spot on the other end of the couch from the Mohican. The Biker sat down across from the couch in a wooden chair, grabbing his bag of pot and rolling a large joint.

Skye's head was still throbbing with a pleasant and warm and electric buzz. She was trying to drink up her Colt 45 to take the edge off of her amp.

"Those are some killer axes over there," said Skye, nodding towards the row of sleek new guitars.

"Yeah, he likes his guitars," muttered the biker.

"He's really popular over at Guitar Center," said The Mohican suddenly.

"I'll bet."

"He really is," said the biker. "They treat him like a king every time he comes in. He buys like, a new guitar every week."

"No shit? What the hell for?"

"Cause he can," said the Mohican.

"He buys 'em all th' time," said the biker, gesturing towards the guitars. "He resells most of 'em. He's got three or four that he always keeps."

Skye leaned over the coffee table, eyeing the guitars. "Those are some pretty fucked up axes." She was observing a brand new black Gibson. "You think it'd be okay if I messed around with one?"

The biker and the Mohican both straightened their backs. The biker shook his head. "No, you don't wanna' do that. Wait till he comes out an' then ask him first."

Skye sank back into the couch, sipping her beer. The biker leaned over his bag of pot, concentrating on a joint he was rolling.

She jumped ever so slightly when a loud buzzing noise reverberated near the couch. The Biker put down his joint and stood up.

"Don't forget to check," said the Mohican.

"Yeah, yeah. I know," replied the Biker as he walked over to the window and carefully peered out of the curtain. Walking over to the door, he pressed a small button and then came back to the coffee table to continue rolling his joint.

A few minutes later a tall and thin man in a black leather trench coat and sunglasses walked into the room. He stopped after closing the door and looked around.

"Is Riff here?" he intoned in a long and low voice.

"He'll be out in a minute," said the Mohican. "You'll have to kick back for a bit,"

The tall trench coat slowly paced into the room. Skye had recognized him. He was Sven Stavanger, the singer for Die Motte, a very popular and successful San Francisco band.

Skye kept sipping her beer as the Mohican lit his joint. She had never met Stavanger in person, but she had heard about him from friends of hers who had dealt with him before. Apparently he was the kind of person who always remained aloof, if for no other reason than for appearances sake.

Skye remembered the days when she would be impressed to meet someone like Stavanger, but she had been around enough musicians, famous, not so famous, and not at all famous, that their status was no longer a factor for her. Experience had taught her that the famous ones were no different from any of the other musicians that she knew. She did not, however, expect to see anyone like Stavanger at a West Oakland dive trying to cop speed.

Stavanger walked by them, looking out to the far end of the room through his jet black sunglasses. Skye kept sipping her beer and watched the biker meticulously prepare his joint.

By now the biker had lit up his joint. After taking a few puffs, he leaned across the table, handing it to Skye.

"Thanks."

Skye took a quick puff and handed it back to the biker.

"That's all you're gonna have?" asked the biker.

"Yeah. I don't smoke weed that often."

"No shit?"

"Yeah. For some reason I never got into it."

"I guess none of us are perfect."

Skye tilted back her beer. She was finding it difficult to finish her tall Colt 45 too quickly. Stavanger hovered by the guitars, apparently studying them.

Leaning back and trying to relax, she was sorely tempted to ask Stavanger to play something, if for no other reason than just to mess with him.

She started standing up, propping her buzzing body against the arm of the couch, trying to keep her balance. Righting herself on her hollow legs, she concentrated on her knees, making sure they were bending the proper way. She was halfway tempted to sit back down again, as the lines of the room were bending.

Picking up what was left of her beer, she decided to grab another one. Taking a few carefully choreographed steps, she knew that she should probably wait a few more minutes before getting another beer, but she did not want to pass up the chance to razz Stavanger before her sky high buzz wore off.

She casually meandered in Stavanger's direction.

Pulling another beer out of the bag, the can felt cold in her warm and buzzing hands.

A door opened.

By the time Skye had turned around there was a new set of lines on the table. Riff Raff had been making new lines for everyone when he had been in the back with Preston and had brought them out on a tray.

Riff Raff and Preston did their lines and then Preston handed the straw to Skye. Still wanting to save face, she walked right over to the mirror this time she decided she would simply snort up her line as quickly as possible.

The line was just as long as the last one. Lining up the straw with the line, she proceeded to snort her line up at a quick pace. Halfway through her line her nostril was throbbing with pain. The front of her face felt as if it were on fire. She drove herself to finish the line, using every ounce of her willpower to finish what was left.

Dropping the metal snorting straw next to the mirror, she quickly turned away, taking a quick sip of her beer to kill the overwhelming metal taste in her mouth. Her eyes were watering and her face was hot. Her sinuses were flush with hot flashing liquid as the drain from the large line kept washing down her throat in waves, filling her mouth with a bitter metal taste. She wondered if her nose was bleeding. Wiping her running nose with the back of her hand and giving it a quick look, there was no trace of blood.

She turned towards the instruments in an instinctive effort to look as if she were checking out Riff Raff's musical collection. A strong throb went through her head, a passing high that tilted the room and nearly knocked her off of her feet. The waves came through her forehead and down into the front of her face where she could feel a full heartbeat go through the bones in her cheeks.

Her entire face was numb, as if she had just done a line of coke. Her head felt weightless.

Risking detection of her state, she brought a hand to her face to wipe away some of her tears.

She could hear the biker talking to the Mohican again. Out of the corner of her eye, she saw Stavanger snort up one of the impossibly long lines as if it were nothing.

It had been only fifteen minutes since Skye's last line. Walking out of the house, the street was almost completely dark. Only a few of the houses on Riff Raff's street had any lights on.

Skye's mind felt sharp and clear, yet her head still felt as if it did not weigh a thing.

Holding her tongue, she got into the driver's seat, dismissing the idea of asking Preston if he could drive.

She wished she had asked for a glass of water before leaving the house. She could taste the thick dry residue of speed on the roof of her mouth.

Adjusting herself in the driver's seat, Preston reached over to the wheel.

"Just stay there. This will only take a sec'."

The center of the steering wheel was a square piece of plastic with rounded corners. Preston gently tugged at it and it popped off. He placed several large plastic baggies inside of the horn and carefully replaced the horn. Skye saw that the plastic middle of the horn was held onto the steering wheel by one large metal clasp.

Scanning the street through the windshield, she could still not feel the weight of her head, but the lines of the street, and the cars, and the houses, and the lines on everything were crystal clear.

Putting the car into first gear, she slowly pulled the car out into the street.

Preston had been calling out directions, but she was virtually ignoring him as she kept her eye on the road, watching the readouts of the car's dashboard out of the corners of her eyes and remembering how to backtrack herself to the freeway.

Getting onto the freeway, the bay bridge was not as crowded as she had suspected it was going to be, but then she also realized that she did not know what time it was. She only knew that it was dark outside.

She caught it in the rear view mirror, a short black sports car. It was getting onto the bridge with them, just right behind their car. She noticed it when she changed lanes and the small black dragster changed lanes right along with her.

She kept glancing in the rear view. Every time she looked, the car was still there.

Halfway across the bridge, she drifted into another lane. The short black sports car stayed within its original lane, but it was still keeping pace with them, driving just behind them and to the right, at the same speed.

Nearing the end of the bridge, Skye reluctantly switched back into the right hand lane. She tried distracting herself by concentrating on the traffic in front of her. Taking Preston's car onto the off ramp, she drove through the wide semi-circle that led back to Mission street.

Stopping at the stop light off of the freeway exit, she snapped her eyes towards the rear view mirror.

The short black car was right behind them.

Her heart skipped a beat, banging violently into her chest.

"Preston!"

"What?"

Preston sat up in his seat, looking over at Skye.

"I think…"

She stopped herself as the short black sports car turned away, going down another street.

Looking around the windshield, the lines were blurring, just for a moment.

"What is it?" asked Preston.

"It's nothing. Just, forget it. Don't worry."

"Man, you must be really tweaked."

Sleep

Her arms were light, her shoulders were heavy. Her skin and mouth were dry, yet she could still feel a layer of film on her arms and chest. The roof of her cotton mouth still had the metallic taste. Her stomach was empty, yet thinking about food made her nauseous.

The worst part of sitting up was her heavy head. Her mind felt empty, but her skull felt as if it were an iron weight. Her matted hair felt as if it were pulling her head down. Despite her heaviness, she could not lie back down, because it made her head and her jaw ache.

It had been at least forty eight hours since Skye had had any sleep, and it had been at least eight hours since she had done any crank.

She went through it in her mind, mentally calculating how much of her stash she had gone through in the past four days. There was the teen she had secured for herself, though she had treated Chasey and Linette to a decent amount of that supply.

She wondered why she was still wired. She recounted all of the lines she had gotten from Preston, and Riff Raff, and the lines she had been given by the quiet yet generous throcker that had been haunting Linette's place when she had stopped by for a few hours to deliver Linette's stash. The throcker's crank was not nearly as good as Preston's stuff, but it still added to the speed in her system.

Skye was getting tired of drinking water all of the time. She felt she needed a liquid refreshment with more substance.

She knew it would not have been so bad if she had eaten something in the past few hours. She kept trying to will herself to the kitchen, to eat another one of Arden's bran muffins, or make some toast, or just have a piece of fruit, but she simply could not bring herself to do it. Her gall forced her back onto her futon.

Water, food, and speed She completely lacked the desire to put anything at all into her body.

She needed to burn out and recharge. She needed to get her skin and her guts back into place. The last time she had slept, it had only been a few hours of half-sleep.

Laying her head down, she concentrated on relaxing her jaw. Closing her eyes, her mind was drained, but she still felt wide awake

Her skin cooled against her bones. The air in the room finally became still. Her ears were wide open and her skin tingled. Slowly the soft rumbling of the city drifted into the room; the muffled sounds of people, cars, honking horns, and the steady urban hum slowly became more distinct as it vibrated through the apartment windows and walls.

Skye heard a door close. It was somewhere in the apartment building.

She heard another door. It was opening. A breath later, it closed with a thud.

Opening her eyes, Skye could not tell if the opening and closing doors were inside her flat or not.

Then a soft knocking, a thudding against a piece of wood, something soft and blunt.

Thuck, thuck, thuck.

Quickly sitting up, she could not tell if the sound had been footsteps or someone knocking, or possibly something else.

Quickly spinning her head to and fro, she looked at both of the walls of her room and listened for the sounds again.

Thuck, thuck. Thuck-thuck-THUD!

Skye quickly stood up and kicked the covers off of herself. She heard a woman's voice. The woman had blurted something quickly and sharply.

Going up to her door, perhaps Arden or Jane had made the noise. Perhaps someone had let Linette in, or maybe even Chasey or Mercy, though Skye could not imagine Chasey or Mercy dropping in on her so suddenly.

She wondered if it could have been the landlord. Skye had never met the owner of the building, even though she had been living there for more than a year. Not even Jane had met her. Arden was the only one who had ever dealt with her.

Slowly opening her door, she peered into the corridor.

The still air was cool. Someone had left the hall light on. Arden always turned it off when she passed through.

Skye tried to listen for any movement within the flat. Her mind was racing, wondering who could have left the light on.

Sticking her head out of the door and then pulling it back in, she strained to sense the intruder. Skye could hear faint clickings and knockings.

Skye shivered when she heard another voice. Retreating partway into her room. she froze as she stared at the hallway light. Who had left it on?

Another flinch. She heard the voice again.

Her legs became tight and her chest grew hot as she stepped out into the hallway.

"Jane? Jane are you there?"

Thuck, thuck. The muffled voice was coming from the kitchen.

"Jane?" called out Skye, louder this time.

Skye walked towards the kitchen. "Jane? Jane is that you? Who's there?"

The kitchen light was on. The dead air pressed in on Skye. She flinched when she heard the woman's voice yet again, but this time it sounded as if she was in the room.

"Mark!" muffled the woman's voice. "Did you grab that six?"

Skye felt another shiver. Her shoulders became heavy as the tension left her chest.

"Oh man," groaned Skye.

The voice belonged to one of the upstairs neighbors. She was walking around her kitchen and calling out to her boyfriend, as she regularly did in the early evening hours.

Looking around, Skye felt her stomach curling in on itself. Quickly going back to her room, she retrieved her flight jacket.

It was just a few blocks to the corner market.

Out of her building and onto the street, the dark city wind was getting stronger, creating a distinct whistling noise through her jacket.

"Hey!"

Stopping in the middle of the sidewalk, Skye spun around.

There was no one there.

"Fuck," muttered Skye under her breath.

Paranoia

"Hey, you're not gonna flip out like Wink's dealer did?" asked Skye.

"Fuck no," gasped Preston.

He was holding his breath over a piece of smoking foil.

"It's cool to smoke this stuff sometimes," continued Preston, "but if you keep doin' it, it'll seriously fuck with your head."

Preston handed the foil and lighter over to Skye.

"I mean, the rush is really fuckin' cool," continued Preston. "But man, the people I know who smoke this alla' time, they always go totally fuckin' psycho."

"No shit." Skye heated up the foil and drew in some smoke.

"I'm never gonna get like that," said Preston confidently.

"That's what they all say."

Tilting her head back, Skye could see wisps of smoke hanging around the top of the room like a fog. She was tempted to try and pry open the one working window, but she did not feel like getting up. The smoke was making her limbs heavy and her chest light.

Trying to balance her head on the top of her neck, she tried to remind herself about her buy. She was there to get the usual supplies as well as a few extras. Linette and Chasey had both made a few more go-between contacts, and she was buying an extra teen to split between the two of them. Linette was even thinking about buying larger supplies for herself so she could start selling quarter bags on the main strip to the local cafe transients.

"Speakin' of paranoia," said Preston, "I was wonderin' if you wouldn't like to do some runnin' for me."

"Hm?"

"I was just thinking, I gotta stick aroun' here a lot, an' I'm gettin' kinda antsy about always having people come over here all the time. It's kinda inconvenient."

"Sure," replied Skye through her foggy high.

"If you like, I could give you a few deals on alla' this stuff you've been buyin' if you do some runs for me. Y'know, deliver some stuff and collect some dough here an' there. Nothin' too big or too far out."

Skye looked around the room. "Like, when would you want me to do this?"

"The weekends is when I would need you the most. You know, when it gets all crazy after payday. You'd mostly be takin' it to a few guys you already know."

"Would I have to drive your car a lot for this?"

"Actually, I don't think you would ever need to drive the car at all. I only need rides when I go out to Oakland. You can pretty much walk to all the places, unless you wanted to drive up to Haight."

"Sure. I can help out," she answered as she slowly pushed herself up out of the easy chair. "Is there any beer left in the fridge?"

"I think so."

Skye concentrated on her legs as they threatened to give out underneath her.

Walking carefully into Preston's short hallway and propping herself up in the kitchen doorway, she could see that the fog bank of speed smoke had made its way into the kitchen.

Bones

Yuri found the edge of his blanket.

His skin was damp from sweat, making his skin colder. The sharp air was cool enough to bite the skin on his face.

Small shivers skittered up and down his forearms and through his shins as he rolled the blanket around his body, trying to get warm. The inside of the blanket was damp and sticky from perspiration. He quickly unraveled himself, braving the freezing air long enough to switch to a dry blanket. His top blanket was made of rougher material that irritated his skin, but he could not keep using the damp one.

The shivers were making their way up his neck. Wrapping himself up in the dry blanket, he realized his legs were shaking. Quickly lying back down, his eyes started stinging. The sweat was running into his eyes.

Grabbing the inside of the blanket, he pulled it tighter against himself. He turned over onto his other side. His eye spotted the small red light of his answering machine. He watched the small glowing and unmoving red dot.

"Well, it's jus' that we know you're trying to stay clean."

He kept looking at the small red light, concentrating on it. The longer he looked, the brighter it got. It was as if it were going straight through his eye and into the back of his head. His eye began to sting and ache, but he did not look away.

Intently watching the light for a few more moments, his vision started to blur. His eye started trembling, and the small red dot was beginning to shake.

Squinting hard, he let his head shake and shiver before opening his eyes again. The light was not as bright. The darkness pressed it down again. He brought out an arm to roll the outer blankets on top of him to try and make it warmer. Lying back down, he could feel his heavy head sink through his pillow and his bed, and then down on the hard floor. Looking back at the small red light, he knew that if he looked at it long enough it would start to become brighter once again.

There was Sue and Zata, there was Holt and Tilden; they all had his number, but they rarely ever called, usually because they would see him at meetings. Once in a blue moon, Zatch would leave him a message from his girlfriend's place.

Yuri remembered what Holt had told him, that he needed to get away from old habits, even if those habits were places and people. Holt lectured Yuri on the importance of avoiding temptation, especially when one was a newcomer. There were too many traps in those people and places that one would associate with using. Perhaps, thought Yuri, it was for the best that they weren't around, and that they were not calling him.

It still didn't stop him from watching the red light, every time he came home.

Skin

Skye was awake.

One moment she was asleep, and then the next moment she was awake. She had awoken in a very matter-of-fact way, suddenly lifting her head, snapping instantly from slumber to wakefulness. No fading into her senses, no slow awaking from darkness to gray to light, just an automatic turning on of her mind and sight.

Slowly putting her head back down on the bed with widening eyes, Skye could hear people talking outside of her window.

Her clear-cut sight and the stark brightness of her room let her know that she was still wired. The previous night's speed was still working her system. The sleep she had just experienced had not been very deep. It was as if she had been partly awake for most of her slumber.

The pale light coming through her gray windows cast a bright pallor over her room. She could feel the cool air against the part of her face that wasn't covered by her frayed black hair. She was wrapped up in her cloth sleeping bag and comforter, curled up in a warm and soft cocoon.

Standing up and letting the covers slide off of her, the cool room air pressed against her skin. Folding her arms and running her hands over her forearms, her skin felt dry.

Reaching for the ceiling, she stretched out her arms and legs. She moved deliberately, letting her body unravel. Bringing her arms back down, she could still hear the voices beneath her window.

Listening more closely, Skye realized that the voices were actually one voice.

Walking around the room, her body stirred the still air and she wondered if she should do another line. The few rays of the high afternoon sun that had wedged in through the curtains warmed her skin where they hit her hands. She thought about how good it would feel to draw back the curtains and stand in the open window, letting the sun and air warm her, if only there wasn't someone right under her window who was incessantly chattering away.

At first it had sounded like a woman's voice, but as she came closer to the window and listened more intently, she could now hear that it was a man's voice. He was talking in a very animated way, describing something to someone. Skye edged herself towards the window, If she moved too hastily, they might hear her.

She carefully approached the curtain, trying not to bump into it and cause it to flutter. Carefully peeking through a small vertical gap between the curtains, she peered down towards the sidewalk.

No one was there.

Only there was someone there. She could still hear them. Moving her head, she looked towards either end of the sidewalk, at least as far as the slight part in the curtains would allow her.

Walking around the room for a moment, she tried to ignore the jabbering outside, but trying not to listen only made it more pronounced.

She had to take a chance. The old faded curtains were completely drawn all the way across her windows. Going to the far edge of the left window, she slowly parted the curtain so she could get a better look at the sidewalk.

Straining her eyes, she was able to see most of the sidewalk. The voice was getting louder.

The sinking sun had left the first floor of her building covered in shadows. Close to her building, she spotted a round protrusion, which appeared to be a shoulder. It was the shoulder of someone standing near the building. It was tempting to move the curtain completely away and open the window so she could get a really good look at them, but she did not want to be discovered.

Listening, she thought she could make some of the words out.

Her heart jumped as she heard her name.

Quickly stripping off her clothes, she wrapped herself up in her large bath towel and dashed out to the shower. She spent a good long while under the streaming hot water.

Getting back into her room, her damp skin stood on edge as she bent her ears towards the window.

Nothing.

Walking up to the window, the voices were gone.

The sun had taken itself out of her room's range. The room quickly became cold. Dressing herself, she remembered an old dealer in South Berkeley, her ex-boyfriend Zeke's dealer, who had a closed circuit security system outside of his house. He had set up a small video camera outside of his door, and had an old black and white television inside of his house that showed everything that was going on. Perhaps she could set up some sort of system outside of her apartment building so she could see what was going on the next time she saw strangers or heard voices.

She reconsidered her sudden idea. Who knew what the hell that man had been doing in front of her building? What kind of loser had nothing better to do than stand in front of an apartment building and talk all day?

She wondered if they had heard her wandering around her room.

She wondered if they had seen her through the curtains.

It was time for another line.

Dragging

The wind was whistling against his walls, yet the interior of his boarded backyard hut was still fairly warm and comfortable.

It had been an off day for Yuri. Even though he needed to get some more food and even though his bedding needed a washing, he had spent his entire day inside, wafting in and out of random naps, half-heartedly cleaning small corners of his sparse place, and thumbing through a novel he had gotten from the library. He had decided he needed to read more often, but he could not read more than a few pages before having to put the book down.

Lying back down on his bed and rustling his covers over himself, he tried thumbing through the book again. He had been sweating inside of his blankets and covers for the past three nights as the weather had been deadly cold.

Yuri wondered what could consume a man enough to make him write about a fat and obnoxious slob with no life. He had gotten the novel on Sue's recommendation, having half listened to Sue's story about the dead author. It was almost too depressing for him to read, but also too good to put down. He remembered the piece of paper that he had been using as a bookmark.

It was a piece of paper with the address and time of an NA meeting written on it as well as Zata's phone number.

He had gotten Zata's number from Sue some time ago, only he had not mustered the courage to call her.

He thumbed through the book for a few moments before taking out the Zata's number again.

He picked up the phone. He decided that her latest absence from meetings was the perfect excuse for calling.

"Hello?"

"Hey Zata."

"Hi Yuri. What's up?"

"Well, I hadn't seen you around the meetings in a while, so I thought…"

"Are you at home?"

"Yeah."

"Where do you live?"

"Well, just a few blocks from the Ashby station."

"I'm close by. Can you come over here?"

"I guess, sure."

"If you help me move a desk I'll buy you lunch."

"Yeah?"

"It's okay if you can't come over."

"No, it's fine."

Zata gave Yuri directions to her place. He quickly leaped out from under his covers, dashing into the main house for a quick shower. Quickly getting dressed back at his place, he set out for Zata's. It turned out her place was only a few blocks away.

Zata lived inside of a plain wooden box apartment, down a side street off of a main South Berkeley street. She was right up the street from a popular Irish pub and music club on Shattuck Avenue. He searched for her apartment number and realized she was on the second floor, up a long flight of wooden stairs that ran along the left side of the building.

Trudging up the long and loud wooden steps, the place appeared to be old, but well-kept. The faded paint had refused to peel or fade unevenly, as it did with so many other older buildings in South Berkeley.

Standing on the deck of Zata's second floor apartment, a charge went through Yuri's chest just before he knocked on the door.

His knuckles almost lost their nerve as he hesitated. He rapped on the door carefully.

A few long moments. The door opened.

Zata was standing by the door, dressed head to toe in her usual black colors. Her jet black jeans and black tank top seemed to blend into each other, forming a dark shield over her tall frame.

"Come on in," greeted Zata with a smile.

"Thanks."

Her apartment was small and sparsely furnished. It was clean and well organized. A small couch and two chairs, and a coffee table with nothing on it save for an empty ashtray that appeared as if it had never been used. There was a small set of wooden shelves with a small television set, an immaculate boom box, and a well organized stack of cassette tapes.

She stood still as he walked into the room.

"My roommate just moved out," announced Zata. "She left her desk behind. She said I could go ahead and keep it."

"Oh. So…"

"Come on," said Zata as she gently closed the door.

Walking into a small hallway and then turning into a small bedroom, Yuri saw a short, long, and dark wood desk. It was the lone item in an empty bedroom.

"It doesn't look that heavy," blurted Yuri.

"It's heavier than it looks, but that's not why I need help moving the desk."

"Hm?"

Zata pointed to the doorway. "I need another person to help me wrestle it through this doorway." She paused. "Plus I can't raise my left arm very high."

"Okay."

Under her direction, he took the far end of the desk and helped her angle it through the small bedroom doorway and through the narrow hall. It took them some time, as the desk was indeed heavier than it appeared, but they eventually brought the desk into the front room, where she completed the move by positioning the desk by the window.

"I like to look out the window while I'm studying." Zata went into the kitchen. "I was going to order some Chinese food. Is that alright with you?"

"Sure," answered Yuri as he sat on Zata's couch.

"Would you like a ginger beer?"

"Okay."

She started speaking softly to herself as she went into the kitchen. Yuri bent his ear, wondering what she was doing. She was on the phone, ordering food.

"The food will be here soon," called out Zata. "It's coming from a place not too far from here."

She walked out from the kitchen with two bottles of ginger beer.

He had seen the top of her tattoo, the snaking dragon claw and mane that had peeked out from the top of her shirt at a few meetings. The dragon tattoos did indeed snake around her chest, as well as over her shoulders and down her arms.

The blue and red dragon scales were only snaking around certain parts of her arms, for on her arms and her chest were thick and gnarled scars, continuous thick lines of ruined skin, skin that looked as if it were in the midst of boiling.

He was trying not to stare.

"Do you like spicy food?" asked Zata.

"Yeah. What did you get?"

"I got the kung pao chicken. This is one of the only places that makes decent kung pao around here. I also got some lemon chicken just in case you don't like the spicy stuff."

"Oh, heck no. I really like spicy stuff."

The roping trails of ruined skin were pulling at Yuri's eyes. He kept trying to make eye contact with her as he talked to her, though her dark eyes were hard to stay with for very long.

"So how are you doing Yuri?"

"I'm doin' okay. Can't complain."

"Yeah?" she replied as if she didn't believe him.

"It's kind of cold in my place, and I wish I could get some more work. There doesn't seem to be much out there though."

Zata's tilted her head and stretched one of the scarred ropes on her shoulder.

"Other than that I'm okay," continued Yuri.

"Where are you from?" asked Zata.

"Nowhere in particular."

"Why do you say that?"

"I guess 'cause I've never stayed in one place to really be from anywhere."

"But you've lived here for a while."

"That's true. But I can't really say I'm from here since I didn't grow up here or start here or anythin'."

"Why not?"

"Mm."

"Just tell people you're from here."

"I mean, I'm from Portland originally, but it's been so long since I've been up there that I don't really call myself a Portlander anymore."

"Is Yuri your real name?"

"Yeah."

"Really?"

"Yeah. My parents emigrated from Russia."

"No kidding?"

"My full name's Yuri Rozhenko."

"Wow. Can you speak Russian?"

"Some. I'm really rusty though. I don't remember enough to really carry on a conversation."

There was a knock on the door. It was the Chinese food. Zata got some plates and chopsticks, spreading everything out \.

They had an amiable conversation over their lunch, as Zata continued to ask him questions about himself. Throughout the meal, Zata's scars would turn and twist with her skin as she reached back and forth for food. The snaking scar on her shoulder would always coil back and forth whenever she talked or turned her head.

He never once asked her about her scars.

A note

The passing traffic vibrated in her ears as she quickly walked down her street. The strings in her shoulders were twisting around. It was an unusually heavy commute on her street for that time of night.

It wasn't until she rounded the corner and stood next to her apartment building's doorway that a wave of fatigue washed over her, causing her to stop in her tracks. The weight of her arms and legs fell out of her as she experienced a wave of dizziness. A familiar tilting of the ground forced her to lower her head and prop herself up against the doorway. Putting out an arm and grabbing the side of her apartment's entrance, she let her heavy head hang down.

As she let her mind get its second wind, she thought about what she had to eat at home.

Her sight began clearing up. Lifting her head, she stopped herself.

There were small bits of paper littering the entrance to her apartment building. They were torn bits of lined binder paper.

Kneeling down to take a closer look, there was something about the white bits of rendered pulp that was attracting her attention. She picked one of them up.

She picked up a few more pieces. It was a handwritten note that had been torn apart. She squinted at a larger piece.

"I hope you understand..." said one ruined section.

She picked up a few more pieces. *"I know that we were close..."*

"If you could only realize..."

Skye began scooping up all of the pieces and put them in her jacket pocket. Looking around, she found at least a dozen more pieces out on the sidewalk.

Taking one last look around the doorway and sidewalk, she decided that she had found all of the pieces that had not been irrevocably swept away by the languid street wind. She felt a charge as she quickly unlocked the front door and skittered up to her flat.

Up in her room, Skye took out her speed baggie and put it in her bottom dresser drawer. She carefully extracted the ruined pieces of paper from her jacket pocket, double-checking to make sure she had gotten them all out.

After having thoroughly searched her jacket pockets, she went to the corner liquor store for a forty of Budweiser and a roll of Scotch tape. She also grabbed a few packages of Chocodiles as well. Coming back from the store, she double-checked the entrance to her building and the surrounding concrete for any more errant pieces of rented note. Spotting one final piece that she had missed, she grabbed it and ran up to her flat.

Carefully setting everything up, she shook out the dregs of her week-old speed baggie and carefully opened her forty. Opening the Chocodiles and laying them out, she snorted a couple of quick lines and took a few hits off of the Budweiser. Lying down on her stomach, just over the edge of her futon, she collected the pieces of paper and arranged them on the floor.

The pieces of paper were bright against the scuffed and dark wooden floor. The note had gone through a fairly violent rendering. Some of the pieces were long and thin, while other pieces were wider and shorter. A few were so small Skye was wondering if she would ever be able to fit them in at all. She laid out each piece flat before trying to piece them together.

A few pieces jumped right out at her. Carefully maneuvering two strips together, she was able to line up the dark blue-inked letters to verify that the pieces belonged next to each other. She laid the two pieces down, side by side, carefully aligning them, and slowly stretched out a piece of tape.

With surgical cautiousness, she aligned and pressed down the tape, joining the two pieces. Lifting up the newly-mended section of the note, she admired her work. She had pressed it back together perfectly. It was quite clear she would be able to read the note if the rest of her joinings were as competent.

Skye spied a corner that read "*Joey*" which she elected as the best candidate for the beginning of the letter. A few moments later she found another piece that read "*Love Always, Eve.*" She put the pieces on either side of the field of scattered paper pieces.

A few more moments of searching and she found a few other pairs of pieces that went together. She was always quite cautious with her taping.

After a while she had several small sections pieced back together. Skye got a small charge when she realized that two re-taped sections had a common edge, and she was able to join them into one big piece.

Turning the piece around, she could make out a few short sentences. The section was large enough that she could read part of the note, but she resisted the temptation.

She lost track of time as she worked. Bringing out her new baggie of speed, she did another line. She could still feel her weekend burn out as a light feeling centered in her skull, but her curiosity kept her energized as she kept plodding through her meticulous task.

After a good long hour of work, she taped together the last few pieces. The note was almost completely intact.

Turning the note around, she examined her handiwork. She had completed the pieces in almost perfect condition, almost as if it had never been torn to tatters at all.

She decided to have one more line before reading it. She wanted to be good and wide-eyed for its revelations.

Snorting up a decently sized line, she did not feel too much of a jolt. She had been running on speed for too long. It did, however, lighten her skin and bolster her eyes.

Taking another few hits off of the Bud, she carefully picked up the taped together note and began to read it.

Joey, you and I have been going out for a long time now. Maybe it does not seem that long to you, but it does to me.

I know a note like this may not seem a proper way to tell you about something like this, but I did not know what else to do. I do not know if I could stand to tell you this face to face, and I think a phone call would be even more hard than this letter.

I'll never forget the first time we met. You were so energetic and you had such a nice smile. I really liked your sense of humor. You were always so crazy and always so willing to make everyone laugh.

But now all you do anymore is get wired, and get stoned, and get drunk. All you do now is get wasted and fucked up and burnt out. I know you said I was a hypocrite because I smoke pot and drink beer and do speed. But I only did speed a few times, and I don't smoke pot all the time. I do drink when I go out, but only when I go out, to a party, to a club, to a friend's house. I don't drink all of the time. I don't smoke pot all of the time. I don't do speed all of the time.

I know you think that woman with the weird and scary black hair in your apartment building is a speed freak, and I know you are thinking about asking her if she knows where to get any speed because you said you don't want to buy speed on Haight Street anymore. I know all of this because you told me all of this. You told me when you were really really drunk. You told me before that you were going to stop doing speed when your dealer stopped coming to the cafe and you couldn't find him. Now you're thinking of asking some stranger who happens to live in your building if they know where they can get you drugs. It's too much. It's too crazy. You don't know what kind of fucked up things that woman does, or what kind of fucked up people she knows. For all I know she's going to get you hooked onto speed even more than you are now. She might even get you hooked on something worse, though I don't know if there is anything worse than what you are already doing. My God Joey, she might even know people who could have you killed. She is a very mean and strange looking person and I wish you would not get mixed up with her at all.

I know what you are going to say. You are going to yell at me that I've done speed before too. I did. I did on that weekend at Nikki's and that other time over at Steve's. I may have done it once or twice before, but not that often.

I would ask and plead with you to stop, but I know I can't get you to stop doing speed all of the time. I don't think there is any way I can still see you anymore, not when you are doing this and planning on getting mixed up in all kinds of things which will just mess things up worse than they already are.

I'm sorry, but that's my final decision.

I know you are probably angry, but please know that you will always have a place in my heart, whatever happens.

Love Always, Eve

Putting the note down, Skye crossed her arms. Lying on her futon, she stared straight out over the floor.

A sudden tightness shot through her. She bolted to her feet.

Taking the note into the bathroom, she quickly tore it to pieces.

She flushed the pieces of the re-rendered note down the toilet.

IV

Sinking

New Binge

Leaning down, she snorted up the line. Tossing back her head, the light expanded inside of her skull and danced around her eyes before melting down through her neck and into the rest of her body.

It was a good charge, lightening her limbs and loosening her chest. Letting out her breath, she fell back onto her futon and waited for the spins to cool down.

It was a good hit and an intense high. She had not done any in the past few days. She had been taking it easy for a while after having completed a decent binge.

She brought herself to her feet and went over to the window.

Parting the curtains and wrenching up her old apartment house window, she stuck her head out and leaned on the sill. The slow wind crept through her tank top and brushed against her still shower damp skin. She shook her head around, shaking her long black dreads out of her eyes, and looked around the street. Looking down at the sidewalk, Skye saw an elderly woman in a white flower hat, walking a small white dog.

It was a new ritual, parting her curtains and observing the world under her window in order to clear her head whenever she was starting a new binge. It took a bit of time, but eventually Skye began to realize that the plaguing chorus of faces and voices that had continuously haunted her only several months before had just been hallucinations, brought on by a lack of sleep more than anything else. For months she had been plagued by voices, talking throughout the building, talking underneath her window. And then there were the shadowy figures, far off in the distance, standing next to lamp posts and mailboxes down the street, just standing around, possibly watching her apartment.

The final straw was when she became convinced that there were people looking at her through her windows. It got to the point where she had almost called the police, until she managed to convince herself that there could not possibly be people looking through her windows, given the fact that she lived on the second floor.

In time, she realized that keeping the curtains drawn and never looking out of the window was only making her hallucinations worse. A good look, even when it was dark, was enough to help dispel any coming wraiths that her mind threatened to imagine.

The habitual lack of nourishment during her binges had not helped her senses either. She was now making it a point to eat on a regular basis, forcing herself to eat even if it was just a snack. She also kept it in mind to drink a lot of water.

It all took some practice.

Her window ritual had taught her a few new things about her neighborhood. She rarely ever saw anyone else looking out of their windows. Many of the windows of the apartment buildings across the street were always closed and curtained. A few times she saw some kids looking out of their windows. One of them even waved to her one day.

She turned away from the window. Before Skye had gone to sleep she had unplugged her phone. She plugged it back in.

A light and pleasant shiver raced over her skin as random people passed through her mind. She wondered about Linette, and where she was heading as Linette weaved in and out of her junky and tweaker worlds. She thought about Mercy, and whether or not she should try calling her again. For some reason, a reason which she couldn't fathom, Deep came to mind. She ruminated about her former dealer, about how she had never heard from him again after their last get together.

An unpleasant wave shook itself through Skye's shoulders. She had managed to avoid any memories of their unpleasant coupling for the last several months.

Skye started on another curious and random rumination. She was thinking about Johnny Trash. Preston had mentioned him in one of their many conversations about music. Preston told her he had run into him. She always remembered Johnny Trash as a shameless glam hipster who was always trying to start a band but could never get anywhere with the idea, not even ever coming close. Trash could never get around to mustering a band that would last long enough to play more than a few club dates before falling apart.

The only time she had ever hung out with Trash was the one night that her old friend Dex had invited him over to his place. They had been doing a lot of speed, and Dex wanted to get back at his noisy roommates and the upstairs neighbor, the ones who were always making too much noise in the morning by playing music and stomping on the floor. Dex fed Johnny Trash a bottle of vodka and had him sing some Led Zeppelin and Jane's Addiction tunes through a bass amp. Trash screeched into the microphone, barbarically warping the lyrics to When the Levee Breaks and Mountain at wall shaking decibels.

Suddenly Skye remembered that she was supposed to drive Preston out to see Riff Raff again. She thought about contacting Chasey and friends, seeing if they wanted to get in on any scores before she went. No doubt Preston would have a few delivery tasks for her as well.

Moving away from the window, she stretched herself out onto her futon. The cool air had made her head too light, as her speed high was gently swimming in place.

Rolling onto her side, she picked up the phone.

Dredge

Following the lines, they wavered side by side, as if they were trying to align themselves with each other, but never quite getting it right. Spaghetti trying to right itself, trying to remember their dry state. The trails of drunks, staggering home after the bars had closed.

A curling wisp of a smoke brushed his eye. Looking up and lowering his cigarette to hide the long stem of ashes, he brought up his coffee cup. He had been studying the patterns in the old varnished wood floor. He was in the basement of an old Presbyterian church, a place close to the more dilapidated sections of West Berkeley. Holt had given him and Sue a ride, as Yuri was trying to fulfill his obligation of ninety in ninety, or at least show up to enough meetings so that people would believe him if he claimed to have done so.

Yuri's eye watched one of his curling wisps of smoke rise and dissipate. Someone was sharing.

It had been the first time that he had shown up to a meeting late.

They had come in during the initial readings, the opening of the meeting when they read the credos from laminated cards. He had heard the twelve step preambles so many times that he was starting to weary of the whole ritual.

Shifting his gaze, he could see Holt leaning on his knees and balancing a cigarette, looking askance towards a far wall. Sue was looking down into her coffee cup, staring motionless.

He resisted the temptation to shift himself around. The metal chair that he was sitting in was quite noisy, letting out painful high-pitched squeals with even the slightest movement.

Looking up, he tried to spy the person who was sharing. He felt an inner urge to at least oblige the meeting by trying to pay attention to some of the things that were being said. There was actually enough smoke in his section to make it difficult to look around, especially at anyone across the room.

Looking around the sides of the room, he scanned the crowd, searching for familiar faces.

He saw a few people he recognized, but they were people he had seen at other meetings. Virtually all of the members whom he recognized were people he had rarely talked to, and many he had never talked to at all. There were more than a few circles that he had yet to break into.

Then he saw her. He was wondering how he could have missed her.

Zata was standing on the other side of the room, leaning back with her standard expression, looking out over the room as she squeezed her shoulders forward so her open black jacket would fall in front of her.

After he had been over to her place for the first time, Zata started approaching him after meetings. She had invited him over a few more times, sometimes asking him over for an afternoon lunch now and then, as well as a few times after seeing him at meetings.

Even so, she had kept him at a distance. Every time he had been to her place she would let her scars and her tattoos show. She would keep them fairly well hidden in public places and at meetings. She had not been to his place yet, probably because it had not crossed his mind to ask her over.

He had asked Sue about the scars. "I'm not entirely sure where they came from," she had told him. "She doesn't talk about them too much. I heard somewhere that some of them were self-inflicted."

Sue had also added that she was surprised he had seen them.

Straightening his back and lifting his head, Yuri bent his ear towards the current speaker, trying to concentrate on what he was saying.

Dealer

Coming back from Preston's, Skye had to move a few things around in her bottom dresser drawer in order to make room for her new stash. She had bought a supply for Chasey and Linette, as well as an extra surplus supply for later in the week. She was getting tired of running to Preston's every time someone had a new order, so she decided to plan ahead with extra speed.

Dashing out of her apartment, she took off down her street and turned on Valencia, making her way to Wilkins, the local smoke and bong shop. She waited in the narrow store for a few moments, perusing the postcards in the back until the counter was clear of customers. She bought a small plastic scale and a supply of small plastic baggies. One more stop for a forty ouncer of Budweiser at the corner liquor store and she was on her way back home.

Back in her room, she dug the new supply out of her dresser. She retrieved a metal baking sheet from the kitchen and carefully set up the scale and baggies on the baking sheet, just on the floor at the head of her futon. She opened the forty and carefully placed it on the side of her bed after taking a few sips. Her new small blue plastic scale looked like a children's toy.

Lying on her stomach and reaching out over the edge of her futon, she started scooping out speed from the eight ball bag and weighed out half grams. Eyeing her task, she carefully tapped out wisps of crank into the scale's small bowl. She was being extra careful not to make the baggies too light or too heavy.

Linette had stopped by her place the other morning, telling Skye that somewhere around three or four of her friends were interested in scoring some speed, and could she give them her number. Skye immediately vetoed any idea of having Linette's friends walking around with her phone number, carelessly blurting out to anyone they knew that they had connections to a speed dealer. Even worse was the idea that her name and number could get spread around. She stressed that point to Linette, even going as far as implying that her supply would dry up if her name got out around the cafes on Haight Street.

Linette called a few hours after leaving Skye's place.

"I don't think they wanna go for it," she explained.

"What? They don't wanna buy no more?"

"Nah, it's not that. They're just nervous."

"What?"

"They don' wanna do it that way, the whole givin' me the money deal."

"Well what the fuck? Do they want any or not?"

There was a pause. "I don't think they wanna trust me with the money."

"Well, you tell em' they can't have my number, and if they want any a' this they gotta go through you."

"What if they still don't wanna?"

"Then tough shit. Tell 'em I said so."

There was another pause. "Okay."

"Otherwise it's all just for you."

"Okay," brightened Linette.

It was later in the day that Chasey came by, letting her know that a lot of her friends wanted to score.

"Couldja make 'em into halves?" asked Chasey.

"Huh?"

"Like split the stuff into half baggies. Everyone's scorin' a half."

"Sure."

Shortly after Chasey left, Linette came by with an order for two halves and four quarters. She came by with a large stack of bills, most of which were one and five dollar bills.

Holding the spoon above the small plastic cradle, Skye carefully eyed the indicator. She assumed it was not a very accurate scale, so she always tipped in just a little bit extra. She could have bought a better scale, but the really good ones were fairly expensive.

After making a few more baggies she took another long drag off of her Budweiser. She carefully set it on the side of her futon, far away from her work area.

She was keeping careful track of her baggies, making up Chasey's first, and then Linette's. She kept her own stash nearby in case she ran out from all of the extra tapping she was putting into the baggies.

As her work went along, she got better at handling the small and rickety scale. She had her task completed just in time for a phone call from Chasey.

"Y'got th' stuff?" asked Chasey.

"Yep. Should I come on over?"

"I can come over there."

"Okay. I gotta wait for someone else anyways."

Chasey agreed to be there in a few minutes.

Skye placed the baggies in her bottom dresser drawer, keeping Chasey and Linette's piles carefully separated. She went out into the kitchen to pace, trying to remember when Linette was supposed to come by.

The door buzzer went off. She pressed the buzzer to let Chasey in. When Skye went to answer the knock at her flat door, she found both Chasey and Linette waiting for her. Chasey was carrying a paper bag suspiciously shaped like a six pack of beer.

"Look who I ran into," smiled Chasey.

"Hey Skye," greeted Linette. "I got here early."

"More for your money," said Chasey. "Or double your trouble."

"Hey guys. Come on in."

In Skye's room Chasey took out a six pack from the bag, offering everyone a beer. Skye was sitting before the baking sheet at the head of her futon as Linette sat in the one kitchen chair and Chasey sat against the wall.

"I've gotten pretty popular these days," commented Chasey.

"Why?" asked Linette.

"Why do you think?"

"I dunno. What y'do? Win the lottery?"

"I'm the man! I'm the babe! I got th' connections."

"Yeah."

"Ain't that right Skye?"

"I guess," replied Skye quietly as she concentrated on making lines for everyone.

"Aren't you th' man Lin?" asked Chasey.

"What?"

"Aren't you the man on your street?"

"What the fuck are you talking about?"

"That's it," said Chasey, pointing at Linette, "she's the man."

Skye went ahead and snorted her large dealer line. Standing up, she handed the straw to Linette. Linette quickly did her line. Chasey took a little time before getting around to snorting her line, as she was still chattering away. Linette got back in her chair, sitting up straight and sipping her Red Hook.

"Fuuuck," groaned Chasey.

Picking up Linette's stash, Skye could hear footsteps in the hall. Most likely it was Arden. There was an outside chance that it could have been Jane. Putting down Linette's stash, Skye went over to her small boombox and put on a Motorhead tape.

"Damn, this is some good shit," groaned Chasey.

"Fuck girl, you're hella tripping offa' that shit," commented Linette.

Skye went back to double checking Linette's order, as she was trying not to wonder who had been walking through the hall.

Drag

"Can you stop off at Drag's house?" asked Preston.

"Sure."

"He wants a teen."

"Okay."

Preston finished weighing out Skye's supply, snapping her portion into a large plastic bag.

"Make sure you get the money from him," said Preston as he carefully checked his metal scale.

"He hasn't paid for it yet?"

"Nu uh." He looked right at her. "Is that cool with you? Picking up the money when you make the delivery?"

"I was plannin' on just goin' home and gettin' wired after the deal," admitted Skye.

"Yeah? Well, if you do this for me I'll give you an extra half."

"Okay!" That was all she needed to hear.

Preston picked up a pre-weighed baggie. "That's his stuff."

"This is sorta a trip," said Skye as she stored the supply in her backpack.

"Don' worry about it. Drag's cool. I trust him just as much as I trust you."

"You actually trust me?" she said with a smile.

"Sure I do. Why not?"

"Sucker! For all you know this'll be a half when I get there."

"I'll just tell Drag to look out for a gal with her eyes hanging out of her sockets."

"Wait, I gotta do a line first."

"I got it."

She sat down in the easy chair as he made up a dealer line for her. She noticed that Preston's lines had been getting slightly bigger every few weeks.

Her body felt weightless as she tried balancing herself down the street. She stopped at a corner liquor store for a soda and a candy bar to give her some weight.

Walking briskly after she consumed a Snicker's bar and a Coke, Skye thought about how she wanted to get the deal over with quickly so she could get back to Preston's and then finally head home so she could enjoy some isolation.

It did not take her long to get to Drag's place. After double checking the address, she walked up to Drag's apartment building and buzzed the apartment number on the gray intercom panel.

"Who is it?" asked a static voice.

"It's Skye."

"Who?"

"Is this Drag?"

"Who is this?"

"Skye. Preston's friend."

"Oh yeah, hey. I'll buzz you in."

The door buzzed and she pushed it open. Drag's place was three flights up. She had met Drag only a few times before. It seemed rather odd that a person such as Drag was living in such a nice place for the sketched-out guy that he appeared to be.

She could have taken the elevator, but her amphetamine blood inspired a quick sprint up the stairs.

She could hear talking and music behind an apartment door down the long hallway. The door opened before she even knocked.

"Hey Skye," greeted Drag.

"Hey."

Drag stepped out of the way and Skye walked in. The thick beige living room curtains were drawn. Several cheap second hand lamps provided shadowy lighting between the two couches and small wooden chairs that surrounded a long and wide coffee table. The table was covered with a plethora of junk: magazines, beer cans, and various junk food wrappers. There was a large mirror and blade that covered the far end of the table.

Two very young women were sitting quietly, trying to hide their impish expressions with carefully strained scowls. Skye assumed, from their excessive black eyeliner and round baby fat faces, that they were still in their teens. The minor league throckers sat on opposing couches as thrash music played at a low volume in the background.

Drag was tall and lanky, not unlike a lot of the hipsters that haunted the city. He looked like a lot of the dime-a-dozen spike haired Danzig t-shirt wearers that she always saw on Haight street. He had a gaunt pale face and a nose that was so pointy that she imagined it was capable of punching holes in wall board. A few pale red spots of acne accentuated Drag's beady eyes. Even so, he still looked amiable enough.

"Thanks for bringin' the stuff," said Drag.

"No prob."

"You do have the stuff with ya', don'tcha?"

"Yep," she replied as she stopped and stood firmly.

"Aw man, thanks a lot for bringin' it over," he said, smiling widely.

"No big."

"Naw, really, I'll line ya up for it."

"Okay. I wouldn't say no."

One of the young women uttered an anemic hello. Skye nodded back.

"Hey, y'wanna beer?" asked Drag.

"Sure."

Drag went over to the partitioned kitchen area and grabbed a few Meister Braus out of his fridge.

"Here ya go," said Drag as he handed her a beer.

"Thanks dude."

"Have a sit."

Skye managed to forget that she was in a hurry and sat down on the couch against the wall, on the opposite end from the wide-eyed young woman who had not said hello to her.

She opened her beer as Drag sat down in one of the wooden chairs, just off to Skye's right. He was looking at her anxiously.

"So why don'tcha bring it on out?" he asked with brightening eyes.

"Not so fast there killer," she replied, "I gotta see a hundred clams first."

His face tightened up and he looked slowly around the room. He exchanged glances with the young women.

"That's what I wanted to talk to you about," said Drag finally.

Skye straightened herself up. She had more or less tossed her backpack to her side, even though she still kept her left forearm through one strap. She pulled the backpack a little closer to herself.

"Talk to me about what?" asked Skye.

He leaned forward, folding his hands and looking straight ahead. "Well, Skye, I wanted to talk to you about this deal."

"Yeah?"

"About the deal, I wanted to talk it over with you."

"This is Preston's deal, not mine. I'm just a go-between."

"Yeah, well, you know how you usually do a deal, right? You bring him the money and then you get the stuff, right?"

"You know how it's done."

"You know Preston trusts me to give you the money before he gives out the stuff, right?"

Skye shuffled herself around, sitting straight up and pulling her pack higher up onto her arm. "Hey, ask Preston how much he trusts you.

Don't ask me."

"Well what I'm tryin' to say is, you know I'm good for a front, right?"

"You have to talk to Preston about that."

"But I'm talkin' to you."

"It ain't got nothin' to do with me."

"Yeah, but you got the stuff. You know I'm good for the money."

"Again, Drag, I don't know if you're good for the money or not."

He leaned a little closer to Skye. "Yeah, but I mean, you could give me the stuff now and get the money later, right? I mean, you're the one handlin' the stuff, so what does Preston have to do with it?"

"He's sittin' at his place, waitin' for me to come back with the dough. If I don't come back with a hundred bucks for this teen, he's gonna be really pissed."

Drag leaned back in his chair, moving his arms to his side. "Y'see, there you go again. Right now this is between you an' me. I don't see how Preston's got anythin' to do with it right now."

Taking a long drag off of her beer, Skye leaned forward. She picked up the phone that she had managed to spot amid the clutter on the coffee table and held the receiver towards Drag. "Why don't ya give Preston a call, and if he says I can give you the stuff on a front then I'll give you the teen, otherwise I gotta see a hundred bucks for it or it's no deal."

"But I ain't talkin' to Preston, I'm talkin' to you."

The young women were starting to scrunch themselves into their seats.

She put the phone down, hard enough to make the bell ring. "Gee Drag, if you're so good for the money then how come you don't call Preston and ask him for a front?"

"Don't slam my phone around!" hollered Drag.

"This is bullshit," she snapped as she stood up. "Do you have the money or not?"

Drag stood up in front of Skye. "What difference does it make if I give you the money now or later?"

"I dunno. Ask Preston."

"Fuck Preston! You think I'd welsh out? Are callin' me a cheat?"

"You're certainly starting to sound like one," she said as she started walking to the door.

Quickly dashing around the coffee table, Drag jumped in front of Skye, blocking her way to the door.

"Wait a minute," pleaded Drag.

"Whattaya want now?"

"What about I pay part of it?"

"Drag, if you ain't got the money for this stuff then I can't give it to you. I just work for Preston, I don't make the deals. If ya wanna front, you gotta call Preston. Call Preston, Preston! Why is that so hard for you to understand?"

"I can give you sixty for it now."

"Hey, no way!" shouted one of the punk chicks as she bounced in her chair.

"Wait," said Drag as he turned to the bouncing young woman.

Drag and the young woman started arguing. Skye turned and started walking out of the apartment.

"Hey! I ain't through with you!" shouted Drag as he reached out and grabbed Skye's arm.

Drag pulled on her arm, trying to pull her back into the living room. As Skye was thrown off balance, she stumbled to regain her footing. As she began to regain her balance, she felt her right hand running into a soft protrusion, feeling thin and brittle sticks crackling underneath her knuckles.

Straightening herself upright, Skye saw Drag stumbling down his apartment hallway, holding onto his face as a dark color was seeping between his fingers.

"You fuckin' bitch!" growled Drag's muffled voice.

Without even thinking about it, she had punched Drag in the face. She had bloodied his pointed nose. There was a decent chance his nose was broken.

She had reacted on pure reflex. Her hand had shot out on its own accord, a reflex from her younger fighting days. She had not even realized she had hit him until she saw him stumbling down his apartment hall with his hands on his face.

Drag disappeared into the bathroom as she stood her ground, her feet firmly planted as she stood in the middle of the apartment. She turned, looking over the surprised faces of the young women who were shrinking further into their seats with wide-eyed surprise.

Skye turned towards the door.

"What a fuckin' bitch," muttered one of the young women sharply as Skye was reaching for the doorknob.

Every nerve in Skye's body started quivering. All of her muscles twisted up. Her fist shot out again, this time hitting the door with an ear splitting slam. Skye shot over to the couch and loomed over the young Throcker.

"Ya want me to smash your fuckin' face in too you rotten little bitch?" shrieked Skye at the young throcker woman who had made the comment.

She had shot over to the couch like a bolt of lightning. The young women almost jumped out of their seats. The one in front of Skye was actually trembling as Skye's red eyes stared her down.

Skye's hand shot out again. She backhanded the young woman in the face, causing her to yelp and crumple into the couch, trying to protect herself in a fetal position.

Skye wanted to calm down, but her whole body insisted on shivering with rage. She looked over at the other woman, who was actually clutching onto a couch cushion.

"You think I'm a fuckin' bitch? Who the fuck do you think you are you fucking little shit? You're trying to rip me off and you call me a bitch? I'll smash your fucking face! You fucked up little thief! Is that what you fucking want? "

The young woman was trembling even more, too scared to move, yet shaking enough that beer was spilling out of her beer can.

"Answer me!" roared Skye as she brandished her fists.

"No," whimpered the frightened young woman.

Quickly turning around, Skye started for the door. She felt numb. Her muscles were still tense, but her nerves had stopped vibrating. She could not feel her arms or her hands. A hot sensation washed over her face. She walked through the door, slamming it on her way out and quickly walking down the stairs.

Outside, all she could see was the white glare of the street, as she quickly walked back to Preston's.

Wall of Berlin

He had been ambivalent about the suggestion, but Sue and Holt had been rather insistent.

Yuri was sitting at a large round table by the window. Sue was listening as Holt and Tilden talked. Yuri was only half listening, casually watching the gutter punks and high school Throckers who were congregating outside.

Most of the gutter punks were sitting, a few of them were standing, and a couple of others were walking around, circulating around the crowd. A few of them kept tall and wadded paper bags by the legs of their chairs. Some of them were leaning in close to talk to each other. Yuri could pick out the details in the corners of all the dark clothes and accessories.

"Don't you think so Yuri?"

Turning from the window, he saw that Holt was looking at him.

"Mmm."

"You did your ninety in ninety, right?" asked Tilden.

"Yeah."

"You sound like you're not sure," remarked Holt.

"Hey, he wouldn't lie about a thing like that," quickly added Sue.

"I was talking to the new guy at the Wednesday night meeting," continued Holt as he turned back to Tilden.

Sue resumed listening to Holt, turning her eyes and leaning in. Once in a while her head would nod in agreement as Holt carefully related his earlier discussion with a newcomer whose name he was careful not to mention.

Looking back out onto the street, two gutter punks were hunched down, crouching near the outside corner of the cafe as if they were two baseball catchers at the same plate. Yuri bent his eyes to see if he could make out what they were doing when he felt something on his shoulder.

"Zata," said Sue before Yuri could turn around.

"Hello Sue."

"Hey Zata," said Yuri.

"Hi." Zata sat down, sitting right in between Yuri and Sue. "How have you been Sue?"

"I'm good. I've been good," she replied while quickly nodding her head.

"Still working on your steps?"

"Oh yeah. I'm back around to step one."

Leaning back in her chair, Zata stretched out her right arm, resting her forearm on the back of Yuri's chair. She quickly glanced at him, and then turned back to Sue.

"So Yuri tells me he knew you back in your old days," said Zata.

"We used to live in the same house, back in San Francisco."

"Really?"

"We used to get wasted together, when we were living in this ghetto pad called Hell Nose House."

"Hell Nose House?" Zata sat up. "What kind of name is that?"

Sue shrugged. "The people there before us named the place."

Yuri didn't say anything as Sue kept talking about Hell Nose House. He thought it was odd that Sue said they used to get wasted together. He had hardly ever talked to Sue back when they were housemates. Her old nickname, Surly Sue, was more than appropriate for her back then.

Glancing across the table, Holt was still talking. He was leaning farther back in his chair, pressing himself up against the wall as he strained his neck to keep his face turned towards Tilden, even though it put his neck in an odd position.

"Yuri."

Yuri realized he had let his mind wander away from Zata and Sue's conversation.

"Whatever happened to Skye?" asked Sue.

"I have no idea. I haven't seen her since just a few weeks after she moved into Mercy's place."

"Skye's your old girlfriend?" asked Zata.

"Yeah. We were going out back then."

"You'll have to tell me more about her sometime."

His eyes darted around. "Sue could probably tell you more about her than I could."

"I doubt it," replied Sue.

"I should probably get home," said Zata as she started standing up.

Out of the corner of his eye, Yuri watched Zata stand up and stretch her shoulders.

"Early day tomorrow?" asked Sue.

"Yes. Have to be at work early tomorrow morning. See you later Yuri."

"Yep. Seeya."

Stopping for a moment, Zata looked over her shoulder, looking at Sue. "By the way, thanks for giving Yuri my phone number."

"Sure."

Zata deftly turned and resumed her exit. Yuri glanced towards Holt. Holt was still awkwardly turning his head, chatting persistently to Tilden.

Burnt

It was a detour.

At least that's what Skye kept telling herself.

She was sitting in the corner of Beller's cafe, drinking a Vern's ginger ale. There were a few Haight street dwellers she recognized, people she had seen a few times from the upper Valencia and lower Haight scenes. Some of them were spooking in and out of the place as they made their rounds.

She didn't know them well enough so that social graces forced her to say hello to them. She didn't need to do that in any case. Linette was off in the back of the cafe, talking to a couple of young punks.

Linette was taking her time and Skye kept trying to watch the street scene through the bright window rather than look around the cafe.

Linette finally came back to her table.

"Fuckin' a'," groaned Linette. "Those idiots kept tryin' to talk me down."

"For what?"

"Just a couple a' Q's."

"Damn."

"They said they'd be back later. I already fronted 'em once, I don't feel like doin' it again."

Skye had only glanced at her customers. She knew that a few of the other youngsters scattered throughout the cafe were also regular customers of hers. She did not think they looked like tweakers. They did not have the eyes or the gaits of hardcore users. Their eyes were too bright and their lines were too bland.

Linette, on the other hand, appeared very out of place in the Beller cafe. The creases on her face and her darkening eyes were out of place amongst the younger faces.

"Thanks for comin' to meet me," said Linette as she leaned on the table.

"S'okay. I should get outta the house more often anyways."

Linette's nose started pointing towards the table as her curls floated in front of her face. She tossed her head.

"Fuck. I need ta chop my hair."

"How's this place workin' out for you?"

"It's all right," replied Linette, nodding her head a bit. "I pretty much know most a' the people in here."

"You don't get worried about…?"

"Naw. It's all just high school and cafe kids anyways. There ain't nobody here to worry about. They really like me too, because I don't cut th' stuff too much."

Skye leaned on the table. "I don't do that shit either, no matter what Chasey says."

"I remember when we used to come into places like this, tryin' to score in the scene when we really didn't know anyone. We'd end up with really bunk stuff most of the time."

Skye saw a few young punks eyeing her and Linette.

"You remember that?" ask Linette.

"What?"

"Screwing around these places in the old days."

"I didn't hang around the cafe scenes that much."

"Didn't you used to go hang out with them street dudes out in Berkeley?"

"Sometimes."

Linette slowly slumped onto the cafe tabletop. "Fuck, I remember alla' that stupid stuff I used to do. I kept saying the 's' word alla' damn time, and my friends would get really fucked up about it. I remember doing lines on the table, right out in the open. Shit."

It was because Linette insisted on talking about it that the memory started floating around Skye's head.

It was the first time she had ever tried it. She was only fifteen, living in a squat in Oakland and hanging around Telegraph Avenue in Berkeley. It happened in a cafe called Botega. She had been hanging out with her gutter punk friends and a few older hippies from the squat where she had been crashing. They were talking about scoring speed, only none of them were hardcore speed freaks. She had never even tried it before. Her friend told her to wait while she approached a brooding and shaggy haired man sitting in the corner of a cafe, someone who always kept himself wrapped up in an old olive green army jacket.

Skye had enjoyed her first speed experience, even though her friends said it was not the best stuff. She enjoyed it enough to look for the army jacket man, eventually finding him in a corner of the same cafe where she had seen him before.

She had just walked up to him, looking right at him and asked *"Hey, can I get any speed?"*

The man had quickly stood up, roughly putting his arm around her and guiding her to the back, warning her in a low yet serious tone that she was never to say the word "speed" out loud in a public place, and that she was never, never to approach him again. He had told it to her as a warning, but she had also heard it as a threat.

The nerves in her shoulders tightened at the memory. Her teenage ignorance at the time was not enough to forgive herself for being so reckless.

She wondered whether or not any of Linette's young customers would start harassing her out of reckless ignorance.

"You gonna stick around?" asked Skye.

"Yeah, for a little while, I guess." She lifted her head and shook her hair around. "I'll probably give you a call later tonight."

"I might be at Preston's. Try me tomorrow if you don't get me tonight."

In the corner of the cafe a young woman was yelling at her friend from behind her black hair, sending a quiver through Skye's back.

Skye was making her way down Mission, towards Valencia. She did not like walking around the streets in midday because it meant walking through crowds of people. She especially did not like it when she had a heavy backpack with her.

Linette's cafe business was getting quite brisk. Linette had gotten off a double order, buying two teens as well as an additional eight ball. Skye had already sold a teen to one of Chasey's Danzig friends, as they usually bought a teen directly from her once or twice a month.

Now she was walking down the main part of Mission with a great deal of money. The weight of the currency was making her edgy.

Bumping into someone as she turned the corner, she realized she was only a few blocks from Chasey's place. She kept going as the offended bumpee was yelling threats and curses in her direction. She knew that she did not currently have the nerve to contain herself in the face of an angry pedestrian, so she just kept going. She decided she needed to get off the street, cursing herself for having let Linette cajole her into a daytime delivery. She would stop by Chasey's place, just to get off of the streets if nothing else.

She made quick time to Chasey's. Standing in place and ringing her apartment, she suddenly felt her aching feet. After a few more moments she pressed the apartment buzzer again.

Looking around, trying not to shuffle her feet too much, she looked out toward Valencia, hoping the foot traffic might thin out in the next few minutes.

Starting down the steps, she was trying to plot out a decent side route to her house when the front door buzzed.

Darting quickly up the steps, she caught the door just in time.

"Wassup Skye," bemoaned a dark-eyed Chasey.

"Hey Chase."

Chasey turned to the couch, slumping down and lighting a cigarette.

"What's up?" asked Skye as she carefully maneuvered herself around the dark living room.

Chasey kept puffing on her cigarette as Skye sat down in the easy chair across from the couch. The rising plumes of cigarette smoke were bright against the backdrop of drawn shades and dull yellow light bulbs.

"Y' wouldn't happen to have any stuff on ya?" drawled Chasey.

"Yeah. I got some a' my stuff left over. I'm gonna make another buy tonight too."

"Yeah, I know," she affirmed as she slowly sat up. "I'm gonna hook up with Paul an' alla' them later."

Skye slowly put down her backpack. Chasey sat forward with her head hanging down and cigarette smoke creeping through her hair.

"Chase."

Chasey brought her head up. "Sorry, I'm kinda burnt. I hadda call in sick for work." She took a slow drag off of her cigarette. "A line would pick me up though."

"Sure."

Skye brought out her kit. She had a reserve half stuck in the small pocket of her backpack.

Chasey rubbed her eyes with her free hand. "Fuck. I hadda ask you somethin'. What th' fuck was it? Right, I need to get another couple a' teens from you."

"It'd be cheaper if you just bought a whole eight."

"Yeah, I guess it would be. I dunno. I'm tryin' to keep alla' my buyers straight. I guess I don't need two teens except for an eight. I gotta split alla that stuff up."

"Sounds like you need an accountant."

"I needa lotta things." Chasey hung her head back down. "I'd be making a lotta extra money if I was able to get to work." She stopped herself, hanging her head down lower and then bringing it back up again. "So what are you doin' tonight?"

"I dunno. I might be goin' out to Preston's. I could get your eight for you then."

Chasey waved a dismissing hand in the air. "I gotta collect th' money first. I can give you enough for one teen and buy the other later."

"Sure. If you want to do it that way."

"You could come hang out over at Paulie's."

Skye knew that Chasey would be hanging out with a decently sized group of speed freaks.

"You should really get out more," said Chasey. "Jus come hang out an' relax. You never do that no more."

"I gotta see what Preston's up to first. I might have to make another run."

"Sure."

Skye finished making the lines. She did hers first, quickly snorting up her line before handing the straw to Chasey. .

Chasey brought her head up, sniffing and slowly lying back into her couch. "Fuuuck yeah." Skye finally decided to stand up. Skye paced around the room, slowly, watching her feet so she did not trip over anything.

"You rearranging your room?" asked Skye.

"Nu uh."

Skye deftly shuffled herself around a few boxes. She looked towards the kitchen. She glanced back at Chasey who was still leaning her head back on the couch. Into the kitchen and looking into the fridge, there was barely anything in there. A quarter gallon of milk, a few packages of unopened tofu, and a half empty open bottle of Budweiser. She had been hoping for an unopened can of beer.

Shutting the fridge, she could see Chasey pacing around the small lane between the coffee table and the couch, actively puffing on another cigarette.

"You really need to come out with us tonight," said Chasey.

"If I don' have to hang out with Preston. You know how it gets, you gotta hang out. I might not be able to get away for a while."

"You couldn't cut it short?" she asked as she rounded the couch.

"I really shouldn't, especially with Preston."

"You remember where Paul's place is?"

"Yeah. I was just by there today."

"Come hang out."

The more she thought about it, the less appealing the idea of Pauls' place was.

The front door was calling her, though her social graces would not allow her to leave Chasey so early, especially since she had unexpectedly dropped in on her, and especially since she was upping her orders.

Questions

"Have you done your ninety in ninety?"

"Mmm," replied Yuri.

"What?"

"I'm on it."

"Because it's really important to get that in. Who's your sponsor?"

"What?"

"Who's your sponsor?"

"I don't have one right now."

"You really should have a sponsor."

"I tried one, but he didn't work out."

"What?"

"My sponsor. It didn't work out."

"You really should get another sponsor."

"Yeah, I just got rid of this one."

He had tried a sponsor. He had asked Tilden if he would be his sponsor, and Tilden had readily accepted.

Tilden told him to call him the next day. When Yuri got him on the phone, Tilden emphasized how serious he was about step work, and began explaining to Yuri what he expected out of him as a sponsee.

After talking to Tilden for about five minutes, Yuri realized that Tilden was not going to be the right sponsor for him. Not at the time, in any case.

He still talked to Tilden for about twenty more minutes, but he already knew he would not be calling him again.

"It's really important to have that sponsor, especially when you're just starting out," said the man whose name Yuri had just forgotten.

"Excuse me, I have to find a friend of mine."

He quickly turned away from the anonymous twelve stepper who had been peppering him with questions.

Walking through the crowd, a good number of people were still milling around the hall. Turning to look down the aisle, he saw Holt walking in his direction. Holt casually looked around the room as he strolled down the meeting room aisle, but Yuri could tell that he was approaching him. He pretended not to notice Holt's approach.

"Hey Yuri, how's it going?"

"Pretty good. I've been okay."

Holt looked right at him. "Say, have you done your ninety in ninety yet?"

"Yeah."

"Seriously?"

"I've done my ninety in ninety."

"Mm," grunted Holt. "So have you been hanging out with Sue a lot?"

"Now and then. Sometimes we talk about the old days."

Holt scrunched up his face. "Are you hanging out with Zata?"

Yuri looked around, scanning the room behind Holt.

"Not as much as I hang out with Sue."

Holt gave an approving nod. "You gonna make it to Saturday's meeting?"

"Probably."

"Well, I gotta go. See ya."

Holt resumed his casual walk through the aisles. Yuri kept looking around the room. He was hoping to see Sue. He had not seen her earlier, but was hoping she might have stopped by late.

The crowd was moving out of the meeting room. Yuri told himself that he needed to attend more small meetings. He was also telling himself that he needed to call Sue.

Absence

It was with a momentary sense of alarm that Skye had discovered a stack of boxes by the front door of her flat. She had just gotten back from work, still riding several maintenance lines that she had snorted in order to endure her video store job.

It was a rare occasion that she would ever do so, but she felt the need to knock on Arden's door.

"What's up with all the boxes?" she asked as Arden ghosted into her doorway.

"Jane's moving out."

"I guess we need to find a new roommate then?"

"Uh huh," replied Arden anemically.

Making her way into her room, Skye thought over these new events. It made sense for Jane to move out. She was hardly ever home in any case. No doubt she was going to live at her boyfriend's full time.

Getting back into her room, she went to her dresser drawer to check on her supplies.

She looked at her door. The thought had never crossed her mind until now that she should buy a lock for her door.

Standing up, she became uneasy, anxious at the thought of leaving her flat. No doubt Jane would have a few people over to help her haul things away. She wondered if Arden knew when Jane would be coming back for the rest of her things.

Checking her phone, there were two messages waiting for her. There was an outside chance that one of the messages could be from Preston or Paul rather than Chasey or Linette.

Looking for her laundry bag, she kept reminding herself to check her messages and call her people. It was another new ritual she had recently adopted: avoiding her answering machine for as long as possible.

The phone started ringing. She decided she should let the machine get it. Hesitating long enough, the phone stopped ringing. No message was left.

The thought came back to her. She had to find the new roommate.

And it could not be just anyone.

It would have to be someone she could trust, Someone who would not freak out and who was down enough to at least tolerate what she was doing and not make things more difficult for her. The wrong person could end up calling the police, or ripping off her stash, or simply start talking too much. She trusted Arden, though she didn't know why. She still knew very little about Arden and her habits. She didn't even know if Arden was aware of her speed activities, though she could hardly believe Arden was ignorant of them.

Her mind raced.

Skye tried to remember when she had last seen Preston without his baseball cap. Parts of his slicked out bleached blond hair were sticking out from under his plain black baseball cap. She was trying to get a better look at him through the floating plumes of cigarette and speed smoke.

Leaning over, he picked through all of the flat pieces of blackened tin foil. "I'm gonna have to get some more foil from the kitchen. These are all baked."

"I'll get some."

Skye never smoked it unless she was with Preston, and even then she would not always indulge.

Coming back from the kitchen, she handed him a new piece of clean foil.

"I brought back a couple a' more Mooseheads," said Skye.

"I'm still working on my last one."

He started folding the foil as she sunk into the easy chair. He dumped some speed out onto his folded piece of foil. Putting a straw in his mouth, he heated the underside of the foil with his lighter. White wisps of smoke floated up into the air, most of which he caught with the straw in between his teeth. The fog in the room was getting thicker.

"You've been smokin' that stuff a lot lately."

"Yeah," he gasped between puffs. "Once in a while I smoke some up. I've been snortin' it mostly still. Mostly I just smoke it when people are over. Helps me deal with the cramped spaces and all. Y'know, like I'm not sayin' that I mind you being over, it's jus' I get a lotta people out here sometimes." Leaning forward, he carefully put the hot foil down. "At least I'm not shootin' it. That's when you start gettin' really fucked up."

He only waited for a moment before picking up the foil and heating it again. He held the foil out for Skye.

"No thanks," she said, waving off the offer. "I'll take a hit later."

"Sure."

He leaned back against the bedside wall. "How's it goin' with you lately?"

"Everythin's goin' fine, except my roommate Jane's movin' out."

"What?"

"You know my roommate Jane?"

"Naw. I don't think you ever mentioned any Jane before."

"She's my other roommate. I guess I never mentioned her because she's hardly ever around."

"You mean like your spooky roommate Arden?"

"Oh, Arden's around plenty, it's jus' that she hardly ever comes out of her room. The whole thing about it is I gotta find someone new for our flat."

"You know who's gonna move in?"

"I dunno. I don't know anybody offhand. I would ask Mercy to move back in, but there's no way she'd ever leave that place of hers. I was thinkin' about Linette, but I'm not too sure about that idea."

Leaning forward, Preston picked up his supply baggie. "Maybe I could move in."

A spasm went through Skye's back. "What?"

"Y'know, maybe I could get that room."

"Hm," she grunted as she pressed her lips together.

"Did Jane move out yet?"

"Mm, is there something wrong with your place here?"

"Naw, I like this place fine. It's just that if we were livin' in the same flat then we could coordinate our deals way better."

"Hm."

"I mean, you wouldn't have to walk all th' way over here, and you also wouldn't have to call me all th' time to see if I was awake and all, and it might do me good to get out of here."

Preston looked in her direction.

"I have to see if Jane or Arden has found someone yet," she finally replied.

"Yeah?"

"I'm not sure, I'll have to double check."

"Yeah, let me know if it's available. Call me after you've talked to Jane."

She looked around the top of the wall, studying the few places where the bare wall was exposed from behind all of Preston's band flyers and shelf space. She was looking at the previously overlooked details, the lines in the cracked wallpaper, and the uneven colors where the wall and the ceiling had been fading.

"So what was you gettin'?"

"Hm?" His question had snapped her out of her trance.

"You were gettin' an eight?"

"Right! An eight and two teens."

"Why not just get two eights?"

"Yeah, I could do that, but could you weigh an eight into two teens?"

"Sure. We's aims to please."

"One of the teen's is for me," said Skye.

"Sure. Just don't forget to call me about the room."

"Yeah."

Ninety in Ninety

Looking over the bus schedule, he realized he would never be able to get back.

He had gotten the schedule to see if he really could make it to the closest Thursday night meeting after work. He found that he could take a bus to get to the meeting, but the line stopped running well before the meeting ended. He would have to hassle people for a ride back to Berkeley. It was too far away to walk.

He could make the walk, but he had been walking home from work in order to save more money. He had nearly worn through his better pair of shoes, to the point where he was considering taking the bus simply for the sake of his feet.

Putting down the bus schedule, he made his way to the fridge. Earlier Yuri had thrown out a half can of Budweiser that Zatch had left in the fridge. The smell of the lager had been making him nauseous.

He did not think it was very likely that Zatch would be upset about the disposal of a stale can of beer, but he was bracing himself for the possibility.

He came back from the fridge with a soda and what was left of last night's chicken burrito. Sitting on his bed, the thought of walking all the way across town got him to pondering his weight again. He had been trying to eat more protein, to see if he could at least keep his weight up.

He was unable to finish his leftover burrito. It was too much food for his fragile stomach.

Lying on his back, he eyed the spot where his television would be if he had one. He thought about a walk around the industrial areas to see if he might be able to find an old television that might still work. People in those neighborhoods oftentimes disposed of appliances by leaving them out on the street, rather than taking them to the dump and having to pay an expensive dumping fee.

Picking up a meeting schedule, he thumbed through it when he suddenly felt a charge.

Standing up, Yuri grabbed his coat and left his place. Out in the cool early evening air, he quickly walked towards Telegraph.

There was a women's meeting near the main drag of Telegraph. He knew that Sue almost always attended that particular meeting.

It had been almost a week since he had seen her. He had just enough time to get up to Telegraph and get to the meeting as it was ending.

Walking by the meeting hall, he could see people walking and milling outside of the building. Standing by the bus stop, he kept an eye out for Sue. After only a few moments the crowd trailed off. No one short and skinny enough to be Sue had walked out of the building.

He began making his way to the main drag. Walking into the main section of Telegraph, he spotted a familiar head of short hair, standing by the Med cafe, looking through her backpack.

"Hey Sue."

"Oh, hey," replied a wide-eyed Sue, looking up as if she had been caught doing something wrong.

"Whatcha up to?"

"Nuthin. What are you up to?"

"Goin' to get a slice of pizza. You wanna come?"

"Sure, hang on a sec'." She resumed rooting through her backpack. "Whatcha doin' up on the 'graph?"

"Looking for you."

She shot him a surprised glance.

"Only joking," said Yuri quickly.

"Here it is." She finally pulled out a pair of glasses and carefully put them on.

"I didn't know you wore glasses."

"I don't have my contacts with me right now."

They started walking towards the pizza stand. Sue seemed to insist on walking slightly behind him as she continued to fuss with her backpack, zipping and unzipping pockets and shuffling the contents of her pack around.

She turned down his offer of a slice. Sitting down at a corner table in the midst of the Thursday night throng, he contemplated the potential effects of an entire thick slice of cheese pizza on his flat stomach as Sue sat across from him.

"I was wondering about something," asked Yuri.

"Something, like in NA?"

"Some people actually."

"Is this about your recovery?"

"Not exactly. You remember the last time we were in the Wall of Berlin?"

She rolled her eyes around in thought. "I don't know. I'm in there a lot."

"We were sitting with Holt and I think Tilden. I'm not sure who else was there, and Zata came in and sat between us."

"Mmm."

"It was jus' kind of weird. 'Cause a couple a' days later I run into Holt at a meeting, and he asks me about her."

"He did?"

"Yeah. It was... I dunno. Is there something between Holt and Zata?"

"Something between them? Like what?"

"Holt was like, not even lookin' at us while Zata was sitting with us. An' then he goes an' asks me if I've been hanging out with her. Did they used to go out or something?"

"No, it's nothing like that."

"Then what's up between them?"

"Why do you want to know?"

He shrugged. "Well, they're two people from the program that I hang out with." Yuri picked up his slice and then put it down again. "An' I was also just curious."

"I guess, they kind of don't get along."

"Yeah, I gathered that much."

"They don't get along is all."

"Yeah? It just seems weird."

"How so?"

"Well, they're both in the program and they both hang around with pretty much the same crowds."

Her eyes stopped. "Well, they disagree with each other. I don't want to get into why. It's really nothing for you to worry about."

"Okay."

"Really."

"Don't you hang out with Zata also?"

"I do, but it's kind of weird." she said as her voice began to drop down. "I go over to her place once in a while, and sometimes we hang out over at the Ashby cafe, but it's like, we only really hang out one-on-one. We almost never hang out with a crowd."

"Does she want your friendship to be a secret or something?"

"She's not worried about anyone finding out. I get the feeling she just doesn't want to talk about it. She wouldn't go around saying 'I was hangin' out with Sue the other day'. It's not that she would be upset if someone found out, I mean if there were anything to find out about." She sat up and shook her head around. "Never mind. It's hard to explain."

"It's okay. I think I know what you mean."

Employ

Skye lost her job.

The thought occurred to her as she struggled out from under her covers. The whole idea was almost an afterthought, as if something was needed to jog her memory about her employment. With her turnstile calls to Preston, Chasey, and Linette, she had lost nearly all of her concern for her retail job.

Skye had not received any official confirmation that she had been formally terminated from her customer service position at Levigate Videos, but she had not bothered checking in with her place of employment for about a week. She vaguely remembered the voice of her supervisor on a few of her answering machine messages, but she had not bothered to listen to them.

More speed deals had been coming down. She was making more deliveries for Preston, and Linette's new quarter bag business was booming. Chasey was coming through on a regular basis, except in the middle of the week when she would eventually crash and burn. Skye was bracing herself for the possibility that she might have to curtail her supply to help Chasey keep her grounded. At the very least Chasey might be due for a lecture.

She brought herself upright and paced around the room, stirring the stale air. Picking up her heavy legs, she took herself into the kitchen. Her light chest and heavy feet were telling her that she needed to eat.

Even though she had lived with her for over a year, Skye was always surprised whenever Arden appeared.

Arden was standing by the fridge, wearing her traditional white terry cloth bathrobe.

"Hey Ard."

Walking over to the sink, Skye rinsed out a large plastic cup and filled it with water. Gingerly sipping her water, she looked around the floor as the statuesque Arden stood, sipping on a cup of coffee.

"I found someone for the room," ghosted Arden.

Skye's eyes grew wide. "Who?"

"She's one of my cousins."

"Mind if I have some coffee?"

Arden didn't say anything, which was her way of saying yes, one of the more important idiosyncrasies that Skye had learned about Arden.

"She's only going to be staying here for about five or six weeks," continued Arden. "She just needs a place to stay until she can get settled in for school."

"Okay."

"She just got out of high school. She'll be coming by next weekend. Don't give her any speed."

"What?"

"Don't give her any speed."

Skye gritted her teeth. "Is she gonna be uptight about that?"

"No, nothing like that."

"Ah. Okay."

Picking up her coffee, Skye started out of the kitchen. She stopped before the hallway and turned towards Arden.

"Hey Ard, I don't suppose you want any crank?"

Arden said nothing.

Skye stood for a moment, and then turned into the hallway.

She reminded herself to let Preston know that the room was no longer available.

The Scene

Standing on the sidewalk, looking over the front of the Trevor House, he was trying to remember what it had felt like when he had first seen the large and bright house. For the moment, it did not seem as big as it did before.

Holt in one huddle and Sue in another. Tilden and Jesse were hovering near Holt and a group of very familiar people who had never bothered to introduce themselves to Yuri. Rod was posing in a far corner. Rod had cast a glance in his direction when he came in.

Holt was being very quiet that evening, which was unusual, but not unheard of. Yuri would not have minded except that his silence had prompted Tilden and Jesse to become very quiet as well.

He almost thought the group had grown quiet when he had approached.

Sue was off talking to a cluster near the Holt and Jesse crowd. It was occasionally difficult to identify particular groups when they would mix closely together, though he had come to recognize certain sections and their sub-groups over time.

Scanning the crowd, he was still looking for old friends. He still clung to the hope that he would eventually run into some of his old partners from some of his old scenes. It was during these times that he would contemplate going out to San Francisco to try some of the meetings out there, though he would always eventually reconsider such a trip.

Peering through all of the facial piercings, black clothes, and bald heads, he recalled how Holt had introduced himself, simply walking up to him and saying hi, even though he was, at the time, a total stranger. Occasionally he would see Holt talking to unfamiliar newcomers, but for the most part he rarely ever saw Holt or any of his clan talking to anyone outside of their circles.

Watching a few of the stray loners wandering in between the clusters, he wondered if perhaps he could do the same thing.

But then again he didn't have that much clean time. No one had told him so, but his still-hazy perceptions about the cryptic unwritten laws of the scene told him that cold-start introductions were best left up to people with a lot more clean time and more experience.

He scanned a group of punks who were clustered by the stairway. There were three of them, all decked out in black with their wandering wisps of dyed black hair. They were standing in a semi-circle, mildly chatting with each other, waiting for the meeting to start. Perhaps he could talk to one of them. He could just pass by and calmly introduce himself. He recognized one of them from past Trevor House meetings, the short and chubby one with the Operation Ivy patch and the skinhead haircut. He could always claim to have talked to her before if she expressed any puzzlement or disdain at his introduction.

Just past the punk trio, he spotted a lone punk. He was about Yuri's height, wearing a cloth cap and brooding by himself in a corner.

Yuri went into the house, walking quickly past the trio and the lone punk, going in ten minutes before the meeting started. It meant that he was putting himself in danger of being asked to read one of the preambles by the wandering secretary, but he simply could not deal with his thoughts and the crowds at the same time.

He headed straight for the coffee. Keeping his back against a wall, he kept watch over the room as he sipped his coffee. Carefully looking out of the corner of his eye, there were still only a few people inside. He shrank into his corner when he saw the secretary wandering around the room with the laminated colored cards in his hand.

Looking to his left, the lone punk that had been outside was getting himself a cup of coffee. He had been wandering, very much alone, around the crowds outside.

"Hi, I'm Yuri," he risked with an extended hand.

"Hey. I'm Jasper," replied the young punk, turning towards Yuri with bright eyes.

"Hey. Are you new to the program?" blurted Yuri.

"Oh, a couple of years," nodded the now grinning Jasper. "How about you?"

"About six months now."

"Oh, great! Congratulations. Have you done your ninety in ninety?"

"Yeah."

"And you're working the steps?"

"Yup."

"So which step are you on?"

"I've been doing my third step."

"That's great. And you have a sponsor?"

"A temporary one. I had to let one go."

"Awright. Well, get that permanent sponsor then!"

"Sure."

"It's really important to have a sponsor."

"Yeah."

"And you really did your ninety in ninety?"

"Oh, yeah."

The secretary had sidled up alongside Yuri. He did not even notice him until he was handing him one of the reading cards.

"Would you like to read?" asked the secretary.

"Sure," he replied automatically as he took the card.

Looking around, the room was starting to fill up.

"I'll see ya aroun'," said Yuri quickly.

"Sure thing. And don't forget to get a sponsor soon!"

Looking for a seat close to the center since he had to read, Yuri watched as the clusters began crowding in. Holt came in with his group. Sue came in with her group. The circle of punks came in together. The room was filling up with random chatter and the shuffling of metal and plastic chairs.

Looking down at his card, he had gotten the twelve traditions. It was one of the longest ones to read.

Sidebar

The West Oakland light was low. They had driven out in the late afternoon.

Skye had been driving Preston out to Riff-Raff's at least once a week for the last several months. Preston had convinced her to be his regular driver.

For this particular visit there were a few amiable longhairs in Riff Raff's place. One of them was wearing a tie-dyed t-shirt while the rest were plunking on guitars and talking animatedly about music.

Skye sat in a corner, feeling somewhat tense after the drive. She sank into an old easy chair. The tie dye shirt was over by the drum set, looking over an old clarinet that had somehow made its way into Riff Raff's place.

Standing up, she looked at Riff Raff. "I'm jus' gonna go grab my forty from the fridge."

"Sure. I need somethin' from th' kitchen too."

Riff Raff followed her into the kitchen. He sided up to her while she opened the refrigerator to retrieve her forty.

"Hey, c'mon into my room for a sec'," he hushed "I got somethin' to show ya."

"Okay."

She started walking back into the living room.

"Not that way!" he hissed between his teeth quickly. "Let's go through here." He pointed towards the hallway at the other end of the kitchen.

Walking straight and clutching her forty. It was a part of the house she had never seen before. Her stomach made a few turns.

He led her into a sparse bedroom. It only contained a large bed and a tall dresser. The bed was very long and wide, with an old thick cloth comforter covering it. The dresser looked like an antique, made of strong, thick wood with a dark finish.

"Have a seat." He knelt down and opened the bottom drawer of his dresser.

She sat down on the edge of the bed. Standing up, Riff Raff carefully clutched an old lacquered black serving tray with both hands. On it was a crystal clear mirror and a few baggies of speed.

He sat down on the bed, carefully placing the tray between himself and Skye. She sat quietly and cautiously, carefully holding onto her beer. The bed was soft and moved too easily.

"I got some extra special stuff I'd like you to try."

Using a blade, he brought out some white substance from one of the baggies. It was very white and had a particularly chalky residue. She thought that it looked more like wet baking soda than speed.

"Now I don't jus' give this to anyone," he cautioned.

"Okay."

He raised a hand. "Don't worry, I ain't hittin' on ya," he said seriously. "I'll do that when Sharon ain't here," he said with a wink and a playful grin.

"What is that?" she asked as she leaned over to get a closer look.

"This, my fine feathered friend, is some extra special stuff I get straight from the manufacturer."

"I ain't never seen crank like that before."

"You ain't never had crank like this babe. I know that for a fact. This shit is completely pure, extra primo."

Riff Raff quickly made a small line for her. He held up a small mirror and a metal straw.

"That's all I need?"

"Be careful. This shit'll knock your socks off."

He handed her the metal snorting straw. Putting her forty down on the floor, she leaned down and quickly snorted up the line.

She couldn't feel the burn. Her nose simply went numb. A spasm in her neck sent the front of her face throbbing.

An ethereal hand pushed her head, almost knocking her down. A muscle in her neck began twisting her around. She let out a gasp as her heart started beating throughout her body, followed quickly by a numb wave that came down from the top of her head, glided through to her feet and then back up again.

"Oh fuck."

Her foot bumped into her forty as she wobbled in place. She quickly leaned down and grabbed the bottle while trying to keep her head from pulling her down.

"Don't say I didn't warn you."

Riff Raff busied himself with making a line for himself as Skye leaned back on the bed, hitting her forty a few times to try and calm down the spins. The bitter lager only made her head throb and spin more.

"I was thinkin', you been doin' a lotta business with Preston," said

Riff Raff.

"Yeah." She let herself fall back on the bed so she could concentrate on talking. "I'm basically his driver for these runs, but I also get a lot of stuff for people I know."

"On the under, right?"

"Oh yeah, I have a couple a' friends who go-between for me."

"Yeah." Riff Raff paused. "So how is Preston doin' these days?" he asked as he kept his eye on his black tray.

"Okay, I guess."

"'Cause I been kinda worried about him lately."

She gripped her forty. "Okay."

"Don'tcha think he's gettin' kinda sketchy lately?"

She could feel her eyes getting wider. Skye was having a hard time digesting Riff Raff's question while she was fighting the swimming high of her line.

Balancing her head on the top of her neck, she looked more or less in Riff Raff's direction. "Why are you asking me about Preston?"

"I'm jus' thinkin' that maybe he ain't been all there lately."

Shifting her eyes around the room. "Well..."

"The fact of the matter is, he ain't exactly been keepin' up his end like he used to. He hasn't been calling me as regularly as he used to. He's been takin' longer to get places, and he's been..."

She swiveled her head around. Riff Raff was looking right her.

"He's been gettin' too tweaked out," he continued. "He's been sayin' and doin' some shit that's got me a kinda concerned."

"Like what?"

"What?"

"Well, I mean, can you give me an example? I'm tryin' to get this down."

He put down his blade and picked up the straw. "Part of it is the way he's been actin' around here, just a bit off and tweaked out, at least enough so I can notice it. It's also, I can't say exactly who is doin' this, but I know one of his regulars ain't been able to come over to his place for a while. Now it ain't none a' my business what Preston does with his own place, but I can say I ain't too happy that this one guy can't get in, 'cause he ain't done nuthin' to be treated like that. The fact a' the matter is, Preston's been callin' me about this guy, goin' off about how he's gonna try an' do this and he's gonna go and report that. He's convinced this guy is going to get him busted, an' he ain't even close to bein' any kind of narc. Then he starts asking me about people this guy knows, starting' to wonder if they're narcs as well. It's all just a buncha crazy shit."

He leaned down to do his line as she looked across the room.

Right after he quickly did his line, Riff Raff went up to his dresser and wrote something down on a small piece of paper.

"Here's my number. If you'd like, you can come out here by yourself. You don't need to bring Preston along anymore or nuthin' like that."

"Thanks."

He sat back down on the bed. "Also, if you want, there's some guys in the city who could use a new connec'. I can hook you up, but only if you're willing to take up new business. They take their stuff in teens an' eights alla' time." He held up his hands. "No pressure though. Think about it, and if you aren't into it don't bother with it."

"Sure."

Suddenly Riff Raff appeared thoughtful. "I understand if you don't want to get any deeper into alla' this. Believe me, it's more work comin' here than goin' through Preston, but I can tell ya that you'd make a lot more money than you would be now. I won't lie to you though, it'll be a bigger hassle, so think about it before you agree to anythin'."

She was still dizzy from her hit of speed.

Hitting her forty again, the electricity in her head was still growing. It felt as if the high was getting stronger by the moment rather than receding.

A Visit

He wasn't sure why he had done it. It was a spontaneous act. He would not be able to tell anyone why if they had asked.

He had invited Zata to visit him at work.

It occurred to him that he had no idea what his boss would think if she came by when he had a friend visiting. The guarded thought only occurred to him shortly before Zata was supposed to arrive.

He had asked her to come by the warehouse just after his shift was ending. He was sitting by the shipping desk near the warehouse doors. He did not want to miss her because he was lost somewhere deep in the dark maze of the warehouse.

The knock came, just a few minutes after five. The sound had surprised Yuri. He was not used to people being so punctual.

Opening one of the large wooden doors, the sound of heavy rain poured through the opening. He had not heard anything at all with the doors shut.

Zata was standing tall and straight, underneath a large black umbrella, holding onto a brown grocery bag.

"I wasn't sure if this was your work or not," said Zata. "This place really is out of the way."

"Come on in." He closed the door behind her. "Sorry it's raining so bad."

"It's not your fault it's raining."

He locked the door shut as Zata set aside the umbrella. She looked around the dark warehouse.

"Wow, you work here all day?"

"Yup."

"How far back does it go?" She craned her neck, trying to see down a shadowy corridor.

"All the way to the end of the building."

"You mean it goes all the way to the other side of the block?"

"Yeah."

"Cool!"

He was surprised again. It was the first time he had ever heard Zata use an exclamation. "I can give you a tour if you like. I don't know how interesting it will be."

"What's back there?" she asked as she continued stretching her neck and standing on her toes.

"All kinds a' junk. It's supposed to be just books and records, but they dump all kindsa' stuff in here. I always gotta figure out where to put it."

Turning around, she went over to the shipping desk. She took a couple of fancy brown bottles out of the bag. They appeared to be beer bottles.

"I brought us ginger beer and some sushi."

"Okay."

"Don't worry, this stuff ain't alcoholic."

"I didn't think you would bring…"

"What's back there?" she interrupted as she peered down another aisle.

"Did you want to have some sushi?"

She started walking down one of the aisles, bobbing her head around and widening her eyes.

"Wait," cautioned Yuri. "I better go down there first. There's a lotta junk down there."

Dashing ahead of her, there were still some boxes on the floor that he had not yet organized.

That's when he noticed a box full of doll clothing, sitting next to a shelf full of cassette tapes.

Stopping and turning around, he had lost her. She was a half aisle length behind him, looking over a box of records.

"What is this stuff?" she asked.

"Inventory. Backlogged stuff and stuff they can't sell. Some of it's just here temporarily until they can make room for it at the stores, but most of it's here to stay."

She took a John Coltrane record down from the shelf. "Would they miss any of this stuff?"

"Probably not."

She put the record back. "Sorry. That's my old addict talking. I'm not really going to take anything."

"Yeah, I know."

"You should be more suspicious," she replied with rolling eyes.

"Fuck it. I know you ain't no fuckin' burnout."

She walked up to him and put a hand on his shoulder. "I am a burnout, an old burnout who's not burning out anymore, but that doesn't mean you should still trust me."

"What are you talking about?"

"Never trust drug addicts. Not even the sober ones."

"Not even you?"

"Especially not me," she replied with a wink.

Moving further into the warehouse, she found a break in the shelves, a small section filled with boxes of random items that was right under an old and bright metal lamp.

"Let's have our sushi here."

"Sure."

She dashed back to the shipping desk and quickly came back with her grocery bag. She opened her ginger beer and set the sushi down on a wooden crate.

"What is all of this junk for?" she asked as she was picking through a group of old kitchen appliances.

"Beats me. I don't think it has anything to do with the stores though. She jus' puts all of her junk in here."

"She does?"

"My boss. The lady that owns the bookstores."

"Damn, there's a milkshake machine in here!"

"What?"

"An industrial milkshake machine. It's the kind a restaurant would use."

"Yeah?"

"Didn't you notice it before?"

"Not really. I just dump this stuff in here."

"Look at this." Reaching into a box, she pulled out an old and rusted handgun. "Damn dude! You've got firearms in here."

"I don't think it's real. It's just a toy."

She took the clip out of the gun.

"It's real." She examined the clip. "It still has bullets in it."

"Holy shit!" he gasped as she handed him the clip.

"Yep."

"I thought it was just some rusted out old toy."

He could see a rust-covered bullet on the top of the clip. He carefully handed it back to Zata.

"Don't put it back in," he said.

"I won't, though I doubt this thing still works." She checked the gun chamber and carefully put the gun down on the crate. "Man, I can't believe you have all this cool stuff in here and never told me about it!"

"I never really thought about this stuff before."

She handed him a ginger beer. "You like sushi?"

"Oh yeah. I hardly ever have any though. I can't really afford it."

"Well, you have to spoil yourself once in a while."

She was eyeing the milkshake machine.

"Hey Zata, when you said not to trust addicts, not even the sober ones..."

She turned and fixed her eyes on him. "Yes?"

"I don't get it."

"What?"

"Aren't you one a' them?"

"One of what?"

"One of those twelve steppers."

She took a sip of her ginger beer. "That depends on who you ask."

"Yeah?"

"If you asked Sue she would tell you I'm in the program, only she would say it in a way like she wasn't sure, like, she was almost apologizing for having said it."

"Hm."

"You know what I mean?"

"Yeah, I can imagine her doing that, even though it's kinda weird to think about."

"Is it?" she asked as she leaned forward.

"It's just that, when I knew her back at Hell Nose House, she was totally, and I mean totally different."

"No kidding?"

"She was always skulking and scowling. She always tried to avoid people, except for her friend Skye."

"Isn't that your old girlfriend?"

"Yeah."

"The one you never told me about?"

He shrugged. "There's not much to talk about."

"Oh. Bad subject?"

"No! No of course not. She was pretty cool, it's just that we never really ever got that serious." He started looking through the wooden crates and boxes, wondering if there were any more weapons in them.

"And now Sue is totally different," said Zata. "Now she's quite positive and happy." Her voice almost sounded sarcastic.

"Well, I don't know if I would go that far. Maybe she's happier compared to what she used to be like."

"Sure. I know the type."

"The type?"

"Yeah. The cynical drug abuser turned chirpy NA member. They're all over the place. What do you think Holt used to be like before he came here?"

"You knew Holt when he was using?"

"Yeah, I did know him back then. And he knew me too."

"Uh huh."

"Not like that. We were just friends."

He clasped his hands. "I kinda noticed something the other day, when you came by the Wall of Berlin."

"Yeah?"

"It seemed, like Holt was kinda…"

"Me and Holt don't get along."

"I sorta figured."

"Let's just say we don't agree on a few things."

"Hm."

"I don't get along with program fascists."

Yuri straightened his back. "What do you mean by fascists?"

"You know, those regulars who are always asking you the same questions over and over again? You know who I'm talking about."

"Well, I know a lot of people were talkin' to me when I first got there."

"But they were always saying the same things, right?"

"Sure."

"And what do they always talk about? What are they always asking you?"

"Well, the program."

"And do you know why?"

Yuri had been looking at the floor. Now he looked at a bright light overhead.

"They want me to stay clean, right?"

"Not exactly."

Dropping his eyes, Yuri looked Zata right in the face. "I don't understand."

"They want you in the program."

"Right."

"And that's it."

"So I can stay clean."

"No."

Yuri's eyes wandered again.

"I still don't get it," he confessed.

"All they care about is getting you into the program. It's not about sobriety. It's about the steps, the traditions, doing a ninety in ninety and having a sponsor. They don't care if you stay clean or not."

"But that's the whole point, isn't it?"

Zata was looking right at Yuri. "Do you know what you have to do to stay clean?"

"Follow the program?"

"Well, the program may or may not keep you clean. You have to find that out for yourself, but ultimately you need to do what you have to do to keep yourself clean and sober. That might be the program and it might not. They want you to have a sponsor, and follow the steps, and do a ninety in ninety, but the thing is, you can be relapsing over and over again, still taking drugs, and they'll still accept you, as long as you stay in the program."

"Okay."

"And let's say you stay clean and sober, that you work on your own stuff, but you aren't in the program. You aren't following the steps, and you don't have a sponsor, you know, all of that stuff. They simply wouldn't care that you were clean. They would shun you, because you weren't in the program. The whole point of being clean and sober is lost for them. All they care about is the program."

"But that's what the program's about. It's about staying clean and sober."

"That's why it was started, but no one seems to remember that. They keep talking about being clean, but it's the program that they're worried about. That's it."

Yuri leaned forward. "Why are you saying all this? What makes you think they would shun you if you dropped out of the program?"

"Not just if you drop out of the program. They'll also shun you if you don't follow the program the way they want you to."

"Well, I mean…"

Zata leaned closer to Yuri. "Tell me, what happened when you quit drinking, when you went full on clean and sober."

"Like, you mean going to the meetings?"

"Didn't you suddenly lose a bunch of friends? Do you remember you told me how you used to hang out with some guy Dex, and some girl named Sweepy or Swishy or something weird like that?"

"Yeah."

"And what happened when you went totally clean?"

"I didn't really see any of them after that."

"Yeah. That's what all these twelve steppers will do to you if you didn't stick with their program, and that's regardless of whether you stay clean or not. You have to find your own program, what works for you, not what these guys tell you to do."

Zata became quiet. Yuri tried to digest what Zata had just told him.

Newbie

Looking through her backpack, Skye wanted to make sure she didn't have any errant baggies cluttering it up before she went out to Riff Raff's. Paul and Linette had both come up with new demands, and Skye was interested in increasing her personal supply with an extra teen so she would be able to treat her various go-betweens and friends when she stopped by for drops.

She could hear Molly, yet again, making her way back and forth from her new temporary room to the kitchen. Molly was Arden's cousin, the roommate who was going to be in the apartment for five or six weeks.

Only a few days before, Arden had brought home a young, short, and round-faced woman dressed in bright pastel clothing and introduced her as their new temporary roommate. Molly had come up from Fairfield. Molly had described her situation to Skye from under her bright green hat and bobbed black hair, relaying her decision to move to the Bay

Area for a few months before her semester started since Arden had an available room. She went on about going to college across the bay in a few months, and how her parents weren't happy with her leaving early. She had also enthusiastically talked about several other random topics that Skye had only half-heartedly listened to.

Skye did not refocus on Molly's kitchen conversation until Molly leaned in and asked Skye where she might be able to get some magic mushrooms. Skye told Molly that she did not know where to get mushrooms, which was only a half-truth. Skye did not know specifically where to go to acquire mushrooms, but that kind of excess would be easy for her to find with her contacts.

Molly then went on a short yet spirited diatribe about the differences between acid and mushrooms until Arden walked back into the kitchen.

Skye was partially relieved that Molly was not all that ignorant about recreational drug abuse, but she was concerned that she was not ready to be in the vicinity of a speed dealer.

Molly did a lot more moving around than Arden. It was bad enough that she was home most of the time, but Molly also found it necessary to constantly move back and forth around the flat, constantly making trips from her room to the kitchen or to the bathroom and then back again.

Neither Jane nor Arden ever made so much noise walking around the flat, even when they were wearing boots.

Skye wondered how quickly the five to six weeks would go by.

The trip had taken a lot longer than usual. Preston had gotten into elongated speed-induced conversations with a few musicians who had been hanging out at Riff Raff's. Skye mused on the idea that Preston's concentration had been slipping, and she thought about what Riff Raff had said to her a few weeks earlier.

Returning to her flat, Skye had brought Preston's car back with her. She was sure there were a pile of messages for her on her answering machine.

A slight tremor went through her shoulders when she opened her apartment building door.

Trying to keep her mind clear, she made her way into the flat, making sure the front door was shut behind her.

"Skye."

Skye held in a start as she came to a stop by the kitchen door. The voice had sent a jump through her because it was not Arden or Molly's voice.

"What," gasped Skye.

"Sorry," said Linette. "I didn't mean to startle you."

"What are you doing here?"

"Your roommate let me in."

"What?"

"That trendy gal let me in, the one in Jane's old room. What's her name? Polly or something?"

"Molly. Let's get into my room," said Skye, putting a hand on Linette's shoulder and guiding her into her room.

"What are you doing here?" asked Skye as she shut the door to her room.

"Well, you had been takin' so long to come back I thought I would stop by and see what was goin' on. I mean, normally I wouldn't, but you had been gone for such a long time I was startin' to get worried."

Kneeling down, Skye kept her back to Linette as she put her stash into her dresser. "How long have you been here?"

"Damn, I'm not sure. I've been hangin' out with Molly in her room."

Skye stopped and turned to Linette. "What were you guys doin'?"

"Nothin'!" replied Linette defensively. "Just talkin'."

Skye saw the quickly blinking light on her answering machine. The skin around her temples stretched thin, causing her head to throb.

"Lin, can you stay here a sec' while I run down to the corner store? I gotta get a beer in me or I'm gonna explode."

"Sure."

"I'll get you one too. Just stick around here."

"Should I answer your phone if it rings?"

"Yeah yeah. Don't say anything except that I'll be back."

With that, the phone rang.

"You wanna get that?" asked Linette.

"Fuck no. Just sit tight an' I'll be right back."

Skye quickly sprinted down the hallway and out of the building. Walking down the street, she could feel her skin crawling for a bottle.

There were only a few people in the corner liquor store. The cashier nodded to Skye as she walked in. She grabbed three forty ouncers of Budweiser. Standing in line, a man was arguing with the cashier.

"They's only a dollar fifty."

"That was last week. They're a dollar sixty five now."

"You can't sell me it fer, you know, less fifteen cents?"

"No I can't."

"It's only fifteen cent!"

"It's a dollar sixty five now."

The argument went on for some time. The bottles were warming in her arms. She finally barged up to the counter.

"Can I just pay for these an' get outta here?"

Skye ignored the other customer's complaints as she convinced the cashier to let her go ahead. Making the quick sprint back to her place, the delay at the corner store only added to the strain.

Walking into the flat, Skye could hear Linette and Molly in the kitchen. Looking through the kitchen doorway, they were drinking Anchor Steams.

"Hey Skye!" chirped Molly.

"Hey."

"I hope you don't mind that I let your friend in."

"Naw. No big."

"Have a beer. I got plenty."

"I just bought some myself."

"Lin says she thinks she can score me those mushrooms!"

"Really?" drolled Skye as she put away her forties.

"Well, I don't know exactly where to get any," said Linette. "But I'm sure they're pretty easy to find. I can ask a few friends."

"That's cool," commented Skye as she opened her forty. "There's a forty in there for you," said Skye to Linette. "You can have the other one if y'like," said Skye to Molly.

"That's okay," replied Molly. "There's ten Anchor Steams left in the fridge. You can have one of those too if you want."

"I'll be right back," said Skye after taking a large swig off of her forty.

Skye went into her room. She made sure there was no speed paraphernalia out in the open as she carefully checked her stash. She quickly called Chasey, asking her if it was okay to drop off her stuff.

"Yeah, come on over."

"I'll be there in five minutes."

Skye let Linette and Molly know she would be right back. She dashed out of the door and quickly walked to Chasey's place.

Chasey was more than amiable to take the stuff and have Skye leave straight away, forgoing the usual socializing, especially since it had taken longer than usual for Skye to get the supply.

It only took a few minutes for Skye to get back to her flat. Walking into the flat, she looked into the kitchen. Looking in her room, Linette was not in there either. Skye walked down the hallway and knocked on Molly's door.

"Who is it?" quickly asked Molly's muffled voice.

"Skye. You got Lin in there with you?"

"Yeah. Come on in."

Skye opened the door and walked in.

"Shut the door!" snapped Molly.

As she was carefully closing the door, Skye looked in disbelief. There was a small mirror lying flat on top of one of Molly's boxes where Linette was forming two lines of speed.

"What are you doing?" blurted Skye.

"Hey Skye," chirped Linette. "Molly wanted to try some of this stuff."

"Can I speak to you for a moment?" commanded Skye to Linette.

"Sure thing." Linette looked at Molly. "Don't do anything until I come back."

"Gotcha," replied Molly with a thumbs up.

Skye quickly led Linette into her room. "What the fuck are you doing in there?"

"What?"

"Arden told me not to give her any crank."

Linette shrugged. "So? You're not. I am."

"What the fuck."

"She asked me if I was doin' any kinda stuff this weekend an' I said yeah, jus' some speed. So she tells me she wants to try some."

"Fuck. Did you tell her where you got it from?"

"Hell no. I didn't tell her nothin'."

"Dammit Lin, Arden's gonna know she's wired."

"Well she's all askin' me about mushrooms an' X an' stuff, so I figured I could help her out. I mean, you wanna have her go on th' drag and ask the cafe scum for that stuff?"

"Fuck."

"Lemme get back in there before she tries to snort it without me."

Linette dashed out of the room. Skye had to let herself breathe for a moment before picking up her forty.

Skye let herself into Molly's room. Linette and Molly were leaning over the mirror.

"Watch out for that beer," cautioned Linette. "You don't want to dissolve your speed."

"Gotcha."

Skye stood against a wall, nursing her forty, as Linette gave Molly an elaborate snorting lesson.

"Don't forget to breathe out before you snort, but don't breath out over the mirror, or you'll blow the stuff off onto the floor. Don't try to snort the whole line if you can't handle it. You can always snort the rest on a second try."

Molly turned and looked at Skye. "Have you ever done this stuff before?"

"Yeah, a few times."

"I hear it's a lot of fun."

Skye shrugged. "It can be. It's also pretty powerful stuff."

Linette leaned down and did her line as Molly closely studied her.

"Don't snort it as fast as I did," gasped Linette. "I've been doin' this stuff for a little while now, so I'm more used to it."

Leaning forward, Linette carefully handed the straw to Molly.

"Don't forget what I told you. And brace yourself for the punch. It's a nasty one."

Molly took hold of the metal straw as if it were a scalpel.

"Have you ever snorted anything before?" asked Linette as Molly started lowering her head toward the line.

"Quiet," commanded Molly. "I'm trying to concentrate."

Carefully leaning over, Molly started snorting before she even reached the line. She snorted up half of it before bringing her head back up.

"Ack! Ouch ouch ouch!"

"Toldja," snorted Linette.

Molly leaned back as Linette took hold of the mirror. Molly's face was red and tears were streaming down her face.

"Shit! This stuff hurts!" muffled Molly from behind her hands.

Linette carefully put the mirror back down on the box where she was sure Molly would not knock it over. Linette looked at Skye. "You wanna line?"

"Sure."

Skye sat down against a wall while Molly was rubbing her red nose and Linette poured more speed onto the mirror.

"Sorry I don't have any place to sit down," apologized Molly.

"Don't worry about it."

Molly paced back and forth, breathing heavily and shaking her limp hands around. "Hooo! Damn! Fuck." Stopping in place, she craned her neck and looked at the ceiling. "I know this is good stuff because I hardly ever say 'fuck'."

"Fuckin' a'," interjected Linette.

Linette leaned over and did her line, quickly handing the straw to Skye. Skye snorted up her line.

"Damn!" exclaimed Molly. "How the hell can you snort that stuff up so fast?"

"Practice," replied Linette.

"God, my nose still hurts. It felt like I was snorting glass."

"That's what the good stuff tastes like."

"Damn, what does the bad stuff taste like? Is it even worse?"

"Naw. If it's chalky an' doesn't taste like battery acid then it's usually bunk."

"Yeah, that's what it tastes likes! It's like eating a battery."

Molly started pacing around again.

"I need a cigarette," gasped Molly as she started digging through her pink vinyl purse.

"Don't forget the rest of your line," added Linette.

Skye put her back against the wall. She kept in mind that she had to contact Paul after another hour or so. Molly started vigorously smoking a cigarette as her fishbowl eyes darted around. She nervously shuffled her feet for a few minutes before she began pacing again.

"Damn, damn, damn."

"You gonna do the rest of your line?" asked Linette.

"Fuck no. I don't think I can handle it right now. Fuck. There I go again, saying 'fuck' again. Damn." Molly waved her hands towards her chest. "I'm not going to have a fucking heart attack, am I?"

"It would be a first actually," commented Linette as she started pouring more speed out onto the mirror.

"No shit? Fuck. There I go again. Shit. I don't think I've said 'fuck' so many times in one day."

They had moved into Skye's room for more privacy. It was Skye who had brought up the possibility that their activities might attract the attention of Arden.

Linette was lying down on the futon, leaning over a baking sheet, making new lines as Skye sat against the wall. Molly insisted on pacing.

Linette turned to Skye. "So, when was the last time you saw someone do their first line?"

"What?" snapped Molly. "Did I do something? Did I say something? What?"

"Slow down," cautioned Skye.

"Drink some more beer," suggested Linette.

"Should I do that? Isn't it dangerous?"

"How is it dangerous?" asked Linette.

"I mean, isn't that something you're not supposed to do? I mean, can't you get a heart attack or something. I think Thompson said something like that once. I mean, I guess you guys would know more about that."

"I'm gonna get th' other forty," grunted Skye as she stood up.

Going into the kitchen, she brought out the two forty ouncers. Back in her room she carefully shut the door behind her. Molly had stopped pacing long enough to observe Linette forming lines.

"Here," said Skye, handing a forty to Molly.

"Jus' a sec'," replied Molly, holding up the metal straw.

Skye looked down at Linette who was trying to make the modest lines as straight as possible.

"Jeez Lin, jus' let her have some!"

"Sorry."

Linette sat up.

"What do I do now?" asked Molly.

"What you did before," instructed Linette.

"Like, I kinda forgot."

Linette waved her hands around for emphasis. "Breathe out, but not over the surface so you don't blow the stuff away, line up the straw, and then breathe it in through your nose steadily and evenly."

"Right. All I remember from the last time is the pain. My nose still hurts."

"Use the other nostril," suggested Skye.

"Oh. Right. I got two, don't I?"

Skye bent an ear towards the hallway, listening over Molly's giggling for any faint sounds of movement or slippered footsteps. The corners of her eyes watched as Molly managed to snort up her entire line.

Molly fell back, coughing and sniffing with a beet-red face that was wet from her streaming tears. "Fuck fuck fuck fuck."

"You okay?" asked Linette.

"My fuckin' nose! This shit hella burns!"

"You shouldn't have snorted it so fast," said Skye.

"I didn't want to look like a wimp."

Linette and Skye distracted themselves with their lines as Molly kept huffing away, waving her hands at her face and rubbing her nose.

Linette looked at Skye. "You got my stuff together yet?"

Skye waved a discreet hand, indicating that Linette should keep quiet.

"Damn. I always wondered what speed was like," huffed Molly. "This shit is intense. "

Molly rambled on for a few minutes and then suddenly stopped with a huff of air. "Fuck."

"Hey Molly, you should grab a glass of water," insisted Skye. "It's important to keep drinking water when you're wired.

"Yeah?"

"Yeah. And could you grab the last six of Anchor?"

"Sure!" sprang Molly as she jumped to her feet and darted out the room.

Skye went into her bottom dresser drawer. "Lin, I need you to keep an eye on Molly while I go make a delivery to Paul."

"Okay."

"I'll fix your stuff up there. Can you hang out for a while?"

"Sure. Why not?"

"Cool. Don't let Molly know what we're up to. As far as she's concerned we're just users."

"Of course. You don't have to tell me that."

Molly came back in with a glass of water and the six pack, just as Skye had stuffed Paul and Linette's stash into her backpack.

"Oh wait, I already have the forty," corrected Molly.

"That's cool. You guys can hang out here for a while. I'll be back in just about half an hour."

"Where you goin'?"

"I gotta go meet someone real quick. Don't worry, I won't be long."

"You gonna deliver drugs?"

Skye held back a start. "No, nuthin' like that. I just gotta go return some CD's and talk to a friend. You guys can hang out an' play some music if y'like."

She could sense Molly's next question coming on and dashed out of the door.

Walking out onto the street, she would try and deal with Paul as quickly as possible and then get back to her place and work out the long night.

She kept wondering what she was going to do when Arden found out.

V

Lost

Ring, ring, ring.

"Come on."

Ring, ring, ring.

She kept counting to herself. Nine, ten, eleven, twelve.

She let it ring one more time and then slowly put down the phone, keeping her ear out for a last minute pick up.

Standing up, she carefully made sure that her curtains were completely closed before opening her bottom dresser drawer. She needed to split up her supply into half and quarter bags for Linette's stash.

She had bought a much more accurate scale for weighing out the smaller portions. She thought about asking some of her go-betweens if they couldn't divvy up their own supplies, but they had all been bringing in so much business that she always acquiesced to performing the favor.

It had been two weeks since she had last heard from Preston. His stubborn silence had almost been disastrous for her business. Shortly after his long absences had begun, her go-betweens were hounding her for new supplies. No number of phone calls would get him to pick up. After several more unanswered phone calls, she stopped by his place, but he refused to answer the door. Out of sheer desperation, Skye drove off in Preston's car and made her first solo run to Riff Raff's place.

She could scarcely forget her first solo foray to the West Oakland speed distributor. Riff Raff had appeared genuinely happy to see Skye. When she thought about it, he had actually looked relieved.

Even though she had been nervous during her first solo outing to West Oakland, she still did not hesitate to ask Riff Raff if he knew anything about Preston. He assured Skye that he had been in touch with Preston and that he was still in the same place.

Since that eventful day, she had made several more West Oakland runs. After the last run she had taken Preston's car back to her place rather than leave it by Preston's apartment. Perhaps the absence of the car would finally prompt him to call her.

She kept telling herself that she had been doing Preston a favor by taking the car. At least with her driving it around, it would not get towed away as a derelict, and Preston would not be tempted to drive it, thus risking getting busted for driving without a valid driver's license.

Arranging all of the little baggies, she had to make sure she kept the orders straight. She was working on Paul's order: two halves and three quarters. It was the smaller task, so she was getting that out of the way first. While she sequestered Paul's baggies in a corner, she was trying not to think too much about getting pulled over or busted while driving around. She did not want to lead her mind back to paranoia. It had been a long time since she was convinced that the faraway shapes and sounds were people trying to get into her apartment.

Moving on to Chasey's order, she started up her boombox. Music might distract her worrisome musings.

She decided that she would bring up the subject of Preston again with Riff Raff. She had been reluctant to mention him again, since it seemed that it was a touchy subject with her supplier, but her curiosity was getting the best of her.

The blare of Sonic Youth blasting from her stereo helped her forget about her cart wheeling worries. She had gone through Chasey's portions more quickly than Paul's.

Standing up, a flurry of chores and mental reminders raced through her head. She needed to drop off Paul's supply. She needed to drop off Linette's supply. She needed to call Chasey. She had to eat something. She would need to inventory her room for laundry, baggies, and dry food.

Putting her arms down for a moment and looking around her room, the air was still and light. A faint gray-orange haze forced its way through her covered windows. The room was still sparse, with her large spacious floor and few pieces of furniture. Skye's skin began breathing again with her pause.

She remembered how cramped Preston's room had been.

Meeting

It was an unusual feeling. At least it was unusual enough for him. He basked in the rays of the setting sun and the steady wind as he walked up the lower regions of Telegraph. The weather in the Bay Area was much like a deranged transient on the streets. One day it could be sunny and warm, and the very next day it could easily be cloudy and cold.

Even with all of his concerns over the climate, he had hardly ever taken time to bask in the wind or the sun. Letting the rays of the bright day warm his skin while the sleek wind cooled was invigorating.

At least for the moment.

He still had to wonder over his defiant sense of serenity. His last paycheck had arrived with a warning that his hours at the warehouse were about to be cut. Yuri was hoping that his reduced hours would not last long. Even a reduction of just a few hours a week would make it difficult to keep up with his rent.

He had just done a run on Telegraph, looking for job openings in a few choice retail establishments. There were a few stores on the main drag where he believed he would like to work, mostly the record and comic stores. It was not the work that intrigued him so much as the idea of having unique access to their products. He also thought about applying for another warehouse job.

But the idea of a new job hunt was not bothering him for the moment. He had a new supply of cash. It had been a nice day, and he was on the main drag.

He spotted a young woman outside of the Med cafe. He recognized her immediately. He did not know her name, but he knew her as a meeting regular.

Yuri had not been to a meeting in more than a month. He had been in the clean and sober scene for nearly a year, but recently he had simply stopped going to meetings.

One night, nearly a month ago, he had been planning to attend his regular Wednesday night meeting, but he held himself back at the last minute. He had gotten close enough to the meeting to see the regulars milling about in the glow of the open doorway. His feet simply stopped. He could not find it in himself to make the final steps towards the meeting.

He had given it some thought. Perhaps he just needed a break from meetings, a pause in order to digest what had been going on. Perhaps he had simply been getting tired of the routine, of the endless war stories, the all too familiar meeting preambles, and the same people and the same scenes. He thought about going out to other meetings, other twelve step gatherings in other nearby cities, but he had already attended a few meetings in the South Bay, and he felt they were pretty much the same as meetings in the East Bay, just with different faces.

It did not occur to him to say anything to the familiar woman in front of the Med, even though he was quite certain that she would recognize him. Tilden suddenly walked out of the cafe.

Yuri slowed his pace as he approached the Med. Picking up his stride, he wanted to convince himself he did not have any reason to avoid anyone.

"Y'gotta t time?" asked a passing gutter punk.

"Yeah, almost three."

"Thanks."

By the time Yuri looked back down the street, Tilden and the woman were gone. Turning into the Med, there were a few people already in line. As he waited, he saw Tilden and a few more women from the program, all sitting together at a large round table near the back. Looking around, he spotted Holt, sitting with some of his familiar baldy friends. They were all sitting in a trademark huddle, surrounding the table, talking and laughing.

He kept his place in line and pretended he had not yet noticed them. He thought about approaching Tilden, or maybe even Holt, once he had gotten his coffee.

Looking above the chalkboard menu, Yuri noted that they were preparing to paint over the old and faded mural in the back. The customers in front of him were taking their time, as was the counter help.

He ordered a large latte. While he was waiting for his drink, he thought about how he would answer all of the questions: Where had he been? Had he been going to meetings? Which step was he on? Did he have a sponsor?

Finally getting his latte', he took in a deep breath. He turned around to face the circle of program folk.

The table was now empty. He had been so lost in thought he had not seen where the group had gone. Looking around, he saw them through the window, passing in front of the cafe, no doubt on their way to Trevor House. He suddenly remembered that a Trevor House meeting was about to start.

Walking towards a table, he considered the idea that they had not seen him. Sitting down, Yuri thought about Trevor House. Perhaps he should go by the popular weekend meeting.

Yuri drank his coffee and watched the various characters of Telegraph Avenue walk by.

Isolate

Skye pushed around a good portion of her personal supply on the baking sheet. She had finished weighing out Chasey's supply when the corner of her eye caught the phone.

She had made herself a line, but decided she would wait until after she had made a phone call. During the past week, her calls to Preston had become less and less frequent. It had been almost a month since she had gotten him to pick up the phone. In the past week even his answering machine had stopped picking up.

Nevertheless, she decided she still needed to try getting in touch with him once in a while. She still had Preston's car, and he was still technically her connection with Riff Raff.

With a deep breath she picked up the phone and dialed the all too familiar number.

After Preston's phone rang a few times there was a dead silence followed by a few static clicks. Skye was confused until a telltale high-pitched beep sounded off.

"Preston, this is Skye. I'm going to come by today. I wanted to talk to you about a few things, so I'll stop by later this afternoon if that's okay by you. Gimme a call when you get this message."

Hanging up the phone, she wondered if she had even reached the right place.

She set out for the street after doing a few lines. She delivered Chasey's supply and quickly excused herself from her place, explaining that she had some important business to tend to.

Driving through the Mission, she got to Preston's place in good time. For some reason traffic was not very heavy, even though it was already late in the afternoon.

She parked in the alley right next to Preston's building, the traditional parking spot. Getting around to the front of the building, she buzzed his apartment. After waiting a few moments she heard the intercom click and buzz a few times, but no one had said anything.

"Preston?" she called into the intercom. "It's me, Skye."

A few more clicks and buzzes, then the intercom fell silent.

"Preston? Are you there?"

Standing in place and wondering what to do next, she kept her ears tuned to the intercom, and thought twice about trying to buzz him again. Straining her ears, she could only hear the soft wind whistling through the foyer.

Turning from the intercom, she faced the wind. She thought about trying to call him again, perhaps from her place.

She turned towards the apartment building door. She tugged on the handle. The door swung open. It had not been fully closed.

She quickly ducked into the apartment building, closing the door behind her and making sure it was shut. Walking up to Preston's floor, she made sure that she did not walk too quickly.

She quietly walked up to his door. Reaching out, she knocked, not too loudly, yet not too softly either. She stood, waiting through the inevitable silence. After a few moments, she knocked again.

"Preston?" breathed Skye. "It's me, Skye."

After a barely perceptible turning of the doorknob, the door opened very slowly and only ever so slightly. She sensed that he was peering through the sliver of a crack in the door.

She was about to say something, but stopped herself. She moved her head so that he could see that it was her.

The door remained motionless. She could hear someone breathing. Her right hand tightened up. Her back loosened and her shoulders tightened as she waited for something to happen.

"Pres?"

Someone moved away from the door. The door gently moved open.

Grasping the door and slowly opening it, she kept her arms tensed. Taking a step inside, she could see a silhouette sinking back into the dark apartment.

"Preston?" she hushed as she stepped inside.

"Close the door," hissed Preston from the far end of the dark hall.

She scanned the pitch dark hallway with a final squint before shutting the door. Carefully stepping into the dark apartment, she groped the hallway walls for the light switch. Finally finding the switch, she found that the bulb was either burned out or not there.

He had disappeared into his room, partially closing his door. Skye walked down the hallway, touching the walls as she walked.

Moving up to the doorway of his room, she could feel the thick and warm air settling on her face.

"Make sure you shut the door after you come in." His voice was muffled. There was only one lamp on, and it was covered with an old t-shirt. She tried to avoid all of the boxes and clothes that were spread out over the floor.

Preston had his face pressed up against the curtained window near the head of his bed. There were thick and dark tarp-like sheets over his window, and he was intently looking through the small gap where the tarp parted from the very edge of the window. The sharp sliver of light where the tarp was parted was painful to look at, even from across the room.

"Shut the goddamn door!" hissed Preston.

"Alright!" She pushed the door shut.

Trying to find the easy chair, she noticed a small orange-red glowing light coming from a small metal room heater in the corner of the room.

Skye managed to find the easy chair. She moved aside a stack of magazines and sat down.

"Did you lock the door?" he repeated as he kept his face pressed up to the window.

"I locked the front door."

"What about my room?"

"What?"

"Did you lock the door to my room?"

"No."

Suddenly jumping off of his bed, he ran across the room and locked his bedroom door. He quickly got back on his bed and went back to the window.

Skye sat for a moment, waiting for Preston to start the conversation. He sat unmoving and continued his strained surveillance.

"Mind if I turn on a light?" asked Skye.

He did not say anything. He simply continued to look through the small part in the curtain.

"What are you looking at?"

He did not answer. He did not even move.

She put down her backpack, close to the chair so she would not lose track of it. She leaned forward. "I wanted to do a line, but I'm gonna have to turn on a light." She stood up and turned on the overhead room light. Preston did not move as the light went on.

She finally saw just how chaotic his place had become. Newspapers and dishes and fast food containers were everywhere. He had pulled down most of the boxes that had been on his shelves and had dispersed the various contents all over the place. Old appliances, guitar parts, speaker and stereo parts, books, magazines, all kinds of clothes and various other items were lying everywhere. Some of the appliances had been taken apart. She was surprised that she had managed not to trip over anything when she had walked into the room.

"Where's your stone?"

He remained unmoving and silent.

"Preston?"

"What are you doing here?" sharped Preston as he kept looking out of the curtained window.

"What do you think I'm doing here?" snapped Skye. "I haven't heard from you in weeks. I've been callin' you and stoppin' by." Leaning over, Skye tried to find Preston's snorting stone. "Riff Raff tells me you jus' come by on the weekdays, an' then you're only scorin' a personal stash."

He finally looked away from the window. "You've been talking to Riff Raff?"

"Well, yeah," she replied as she continued to look for the stone. "What th' fuck was I supposed to do? I got customers to feed an' you weren't around."

He looked back out the window. She found Preston's snorting stone. Brushing it off, she cleared a place for it on the coffee table. Carefully bringing out her stash, she noticed Preston's stash box, lying sideways on his bed, with a large baggie of speed tilting just over the edge of the box.

She dumped out a decent amount of speed onto the snorting stone, being careful not to put out too much or too little.

Suddenly he looked up, snapping his head around. He looked directly at the snorting stone.

"Where did you get that speed?" commanded Preston.

She shrugged her tense shoulders. "Where d'ya think?"

He slowly turned around on his bed. He looked intently at the portion of speed on his snorting stone. "Is that from Riff Raff?"

"Yeah."

"What's he been sayin' about me? Has he been talking about me?"

"He hasn't said anything."

"Nothing at all?"

"Well, he asked if I had talked to you lately."

He looked right at her. "What did you tell him?"

"What?"

"What did you tell Riff Raff when he asked if you had been talking to me?"

He leaned forward. She could see that his neck was tight. His glass eyes were sharp.

She kept her eyes askance. She could see the hollow of his cheeks. The darkness under his eyes was more pronounced than usual. His hair was getting unusually long, at least for him. It was splaying out in all directions as if it couldn't decide which way to go.

"Well," said Skye quietly, "I told him you were fine."

"That's it?"

"Yeah," she swallowed. "I couldn't really say much about you since I haven't seen you or talked to you."

Quickly looking down at the floor, he scrunched himself into a ball on the edge of his bed. He grasped his foot with one hand as he balanced himself.

She took out her library card and started moving the speed around on the snorting stone as Preston held himself still.

Forming lines on the stone, she tried to force her shoulders to unwind.

"This shit is pretty good," said Skye. "Give it a go."

He kept his huddled position for a few more moments before turning around and grabbing a piece of foil. He laid the foil down on the stone. "Just put it on this."

"What?"

"Put anythin' you wanna give me on the foil."

She did not say anything. He turned around and began looking out of the window again. She took up a portion of his line and put it in the foil.

"You smokin' it?"

"At least I ain't shootin' it. That's when you know you're getting too fucked up."

Leaning over, she quickly did her line.

Bringing her head back up, she found it was difficult to breathe in the thick and acrid air of the room. Stifling her throat, she tried to bring down the tension. "So what's been up?"

He turned to look at her. "What?"

"What have you been doing? I haven't talked to you in a long time."

"How did you get into the building?"

"Didn't you buzz me in?"

His eyes darted around the room. "Did I?"

"Yeah. Don't you remember?"

"What, why did I let you in?"

"I buzzed the door and you asked who it was, and I said who I was and you let me in."

He looked around for a few more moments. He swung his legs over the edge of the bed and picked up the foil. "Yeah, that's right."

Taking a straw between his teeth, he started heating the underside of the foil. White curling smoke rose from the melting speed. He inhaled some of the smoke through the straw.

"I just wondered what you were up to," she continued. "I've been callin' you once in a while, jus' to see how you were doin'."

He held in a large wisp of white smoke for a moment. "I've jus' been layin' low," said Preston as white smoke billowed from his mouth. "Some strange shit has been goin' on. I don't fuckin' know anymore. Riff Raff's been actin' hella weird."

"Yeah?"

"Somethin' like, he keeps askin' me how I'm doin', an' he keeps talkin' about selling me smaller amounts. I don't even get those big supplies no more. He was tellin' me about how he wasn't gonna sell me no more eight balls, that he's only givin' me teens from now on, an' only one at a time. I've been havin' to take the subway out there because my car's all fucked up."

"Your car?"

"Yeah. It fuckin' disappeared. I think the cops took it. They're probably tearin' it apart tryin' to find somethin'. I dunno. I think someone is trying to rat me out."

"No shit?" She was trying to remember if he could see the alleyway from his vantage point.

"It's like my car is jus' fuckin' gone one day. I don't know what th' fuck happened to it. An' then fuckin' Riff Raff starts askin' me all these fucked up questions. I think there was someone trying to come by. I saw some people out there, just the other night, just standing out on the street an' lookin' up at my place. I'm just not sure what the fuck's goin on."

Preston suddenly looked right at Skye. "You still goin' over to Riff Raff's?"

"Yeah."

"What are you doing out there?"

"Don't you remember? I got customers. I still move just as much stuff as before. More than that actually."

"No shit?"

"Yeah. I just started goin' out there myself."

"How do you get out there?"

"What?"

"I mean, since you ain't got no car, how do you get out there?"
Skye hesitated.

"I get a friend of mine to drive me out there," she finally answered.

He looked up at her again. "You mean he's actually letting you bring people out there already?"

"No. They drop me off and come pick me up later. It's kind of like that." He kept looking at her as if he did not believe her. "I gotta get out there somehow. I need to fill these orders."

"Fuck." He took a few more hits off of his foil and went back to his window.

Leaning over the chaotic coffee table, she started making a few more lines. She had hoped that a few hits of speed might calm him down, but all he could do for the rest of her stay was look out of the small sliver between the curtain and the window.

Call

"Hello?"

"Hey Sue."

"Yes?"

"It's Yuri."

A long pause. "Hey."

"How's it goin'?"

"Can I call you back? I can't stay on the phone right now."

"Yeah."

"'Kay."

Sue hung up.

He put down the phone.

Lying on his mattress and looking across the floor, he resumed trying to get his mind to go blank, but he couldn't stop his churning thoughts.

He hadn't heard from Sue in more than two weeks, despite having left several messages on her answering machine. He decided to wait a few more days before calling her again. The strategy had worked, at least as far as finally getting her to personally answer the phone.

Turning around to lie on his stomach, he pressed his crossed arms into his pillow. He was trying to convince the muscles on his back to loosen up. He thought about trying to save money for a new mattress.

Trying to listen to his body, he could not feel his stomach, only the skin that was stretched out over his gut. His torso felt fine, yet his arms and legs were tingling with aches and pains. His head was heavy, as if it were a stone weight, even though the rest of his body felt hollow.

He managed to force himself to stand up. He did not want to feel the hollow parts of himself.

Gathering his backpack, he started out the door.

There was a decent wind pushing him in the streets. He had left the house without thinking about where he was going. His natural inclination was to go to the main drag. He would head for Telegraph and hang out in one of his usual haunts.

As he walked, he mused on one of his new plans. He was thinking of buying or borrowing a guitar so that he could try his hand at writing songs again. Perhaps he could even practice enough to where he would get in on a band. It was a rather strange thought for him to harbor. He had always dabbled in playing and writing music, that is until the last few years of his addiction when he hardly ever did anything with music at all.

His old girlfriend Skye and his old roommate Preston had both been in bands. He remembered how Skye had virtually cut him off when she was suddenly recruited to play in the Dynamite Chicks, staying in her room for hours on end to practice playing bass. She had even written a couple of new songs for them, as a way of trying to stay in the group.

Preston had always been practicing his guitar, to the point where the rest of the housemates had forced him to keep his guitar amp turned off for the better part of the day. Preston used to sit in the front room, quietly plunking on his guitar, even when he was watching television or was hanging out with friends.

A few blocks before Telegraph, he saw a crowd, right at the top of the drag. Telegraph was usually crowded, but this was an unusual concentration of people.

Further along the street, he saw that it was a street fair. Occasionally the city would block off the main blocks of Telegraph and set up a market. There were always table sellers on Telegraph, selling pottery and jewelry and various other kinds of artwork. During the street fairs there were always a lot more sellers. There might be one or two street performers, but usually it was just people selling their wares.

Making his way into the crowd, he walked down the street behind the tables so he could move more quickly. He started getting looks from some of the sellers and a security guard, so he made his way back to the sidewalk.

Passing by the Med, he decided he would make his way to the end of Telegraph. Maneuvering his way through the crowd, that's when he saw her. It was Linda from NA. She was with a couple of other twelve steppers whom he recognized, even though he could not remember their names.

"Hey Linda," said Yuri as he sauntered by.

Linda's friends glanced at him. Linda kept her eyes down, looking at the table.

She didn't say anything.

He had slowed down. He could tell by Linda's expression that she had heard him, but for some reason she was not responding.

Looking away from Linda, he kept walking.

Floor

Looking around her hardwood floor, she observed the scuff lines, patches of faded wood here and there, marked up and marred by the history of furniture and feet of tenants past.

If she looked at one part of the floor for very long, the lines would start to waver, and the boards would seem to move, slowly undulating and slithering, like a breathing snake. But she never kept her eyes fixed for very long. She was looking for bits of white.

She had finished up the principal amount of her own personal stash just a day before. She had enough left for maintenance lines and had been riding a three-day crystal clear high. She made several runs back and forth from Riff Raff's, delivering to Chasey and Linette, two times apiece in the last three days.

It was an obscure search. She had corralled all of the stray grains on her baking sheet and snorted them up just for kicks, and now she wandered about the floor.

She was also well aware that searching for random bits of white specks was usually the bait of hardcore tweakers. But Skye had no need to search the floor for a supply. She still had at least half a gram of good clean speed. She was thinking about a possible bust. A thin layer of speed residue on her floor might be all that was needed to get her some jail time.

Turning to the base of the far wall, she closed her eyes.

Taking in a few breaths, she let her mind go blank.

She tried to remember when she had last eaten. A cold wave went over her.

Looking at her phone and shuffling her feet around, she thought about calling Preston. She was still wide awake. Perhaps she should try and reach out to him again.

She began to feel dizzy. Slowly lowering herself onto her futon.

Closing her eyes, she was grateful that she had drawn the curtains.

Her mind was going blank, as her arms and legs started sinking into her futon.

It was not long, as Skye fluttered between wakefulness and sleep, when she suddenly started back to her senses.

She sat up quickly, turning her head around and looking at the floor.

She was looking for pieces of white.

Coffee

"I really shouldn't be talking to you about this."

"Well..."

"You should really be talking to your sponsor."

Glancing out of the window was his only reaction. He had taken a table by the window in the cafe where Sue had agreed to meet him. It was a place on the other side of the college campus, far from the main drag where they usually met.

The cafe was surrounded by placid white walls and lightly colored trim, with cross-hatching white trestles separating the various seating arrangements outside. It was filled with college types, either studiously going over their homework or loudly talking among themselves, presumably to let the surrounding populace hear their impressive expertise on various academic subjects.

The place was giving Yuri a headache.

"I don't have one," he said finally.

"What?"

"I don't have a sponsor right now."

"No?"

"Well, not really. I suppose Holt is still technically my temporary sponsor, but I haven't talked to him in weeks."

Sue gingerly sipped her coffee.

"I had a sponsor," he continued. "But he really wasn't working out."

"Did you talk to him about that?"

"No. I just stopped calling him."

"You should really be talking to a guy about all of this."

"What?"

"You should talk to a guy in the program about this."

He looked right at her. "Sue, I just wanted to hang out. That's all. I didn't ask you to talk to me about the program."

"Sure. But are you going to start going back to the meetings?"

"I might go once in a while, but at this point I don't think I would go as often as I had been before."

Sue looked around the cafe.

"I can't believe I did it," blurted Yuri.

"What? Can't believe what?"

"That I actually kicked that stuff. Once somebody asked me why I quit. And I had to think about it. I couldn't really answer him, because I couldn't think of any one reason. I had too many fucked up things happen to me too quickly, and I was all washed out. I think, movin' out here, getting out of San Francisco, had a lot to do with it."

"What makes you say that?" she asked in a serious tone.

"Because all of the junk is out there. The only thing I run into out here is hard booze and speed, an' I know I can always turn that stuff down. If I had stayed in the city I would've gone back, with or without any a' this NA crap."

Even though he wasn't looking directly at Sue anymore, he could still see her narrowing eyes and souring mouth. "It's not just the location," continued Yuri. "I mean, getting my place was a big change too. It's small, and it's really just a shack, and it costs next to nothing, but it's clean and it's nice, and it convinces me that I can make a much better life for myself out there. I don't want to get somethin' really fancy or extravagant. I just think that I can get my own decent little place, a nice clean place to live in by myself."

"You won't stay clean if you don't stay in NA."

"What?"

She looked up. "You won't get any of those things if you don't stay in NA and work your program."

"What the hell are you talking about?"

"Everything you just told me, those dreams of yours, staying clean, you won't get any of it if you don't stay in the program"

"I don't think I get you."

"You've gotten this far because of the program. You won't stay clean unless you stick with the program."

Sitting back in his chair and picking up his coffee, he didn't say what he wanted to say, but he could not think of anything else to talk about.

Sue had fallen silent. She was looking down at her coffee with her arms folded.

Self Inflicted

"You buying again already?"

"Yup."

"All those people goin' on a binge?"

"Yeah. Some of my friends got a few new tweakers hangin' on."

Riff Raff leaned over his phone. "I might have ta' make a run out to my supplier. I just finished a weekend's worth a' business."

"I got th' cold cash right now."

"Yeah, I know. That's not it. I'm just low an' burnt."

The lines in his face were looking deeper and darker than usual. He had just been through his own weekend binge. Skye was still flying high off of a large supply of her own, but she could feel the brunt of her own oncoming burnout deep down inside her head and her skin.

There was also the faint twinge of guilt. She knew she was slightly misleading him, as her need for new supplies was not that urgent. She did have a request from Chasey about grabbing another gram, but in truth she really just wanted an eight ball for herself so she could isolate with her own high and hibernate for a few days.

"I jus' gotta cool it once in a while, y'know," continued a graveled Riff Raff. "I don't wanna get too thin, and start punching holes up there, y'know. I'm gonna end up like Preston or some shit."

"Preston got too fucked up because he smokes it all the time."

"Yeah, I know."

He kept looking over his coffee table, as if he couldn't find his phone.

"I can drive if I have to," she suggested. "I'm doin' pretty good. I didn't get too fucked up over the weekend."

"Mm. I gotta think about it."

Skye searched his eyes and assumed that he was probably too burnt to make the trip himself.

He finally stood up. "I'll be right back."

Going into his room, he shut the door behind him.

Looking across the room, she spaced out on the wall, feeling a shallow buzz going through her head. Her chest became tight as she tried not to get too anxious about making a score.

She sat still, becoming distracted by the silent room.

Slowly turning her head, she realized she was all alone in Riff Raff's living room for the first time. There had always been other people hanging about every time she had been over: other dealers, other tweaks, and musicians who happened to stop by just to jam.

She heard a creak and a light tick from the kitchen. Perhaps it was Riff Raff's girlfriend. Skye had only seen her about two or three times. She would always wander quickly into the room and then quickly scurry out. Skye could not remember having ever talked to her.

She spread her arms apart and started sinking into the familiar old couch, finally beginning to relax.

The door opened. Riff Raff came out.

"Well, that cuts it," he said with a slight grin. "Another one a' my guys needs a' new supply as well."

"Yeah?"

"I can't turn down half an ounce worth a supply. 'Sides, I might as well get some a' my own goin' on as well." He looked right at her. "I'm gonna need you to drive me out there though."

"Okay."

Supply

Riff Raff carefully explained all of the machinations of the deal to Skye as she drove deeper into the East Bay. He was telling her while she drove because he did not want to keep his supplier waiting any longer than he had to, an important point of the deal which he emphasized.

"You drive me up there, and you come with me into the house. You can't wait in the car. But when you get inside you have to wait in the front room. Don't come in any further than that. Just have a seat on the couch and talk to the girl in the front. She'll probably have a beer for you or somethin'."

Skye concentrated on the rows of exits signs as they came off of the Bay Bridge. Riff Raff continued to explain the finer points of their mission.

"There's a small trailer out in the yard, on the left side of the yard as we go in. Somebody may be lookin' at us from the trailer. If they are, don't turn and look at it. Try not to look toward the trailer at all. An' there may be some guy lookin' at us from the kitchen. If there is, don't look over there neither."

"Yeah."

"You got it?"

"So far. Is there anythin' else I need to know?"

"Don't look at the trailer or the kitchen. I'm gonna go in and do the deal, but then I'm gonna come out and sit down next to you on the couch. I'll hang out an' talk for a bit after I come out so it looks like we just came over to visit."

"Okay."

"I'll hang out with you in front for like, fifteen minutes or so. I told him I trust you, that you're one a' my homies, but he's still gonna be kinda suspicious since you're new."

He instructed her to drive out to El Sobrante, a North Bay working class suburb. It was a somewhat long drive, and she was wondering how her bloodstream was going to hold up. She had done a line before they left, yet she still tried to feel her blood's thickness.

Driving just past the Berkeley exits, they had not run into the feared traffic jam that occurred all too often on the crowded Bay Area freeways. Riff Raff had been trying to find a radio station he liked for the past fifteen minutes when he directed Skye to take a freeway exit into a low and flat working class town that lay at the base of a large hillside. The town was wide and low, sporting almost no buildings over two or three stories, with row after row of houses.

They took the fairly crowded main street for some time, driving several miles, and then turned onto a wide road that was sparsely populated with traffic.

They stayed on course, driving a long, lonely, and empty thoroughfare. The traffic was ever lighter, and the houses were getting fewer and farther apart. Riff Raff had stopped talking, outside of giving directions.

"Take your next right and then park."

The next road was a thin concrete trail, looking more like a long driveway than a street.

"Here?" pointed an uncertain Skye as she slowed down the car.

"Yeah yeah yeah."

Skye could feel his nerves jump as she was slowing down. She brought the car to a more respectable speed and continued down the street for a good fifty feet, finally bringing the car onto a dirt sideway.

"Follow me. Just be cool an' mellow," he said as he got out of the car.

There were three houses in their general vicinity, all with long walkways and gangs of trees and bushes around them. He crossed the road with Skye walking after him, trying to stay more or less by his side.

They walked up to a house shielded by tall, untrimmed hedges and a few tall trees. Behind a leafy wall was a long stone path leading up to a long and low plain wooden house on a slightly sloping hillside. On each side of the stone path was a freshly cut lawn, which was the only cared-for part of the yard. As they walked up the path, she saw the aforementioned trailer. It was small and slightly dilapidated. She tried to keep her barely wandering eyes ahead, watching the house up ahead.

The house was covered with fading paint, and all of the windows were covered up with old and graying blinds. But there was also a distinct lack of clutter that usually pervaded tweaker dwellings, and the freshly cut lawn pulled her skin the wrong way.

Walking up to the door, Riff Raff rang the bell. He turned and looked to Skye, raising a flat hand. The door opened up almost immediately.

"Hi!" greeted a saccharine, high pitched voice. He put a hand on Skye's shoulder and guided her inside the house.

A young and thin woman had answered the door. She was wearing an Aerosmith t-shirt and a forced smile, which was the only part of her face one could see since her feathered hair was draping over most of the upper half of her head.

"Hey Lou," greeted Riff Raff. "How's it goin'?"

"Jay's in the back," said the woman as she closed the door.

"Thanks." Riff Raff nodded to Skye and then walked into the back.

The woman's forced smile melted into a more natural grin. Skye could see more of her face as she lifted her head.

"Y'wanna beer?" asked the skinny woman.

"Sure."

The woman led her over to a few black leather couches that were on either side of a glass coffee table. "I'm Lou. That's short for Louise."

"Okay."

"Just so you don' think I'm a guy. I ain't got no tits an' no ass, so sometimes people get confused."

Skye looked around as Lou quickly ducked out of the room. The couches looked rather new. She took note that the room was fairly free of clutter.

Skye deliberately chose to sit on the couch facing the door and the window. The living room was oblong, running the full length of the front of the house. Aside from the couches and coffee table, there was an empty fireplace at one end of the living room, and a set of large wooden shelves on the other end which contained some very complex looking stereo equipment. A few well placed lamps kept the couch and coffee table area well lit, but there was enough darkness to make the air sit still and thick.

Lou came back with a couple of tall Sapporos. She handed one of the Sapporos to Skye and sat down right across from her.

"So how's it goin'?" asked Lou in a curious voice as she quickly opened her beer.

"A'right."

"You known Steve long?"

"Huh?"

"Steve. Oh! I mean Riff Raff!" she laughed. "Don't tell him I told you his real name."

"Sure."

Skye eyed the table. She expected to see a snorting stone, or some empty pen tops. There were only a few auto magazines and an empty ashtray.

Lou leaned towards Skye. "What was your name?" she asked

between her teeth.

"Skye."

"Yeah," smiled Lou as she casually leaned back. "So how long you known Riff?"

"Oh man, it seems like I've known him forever."

"Hm. You're from San Francisco, right?"

"Uh huh. Over in the Mission."

Lou stood up and walked over to the stereo. "What you do over there?"

"Well, I was workin' in a video store, but I ain't workin' there right now."

"You quit?" echoed Lou's voice from the far end of the room as she bent over the stereo.

"Yeah. I jus' got tired of workin' there."

A blast of Alice Cooper emanated from various speakers throughout the living room.

"Welcome, to my nightmare…"

"You lookin' for another job?"

"Yeah, but jus' somethin' part time, I guess. What do you do for a living?"

"How was the drive over here?" asked Lou with her now familiar grin as she sat back down.

"What?"

"Was it crowded on the freeway?"

"Not really." Skye glanced down at the coffee table, trying to see if she could spot any white grains on the tinted glass surface.

"What kind of job are you lookin' for?" asked Lou.

"You got any Aerosmith?"

"What?" replied Lou, as if she had been caught off guard.

"You got any Aerosmith over at that stereo?"

Lou fixed her eyes. "Why are you asking me about Aerosmith?"

"Because of your shirt."

"What?"

"Your shirt," said Skye as she pointed at her t-shirt.

"What the fuck are you talking about?" she growled, clenching her teeth.

"You're wearing an Aerosmith t-shirt."

Lou quickly looked down at her shirt. "Oh, right!" she laughed.

Skye leaned back as Lou sipped her beer. Lou was still sitting cross legged, rocking back and forth a few times before looking at her again. "What kind of job are you looking for?" she asked again.

Skye took a long drag off of her beer and then let out a breath, sinking deeper into the couch.

"Skye."

"I already told you."

"You didn't tell me what kind of job you were looking for," exacted Lou.

"Yeah I did, part time. Somethin' like retail."

Lou tightened her grip on her beer bottle. Skye searched Lou's hair to see if she could find her eyes.

A door opened. Riff Raff came out with a backpack slung over his shoulder. Skye stood up.

"Wassup Riff?" said Skye.

Riff Raff was walking towards the front door. "Hey Lou, how it be?"

Skye watched Lou from the corner of her eye. Lou's lips were pressed together as she kept watching Skye. Standing up, Lou kept her eyes on Skye.

Riff Raff turned to Skye. "Y'ready to go?".

"Yeah."

Skye turned so she was looking directly at Lou. "Thanks for th' beer."

Riff Raff headed for the door. As Skye started following him, Lou skittered up and was walking right behind Skye. Skye instinctively clenched her fists.

Riff Raff turned around and doubled back behind Skye, cutting off Lou.

"You sayin' what to Jenner?" asked Riff Raff pointedly. "You be like, sayin' okay, hey?"

Lou stood close to Riff Raff, so close that her thin nose, which finally started poking through her hair, was almost touching his chest.

"You know, 'cause I was like just going to, y'know, go say hey to Dan, you know, over by the Greeley an' everythin'." Lou stood her ground as she looked right at Riff Raff. "It's going on over there, you know? Like with Dan and Greeley and all?"

Riff Raff reached back and tapped Skye on her arm. Skye walked out of the house.

Standing on the wooden plank porch, she still had her hand on the door. Riff Raff was still talking to Lou as Skye obeyed her instincts and closed the door.

The scent of cut grass wafted in front of her. The tall bushes stood at attention, with the off-white camper still standing guard. She was trying to decide if she should wait on the porch or go back to the car. She could still hear Riff Raff talking to Lou. She had not heard Lou say anything back.

Skye decided that Riff Raff would not have prompted her outside if they weren't about to leave. She started walking towards the car.

The air was still as she walked gingerly across the lawn, trying to look nonchalant. She could feel the wind pulling her back towards the house, towards the trailer. She watched the ground, walking, pacing, step, step, step, watching her boots mark the ground.

Bringing up her head, she turned and glanced at the off-white trailer.

Suddenly snapping her head away from the trailer, she only saw him in a flash. Thin, hewn, and rough, with two stark eyes, opened wide, with dark irises fixed on her. She felt a sting in her shoulder. She reigned in her legs so she would not walk too fast, her heart beating in her head and her throat.

Getting into the car, she got out the keys. She kept her nose down and held back the urge to turn around and see if Riff Raff was coming.

She nearly jumped when someone thumped up against the passenger door.

Riff Raff opened the door and climbed in.

"Don't worry about Lou," said Riff Raff. "She's just a fuckin' tweaked out little spaz."

"Yeah, I noticed."

Marooned

Sitting cross legged on his mattress, he had spent the last hour cleaning up his room and the kitchen. Now he was thumbing through his small paper phone book, reviewing all of the handwritten numbers.

Lying down on his stomach, he hovered over his phone book with a black pen. A meeting schedule was still folded up in the back of the phone book. He took it out and looked over the listings.

He was tempted to start going back to the meetings. He had a strong desire to be around people who were clean. But he did not think that he would really be able to break into any of the circles. They would stand with their backs to him and block him out.

Putting aside the meeting schedule, he went back to his personal phone book. He decided that he needed to cross out some of the numbers.

There was Dex, and Sweezy. He had long given up any hope of revitalizing any kind of friendship with either one of them, at least anytime in the near future.

He decided to cross them out of the book..

He debated whether or not to cross out Sue's number. He decided he should probably keep her number, just in case he ran into any of their contacts. The other twelve steppers, Holt and Tilden and the rest, there was no real need to keep their numbers in his book.

Then there was Rebar. He knew him too well to cross him out.

He would keep Sue's number, to get in touch with the clean and sober side. He would keep Rebar's number, to keep in touch with the users side.

Everyone else was expendable.

There were a few other random numbers he had collected during his time in the East Bay. They were numbers he had collected when he was getting to know the East Bay scene, while he was still drinking and smoking the occasional reefer. Then there were the numbers he had collected at twelve step meetings when he was getting into the East Bay NA scene. They were numbers of friends of friends and of acquaintances and numbers for people he had barely known at all. Only a few of those numbers had ever been used even once.

It dawned on him that there were two other people in his phone book whom he could still call: Zata and Trash.

Turning on his side, he thumbed to the last pages. There was Zata's number.

Eyeing his phone, he felt there was something off about calling Zata. He also felt that there was something off about calling Trash.

But they were the only ones left.

Zata

It was rather odd, walking down Telegraph with the statuesque Zata. At least it was odd for him since it was in the daytime. They had only previously gone out in public at night.

They were coming up on the Med.

"Did you want to grab a coffee?" asked Zata.

"I don't know if I want to go there."

"How about the Wall?"

"I don't know about that place either."

Zata tilted her head. "Let's just stop in the Med. I'm dying for a cup of coffee."

They stopped in the street, standing just outside of the cafe. Yuri was wringing his hands.

"What?" she asked. "What is it?"

"Well, it's just that the last time I was there, Holt and a bunch of other guys from the program were in there."

"Okay."

"They weren't very friendly."

Zata shrugged. "So what?"

Yuri shrugged back. "It was kind of uncomfortable for me."

"Fuck 'em," she replied with a wave of her hand. "Holt is a prick anyways. I don't give a fuck. I'm not going to let some goon stop me from goin' where I want to go."

"All right."

Walking in, he got in line, standing right before Zata. He looked over the large chalkboard menu, even though he already knew what he wanted to order. The Med was not too terribly crowded, only a couple of old denizens, some college students, and a few gutter punks.

Getting their coffee, Zata led Yuri over to the table by the window. Sitting down, he watched the streams of people making their way back and forth along the crowded street.

"If you watch long enough, you see the same people going back the way they came," said Yuri.

"Yeah, I know. Sometimes you see someone walk back and forth three or four times."

He turned his coffee cup on the table and kept watching the street. "I'm always looking out for people I know."

"Like Holt and his gang?"

"That was kind of embarrassing."

"What?"

"Telling you I didn't want to come in here because those guys might be in here."

"Why is it embarrassing?"

"You're right. I shouldn't let it get to me, whether they're in here or not."

"Hey, there's nothing wrong with wanting to avoid those assholes. I completely understand if you don't want to put up with them."

"I guess it's kind of like Sweezy an' Dex."

"Who's Dex?"

"A friend of mine. I used to hang out with him and Sweezy all of the time, at least when I first got out here."

"Along with that Rebar fellow."

He was impressed that she had remembered. "We were all from the city. We all came over here for one reason or another. We just found each other after a while and started hanging out."

"And you don't anymore."

"Naw. They all pretty much stopped talking to me when I went sober."

"Your using friends. They stopped hanging out with you because you weren't using anymore."

"It wasn't because I stopped using dope. They never had a problem with that. It was the drinking. They dropped me when I stopped drinking."

Folding her arms, Zata leaned on the table top, bringing herself closer to Yuri. "It is strange, that people you knew as friends need you to keep abusing yourself in order for them to accept you."

"I never thought about it that way."

"Well, why do you think they stopped hanging out with you?"

"I knew it had something to do with my getting sober. I dunno. I guess, I was just changing too much for them. I know they don't have an easy time dealing with clean and sober types."

"Like those twelve steppers?"

He waited a moment. "Yeah."

"It's amazing what people want out of their friends."

"I guess."

"I got cut off from my own group of people as well," said Zata. "I stopped smoking dope, I stopped drinking liquor, I stopped slamming and smoking heroin, I stopped snorting speed. I stopped doing all of that garbage. I did all of that, and all of these people that I hung out with all of the time, they just stopped talking to me. They stopped calling me, they wouldn't give me the time of day." She leaned in closer. "I'd run into some of them every now and then. I'd ask them why they haven't called, or why they don't ask me to hang out no more. 'We don't invite you along because everyone knows you're trying to stay clean' they'd say. That's what they would tell me, but I knew it was a lie. They didn't want to be around me anymore because I wasn't using. They couldn't stand the idea of being around someone who didn't at least drink or smoke dope. They could handle it if all I did was stop using the heroin and speed. It was the not drinking that really freaked them out."

"No shit."

She looked down at the table. "I don't usually tell people about my conflict with Holt."

"I guess. I was assuming that it had something to do with the program."

"Like what?"

"Like he probably didn't think you were twelve step enough or something like that."

"That's part of it."

"I didn't know what it was all about before, but after you talked to me in the warehouse, I figured it had to be something like that."

"Kind of. Can you keep this stuff between you and me?" She was looking right at Yuri.

"Yeah, I can."

"It's not that a big deal. It's just that I don't go around telling everyone these kinds of things."

"Sure," he replied uncertainly.

"Our conflict goes back to the days when we were using."

"You used to get wasted with Holt?'

"More or less. We ran around a lot of the same circles. Holt was telling some people some of his war stories, about how much dope he was using, and about his clean time, an' I more or less called him on it."

"Called him on what?"

"Some of the stories he was tellin' we're straight up bullshit. There was some things that had a bit of truth to them, but he was goin' on about how much crank he slammed an' how much junk he got people into. He was exaggerating a lot. I told a few people that. He never slammed no goddamn eight ball, especially not all at once. He was kind of pissed that I was talking about it."

"You told other people he was making that stuff up?"

"I just mentioned it to a few friends of mine, but it got around pretty quickly. I shoulda' known that was going to happen, but I wasn't really thinking when I told them."

"Hm."

"And then he kept going on about his clean time, an' that's when I confronted him again."

"What about his clean time? He's got like, something like seven years, right?"

"No, he doesn't."

"No shit?"

Zata folded her arms tighter. "Y'see, I got clean before he did, more than a year before he got himself clean."

"Yeah?"

"Shortly after I had gone full on clean an' sober, he quit using crank an' dope an' other stuff, but he kept drinking. Finally, he got off of booze and got into the program."

"Okay."

"I mean, he really got into the program. He was all on about the steps and the traditions, and the whole sponsorship deal, just a few weeks after he was there."

"He still does that."

"Oh yeah. An' he was always tellin' everyone about his clean time, way more than he does now. When he got clean, he was tellin' people how much time he had. I had like, eighteen more months clean time than he did at the time he got clean."

"Okay."

"But a few months later, he's talking to someone about his clean time, an' I thought it sounded kinda weird. 'Cause when he told them how much time he had been clean, it was only like fourteen or fifteen less months than me. Then a few more months go by, and he's got about thirteen months less clean time than I do. It isn't too long before I hear him bragging about his clean time, but now I only have a year more clean time than he does. It's goin' on for a while. Before you know it, he's tellin' someone else about his clean time an' I only got ten more months clean time than he does. Later on, I only have six more months. Then it gets to three, then only two more months, and then I hear him telling a whole room full of people that he has five years clean time, which was just as much clean time as I had at the time."

"No shit!"

"An' get this, only a few more months after that he's tellin' someone about his clean time, and he had more clean time than me! And I got clean and sober way before he did."

"Fuck."

"So I confronted him about it. I told him that there was no way he could have more clean time than me, and that he knew it."

"What did he do?"

"He went off on about how I wasn't really in the program, and that I didn't follow the steps, and that I was going to relapse if I didn't stop screwing around and get into the program. You know the drill. You've heard it all before."

"What about his clean time?"

"What about it?"

"Did he change it, once you pointed out?"

"No. His time stopped increasing exponentially. He picked out a date that coincided with his current clean time, and he's been sticking to it ever since."

"Damn. Shouldn't you have you told anyone else about this?"

"Only a few people. I'm pretty careful about it, though I sometimes kinda' wish it would get out more."

"So that's why he can't stand you?"

"Well, that and something else."

"There's more?" asked Yuri, surprised.

"Yeah. He tried hitting on me once when he was really drunk."

"Oh man."

"He got way too aggressive and I laid him out."

"What?"

"I decked him."

He thought about it for a moment. "You mean..."

"I punched him in the face and he went crashing to the floor."

"Fuck."

"Yeah."

"You sound like my ex Skye."

"How's that?"

"She had a right hook like a freight train. I saw her clean some guys clock on the On Broadway once. It was brutal."

"Nice. You like the fiery type, huh?"

Yuri grasped his coffee cup with both of his hands.

Zata watched him for a few moments.

"I don't even know what the fuck I'm doing here," he said with trembling arms.

"Just keep trying to find yourself."

"That sounds really tacky."

"Why?"

"It sounds like a line from an after school special."

"Yeah, it does. It's like some of those NA sayings and slogans that drive you up the wall." Zata leaned in closer. "But it's true. That's why you get clean, so you don't keep washing yourself out of yourself."

Raising her hand, she gently put her palm on his cheek.

"You'll be alright," she said. "Find your program. Don't kid yourself, and don't go into denial, but find out what works for you. Don't let some fool tell you what works for you."

A shiver went through Yuri.

His mind went cold.

His body became hot.

VI

Crash Shadow

The Route

"Traffic was a bitch today," grumbled Skye.

"No shit."

"It usually isn't this bad."

Veering to the right, she kept driving towards El Sobrante's main road, breathing a sigh of relief when she saw that the traffic was beginning to lighten up.

Riff Raff continued lecturing her with his theories and thoughts on the art of pornographic movie production as she guided Preston's car down the long and familiar suburban roads. She would always notice the way the houses, cars, and people would thin out as they got closer and closer to the supplier's place.

"I'm always tempted to look into that trailer," she said as she parked the car.

"Don't."

"I know, I know. I won't."

He was still chatting away as they walked up the path.

"Skye! What the fuck."

"Hey Lou. Where's my beer?"

"I thought you were supposed to bring some," she replied seriously.

"What?"

Lou could not suppress a smile.

"Bitch," smiled Skye as she playfully punched Lou in the shoulder.

"Come on you two, mix it up!" said Riff Raff. "I want to see a cat fight."

They did not joke around for long. Riff Raff made his way into the back and Lou brought out the traditional Saporros. Lou started up the stereo and sat down across from Skye.

"You people are back here already," said Lou.

"Yeah."

"You dirtbags. What do you do with all of that stuff?"

"Believe me, our friends are all too willing to help us out with that."

"Sure, we all got friends like that."

"Well, they usually help us out."

"Usually?"

Skye leaned back on the couch. "I haven't heard from one a' my friends in a few weeks."

"Yeah?"

"I dunno. I guess, Maybe she just needed a break. She'd been getting into it pretty heavy. She was doin' a lot of go-betweening though."

"They always wanted to talk to her right? After she talked to you?"

"Yeah. All the time."

"Especially on the weekends."

"Yeah," sighed Skye as she sunk further into the couch. She was trying to think of a new subject. The unwritten rule of the supplier's house was that you were not to do too much talking about the business in the front room.

Skye had added an extra teen onto her order, in addition to her supply and Chasey's supply and Paul's supply. She wanted to make sure she was well stocked with extra speed when Linette popped up again. For the last several months, Linette had become more and more erratic, calling at odd hours, saying inappropriate things over the phone, and showing up very late.

She suspected that Linette might have been getting deep into another scene. Perhaps she had been drinking too much, or smoking too much dope.

"We got tickets to ZZ Top."

"Hm?"

"ZZ Top. We had to shell out for them. The first show sold out in something like, an hour."

"Hm."

Lou sat forward. "Don't you cap on ZZ Top!"

"I wasn't."

"Bullshit," she smiled. "I know you like alla' them sketched out lookin' punks and weirdos like Danzig an' stuff.

"I don't listen to Danzig."

"Yeah, sure you don't."

"An' like there ain't any sketched out people at a ZZ Top show," said Skye as she tilted her beer bottle for emphasis.

"Sure there is, but they ain't those inner city ghouls."

"So? I like inner city ghouls."

"You is one!"

"Right!"

The door opened. Riff Raff came back out with his backpack. "Did you guys fight yet?"

"Naw. Skye's too chicken."

"I just held back because I didn't want her to get hurt."

"See you guys," said Lou as they made for the door.

They leisurely walked back to the car as the front door shut behind them. Skye thought about traffic, if it was going to be heavy on the way back. She also wondered if Riff Raff would continue his ruminations on porn, and she also thought about Chasey, and whether or not she wanted to start doing business with Paul's friend Rachel.

She might do business with a new go-between, if only she could find out what had happened to Linette.

Getting into the car, she tried not to think about so many things at once.

Burnout

The weight of her thermos would always remind her to keep hydrated. The water would slosh around, making her backpack bob back and forth as she walked towards Chasey's place.

She made her traditional stop at the corner store, just down the street from her apartment building. She bought a couple of fruit and granola bars. She was trying to avoid the traditional candy bars and pastries that she was tempted to get when she was strung out.

She brought Chasey her largest order yet, an entire quarter ounce. She also had a teen for Paul. That, along with the eight she got for herself and the spare teen for Linette meant she was in possession of half an ounce of speed, more than she had ever possessed at one time.

Walking along Valencia, her legs and arms felt light from the steady stream of buzzing electricity. The air was still and cool. The sun was setting. Looking through the long shadows, she tried to avoid the sharp rays of light.

It took a few buzzes at the apartment door to get Chasey to respond. She was walking up the stairs just as Chasey opened the door.

"What took you so long?" asked Skye. "You knew I was coming."

"I hadda check out th' window to see who it was," drawled Chasey as she closed the door behind her.

"Got any beer?"

"You know I do. In the fridge."

Grabbing a Red Hook from the fridge, she realized that the new batch of crank was fairly strong and working her nerves a little more than usual.

"I got some killer shit this time," said Skye as she carefully stepped around the dark living room.

"That's cool."

Chasey lit a cigarette and sat down in the easy chair. She curled her legs up against herself.

"Ain't Paul supposed to be here?"

Chasey shook her head. "He ain't gonna be back from his job site for another couple a' hours. You can meet him here later if you like, or you can give me the stuff to give him."

Taking Chasey's supply out of her backpack, she was hoping that the idea of leaving Paul's supply with Chasey would slip by unnoticed.

"Fuckin a'," exclaimed Chasey in a hushed voice.

"It's a lot of stuff." She carefully put the baggies down. "I brought my scale so you can weigh out your friend's stuff."

"Fuckit. I'd like to keep all that shit."

"No you wouldn't."

"You put my teen in a separate baggie, right?"

"Yup. Those two are teens. You can jus' pick one."

"The bigger one right?"

Skye sank back into the couch as Chasey fixed up a couple of lines from her newly acquired stash. Tilting back her beer, she felt the warm liquor heat up her chest. She guided her senses, through her arms, through her legs, and concentrated on the tilt of her head, trying to see how it was holding up.

Chasey tapped Skye's shoulder. She was holding out the straw for her.

"You gonna wait for Paul?"

"Yeah, sure."

Leaning down towards the mirror, she noticed that Chasey's lines were getting longer.

"You got people comin' over?" asked Skye.

"Yeah. Later. I have to call them."

"Ain't they waiting for their stuff?"

"Feh. They haven't even paid me yet. I'm not doing advanced orders just yet."

"Hey, speaking of fellow tweaks, have you heard from Linette lately?"

"Nu uh," said Chasey as she bent over her snorting stone again to make some more lines. "I haven't heard from her at all. She was supposed to call me about a week or two ago, or something like that. I never heard from her."

"Damn. What the fuck happened to her?"

"Who knows."

"Was she hittin' the sauce pretty hard?"

"I dunno. Maybe she just wanted a break."

"Yeah."

"Or maybe she went straight."

Skye sat up. "What do you mean?"

"Maybe she went all clean an' sober. You know, became one a' them annoying twelve steppers."

Skye held her beer bottle in front of her, contemplating the idea. "That would be really fucking weird."

"You never know."

"Well, I didn't think she was that burned out."

"It happened to my brother," said Chasey as she sat up. "One day he just decided he didn't wanna smoke no more weed or do no more coke."

"No shit?"

"Yeah. I try to avoid him now. He gives me a lotta shit because he can always tell when I'm strung out."

"Fuckin' a'."

Skye tried to sink further into the couch

The idea that Linette might have gotten clean and sober had never occurred to her.

Home

Chasey kept making lines while they waited. Before too long Skye insisted that they use some of her stash. When Paul arrived he offered her a line as a gratuity for bringing him his supply, but she had already done so many lines that she turned him down.

Back at her place, Skye was going through her inventory. She still had most of her supply, in addition to the teen that she had gotten for Linette.

Her thoughts wandered to the Haight street denizens who made up Linette's customers.

That's when a shudder went through her, a tremor that shook her spine. Perhaps Linette had run into trouble. Linette took far more chances than Chasey or Paul, dealing quarters and dimes in cafes on the drags. Perhaps she had been arrested.

The idea turned her stomach and knotted her shoulders. She was not sure why she had not considered the possibility before.

Perhaps she would have heard about it if she had been caught. But then again Linette might have been holding back, not contacting Skye or Chasey if she were in trouble, so they would not get into trouble as well.

An empty space began moving up through Skye's chest and into her shoulders. Her arms began to feel weak. Kneeling onto her futon, she took out her food and her thermos. The empty feeling went into her legs.

Bending down, she fell onto her arms. She let the weight of her empty body drag her down onto the futon. She looked at a banana, an apple, a granola bar, a thermos full of water, and an eight ball baggie of speed. Her eyes were working only on waning energy.

Falling over on her side, the emptiness expanded throughout her body, making her heavy bones sink through her gelatin flesh, pinning her onto her beaten futon.

Everything went gray.

Shudder

It happened all at once.

No fading, no focusing, no gradual climb back into consciousness. It happened all at once with a violent shudder.

It was a sharp and unpleasant jolt of electricity that went through her, causing all of the muscles in her body to shake.

Sitting up, trying to breath, her chest was constricting, keeping her from taking in air. The muscles in her forearms and shins were vibrating. Quickly sitting up and losing her balance, her head spun around, tilting the room violently as she flailed her arms, trying to regain her balance.

Twisting her body, she realized her legs were caught in her blanket. Turning herself, she put out both hands, propping herself up on the futon, waiting for her head to stop spiraling.

Finally forcing in a breath of air, her racing mind flashed on the walls.

Where am I?

Her bouncing eyes shot to the walls, glancing quickly off of the too-bright windows.

As suddenly as she shook awake, she realized she was in her own room.

She leaned on her arms with her legs still tangled in her blanket.

Catching her breath, her head was still spinning. She was breathing too quickly. She concentrated on her breathing.

Her arms trembled. They did not have the energy to hold her up anymore. Girding her shaking arms as best she could, she slowly lowered herself back down onto the futon.

Now she was lying flat, feeling embarrassed that she did not even recognize her own room when she had shuddered awake. Her ankles were aching from being tangled in the blanket.

A warm wave overtook her. Lying back and getting her bearings, she thought about grabbing the thermos of water. Her forearms were starting to ache.

As her body slowly shuddered still, she could feel her cold and hard skin sticking to her clothes. She knew it was no use trying to look at the clock. She would still not be able to tell how long she had been asleep.

She started pulling at the covers, trying to untangle her feet. Even lifting her arms was a strain, but her ankles were aching too much.

That's when she saw the bag.

"Fuck!"

She had left an entire eight ball of speed out in the open, right next to her bed.

Her shaken muscles were now tense. Quickly standing up and then dropping down to her knees again, her head took a vicious spin. She was too dizzy to stand. Crawling across the floor, she picked up the bag and quickly put it in her dresser.

Her muscles were throbbing. She was gritting her teeth. Getting back to her futon, she slumped down onto her side.

Reaching out with her arms, she took hold of the thermos. Her temples throbbed as she drank the water. Putting down the thermos, she felt a surge of cold, cool energy running through her. Downing more water, she quickly gained enough energy to stand up. Picking up her food, she made her way to the kitchen while trying to ignore the buzzing that was shaking her skull.

Paul

She had forced enough food down her throat that she began to feel somewhat human again. As she walked out of her apartment building, she could feel the food's energy seeping through her. Making herself stop at the corner store she picked up more snacks and a soda.

She had still not heard from Linette, but she was glad that she had bought the extra teen. Paul had called, asking for more supply.

It was more of a hike to get to Paul's lower Haight place than it was to get to Chasey's, but she did not mind the change of pace. She was somewhat concerned by the way Paul had sounded on the phone. From the sound of his voice, he was probably drunk.

Walking against a strong sun, the cool gray clouds were moving in. The wind became stronger as the sun was slowly blotted out by the windswept clouds. The cool rushing air helped wake her up, as it sliced through her hair and rushed through her clothes.

Paul lived in one of the many San Franciscan Victorians that had been converted into flats. It was one of the more run down buildings near Haight and Steiner. By the time she arrived at his place, the sun had been completely blotted out by the rolling clouds and the wind was whipping the leaves and papers through the streets.

She buzzed his flat. Looking around, she saw that Haight street was unusually devoid of people, especially for the time of day.

She whipped her head around as she heard the front door buzz open. Cautiously pushing the door open, she was rather put off that Paul had not talked to her through the intercom first. Walking up the stairwell, she reminded herself to keep finding the right line between caution and paranoia.

The stairwell was dark. She saw the door to Paul's place was partially open. A stream of muffled music was coming from the back of the flat. Looking inside, The living room was flooded with a dull red light. The doorway to the kitchen was dark.

Walking cautiously into the dark commons, she looked at Paul's bedroom door. It was ajar. There was a thin line of yellow light coming from the crack in the doorway.

Clenching her teeth, she waxed against the strong urge to turn around and leave.

"Paul?" she said quietly, yet decisively. "Paul, where the fuck are you?"

"Is anyone there?" she said, more loudly this time.

A voice barked from the hallway. It was a man's voice. She could not make out what he was saying.

Taking a few steps back into the living room, she peered down the dark hallway when a figure suddenly lurched out of the darkness.

"Didn'tcha' hear me?" yarped Paul.

"What?"

"I was yellin'."

"What the fuck dude?"

"Come on in," he slurred as he lurched into his room.

Turning, she closed the door to the flat and made sure it was locked.

Stepping into the room and looking through the dark blue light, Paul had flopped down onto his bed, propping himself up on one arm.

"Paul."

"Kick it!" he yelped as he rocked on his bed.

Closing the door, the air was thick with smoke. She was surprised to see two more people, two young men, sitting in a corner smoking cigarettes. One had a limp red mohawk, and the other had a curly mop of unkempt black hair. They were both shrouded in black clothes.

"What th' fuck Skye? I'm glad you were able to make it."

"Uh huh," she replied flatly.

"What th' fuck," slurred Paul. "Fuckin' kick it, give it up. Get out th' stuff!"

Standing by the door and smelling the smoke, she could tell that they had been smoking speed as well as cigarettes.

"Siddown. Have a smoke," stumbled Paul some more. The duo of youngsters were sitting still, quietly smoking their cigarettes as Paul wobbled onto his side. Skye's eyes widened when she realized there was also a thin and young green haired woman on his bed. She was curling her thin limbs against herself.

"Fuckin' a' Skye, you used to, you know, ain't you ever done that?"

"What?"

"What? What what what. I fuckin' used to have long hair." Paul tried to sit up again, balancing himself on one arm while the other arm was waving around, beer in hand, trying to correct his balance. "I cut it all off, an' then I baked it in a pie." He slumped back down on his side. "I tried to get somebody to eat it, but no one would take a bite. No one wanted my hair pie."

He started laughing, letting out loud hacking noises while doubling over, rolling over from his side onto his stomach. He spilled his beer and kept threatening to tumble completely off of his bed. The young woman was smiling, apparently not at all irritated by Paul's behavior as she casually grinned and puffed on her cigarette.

Still standing quietly with her hands behind her back, Skye leaned against the door. The two floor punks were sitting very still, holding their smoldering and motionless cigarettes.

"Paul," said Skye definitively. "I need to see you in the living room."

Paul was still laughing and hacking. She thought she saw the two young men sitting against the wall jump when she had addressed Paul in her stern and serious voice.

Opening the door, Skye walked out into the dark hallway and shut the door. Walking out into the living room, she could still hear his drunken laughter which threatened to drown out the thudding music.

The living room was sparsely furnished with an old couch and several wooden chairs. The only appliances were a boom box and an old television set. There were a few beer cans and some newspapers strewn about, along with a few tattoo and porn magazines.

Sitting down, she took off her backpack and laid it down beside her, keeping one arm through one of the straps out of habit. Feeling somewhat foolish, she wondered why Paul's phone call had not tipped her off.

Paul's laughing suddenly stopped. The music was still thudding away.

Only the weight of the teen in her backpack and the money it would bring was prompting her to wait. She eyed the kitchen. Perhaps there was a beer in the fridge, one that she would not feel at all guilty about taking.

Standing up, she was about to walk into the kitchen when the red mohawk appeared, standing in the living room doorway.

"Hello," said the Mohican. "Sorry about Paul."

"Sure."

"I'm his brother, Jack."

"Uh huh."

Jack looked around. "D'ya want a beer from the fridge?"

"I was just about to get one," she said flatly.

"I got it." He went into the kitchen and came back with two tall bottles of Heineken. "I'm sorry again."

"Is Paul coming out here?"

"I don't know." The Mohican sat down on one of the wooden chairs. "I think he's on the floor at the moment."

"Mm."

"Well, basically I'm sorry you came out all this way for this."

"Came out this way?"

He fumbled with his beer bottle. "We just came over because our friend Tina's got a crush on Paul."

"Must be some crush," spiked Skye.

"No shit. I don't know why Paul's all fucked up like this. I guess, I dunno. We was all gettin' tanked an' smokin' up his stuff, an' then Tina was gettin' on his case about getting more stuff."

"I see."

"So, I guess, he really likes her. At least, he'd like to do her anyways. I dunno. So, he's gettin' hella' sauced, an' then he lets her talk him into calling you for the stuff."

"What stuff?"

"He told us 'Skye's bringin' th' stuff' after he made the call."

"Great," she soured.

"Listen, I'm cool with Paul. We've been partyin' together since I was thirteen. I know he ain't bein' cool right now. He told us you were jus' a go-between anyways."

She looked right at Jack.

"I got th' money for th' stuff, an it would be cool if you could still sell it, but if this is all too much an' you just wanna split that would be cool with us too."

She usually saw it in the eyes and the lines of a face. She could tell that Jack was still young, yet there was enough there to tell her that he was not a total stranger to getting burned out. The lines in his face were just starting their deep furrows, and the glass over his eyes was just dull enough.

Sitting forward, she looked right at the nervous young man. "You got a surface on you?"

Jack looked around the room. "I guess we could use the top of the television."

"Okay, bring it over."

She got out a bag of her own stash as Jack pushed the large and old television across the floor.

"Let's do a few lines together," said Skye. "An' then I'll sell you the stuff."

"Okay," said Jack uneasily.

Ache

Dark and cold with a strong wind, she wrapped herself up in her Derby jacket as she quickly walked through the lower Haight. She was moving fast to try and keep warm. Her empty limbs were going numb. Noticing the closed cafes and the crowded state of the bars and clubs, she estimated that it must have been somewhere around midnight.

She had gotten all of Paul's young friends wired as Jack had eventually coaxed them out of the room, leaving a drunk Paul collapsed on his floor. She had stayed quite a bit longer than she had planned, talking to the young trio for some time about music, drugs, and the San Francisco scene.

Whipping her head around, she dashed across Market, leaving the semi-trendy depths of Lower Haight for the South of Market scene. Crossing through a few side streets, she emerged on Valencia.

Passing by the Zeitgeist, there was the usual gang of BMW and Triumph bikers milling out front.

A few blocks later she was passing by the club Slowdive. There was a small crowd milling about the entrance to the small corner club.

Someone did catch the corner of her eye as she passed by the small crowd. She was tall and dark, casually standing against a wall as she ran a hand through her long and thin dreadlocks.

Skye did a double take.

It was Mercy.

"Hey Mercy," said Skye as she stopped.

"Hey," replied Mercy through the stilling air. She stood straight as she turned to face Skye.

"What's up?" asked Skye. "Long time no see."

"Yeah. How have you been?"

"I've been okay. Can't complain. Whatcha doin' here?"

"Just checking out this place." Mercy looked at the ground. "I don't go out that much anymore."

"Believe it or not, neither do I," she replied quickly.

"For different reasons, I'm sure."

Skye felt a pinch in her shoulders. "Well, yeah. Sure. I'm out for different reasons. Why not?"

"Yeah, well, good luck." Mercy stood straight. She was turning to go back into the club.

"Hey, wait up a sec'!" beckoned Skye. "You ain't seen Linette lately, have you?"

Mercy stopped and turned to look right at Skye. "What?"

"Linette. I lost touch with her a few weeks ago. I know you guys had broken up, but I was wondering if you had seen her or heard from her lately."

Mercy looked up and down the street and then back at Skye again, "Are you on your way somewhere right now?"

"Just walkin' home. That's all."

Turning her head again, Mercy looked at her feet. "Let's go talk in the park."

"Talk in the park?"

"Not here," she said as she started walking away.

Skye put up a hand to stop her. "What are you talking about? Talk in the park?"

Mercy took in a deep breath. "Lin, went back to her old habit."

"What old habit?"

"Horse."

Skye stood in place.

"I know she was getting into speed to try to get off of horse," continued Mercy. "But she had to go back for a taste, I guess."

"Oh fuck."

"She OD'd a couple of weeks ago. She didn't make it."

"Didn't make it"

"She's passed away."

Skye looked right through Mercy. "Fuck."

"Sorry I had to tell you like this."

Starting from the top of her head, Skye felt herself down to her shoulders, and then through her chest. "Why didn't you tell me before?"

"I thought you already knew. I guess, I shouldn't have thought as much. I didn't really know if you would have found out or not, if I had thought about it."

Skye stood for a moment, looking at her feet. "I gotta go."

"Skye…"

"Save it."

Turning up the street, Skye kept moving, taking the quick route back to her place with the wind still whipping through her clothes and wrapping around her frozen limbs.

"How the fuck does a speed freak OD on horse?"

"Fuck if I know."

Chasey put down the bottles of Red Hook. She had brought out four bottles for herself and Skye.

"How long's it been since you drank hard liquor?" asked Chasey.

"Why?

"'Cause I got some JD in my room."

"Fuck it. Bring it on out."

Chasey was only gone for a moment before she returned with a large bottle of Jack Daniel's. Skye was already halfway through her first Red Hook.

"I'm thinking she wasn't ever really a tweaker," said Chasey as she opened the JD. "Once a junky, always a junky."

"No shit."

Chasey put the Jack Daniel's down on the coffee table and resumed sculpting a few lines of speed. Skye took the whiskey and took a quick swig. She felt a wave go through her head.

"Fuck."

"It's jus' too fuckin' weird," said Chasey. "It's like something Andy Warhol said about death. It's just too abstract. It's not like they're gone, it's like they went somewheres and they just haven't come back yet."

"I guess I didn't even really know her that well."

"We knew her well enough."

Skye sat still for a moment. Taking up the whiskey, she drank a quick shot and chased it with her Red Hook.

"She was kind of like an annoying little sister, in a way," said Chasey as she kept forming lines on her snorting stone. "Y'know, an annoying younger sister who was always buggin' you, but you couldn't help but like her anyways."

"Yeah."

Chasey watched the stone as she pushed the piles of speed back and forth. She kept tipping the baggie, pouring out a little more, making the lines ever longer.

"What did they do with her?" asked Chasey, breaking the stale silence.

"What?"

"What did they do with Linette?"

"What are you talking about?"

Chasey looked up. "Well, is she buried somewheres, or was she cremated?"

"I dunno. I didn't ask Mercy." She took another swig of the whiskey. "I would guess that her family got her. I don't even know where she's from."

"I thought she was from down South, like San Diego, or somethin'."

"Maybe."

Chasey put down the blade. Picking up the straw, she was about to do her line when she stopped herself. She gave the straw to Skye.

"You sure you wanna do alla' this stuff?" asked Chasey.

"Yeah."

Chance

It had been a week since she had done any speed.

Sitting cross-legged on her futon, her bones had the familiar feeling of being hollow and heavy, but there was much more feeling to them as she felt her stretching and aching skin.

She had started a three-day speed binge, using up her entire stash with Chasey, and then getting some second-rate crank from Chasey's friends for the rest of the stretch.

She had enhanced it all with the Jack Daniel's and beer. Looking back on it, she did not actually drink as much as she had originally estimated. She had spent her entire binge at Chasey's place, only emerging for an occasional walk to the corner liquor store. They staged a three day party, with speed-addicted revelers coming and going at all hours of day and night.

Only when she had been truly spent did she finally walk back to her place. The five block walk was one she would not forget. Her shaking legs and trembling arms tortured every step of her homeward journey. Crushing fatigue, along with aching and throbbing pains throughout her body, all accompanied by a consuming nausea, had flared up throughout her body with every step. She did not know how long it had taken her to make the short and simple walk back to her place. When she had finally made it home, she spent quite some time dry heaving in the bathroom. She then passed out in her room for a dead sleep that lasted at least ten hours, by her estimation.

It had now been a week since she had awoken from her long sleep of the dead. Even so, the binge felt as if it had only ended yesterday.

She still could not bring herself to eat very much. She could feel her clothes clinging to her skin. She could also feel her hair brushing against her face, as her dreading hair moved to and fro, twisting and turning as she moved about.

There were new feelings as well. She could feel her feet, with their rough skin from all of the walking she had done. She could feel the stiffness in her ankles and knees. Short shooting pains would go through her gut, running into the bones of her hips.

The entire binge was becoming much starker to her now. All week long the only true craving she ever had was for water.

The shower helped invigorate her, at least to the point where she felt that she could manage a decent walk through the Mission. Walking back into her room, she looked at her phone. It had been unplugged for more than a week. It had rung once, right when she had gotten back from Chasey's. That's when she had ripped its cord out of the wall.

Plugging the phone back in, she half expected it to ring right away. Silence.

Turning the answering machine back on, she went through her clothes.

It had happened all of a sudden. She felt sharp shooting pains in her gut. She was actually hungry.

Her arms and legs were still heavy, but she found just enough energy to head out to find a decent meal.

A surge of energy went through her legs as she walked out of the door.

Her energy waned back and forth as the burden of a chicken enchilada weighed down her stride and her balance.

"Oh man," muttered Skye to herself as she started down Valencia. Her full stomach tilted her mind as well as her body, putting a drag on her thoughts as she tried to remember the last time she had eaten so much food.

Stumbling down the street in indecision, she did not want to go home, yet she did not want to keep walking.

She was trying to remember where all of the cafes were. Her regular hangouts had always been places such as the Zeitgeist or the Vis club, at least before she had become a full-time drug dealer.

A place popped into her head. Beller's cafe was just a block down from Levigate videos. She now had a direction for her newly energized legs.

When she was a block from Levigate she started slowing down. She wondered what would happen if her old supervisor saw her. She had never officially resigned from her Levigate position, having simply stopped going to work.

Cautiously walking by, she glanced sideways through the doorway.

The sight of the dark shelves struck up old memories. The place was strange and familiar all at once. It was as if she were looking into a place for the first time and somehow remembering it all as well. She saw a few people sitting behind the counter, leisurely passing the time. She did not recognize any of them.

Picking up her step, she saw the sign for Beller's cafe down the block. She was now inspired by a new urge for coffee.

She heard it once, but didn't recognize it. She only stopped when she heard it a second time.

"Skye!"

It was Chasey. She had just come out of Levigate.

"Skye! What the fuck? Where've you been?"

"Chasey."

"What's up Skye? I haven't heard from you in hella days!"

"Damn Chase," replied Skye as her shoulders sank from her backpack. "You still workin' here?"

"Fuck yeah! I still need to pay rent. Where've you been?"

"I've jus' been burnin' out." She glanced back at Levigate. "Don't you got to be at work?"

"Hell no. I can take a break. Where you off to? You wanna' go to Bellers?"

"Sure."

Chasey ran back into Levigate for a moment and then they made the walk to Beller's. Chasey bought Skye a large double latte and they made their way to one of the tables in the back of the cafe.

"I know you had a rough time a couple a' weeks ago," said Chasey.

"What makes you say that?"

"Because of Linette. An' I know Paul was gettin' sloppy as well."

Just hearing Linette's name sent a wave over Skye's skin. She had not thought about her at all for the past few days.

"I mean, I guess you was probably gettin' burned out from all the dealin'," continued Chasey. "An' then you get that news about Lin."

"Yeah."

"So you jus' been hangin' low or what? I tried goin' by your place a few times to see if you were there."

"What's up with Paul?" asked Skye, changing the subject.

"Didn't you hear?"

Oh no. thought Skye.

"Not another one," groaned Skye out loud.

"No no! Not that. He's all right. He just got busted."

"What?"

"He got busted for possession, but that's all. They don't have him for dealin'."

"What the fuck happened?"

Chasey leaned on the table, cradling her coffee cup and speaking quietly. "He was hanging out with some young skank, some dipstick that his brother introduced him to. Apparently she was all hella gettin' on his case to find some crank. Now check this. Paul is like, really gettin' into the booze and the dope. He was fuckin' sloppy as all hell, an' he goes out to the Mission and goes into a club and starts askin' all these strangers where he could get some speed, only these people weren't Danzig boys or throckers or nuthin', so the club had him thrown out an' he makes this fucked up scene. He's all yellin' an' kickin' the walls an' threatening the bouncers, so the cops drag him in an' find his stuff. They got him for possession since he only had like, a dime on him."

"Fuck."

"I haven't heard too much more about it. I think Paul's still locked up. I woulda heard from him by now if he had gotten out."

It was going through Skye's mind, how Paul must have been calling her number over and over again, trying to get in touch with her for more supply

Chasey leaned in closer. "So you still gonna take me out to Riff Raff's?"

Skye's back stiffened. "What?"

"You told me about some guy named Riff Raff an' how you was gonna take me over to his place so I could make some a' your runs from now on."

Chasey was speaking in a very tight voice, as if she were anxious. Skye's face went pale. She had no recollection of talking to Chasey about Riff Raff.

"We should talk about that later," hissed Skye.

"Well, you said something…"

"Later," growled Skye.

"Okay."

Both of them were silent for a moment.

"I should be getting back to the store," said Chasey finally. "I got two new recruits to train."

"I'll call you later."

"Sure thing."

Chasey left.

Leaning forward on her hands, she looked up, holding her head steady. Looking through the small cafe crowd, she was trying to digest what Chasey had just told her. Her thoughts were backing up against Linette.

She realized she was gripping the edge of the table. The thought of the Vis club came to mind. Just a drink or two. She just didn't want to think about Linette.

Looking around, trying to distract herself, she spotted a tall waving mop of bleached blond hair atop a slim body covered in black. He came into the cafe. She realized the mop was walking towards her,

"Holy shit," gasped Skye to the hair. "Johnny Trash!"

Connection

"What the fuck have you been doin'?" asked Johnny casually.

"Not much. I mean, I ain't really been doin' anythin'."

"Nothin'? Not no music? No work'?"

"A little work."

"No tweakin' n' freakin'?"

"Maybe some, here an' there."

"Fuckin' a', I was hopin' you could hook me up sometime."

Skye leaned on the table. "I dunno, I'm not really in the loop with that stuff at the moment."

"Got too burnt out?"

"Yeah. It got to be too much."

"No shit. I remember you used to be really into that stuff."

He was talking about two years ago. It had been at least that long since she had last seen him.

Johnny slumped even further into his chair, trying to assert as much of a casual air as he could with his long and lanky frame. "I remember you were playing with Triple T back in the day."

"Fuck yeah. I sort of tried to stay in her band."

"I only remember a couple a' those shows you played."

"I even wrote a few songs for them."

She looked past her glass, down through the floor. She had not thought about her playing days in some time, back when she was drifting in and out of bands.

Sitting up, she shook the memories out. "Fuckit. Tell me what you been up to Johnny."

He slowly waved his hands around in a casual shrug. "Same ol' shit. Goin' out with a babe, fuckin' aroun', tryin' to get my band started."

"Did you ever get any gigs goin'?"

"I did for a while with this one group, but it didn't work out."

"Fuck dude, I had forgotten about your band stuff."

"Yup. I'm still goin' at it. Someday I'm gonna' get it together."

"Did you ever even get one show going?"

Johnny kicked a leg up onto an empty chair. "We almost got a gig this one time, jus' last month, only our drummer couldn't make it."

"Why not? Did he quit at the last minute or somethin'?"

"Not exactly."

"What d'ya mean?"

"Well, his girlfriend moved back to the East Coast an' he followed her. He took off like, one night before the show was supposed to happen."

"Well, why didn't you jus' get a new drummer when you found out he was leavin'?"

"Because we didn't find out until the day he was leavin'."

Skye sat forward. "You mean he didn't tell you he was moving back East?"

"No! It wasn't his fault. He didn't know he was movin' until that night either."

"Damn."

"His girlfriend just sprung it on him, an' he just followed her out there."

"Sounds like a real flake," said Skye.

"What, his girlfriend?"

"The drummer."

"You remember Jason?"

"Which Jason?" blurted Skye.

"What?"

"Jason Hall, Jason Staley, Jason Herz…"

"Herz! He was our drummer."

She sat back in her seat. "Herz. Damn. I haven't heard about that guy in years."

"He was here last month." Bending himself forward, he leaned on the table. "You ever see any a' the old guys?"

She rolled her eyes around in thought. "Like who?"

"I dunno. Like any a' those ol' crusties from Hell Nose House."

The question had surprised Skye.

She thought better of saying anything about Preston.

"I haven't seen anyone from those days. I thought I saw Dan a few days ago, but I wasn't sure."

"Pel's old girlfriend?"

"Yeah."

Johnny sat back again, cradling his coffee cup with both hands. "I ran into Yuri recently."

There was a moment of silence for Skye as a light and a shudder went through her head and jumped into her throat.

She straightened herself in her chair. "You saw Yuri?"

"Fuck ya I did."

"When? Where?"

"It was earlier this year. He came out to the city for a visit."

"He came out here?"

"Yeah. He lives in the East Bay right now."

"Holy fuck! How's he doin'?" she asked, not bothering to hide her brightening eyes.

"Really fuckin' good. He's cleaned himself up."

"Yeah?"

"Big time. He don't do no drugs or drink no booze at all anymore."

"Holy shit."

"Ain't that some fuckin' trip?"

"You don't have his number by any chance, do you?"

"I lost his number, but I remember where he lives."

Reunion

She knew her trip to the East Bay was based more on faith than anything else.

Nevertheless, she also knew she had to try. The curiosity would be too much for her if she did not at least give it one try. The idea of seeing her old boyfriend again, especially if he had really cleaned up his act, was just too tempting.

She could not stop thinking about what Johnny Trash had told her as she sat and stewed in the stale air of the subway car. Johnny did not have Yuri's exact address, so he described to her, as best he could, the location of his new place in fairly uncertain and ambiguous terms and descriptions.

She had set out to look for a perpendicular street to the South Berkeley subway station, and then look for a punk house with a disheveled yard and a dilapidated porch, an old house that had dull and peeling red paint. Trash had assured her that she could not possibly miss the place, but she had her doubts that she could readily find it without an exact address, or at least better directions.

Trash's instructions were based on his sole visit to Yuri's place, which occurred many months before.

Trash had also instructed her, once she had found the place, to go around the back of the punk house and look for a tall wooden structure, a place that, as Trash had put it, would appear to be 'An extra fancy tool shed'.

Squinting against the dark light of a cloudy East Bay day, Skye emerged from the South Berkeley subway station. She started heading East, as she had been instructed. Cutting across a long and wide parking lot, she found what she believed was the street Trash had described.

The wind started kicking up as she kept looking around, trying to get her bearings. Skye had not been in Berkeley for quite some time.

Berkeley had its own feel. It was a college town with many of the same facets of San Francisco, only it was much smaller and a much shorter city. There were no crowding high rises, and there were not nearly as many bars and dives as there were in San Francisco. The East Bay also had the dubious facet of having far fewer music clubs than San Francisco. The only club Skye could even think of in the East Bay was the Gilman Street club and a small dive called the Berkeley Square, a place that she had only been to a few times.

Walking down the street, she hoped she was recalling Johnny's instructions correctly. She walked slowly, measuring her steps, trying to ignore the wind with a calm reserve. For all she knew she was on the wrong street. For all she knew she was on the right street, but would still not be able to find the house.

But that was not the only reason she was treading lightly.

There was something about Yuri, the one-time boyfriend with whom she had shared a rather strange acquaintance. She had been doing speed when he had been doing heroin. They had lived together in the same house, yet not in the same room. If anyone ever asked her, she told people that they had lived together, omitting the somewhat complicated circumstances of their former coupling. Even so, the idea of seeing him again was captivating.

She kept looking around, trying to listen for any sounds of the local populace. The neighborhood was eerily quiet, devoid of any shouting kids or moving cars or barking dogs. She was trying to ignore the empty part of her chest as she rounded the corner.

Her feet came alive. Half a block up the street was the disheveled punk house. She could see the peeling and fading red paint. The front stairs were worn and warped with a listing awning, shading a porch crowded with various derelict items such as milk crates, motorcycle parts, and old bits of broken furniture, among other things.

Crossing the street and walking towards the punk pad, she could make out more details about the place. What little bit of yard there was in front of the house was overgrown with tall grass and weeds. She could see various dark metal objects among the grass which she reasoned were either car or motorcycle parts.

Going down the right side of the house, the driveway was blocked by a tall and crudely built wooden gate. The gate was already partially opened. Skye knew that if there really were people living in the back, then they should be used to people coming and going along the side of the house. She knew she looked the part of a punk house patron, with her faded black jeans, Derby jacket, and frayed black dreadlocks.

Her heart skipped a bit when she saw the tall wooden shack through the opening in the gate, just as Johnny had described it.

She braced herself for a clean and sober Yuri. She thought about how she had kept her distance from him back in those days, even when they were a couple, and how he had always respected her distance. It was that, more than anything else, that made her feel that she might have made a mistake in letting him fade away with so many other past friends, roommates, acquaintances, and old boyfriends.

Then she remembered why she had let him slip away. He had sunk too deep into the heroin scene.

Taking a deep breath, she knocked on the door of the small structure.

A few moments. No answer. No noise. Nothing.

Skye knocked again. She would wait for a moment and then go to the main house.

After a few more moments she was about to turn away from the place when the door suddenly opened. A tall and thin woman with long and frazzled brown hair answered the door.

"Yes?" murmured the woman.

Skye held herself for a moment.

"Is Yuri here?"

"No. He's not here right now."

She felt a rush and then a fall.

"You might check back later," continued the woman. "He might be at work."

"Like, later this evening?"

"Yeah," moaned the woman as she fluttered her sleepy eyes.

"Thanks," said Skye who started backing away from the door. The woman closed the door quickly, shutting it with burned out irritation.

Skye tried keeping the spring in her step subdued as she walked out of the yard. She wondered if the frazzled bush of hair was Yuri's current girlfriend.

Carrie climbed back up the ladder to find Zatch turning over in his bed.
"Who was that?" he asked.
"Some chick looking for Yuri."
"Some chick?"
"I didn't get her name. She looked like one a' those stuck up city punks."
Zatch sat up. "She was lookin' for Yuri?"
"Yeah."
"What did you tell her?"
"I figured he was at work, so I told her to come back aroun' later."
"Oh shit."

East Bay Chance

She had gone to the trouble of coming all the way out to the East Bay, so she decided she might as well stop by Yuri's again in the evening.

She made the fifteen minute walk to the main drag of Berkeley, Telegraph Avenue, to kill some time. It was the only decent main strip that she knew of in Berkeley. Perhaps there were a few other places to go in Oakland or even elsewhere in Berkeley, but she was not familiar enough with the East Bay to know about them, if they even existed.

She had been to Telegraph Avenue many times in her younger days, when she was an underage runaway squatter in South Berkeley. She had always described Telegraph as Berkeley's version of upper Haight, only without any clubs or bars.

She only spent so much time browsing through the record stores. It was a habit that she tried to avoid, since she would invariably find too many things to buy.

She took quite a bit of time going through Moe's bookstore, going through the books, wishing she had spent more of her time reading. Thinking about the rest of Telegraph and what it had to offer, she decided her time would be best spent by getting a cheap paperback and finding a decent bar to wile away some of the hours. She found an old and ragged copy of On the Campaign Trail '72 and went to the front, where a cheerful balding man, chewing on an unlit cigar, rang up her meager literary purchase.

Walking up and down the four-block stretch, the only bars she could find were uptight places full of college students. She would have to settle for one of the many cafes that infested the street.

She found a small cafe on one of the busier side streets called the Wall of Berlin. There were a lot of young punks and throckers hanging out around the sidewalk tables.

Before long, Skye was brooding over a large pint glass full of coffee, reading her book and glancing at the punks and throckers outside. She saw two young men at a corner table, making a deal. The way they talked, the way they moved, and the way they were hunched in the corner made it all too obvious to her what was going on.

It was as if it were pushing its way through cotton, the dull attraction and the now stronger revulsion at the thought of making deals, getting the stuff and getting strung out. It was an odd feeling for her, but it simply would not leave. Not at the moment, in any case. She knew that her real craving for the stuff would return in a week or two. It was only a matter of time.

She assumed that Riff Raff would probably be wise to her burnout and would let her back in to keep doing deals, as long as she didn't wait too long to return to the scene and he was satisfied that she had not been in any trouble with the law. She thought about all of the phone calls she would have to avoid in order to stay away from the stuff, even for a week. A few days before, she had pondered the idea of just dealing the stuff without using it, but quickly dismissed the concept as ridiculous.

Skye returned to her book as a crowd of short punks and tall baldies came clamoring up to the cafe counter.

Looking up from her book, she was curious as to how the outdoor corner table deal was going. She quickly looked back down at her book as the crowd of clean-cut punks started moving in her direction.

"Skye."

She was most definitely not expecting to hear anyone in the East Bay say her name out loud. Quickly looking up, there was a thin woman with short, buzz-cut black hair, standing next to her table, looking right at her.

"Skye! How are you?"

"Hi."

"I haven't seen you in such a long time!"

"Yeah."

"How are you?"

" I'm doin' all right."

The short-haired woman was looking back at Skye curiously. "Don't you remember me?" said the woman softly.

It hit Skye all at once, out of the corner of her mind. A rush went through her chest.

"Holy shit, Sue?"

"Yeah!"

Skye had to stare at her for a few more moments to fully grasp that the polite and well-groomed woman standing in front of her was truly her wild and violent ex-roommate.

"I don't fuckin' believe this!" gasped a wide-eyed Skye. "Surly Sue!"

Sue rolled her eyes. "Oh man, no one's called me that in a long time."

Thinking through her astonishment, Skye realized she had not seen Sue since she had left Hell Nose House. Memories quickly flooded her head.

"Y'wanna join me for a minute?" asked Skye.

"Well, I came in with my friends."

"Come on Sue, I haven't seen you in years!"

Sue's smile became softer. Skye could see Sue's eyes searching her face.

"Okay," said Sue.

As Sue sat down, several people from her crowd glanced in her direction, turning their heads just enough to cast a pointed glance.

Skye tried her best to ignore them. "So what the fuck Sue? What have you been up to all this time?"

She shrugged, keeping her arms folded together. "Oh, you know, jus' workin' and going to meetings." Sue was talking as if she were a shy teenager. "Y'know, I've been through a lot of changes since I last saw you."

"No kidding. Your hair is so short!"

"Are you in the East bay now?"

"Naw. I jus' came out for the day from San Francisco. I was jus' tryin' to find some old friends."

"Really? Have you seen any of the old gang?"

"I've run into Mercy a couple of times."

"Mercy," wondered Sue out loud as her shoulders started to soften. "Wow. I haven't heard about her in a long time. Is she still playing music?"

"No, not for a long time. She's got her own place, all to herself. She found a straight job that pays pretty well."

"Man, I haven't seen her since she was going out with, what was his name?"

"I dunno. She went out with a lot of people over the years."

"That guy, when she was sharing a room with Sweezy in the city."

"Oh, what was it? Rebar!"

"Yeah. I heard Rebar's over here now."

"I never really knew him," shrugged Skye.

"He was hanging out with Yuri last year."

Skye sat up. "You've seen Yuri?"

"Yeah," she answered as she started folding her arms tighter.

"Where is he? What's he been up to?"

"I ran into him at a meeting actually."

"No shit? An AA meeting?"

"An NA meeting."

"Yeah."

"I just ran into him. He said he had moved out here to Berkeley after he kicked his habit."

"I already heard about that. That's the part that gets me."

"We were hangin' out now and then. For a while he was doing really well. He was coming to a lot of meetings. He was trying to get a sponsor."

"What was he up to?"

"Mostly just going to meetings. He was calling around."

"No no, I mean, was he working? Was he going to school?"

Sue hesitated for a moment. "He was just working. He had some sort of warehouse job in Oakland. Other than that, I think he was considering getting back into music."

Leaning forward, Skye decided to confide in Sue. "Actually, I came over here to find him."

"You did?"

"Johnny Trash gave me his address. I stopped by his place earlier, but he wasn't there."

"Wow, that's a trip."

Folding her arms, Skye leaned onto the table. "I know it sounds weird, especially since we didn't seem like much of a couple back at the house in SF. I mean, I dunno, when I think back, if you don't mind me telling you this."

"No, of course not."

"When I think back to alla those guys I went out with in the old days, when I was in Berkeley, back in my old San Francisco days, do you ever have those regrets?"

"I have more than enough regrets."

"You know, did you ever think about the ones who got away?"

Sue shrugged. "Not really. I don't think I ever really had anyone worth keeping."

"Well, I sometimes think I should have kept up with Yuri. He's the only ex-boyfriend I ever think about. He's the only one I'd want to talk to again."

"Yeah, but he was such a junky back at the old house."

"I know. That's the only reason why I didn't keep in touch with him. Now I hear he's cleaned up his act, and he's gone all clean an' sober, which is pretty amazing for someone like him."

"No shit."

"Hearing all of that made me want to find him even more. I'm supposed to go back to his place tonight to see if he's there."

"What?"

"Some woman over at his place told me he wasn't there, and that I should come back tonight. She said he'd probably be back by then."

"Well..."

"It was some skinny woman with long frazzly hair. Is that his girlfriend? Is he living with someone?"

"Skye, there's something..."

"Sue!" A blonde bobbed rude girl in a black flight jacket was beckoning to Sue from her group.

"Jus' a sec'." Sue stood up and walked up to the rude girl. The blonde bobbed rude girl was stood close to Sue, talking right into her face.

Skye was sat and waited with rapt attention for Sue to rejoin her.

"Why are you talking to that burnout?" said the blonde flight jacket.

Skye felt her face become flush. It was as if she was experiencing a speed rush. She could feel her nails digging into her palms.

Sue and the blonde flight jacket kept muttering to each other, talking between their teeth. Skye tried not to listen, at least for the moment.

Sue came by the table. "Hang on a sec' Skye. I gotta go talk to someone."

Sue and the blonde flight jacket went back to the group. Sue was talking to a tall and skinny bald man. Skye was looking in their direction. Not one of them was looking back at her.

Skye went to the counter to get a refill of coffee. She wondered why the blonde bob's comment was tugging at her nerves so badly.

Turning around with a fresh pint of coffee in her hand, she saw the blonde bob get up and start walking towards the counter as Sue's group huddled closer together.

The blonde bob was looking straight ahead as she walked in Skye's direction.

A clear silver spike shot right up the back of Skye's spine, as her hands grew cold and hard.

She set her coffee down on the counter and started turning as if she were about to walk back to her table, just as the blonde bob was walking by.

Skye ran into her, putting a shoulder into her.

"Hey!" yelped the blonde bob. "Watch where you're going!"

"Fuck you."

"What is your problem?" squealed the blonde bob as she started backing up.

"What's the matter? Afraid you'll start using again if you brush up against a 'burnout'?"

Skye could see the tall talkative baldy rounding the corner of the counter.

"Hey! Jus' cool it," said the baldy as he put a hand on Skye's shoulder.

She knocked his hand away. "Fuck off bitch. Why don't you go home and pull that pole out of your ass."

"Hey, just because you're still getting burnt out is no reason to …"

She did not let him finish his sentence.

It was not the same as when she had hit Drag. Her arm had shot out, just as before, only this time it was not a reflex. She could feel her knuckles hit the bone of his jaw through the thin skin on his face.

The tall and slender baldy went crashing to the floor, his legs flying up from a pile of clattering chairs and tables.

Glass jaw.

The whole of Sue's gang had shot up, standing up quickly from their chairs. They were backing up, everyone except Sue, who was grabbing Skye by the shoulders.

"Come on asshole!" shouted Skye at the fallen baldy. "Put your hands on me again motherfucker!"

"Fuckin' cool it Skye!"

Her hands shot out, pushing Sue away. "Fuck you Sue! Fuck you and all your stuck up asshole friends!"

Standing her ground, she was looking right into Sue's eyes. Sue's dark eyes were pleading with her.

And they were also swimming with fear.

Holt's group was standing still, even the baldies. Pushing Sue aside, she walked up to the blonde bob and grabbed her by her flight jacket. She let out a yelp.

Hesitating for only a moment, she pushed the blonde bob onto the floor.

Crumpling to the ground, the blonde bob flattened herself onto the floor.

Skye was backing out of the cafe, in case anyone tried anything. Holt was still on the floor, moving very slowly, holding onto his face. Sue was starting intently back at her.

Finally walking out of the cafe, all of the outdoor table punks watched her walk away. She could feel her knuckles stinging and throbbing.

She also walked quickly to try and churn out her stress. The strings in her muscles twisted up and tightened her limbs.

Reaching the corner, back on the main drag of Telegraph, she looked around, trying to remember which way to go.

Turning down the street, that's when it hit her. She had left her brand new used book in the cafe. She thought for a moment about going back to get her book.

Turning around and looking back up the street, a few police cars had pulled up to the cafe.

She started walking back to South Berkeley.

To The South

She was only lost for a few minutes. She remembered that all she had to do was keep walking south to get to Ashby Avenue, and that led back to the subway station so she would be able to get her bearings again. The dark gray clouds were bringing an early evening.

Her knowledge of Berkeley had deteriorated even more than she had suspected. Many of the old landmarks from her early runaway days were gone. Her life had become such a part of the San Francisco scene that her short lived yet intense Berkeley days were only a dim backroom fog for her now.

Putting her hands in her jacket, she scrunched her arms to her side, trying to keep warm. She kept thinking about the book she had left back in the cafe.

Finally reaching the long Ashby street, she turned the corner and headed back towards South Berkeley. Even seeing it from a distance, the forms and faces of her old Berkeley gang were floating by. The shark-toothed Kasi, the Amazon Izzy, her apprentice Caitlin, and her toxic twin Serena.

And even Justine, the only soft spoken one from her old group.

She had only been a simple alcoholic and casual drug user back then, but the wild days of her Berkeley home were instrumental in bringing her to her current state of affairs, even if the memories were so far away that they hardly felt like a part of her anymore.

She was on familiar ground, only a few blocks away from the subway station. Her pace quickened as she turned down Yuri's street.

Walking up to the dilapidated punk house, her pace slowed down as she started down the dead grass walkway along the side of the house.

After Skye was halfway down the walkway, a tall and dark eyed woman with splaying black hair, dressed head to toe in jet black clothes, was coming out from behind the crude wooden gate. Skye's step stuttered, only for a moment, as she saw the rather imposing throcker move from behind the wooden gate.

The woman was looking right at her.

"Hey, you know if Yuri's here?" asked Skye.

"Are you a friend of Yuri's?" asked the tall woman.

"Who are you?"

"Zata."

"Okay."

"So?" stood Zata.

"So what?"

"Are you or aren't you?"

"I'm an old friend of Yuri's, out from San Francisco."

"Oh. One of his old Hell Nosers?"

Skye straightened up. "Yeah!"

"You wouldn't happen to be Skye by any chance, would you?"

Skye snapped her head back. "How the hell did you know that?"

"He's mentioned you a few times."

"Is he here?"

"No. He's not."

"Fuck. Do you know when he'll be back?"

"I don't know."

The wind kicked up. "Damn."

"He's not coming back."

The dull and electric charge went from the back of her neck and through her face, down her neck and into her stomach. Her eyes grew wide as her heart pulled at her throat.

"No…" cried Skye as tears started forcing their way to her eyes.

Zata started waving her hands around. "No no no no! Not that!"

Skye let out a deep breath. "Jesus fucking Christ!"

"I'm sorry."

"I already had one friend drop dead on me this month. You fuckin' scared the shit outta me."

"I'm truly sorry. That was a stupid thing to say."

"So..."

"Actually, nobody knows when Yuri will be back, if he ever does come back."

"What are you talking about?"

The Friend

Up the creaking side stairs of the wooden apartment building, Skye followed the self-proclaimed friend of Yuri as she had promised to explain everything once they had gotten back to her place.

Skye was right behind Zata as they steadily climbed the long stairs. Zata's whole body looked strong and powerful. Skye was trying to imagine what a fight with her would be like. Certainly she would be no toothpick-nosed Drag or tall skinny baldy with a glass jaw. But it was more than just her appearance. Her sixth sense knew that Zata was no pushover.

Entering the apartment, Zata closed the door, shutting out the wind behind them.

"Would you like something to drink?" asked Zata politely.

"Y'got any beer? I'm dying for a beer."

"Sorry. I have some tea and some pear nectar."

"I'm cool."

The place was sparsely furnished. Skye sat down on a short green couch. Zata sat down across from her. Skye was at least happy enough to be in a place that was warm.

"So what's up with Yuri?" asked Skye.

Crossing her legs and folding her arms, Zata cleared her throat. "Well, it's like this. I met Yuri some time ago."

"At those meetings?"

"Yes."

"That's why you don't have any beer."

"Yes," replied Zata.

"Sure." Skye squeezed her arms together underneath her jacket. "So how do you know about me?"

"He talked about you."

"Yeah?"

"All about you."

"What, like all of the time?"

"No. Usually he hardly ever mentioned you, Until the other night, just last week."

"Really?"

Zata leaned back in her chair. "Yuri had stopped going to meetings. He had been getting tired of the local clean and sober scene. The other day he told me he was getting tired of the Bay Area, and tired of his job, and of his place."

"Yeah, I know the feeling."

"He was talking about his job, about how he wasn't getting enough hours, and about how he was cooped up in this small little place, usually all by himself."

"That sounds familiar."

Zata leaned forward. "Sure, we're all familiar with those kinds of things. It was just this one night, last week when we were talking about the usual things, and then he started telling me a lot of things about his past that he had never mentioned before."

"Yeah?"

"He never really talked about his past, at least not to me. The first time I had ever heard about you was from our mutual friend Sue."

"Yeah, our old housemate."

"She's in the program as well. Are you also a friend of Sue's?"

"I used to be."

"Well, he told me his whole life story, about how he came here from the Northwest, about how he came up to the Bay Area, how he was just an alcoholic before he started getting into the harder stuff, which he started getting into when he got to San Francisco."

"Yep. That's what San Francisco does. It really turns out the junkies."

"That's what he said. Yuri told me about all of his past problems with the usual big city bullshit. The shitty jobs, moving every six months, but he never really mentioned any of his old friends. He told me about a dealer or two, and some stuff about some of his housemates, but you were the only one he never really talked about."

Skye could only look back for a moment. "No shit," she said in surprise.

"He was telling me about your relationship, back at some place called Hell Nose House. That's back when he started getting into horse pretty heavily, so he said." Stopping for a moment, Zata leaned forward, folding her hands in her lap. "I don't know if I should tell you this or not, but I know an awful lot about you."

"Like what?"

"That you were heavy into speed, that you were playing bass and guitar, and that you used to play with Triple T. Did you really play for them?"

"I replaced their bass player for a few weeks. That's all."

"Well, I'm still impressed."

"What else did he say?"

"He told me about the fights you used to get into, how you partied it up, and what you did at the clubs. He mentioned how you just disappeared one day from Hell Nose House, how you had just packed your things up and left without telling anyone that you were leaving. He knew that you had simply gotten fed up with the place, and you just needed to get out." Zata sat back in her chair again. "He was telling me about how he thought he had missed out on something."

"Yeah?"

"How maybe if he hadn't been so wiped out on junk, that maybe you two could have gotten somewhere."

Zata stopped, long enough for the silence to soak into Skye.

"No shit," said Skye finally.

"I'm sorry."

"For what?"

"For laying all of this on you."

Folding her hands, Skye straightened up. "Everything you're telling me just makes me want to find him even more."

"That's just it, no one knows where he is."

"What?"

Zata shifted around. "The night after he told me all of this, he took off."

"Took off?"

"He just left his place. His roommate said that one day he noticed that Yuri and all of his things were gone."

"Fuckin' a'."

"I asked around," continued Zata. "I asked all of his meeting buddies, and then I tried to find some of his other friends, the people he had been hanging out with before he had gotten clean."

"Oh. Y'mean..."

"People who are still using. I suspect they're originally from the city, like Yuri."

"I probably know some of them."

"Zatch might know who they are, but that's a long shot."

"Yuri just took off?"

"No note, no mention to anyone of what he was doing or where he was going, at least not to his roommate, or anyone else that I know. I thought perhaps he might have gone back to the city, but after a while I realized that wasn't too likely."

"You don't think..."

"I can't believe he's back on the horse. He was determined to stay clean and keep going."

"Yeah."

Zata shrugged. "But then again, who knows? Sometimes it's hard to say what people like us might do. Maybe he is using again."

Turning her head, Skye looked away from her. "So you think he's not in Berkeley anymore?"

"I know he's not in Berkeley. If he were still here I would know"

"So what do you think?"

"Where he went? Like I said, I have no idea."

"I know you don't know, but I still want to know what you think he's done."

"I already said…"

"Just your best guess."

Zata looked at the table for a moment. "I guess," stuttered Zata, "I think he went so fast. I mean, from getting loaded on horse, to moving out here, to getting completely clean, and then, the whole NA thing. It doesn't always help you find yourself. He just had to run. That would be my guess. I'd bet good money that you won't find him in San Francisco, or even up North. That's too close to his family, and you don't want to be around those kinds of people at a time like this, believe me."

"No shit."

Skye could not help running her eyes along Zata's outline. Zata was sitting, quite demurely and properly, with her straight back and gently crossed legs, yet she could see the ripple underneath the skin of her shins and her thighs. She could see the edges of her scars, just peeking over the top of her t-shirt. She had a powerful and battle-scarred body. Skye knew, despite all of her good manners and appropriate behavior, that she was a woman who could do some pretty decent damage if she wanted to. She would have to really stand her ground and take some punishment if she found herself in a fight with this woman.

Not that she believed Zata was about to attack. But Skye couldn't help wondering how she would do against her.

"I'm sorry I wasn't much more help," said Zata apologetically. Her remark shook Skye. "Don't be ridiculous."

Crash Shadow

She began to feel her skin again. Her bones were lighter, yet stronger. More often than not, there would be a gap in her gut, and an unfamiliar rumbling, as her stomach talked again, turning her blood with its growling.

She was feeling the sober high now. A strange lightness filled her head, as she could feel her thoughts dancing back and forth at a steady pace. She knew that there would be a come down, that the craving would fill up again, and the press of her place would be prodding her to take in another speed binge.

She could barely feel the last remnants of her last string of binges. There was only a faint light feeling in the back of her head where her mind was still recovering, a crash shadow of her last binge.

She finally returned Preston's car by parking it next to his apartment building. She wasn't even sure if it was still Preston's apartment building. His phone had been disconnected, and he may well have been evicted from his place or perhaps just left of his own accord. He might even be in jail, or locked up in a mental institution or a government rehab.

If nothing else, the car would eventually get towed. She had kept the keys, knowing that Preston would, most likely, be in no condition to drive it. If he really wanted to use it again he could always call her, should his ruined mind ever realize that she had still been using his car.

Finally getting back to her flat, she knew that Arden was gone. She had moved out several days ago without having said anything to her whatsoever to Skye. She knew Arden was gone when she had walked into the kitchen. The coffeemaker was missing, as well as the few telltale bowls and glasses. Arden never had many possessions in the kitchen, but they were few enough to be conspicuous by their absence.

Walking down the hall, her legs swelled with new energy. Going into her room, the red light was blinking quickly on her answering machine. It was full of messages. She had not taken any calls in more than a week. No doubt it was the same people, over and over again, wanting to cop some more speed. Chasey was on there, Paul was on there, and perhaps there were even a few messages from Riff Raff, wondering where his driver had gone.

She wondered how many messages were from Linette, until she stopped the thought with a start.

It flashed in her mind, just for a moment, as she lied down on her futon. Would she have to move out of the flat? Did she get someone else to take the lease, or did Arden simply leave? She wasn't even sure how to get in touch with the landlord. Arden had always collected rent from her and Jane since the lease had been in her name.

Thoughts about the flat quickly left. She would not have to worry about it for at least a few weeks when next month's rent was due. Her heaviest concern was her answering machine and all of the clawing calls that were still on it.

Stretching herself across her futon, she unplugged her phone.

Skye looked over Valencia again, the same stretch that she had traversed so many countless times before: Beller's cafe, the corner liquor store, and Levigate Video. At one time they had all felt as familiar to her as her own room.

Now Valencia was a new street. The shadows of the windows and doors were darker and the neon signs were brighter. The glowing curtained windows were all staring, asking her why she had never seen them before.

Then there were all of the people. The sidewalks were continually crowded by wandering people. Valencia was not usually as crowded as the main drag on Mission or the upper Haight, but it was almost never without at least a steady stream of interspersed people, wandering in every direction like trails of urban ants.

Valencia also had many side streets and alleys, thin concrete roadways curtained by the brick and stone backsides of the bars and clubs. Most of them were just narrow throughways that had street signs, even though they could barely be considered streets. Skye frequently took them as shortcuts, but hardly ever gave a thought about them otherwise.

The bright lights and snaking swarms of people were enough to prompt her off of the main street. She made her way through the back alleys and side streets. She sauntered down one side street after another, looking around, taking note of everything. Occasionally she would see someone carting crates of food and drinks off of a delivery truck, or a few haggard roadies shoving stage amplifiers through small back doors.

Some of the doorways were the openings to apartment buildings, small two or four room domiciles that had been squeezed into the small spaces between the clubs and stores. Usually they were nondescript apartment buildings, given character only by unattended wear and big city neglect. Some windows and doorways were decorated with paintings, graffiti, or small toys. She wondered what it would be like to live in one of the small side street apartments, squeezed in between clubs and corner grocery stores.

Occasionally Skye would spot a small store, usually an antique store or a junk store, its storefront facing on the side street. Usually they would be close to the corner, but occasionally they would be in the middle of the street. Skye wondered how such places could ever get any business.

It was a search. She was finding and observing seldom-seen parts of San Francisco. They were small and out of the way to everyone else, she thought, except to those few people who had to go in and out of the back doors, go in and out of their small cheap box apartments, or tended their small and rarely visited junk and antique shops. To some people, these obscure places of life and work were a big part of their lives. Levigate had been part of Skye's life for an entire year, yet it was out on the main drag, and everyone she knew had at least heard of the place, even if they had not actually ever gone there.

Popping out of the alleys and sideways, she would emerge back out onto Valencia and skitter down the block to move into the next side street. Her search for the urban obscure was prompted in part by an old memory. Skye remembered a long gone day when Mercy's roommate Sweezy had taken them to a small and neurotic yet cool cafe, a place that qualified as one of the weird backstreet stores near Nikki's bar and the Huy club. Even though Skye had only been there once before, she felt an urge to find it again.

That long lost memory had become very pointed in her mind. It was the day that Skye had met Sweezy for the first time. It was also one of the more curious memories from her Hell Nose House days, a strong memory that did not involve loud music, sex, drugs, or fighting.

Crisscrossing a few more streets, she was getting farther down Valencia. The side streets were getting less and less interesting as she started traveling outside of the retail drag and into the more residential stretches of the long and populous street. She knew that the cafe was farther down Valencia, but she could not exactly remember where it had been. She wondered if the place even existed anymore, or if her memory was in any shape to find it again.

She decided to walk the rest of the way down Valencia, rather than zig zagging through the back streets.

She thought about turning around and giving up her search when the corner suddenly appeared. She recognized the spot right when she saw it: a red brick corner, right before an old style iron lamppost.

Moving around the corner, she could see the cafe down the thin side street. It was a small doorway with nothing more than a thin green awning to indicate that anything was there. Its only window was a collage of dingy glass brick. Walking up to the doorway, she could see a few people moving around inside. Taking a chance, she walked in.

The cafe was still there. A tall and thin woman was tending the coffee bar. A few quiet customers were sitting towards the front, while a group of younger and noisier patrons were engaged in a muted clamor in the back.

The cafe was very bright. Multi-colored lights of every shape and size populated the place, hanging from the walls, the ceilings, and even the railings. Chaotic strings of Christmas lights crowded the ceiling and railings, mixing the atmosphere. Most of the tables had white reading lamps fixed in place, guarded by all manner of chairs.

Virtually every square inch of the place had been painted, either with abstract art, portraits, or graffiti. There were paintings and sculptures, large and small, all over the place. Miniature sculptures had been glued onto wooden posts, walls, chairs, and tables. Small pieces of paper with poetry had been tacked, taped, and stapled up in random spots throughout the cafe. Skye remembered that the bathroom had every inch of it covered with graffiti, even the pipes and plumbing. The last time she had been in there, she had spent several minutes in the bathroom just reading the walls.

"Can I help you?" smoothed the tall and slender woman in a heavy European accent.

"Just a large coffee please."

Skye took her coffee to the unpopulated mid section of the cafe, strategically locating herself in between the brooding book readers in front and the chattering young punks in the back. She wanted to get a good look at the place while wallowing in memories of Mercy and her friends.

Her eyes ran around the walls, trying to take in all of the details.

The caffeine was starting to take effect. Her flushing skin made her realize just how cold she had become during her walk.

"Spare change for a skinhead ma'am?"

A slight startle. She turned around and saw a tall young baldy standing right behind her.

"What?"

"Spare change for a skinhead?" he repeated as the tall and bright young man facetiously prostrated himself.

"No, I don't think so."

The young baldy quickly straightened his stance. "Okay. Then how about spare change for a boot boy?"

"Aren't they pretty much the same thing?"

"Hell no!" snapped the baldy, trying his best to look offended. "There are subtle differences y'know."

"Like what?"

"Well, you listen to a lot more Ska when you're a boot boy."

"Right," she replied with a roll of the eyes.

"No, it's true!" The young baldy quickly sat down across from Skye. "It's important to know the intricate social protocols developed by each subculture."

"Well if it's so important how come you trying to be one or th' other?"

"Hey, I need the money. These boots are really expensive!"

Suddenly a short and very young Mohican was standing next to the table, his bright green mohawk drooping slightly to one side. "Is this guy bothering you?" asked the Mohican as he pointed to the baldy.

"No," said Skye. "He's not."

"He isn't?" The Mohican looked at the baldy. "You feelin' okay?"

The baldy looked at Skye. "You know what they say, mohawk, no cock."

"Bitch!" yelped the Mohican. "I'll slap you with nine inches a' limp dick!"

"Just calm down Easy E."

"I'm gonna tell."

Skye was now aware enough of the backroom group to see a young woman with flayed bleached blonde hair walking up behind the Mohican.

"Hey, what you think you doin', bitch?" asked the bleached blonde, looking in Skye's direction.

"You talkin' to me?" growled Skye as she straightened herself in her chair.

"No, I'm talking to him." The bleached blond pointed at the baldy. "He loves it when I call him bitch."

"It's true, I do."

"You don't like it when I call you bitch!" yelped the Mohican.

"No, I like it when you call me daddy."

"Fuck you."

"No, fuck you."

"No fuck you."

"No fuck…"

"I haven't seen you in here before," interrupted the bleached blonde as she nestled herself between the Mohican and the table.

"I haven't been in here for a long time," replied Skye.

"Yeah, no shit."

The Mohican suddenly darted off to the back. The tall baldy ran after him.

"Fuckin' kids," facetiously growled the bleached blonde. "No, really, what are you doin' in here?" asked the bleached blonde as she leaned onto a chair.

Skye shrugged. "Just checkin' this place out again."

"It's just that most people in here know someone who knows someone. This place is run by some weird rich Norwegian guy who kinda uses it as his own private place, most of the time anyways. It's only open for a few hours a day."

"Hey! Stop that right now!" yelled the slender bartender at the crashing punks in the back.

"You know you love it!" yelled the baldy.

"I love you and I hate you and I throw you out if you don't cut it out!"

"So who do you know?" asked the bleached blonde.

"I gotta know somebody?" replied Skye.

"Yeah," the bleached blonde turned the chair around and sat down. "Nobody don't find this place unless somebody shows it to 'em."

"Nobody ever just walks in here because they happened to come across it?"

"That happens like, once a year or somethin'."

Picking up her coffee cup, Skye let herself relax. "Yeah, someone did bring me here, like a couple a' years ago."

"Yeah? Who?"

"Your mother."

"Nah. Couldn't be. I told my mother I'd take her Demerol away if she brought anyone else in here."

"You wouldn't know her anyways. It was some gal named Mercy."

"Mercy. I think my sister knew a Mercy."

Skye tilted her chair back as the bartender started for the back. "I once knew a pit bull named Mercy."

The bleached blonde looked into the back. "Knock it the fuck off you assholes!" she yelled to the still battling Mohican and baldy. Skye could hear the commotion suddenly stop at the bleached blonde's command.

"My sister was Marie," continued the bleached blonde. "She used to strip at the Lusty Lady under the name Charlie Tryst."

"No shit? Is that the same Marie who used to sing for a band called the Dynamite Chicks?"

"Fuck yeah. I saw her play a few times."

"Did you like that band?" asked a now wide-eyed Skye.

"Fuck yeah I did. The music totally sucked, but the band was great anyways."

"D'ya remember Skye?"

"Skye? Who's that?"

"Me. I used to play guitar for them."

"Get the fuck outta here!"

"Yeah. I was friends with Natasha and Triple T."

"I fuckin' remember you!" yelped the bleached blonde as she jumped in her seat.

"From my playin' days?"

"Fuck no. You used to come over to my house."

"I did?"

"Yeah. Remember Marie's sister, th' one who was always messin' with her room?"

Skye's eyes grew. The bleached blonde's eyes were familiar to her now. Many times, several years ago, she had gone to the tall and statuesque Marie's house and saw her short and thin wide eyed little sister running around in flower print dresses with flat black hair, teasing her sister. Once she had snuck up on them when they were making lines. Marie was furious, chasing her sister out of the room, and then they heard her little sister starting to cry, because she did not understand why Marie had suddenly gotten so angry.

Now she was looking at the same spontaneous little sister, with bleached and burnt hair, eyeliner, and dark circles under her eyes.

The slender bartender briskly walked back behind the bar, with the Mohican and the baldy walking behind her in grudging restraint.

"Hey, invite her to the party!" yawped the baldy.

"It's not a party, it's a club," hollered the Mohican.

"Why the fuck should I invite her?" asked the bleached blonde.

"Because she looks like she's old enough to buy beer," said the Mohican.

"You know her, don't you?" asked the baldy.

"She used to play with my sister!"

"Play with your sister? You mean play with her tits or something?"

The bleached blonde took a swipe at the baldy. "Fuck you bitch! They were in a band together."

"Damn, you must be hella old then!"

"Don't worry," assured the bleached blonde "Anyone over eighteen is old to these bitches."

"What's your party like?" asked Skye.

"It's not a party, it's a club," said the Mohican.

"Okay, club."

"It's not a club, it's a party," said the baldy.

"It's a two tone club, down by the warehouses," interjected the bleached blonde. "There's a lotta skins an' rude boys goin', but it should be pretty mellow."

"Fuck no it won't," said the baldy. "It's gonna' be fuckin' wild man."

"Yeah sure," scoffed the bleached blonde. "Everyone's gonna be too slushed to do anything."

"Not us," said the Mohican. "We ain't got no fuckin' money."

"We do so have money."

"I know, but I'm tryin' to get some money outta her," replied the Mohican as he pointed to Skye.

Skye looked at the bleached blonde's dark eyes one more time.

"Sorry, but I gotta get goin'," said Skye, as she stood up.

"Aw, come on!" pleaded the short Mohican.

"Yeah, don't be so lame," said the baldy.

"I just can't."

"We don't bite," said the Mohican.

"Yes we do," said the baldy.

The bleached blonde leaned in towards Skye. "Could you at least buy us some liquor before you split? We'll sport you for a bottle if y'like."

"Yeah, sure."

"Cool!" smiled the bleached blonde, with an air of relief. "You sure you don't wanna come with us?"

"Yeah."

Skye waited for them to collect themselves and then walked a few blocks to the nearest liquor store. She ended up buying them a twelve pack of beer and a bottle of Bacardi. The baldy and the Mohican kept cajoling her to accompany them to the club. When she parted ways with them, the bleached blonde admonished her to find them in the cafe again.

Walking back down Valencia, she knew from her short time with the cafe trio that there was something else in their blood. Liquor was not their only poison. She wasn't around them long enough to know exactly what it was, but she knew it was something strong.

Skye started walking back to her apartment.

It was nighttime.

Valencia was a long street.

Out

It had taken some time and an awful lot of talking, but Skye managed to finally convince the landlord to let her take on the lease and stay in the flat.

Now all she had to do was find new roommates. She could pay the rent for the next two months without roommates or a job, but then she would be nearly broke. She needed to get a straight job and get at least two roommates.

It was an all too familiar task, but one she had not practiced in some time. Her friends, acquaintances, and enemies were always constantly moving around. Even though the search for new roommates was definitely not a new chore, it was something that Skye was giving much more thought to than she ever had before.

Certain kinds of roommates would be more than willing to lead her back into more than a few bad habits. Nearly everyone who had been living under the tutelage of Arden had more or less kept to themselves, leaving Skye in peace to do her own thing.

For a brief moment, Skye thought about what it would be like to have the place all to herself. She quickly pushed the daydream out, not wanting to wallow in impossibilities.

She wandered to the far end of the kitchen with the weight of three bedrooms on her shoulders, she cautiously mused about why she was so determined to stay. She had broken off from Riff Raff. He had not made any inquiries with her one way or another, and enough time had passed that it would be awkward enough to try and get in touch with him again.

Preston had disappeared. Only the day before, she had risked an impromptu visit to Preston's place, only to find his apartment cleaned out. Everything of his was gone from his place, so much so that it had become impossibly clean.

Then Skye had tried to locate Chasey, just to let her know where she was. Chasey was no longer working at Levigate Videos. Going by her place, she was informed by one of Chasey's roommates that she had gone back up North to live with her mother in Seattle. She had not heard from Paul, and she was not sure whether or not it had anything to do with his trouble with the law, but she could hardly believe he would hold himself back if he really wanted to get in touch with her. Still, her intuition told her that it was not likely that she would hear from him again.

Mercy had been slipping away from Skye, going in another direction. She wondered if her own newfound direction might impress Mercy enough to get her to try and reinitiate their now defunct friendship, but when she thought about the possibility she wondered if it was even worth the effort.

Especially because of Linette.

Walking back out into the hallway, moving through the unfamiliar echoes, a spear of razor bright light was cleaving through her curtains. She knew what it was. It was the glare off of a slick and steel high rise apartment building in the distance. The very bright rays of light came into her room for a few minutes every day, when the sun was in a certain position.

She had rarely given the tower much thought. She had only ever considered it when it had subjected her place to its too-bright rays of reflected light. Now she was prompted to glance as much as she could at the high silver tower.

She had never given the high rise much thought simply because the place was too alien for her. It was obviously a very expensive place to live, and it was no doubt filled with all kinds of well groomed and straight-laced people, the kind of people whose plastic and placidly preconceived lives made Skye's skin grow cold. For the moment, she wondered what it would be like to live in such a place. She had never lived in any place that was very well kept or in good condition. Her family had never had very much money, always living in small houses or apartments that were always too cramped.

The idea of living in a large, comfortable, and clean place, or of even having a place, even the current flat all to herself, was something she rarely thought about, simply because she would not be able to handle having with such an unreachable desire.

Now she was in charge of a three-bedroom flat, in an old building, with scuffed floors and fading walls. At least everything in the flat worked. The plumbing did not leak, the heat and the kitchen appliances were actually in good working condition, and you could actually open the windows.

That was good enough to want to keep the place. But who knew when one of the pipes would burst, or the fridge would die in the middle of the night, or when the heat would conk out, and the circuit breakers would start snapping off all of the time.

Watching the sharp ray from the tall silver apartment building slowly fade away, she considered Arden's old room. It was smaller than Skye's room, but it had the advantage of being tucked away around a corner at the end of the hallway. The first two rooms were much more conspicuous.

Walking into the back depths of the hallway, her eyes had to adjust to the darkness. Finding the handle to the door and walking into Arden's room, Skye turned on the light. She was seeing Arden's dark blue walls and dark wood floors for the first time.

Arden had done a very thorough job of cleaning out her place. It appeared as if she had even taken the dust with her. The room was much larger than she had imagined. The walls appeared to have been freshly painted. The floor appeared as if it had actually been varnished in the past few years. The scuffs and scrapes and faded, cracking spots that characterized the rest of the flat's interior were nowhere to be seen in Arden's room. The one window in the room had a clean black curtain, just the right size for covering up the window frame.

She took a short step inside, and then quickly extracted her foot.

Quickly walking back out into the hallway, she went into her room. She tipped over her futon, throwing off all of the blankets and sheets. Hoisting the beaten pad of foam over her shoulder, she quickly brought it into Arden's old room.

Back in her room, she grabbed her boombox and her jacket and ditched them quickly in Arden's room. Getting a plastic milk crate from the kitchen, she gathered up all of her tapes, quickly tossing them in, as well as her few books and her other few possessions.

Going back and forth between the rooms, she quickly transferred all of her possessions as if Arden's room, as if it might be taken over by some unforeseen phantom if she did not move quickly enough. She only slowed down when she came back into Arden's dark room, carefully positioning her futon and her belongings. She resisted the urge to look behind the curtain.

After carefully positioning the one and only chair left in the flat within her new room, she went back to move her most significant piece of furniture: her four drawer dresser.

She went through each dresser drawer, removing them and tossing out the contents onto the floor. The items that she had already moved had created a surprising amount of debris. Dust and dirt and bits of paper and crumbs of various other artifacts were scattered all over the floor. There were ragged bits of unwearable underwear and socks, lost and forgotten clothes that she had long ago lost interest in wearing, and various bits of paper or old makeup that she had no use for anymore.

Back and forth, she stacked the disembodied drawers in Arden's old room. It didn't hit her until she was going back for the last dresser drawer: the speed drawer.

She had not bothered to look into it since she had recovered from her last binge.

For a long moment she only stood before it. She kept trying to feel the strings in her limbs, wondering if her speed cravings would start eating the air around her again. She had to force herself to kneel down and open the drawer.

Opening the drawer slightly, she could see the edge of her snorting stone, with her old black speed kit peeking out from under the few old t-shirts that had been thrown in to cover it up.

She had to know.

Bending her muscles against her bones, she picked up the bag and undid the velcro latch.

A baggie.

Two baggies.

They were full.

They were small baggies, probably containing about a half gram altogether. It was enough to give her a good rush and keep her up for at least a few days.

The warm flutter in her gut and her throat told her that she had plenty of time to find a new job and find a few roommates, and if nothing else she could simply risk a call to Riff Raff and see if she could get back into the trade so she could make enough money to get by.

Her fingers went numb.

Quickly opening the window, it felt as if she was flinging herself off of a bridge as she ripped open the small baggies and let the grains of speed float down to the street. It was a reckless amphetamine suicide as she let the sparkling grains diffuse into the city air.

With a jolt of electricity, she picked up the drawer and hurled it across the room, her snorting stone flew out of the drawer and broke itself into pieces against the wall.

Straightening herself out, standing suddenly still in the middle of the room, she would have to come up with a quick explanation for the hole that was left in the wall from the stone's impact. Her scalp was tingling.

Collecting her scattered possessions, she took the last of her things into Arden's room.

Now it was her room.

It was a new place.

Lying down on her futon, she decided she would go to the roommate finder service on upper Haight Street and put in a listing. She already knew what kind of people she had in mind. They should be cool, but not full on addicts or junkies. She had the idea that she would not even want casual addicts in the place. Even weekend speed freaks would not be an option. She would put in the roommate ad later in the day. She would get herself ready for job hunting tomorrow. If she was lucky, she might be able to find a warehouse job where she wouldn't have to put up with customers.

Closing her eyes for a few moments, she opened them to see the black curtain, smartly covering the lone window in the room. Sitting up, Skye tried pushing it aside.

It had been nailed into place. Skye would have to remove the nailed-in tacks in order to get to the window.

Lying back down on the futon, she kept running the list of leaseholder chores through her head.

The new thoughts were a welcome change. For reasons she could not yet explain, she settled into her new and busy thoughts as if they were a new bed.

Closing her eyes, she took a deep breath and felt content. Her board was set. She knew what she would have to do.

A whole flood of unfamiliar feelings and sensations washed over her. The futon actually felt soft. The blankets were actually warm.

Fading into the fog of sleep, her hard bones softened.

A jolt went through her. She opened her eyes.

Damn. What the hell happened to Yuri?

Made in the USA
Middletown, DE
10 April 2022

63967142R00190